LETTER FROM

A Dead Man

DAWN HARRIS

ISBN-13: 978-1484979983
ISBN-10: 1484979982

1

1793

Not a year passed without someone falling off a horse at the east gate. I had done so myself once or twice in my six and twenty years, for the gate was higher than any other on the Ledstone Place estate, or on my own land at Westfleet Manor, or anywhere else in this quiet western corner of the Isle of Wight. It stood at the end of a long straight gallop through Ledstone woods, where few riders could resist the temptation to jump it.

But, when four separate mishaps in February caused a concussion, a fractured shoulder and two broken legs, Cuthbert Saxborough, my godfather and the owner of Ledstone, ordered the gate to be left open whenever possible. Which it was whenever I rode that way, until one glorious morning in April when, to my delight, I saw it was closed.

I glanced at my groom, John Mudd, who had dismounted to examine his hack's near hind foot. 'Anything serious, John?'

'No, my lady, it's just a stone.' He took a hoof-pick from his pocket. 'I'll soon have it out.'

Indicating the closed gate, I informed him cheerfully, 'I'll wait for you in the parklands.' This being the area beyond the gate.

Casting a look along the track, he grinned up at me. 'Very good, my lady.' John Mudd had come to Westfleet at the age of fifteen, when I was three, and everything I knew about horses I had learnt from this quiet man. He was, as I well knew, totally devoted to me, and despite becoming slightly more protective since my father's death in December, he had never fussed over my jumping this particular gate. And I knew he would not now, just as he knew nothing he said would stop me.

But as I thundered down the long track, I saw someone on the ground on the far side of the gate, directly in my path, and hastily pulled up. I knew it was Mr. Saxborough the instant I caught a glimpse of his forest green riding jacket; the colour, style and elegance of which made this rich and powerful man instantly recognisable in this part of the Island.

Slipping from my saddle, I looped the reins round a bush, lifted the skirts of my black riding habit a trifle, and ran to his aid. Being a mere quarter of an inch under six foot, I had no difficulty in opening the high gate, but on seeing my godfather clearly I gave a horrified gasp, for his eyes were open and staring.

I was not fond of him in the same way as I was of Marguerite, who was his second wife; or of Giles, his younger son of my own age, but it seemed so impossible he could really be dead, I dropped to my knees beside him on the muddy track, unbuttoned his riding coat with fumbling fingers, tore off my wide brimmed hat and put my ear to his chest.

His shirt was damp with perspiration from his morning ride, his body still as warm as the Spring sunshine on my back, but the only living sounds came from a nearby song thrush, the jingle of my horse's bridle as he shook his head, and my own ragged breaths coming painfully from my chest. Shuddering at the staring eyes, I hurriedly closed them, and staggering to my feet, leant against the gatepost.

The ring on his right hand, worn by every head of the family ever since Queen Elizabeth presented it to the notorious William Saxborough two centuries before, sparkled in the sunlight. It had belonged to Cuthbert for fifty of his seventy years.

His horse being nowhere in sight I assumed it had bolted, or gone back to its stable. I doubted it had actually struck the gate, as I couldn't see any fresh marks. The mud on the track was noticeably flatter near the gate, yet I saw nothing significant in that at the time.

Nor was there any question in my mind then, how Cuthbert Saxborough had died. I assumed he'd been thrown from his horse when attempting to jump the east gate, for that was how it looked. And I thought of the impact Mr Saxborough's death would have on the lives of his family; and on Marguerite and Giles in particular, for it was Thomas, Cuthbert's son from his first marriage, who would inherit the estates.

Mudd came galloping down the track, and leaving him with Mr. Saxborough while I fetched help from Ledstone Place, I got back on my horse, my mind on how I was to break this terrible news to Marguerite. She was my godmother and I loved her dearly, and the dread I felt at the ordeal that lay ahead must have shown in my face, for Mudd said quietly, 'Mr Giles or Mr Thomas might be at home, my lady.'

I looked down at him. 'Yes,' I said. 'I pray you are right.'

When Queen Elizabeth bestowed the Ledstone estates on William Saxborough in recognition of his daring exploits against Spain, he built his house in a sheltered spot, surrounded by pretty undulating country, a short ride from the Island's west coast, and the fishing villages of Dittistone and Hokewell. Later Saxboroughs, adding to the building, had increased its charm, and Marguerite had refurbished every room with a stylish elegance that could only please.

For her own bedchamber she had chosen a delicate pink wallpaper, with matching curtains and chair coverings, and it was to this room that she retired after Giles had broken the news to her. And where I remained for many hours, doing what I could to comfort her, while Giles and Thomas brought their father's body back to the house, and attended to all the practical matters that inevitably followed the death of the head of this powerful family.

Dr. Redding had given Marguerite a sleeping draught, bringing her a much needed respite from her distress, and as she slept, I sat in a chair by her bedside, her hand still in mine. My heart went out to her, for her face was red and puffy from crying, and her golden curls, which showed no sign of grey despite her forty-four years, were dreadfully tangled where she had moved her head from side to side in fretful fashion.

Heavy rain had been falling for some time, and as the fading daylight plunged the room into even deeper gloom, Giles brought in a branch of candles, which he set down on a stand. I smiled at him, grateful for his thoughtfulness, and he waited by the door, indicating he wanted to speak to me. Sleep having relaxed Marguerite's tight grip on my hand, I gently removed it, and went to join him.

Giles, slim and slight, and born with the blond hair and blue eyes of his Saxborough ancestors, looked anxiously across at his mother, and I whispered, 'She's slept for the last hour.'

'Thank heaven.' He looked at me, anguish in his eyes, for he adored his mother. 'I can't get the sound of her sobbing out of my head, Drusilla. Her whole body shook with it----- and nothing I did-------' His voice choked with emotion, and I put a comforting hand on his arm.

'There's nothing you could have done. None of us could.' Tears misted my eyes, for I'd found her sobbing every bit as heart-rending as he had.

'I shouldn't have left you alone all this time, but------'

'You and Thomas had other things to attend to.' Wanting to take both our minds off his mother's distress, I asked, 'Did you find your father's horse?'

'Eventually. I had to put the poor thing down.' He ran a hand across his eyes at the memory of it. 'It had got caught up in a thicket and broken a leg trying to escape.' I asked which horse it was and he said, 'The young chestnut.'

'The horse he bought three days ago?' I blurted out in surprise, speaking so much louder than I'd meant to that Marguerite stirred in her sleep, silencing us both. Giles merely nodded in answer, as if it didn't matter which horse it was. Marguerite settled back into a deep sleep, and not wanting to disturb her again, I said nothing more. But, to me, that one fact couldn't have been more significant. For, to my mind, it changed everything.

Meanwhile, Giles informed me in his gentle way, 'Mudd is waiting to escort you home, Drusilla. I'll sit with Mama until you come back with Lucie.'

Lucie, my cousin, was betrothed to Giles, and the wistful note in his voice betrayed how very much he needed her by his side. She and my Aunt Thirza, who had been my guests at Westfleet since September, had gone on an outing with friends and weren't expected back until dusk. I knew that when Lucie heard about Mr. Saxborough, nothing would keep her from Giles, or from helping me with Marguerite.

Riding the four miles home across the Downs, I thought about what Giles had told me; that his father had been riding the powerful, highly-strung young chestnut horse he'd bought a mere three days earlier. For, as I saw it, this meant the circumstances of Mr. Saxborough's death no longer fitted together as they should. The kind of situation I had learnt to recognise when helping my father solve the puzzles encountered in gathering facts for his highly praised book, "The History of the Isle of Wight." An experience that had taught me things were not always what they seemed.

But I wasn't able to speak to Thomas and Giles about it until after breakfast the following morning. They had so much to see to, what with the funeral to arrange, letters to write, people calling to offer their condolences, estate matters to be dealt with, and thirteen year old Tom, at school at Winchester, had to be brought home. Thomas was a widower, Tom being his only surviving child.

I found Thomas and Giles in the library discussing the funeral arrangements, but as soon as I entered the room, Thomas stood up and set a chair for me, inquiring how Marguerite was this morning.

'As well as can be expected,' I said, seeing no point adding to his troubles by describing how very distraught she still was. 'She's sleeping at the moment, and Lucie's sitting with her.'

'Poor Mama,' Giles sighed, glancing at the clock in the corner of the room. 'This time yesterday father was bursting with health----no wonder she can't take it in.'

Thomas reflected sadly, 'When I think of the times he jumped that gate----'

Looking at their grieving faces I wished what I had to say could wait, but that wasn't possible, so I said quietly, 'Perhaps it didn't happen the way it looked.'

Thomas stared at me, puzzled. 'How do you mean, Drusilla? There's no mystery, surely? Father was on one side of the gate, and his horse half a mile away on the other. Isn't it obvious what happened? Father found the gate closed, and decided to jump it, as any of us might have done.'

Gently I insisted, 'Not on that horse.' If it had been any other, I would have accepted it as easily as they had.

There were many things I had not liked about Cuthbert Saxborough; his harsh treatment of servants, his arrogance, his belief that a woman's opinion was of little consequence, but I had always admired his ability with horses. To them he showed only patience and love, taking his time over schooling them, gaining their confidence, learning all their little idiosyncrasies. And for him to urge a newly-acquired, nervous young animal over that particular gate, was so utterly out of keeping with everything I knew of him, I simply did not believe he had done it.

When I asked Giles if he didn't think it odd, he lifted his shoulders a little. 'Dr Redding believes father broke his neck when he fell from his horse,' he said, as if that settled the matter. Convinced he hadn't had time to think about it properly, I said nothing, but he instantly made it clear he had thought about it, and drawn a different conclusion. 'We all do stupid things on occasion Drusilla, things we'd never even consider normally. Like that time you were caught in a thunderstorm

when out walking, and took a short cut home through a field.'
Giles had seen it all from a nearby hill.

Thomas looked puzzled. 'What was wrong with that?'

'The field had a bull in it,' Giles grinned, savouring the
memory. 'I didn't know Drusilla could run that fast.'

'You're never going to let me forget that, are you,' I
groaned.

A faint smile tugged at his lips. 'The thing is Drusilla,
the fact that it was risky didn't stop you. You gave way to an
impulse. And that's what father must have done.'

Unconvinced, I asked, 'Did you find out who shut the
east gate?'

He shook his head. 'I spoke to the gamekeeper, and every
groom and gardener. No-one was anywhere near that part of
the estate. Except me, that is. I rode that way half an hour
before the accident, and the gate was open then.'

'Did you see anyone in the woods?'

'Not a soul.'

'Well, someone shut it,' I pointed out reasonably.

'Does it really matter? All Father had to do was stop and
open it.' This was true, but nothing they had said removed the
doubts from my mind.

Nor was I convinced by the inquest verdict of "Death By
Misadventure." Mr Saxborough had certainly broken his neck
when he fell from his horse. But what was it that caused him
to be thrown?

In the difficult days following the funeral, I still hoped
the truth would come out, as such things often did. But that
didn't happen, nor did I learn anything new from my own
discreet and thorough inquiries. Everyone believed it was an

accident, and as life slowly returned to normal, I even began to wonder if they were right.

Yet, something deep inside of me kept insisting it wasn't so. A persistent nagging conviction, of the kind I'd experienced on the day my father died of a seizure, when I couldn't rid myself of the feeling, soon after we parted to dress for dinner, that something was wrong. That had taught me never to ignore instinct.

I still missed my father badly, and the happy life we had led. I'd loved working on his book, and revelled in the sheer exhilaration of solving a mystery that had puzzled us for weeks. We began by listing the known facts on large sheets of paper, and fixing them to the walls of the workroom where they could be seen at a glance. Sometimes, a small detail, of the kind easily forgotten if we hadn't written it down, led us to the solution of a problem. And we would dance around the workroom like mad things, clapping and laughing.

The idea for the charts had been mine, and thinking of those happy times one night when I couldn't sleep, I decided to use the same system to try to find out what had really happened to my godfather. If I was capable of solving anything by myself, I thought ruefully. And if I could bring myself to spend any length of time in the workroom; something I'd avoided since father's death, for everything in it reminded me of him in a way no other room did, this being where he was at his happiest.

It was time I faced it, I told myself, ignoring the lump in my throat, but before I could do so, my aunt's situation, which had worried me ever since September, when she and Lucie first arrived at Westfleet, suddenly became far more frightening. So frightening, it wasn't easy for any of us to remain calm, my aunt least of all, as became very plain one morning when I returned home to find the house in an uproar.

Aunt Thirza stood at the top of the sweeping staircase, her skirts wrapped tightly round her ankles, her eyes fixed on the servants scurrying about the hall with brooms. Jeffel, my butler, who had been at Westfleet since just before I was born, was directing operations in his usual calm manner, while Lucie watched from beside the staircase. Joining her, I asked quietly, 'What on earth is going on?'

No-one, seeing us together, would have taken us for cousins, for she barely reached the top of my shoulder. In fact the only thing we had in common was a snub nose. My light brown curls, hazel eyes and good complexion were nothing out of the ordinary, whereas Lucie had the most ravishing looks. Lustrous black hair framed a flawless oval face, her smile revealed even white teeth, and her figure, at just nineteen, was perfect. It was no wonder, I thought, that Giles had fallen in love with her, and their betrothal at Christmas had pleased us all.

Startled, she turned quickly. 'I didn't see you come in, Drusilla.' And she confided, 'There's a mouse in the hall. The cat brought it in through the drawing room window when Mama and I were sewing.' Jess, the kitchen cat, was sitting on the bottom stair, innocently grooming herself, and casting an occasional disdainful eye at the antics of the servants. Aware of my aunt's dislike of mice, I put up a brief, but vain, struggle against my worst instincts, and urged Lucie to go on.

'Well---'she said, her lips twitching at the memory, 'Mama jumped onto her chair and begged me to *do* something.'

I inquired, rather unsteadily, 'And did you? Do something, I mean?'

'I rang for Jeffel.'

'Was she - er - standing on the chair when he came in?'

She giggled and nodded. My shoulders shook, for I wished I had seen his face. Wondering how he'd managed to control himself, I spluttered, 'W-what d-did Jeffel do?'

'He got it out of the room, but only into the hall.'

At that moment one of the servants shouted out he'd got the little varmint with his shovel. The mouse was removed and we watched in amusement as Jess, deprived of her prey, stalked out the hall in disgust, her tail held high.

My aunt came downstairs, visibly trembling, and my amusement changed to concern. For we all had weaknesses, and she was easily distressed at present. Ordering some reviving tea to be brought to the drawing room, I persuaded her into a comfortable chair, whereupon she insisted the whole episode was the fault of the servants. 'They always leave the windows open too wide, Drusilla. None of them can be trusted to do even the simplest task correctly.'

I managed to hold my tongue by reminding myself, as I had a hundred times throughout these past months, of the terrible strain she was under, and that I ought to make allowances for her behaviour. If only I had more patience, I thought. When helping father with his work I'd had all the patience in the world, but I had none at all for the kind of trivial matters my aunt fussed over.

Aunt Thirza was my mother's sister, although the only portrait I possessed of my mother showed little resemblance between them. My aunt's hair, on which she had set a cap of the finest lace, was very much darker than mother's fair curls, which I had inherited, and her features were rather plain, but at forty her figure was still trim, and in elegance she outshone us all.

She was married to Charles Frere, a Frenchman by birth, whose father had died when he was a baby. His English mother had soon returned to London, bringing up her son as an English gentleman. But when his French godfather unexpectedly left him a property in Normandy, offering a degree of affluence he'd never thought to enjoy, my uncle sold his London home and moved his family to France; which seemed the sensible thing to do early in that year of 1788. Just eighteen months before the storming of the Bastille, and the start of the revolution.

His property was not large, nor was he very rich, but in France landowners were now the enemies of the people. When Charles Danton, one of the revolutionary leaders, became Minister of Justice, my uncle had sent my aunt and cousin to Westfleet for their own safety, while he stayed behind in the hope of saving his estate from the Revolutionaries. His weekly letters, arriving fairly regularly throughout the autumn and winter, were optimistic; unlike the newspapers, which were full of reports of murder and mayhem, and of hordes of sans-culottes running riot.

Even so, it wasn't until February, when France declared war on England, that my aunt began to despair. For, without my uncle's letters, how was she to know if he was safe? Giles, seeing her distress, arranged for an exchange of letters to take place every Saturday, at a secret location in Normandy; my uncle's letter brought by a loyal servant, my aunt's by an Island smuggler, paid by Giles. For the last two weeks, however, my uncle's servant had not arrived. Anxious as I was too, I suggested the man must be ill, for my uncle dared trust no other servant. Meanwhile, we could only wait and hope. A situation that made her increasingly difficult to live with, for she picked a dozen arguments a day with servants, Lucie, myself, and even it seemed, with poor Jess, the kitchen cat. I had never in all my life had to bite my tongue as much as I did now.

2

What Aunt Thirza needed was some useful occupation, something to help take her mind off her fears for my uncle. I knew exactly what she would enjoy, and I meant to suggest it to her if the situation didn't change soon. But in the morning she was much more cheerful, even insisting I went for my usual ride. Thus, I sent a message to the stables for Orlando to be saddled, meaning to return within the hour. Utterly unaware that this was to be no ordinary morning ride.

After a fast gallop across Hokewell Down, I stopped at the highest point to enjoy the view, patting Orlando's neck and murmuring soft words of endearment. Glancing in the direction of Ledstone woods, my eyes were inevitably drawn to the spot where I had found Mr Saxborough's body, and I shuddered. I hadn't had time to write down the facts about his death yet, but I was determined to do so this afternoon, when my aunt and cousin planned to visit friends.

I was about to urge Orlando on again, when I saw the parson cantering through the Ledstone Place parklands towards the woods, his ungainly manner of riding being quite unmistakable, even from up here. If he was heading back to his parsonage at Westfleet, I could not hope to avoid him up here on the open Down, and I was thoroughly sick of the wretched man, having bumped into him every day for the past week.

And that was why I did it really. Spurring Orlando into a gallop, I soon reached the woods, and seeing no sign of the parson on the bridle path, I plunged into a dense area of shrubs and trees, meaning to wait until he had passed by. If only it had been that simple.

The deafening report of a gunshot was my undoing. Fired from a spot so near to the tree I was hiding under, that my horse whinnied and reared up in fright, pitching me straight into a mass of vicious looking stinging nettles. I failed to hang on to Orlando's reins, and as the tall nettles closed over me, stinging every bare inch of my face and neck, I heard him crashing through the undergrowth in panic. Thrusting the nettles aside with gloved hands, I scrambled up onto my knees, and uttered a word that would have shocked my old nurse. At which point, from somewhere behind me came a deep male chuckle. 'Dear me. How very unladylike.'

A tall man, in a fawn shooting jacket, strode into sight, laid his gun against a tree trunk, and clasping his hands firmly round my waist, lifted me out of the nettles with commendable ease, for despite my slender build, I am no featherweight. But my face was smarting too much to dwell upon that, or to care what he thought of my language, and I simply pointed to some nearby dock leaves, uttering a heartfelt, 'If you would be so good, sir.'

Grabbing a handful of the healing leaves, he passed them to me. 'Can I assist?' I shook my head, rubbing the leaves vigorously over my face and neck, until I began to feel a little more human again. But instead of expressing regret for his behaviour, as I had expected, and which I would have happily accepted, he said, 'I don't wish to pry into your affairs ma'am, but may I ask why you were skulking under that tree?'

'I was not skulking,' I retorted, choking with anger, for his tone of voice clearly implied that whoever was at fault, it certainly wasn't him. 'I suppose I must count myself fortunate not to be lying dead at your feet.'

His lips twitched in amusement. 'Impossible. I was aiming in the opposite direction.' Utterly unperturbed he also advised, 'Dark clothing is not easily seen in the middle of a wood. I might have noticed red.'

'Indeed?' I retorted icily. 'Unhappily I cannot wear red at present. I am still in mourning for my father.'

He was instantly contrite. 'I do beg your pardon, Lady Drusilla. It slipped my-----'

I gasped. 'How do you know my name?'

His brows rose in prim reproach. 'I learnt it ma'am when we were formally introduced.'

My anger subsided quickly, as it always did, and I stared at him, utterly baffled, having assumed him to be a guest of Thomas Saxborough at Ledstone Place. If we had met, I was certain I would have remembered him, if for no other reason than I had to look up at him. A situation I did not often find myself in, but he was at least three inches taller than me, slim yet muscular in build and about my own age. His countenance was interesting rather than handsome, he had jet black thick, wavy hair, and bushy eyebrows; a combination that made his eyes appear a much deeper shade of brown than perhaps they really were.

Smiling down at me, his dark eyes assessed me with practised ease. 'Admit it ma'am, you have forgotten me. Whereas I remember you very well. Your pretty fair curls, sparkling hazel eyes, and so much firm resolve in your nature, that I am at a loss to understand why you were under that tree. Who were you hiding f-----?' He stopped speaking on seeing Mr Upton riding slowly along the track some fifty yards away, leading my horse, and asked in disbelief, 'Him?' I felt my cheeks flushing, for I saw how absurd my behaviour must appear to him. But, before I could answer, he said, 'I had the dubious honour of meeting the parson yesterday. I grant you the man's a dead bore and rides like a demented wasp, but----'

'He is also the most pompous, irritating little man it has ever been my misfortune to meet.'

Feeling decidedly foolish, I started to explain why I wished to avoid the parson, but he wasn't attending, his eyes being on Mr Upton who, having tethered the horses, was forcing his way through the tangled undergrowth towards us. 'Nothing seems to be going right for you today, does it,' the anonymous gentleman murmured under his breath.

Mr Upton, now within hailing distance, called out, 'Lady Drusilla, thank goodness I've found you.' Struggling through a patch of low brambles, he gasped, 'Oh, and Mr Reevers too.'

'Reevers?' I repeated, turning to that gentleman in surprise. 'Radleigh Reevers? Giles's cousin?' We had met at Ledstone as children; but only once, Cuthbert Saxborough having discouraged visits from his six sisters and their families, who all lived on the mainland.

'Giles's *obnoxious* cousin was what you used to call me,' he reminded me provokingly, his eyes alight with laughter.

'Yes, I did, didn't I.' Reflecting on the episode with the nettles, I murmured, 'I really should have guessed.'

I was still thinking of that when Mr Upton reached us. He was a short, skinny man of around fifty, with thinning grey hair, whose sermons were long and tedious, and who was too fond, in my opinion, of preaching to his congregation that it was their duty to bear, without question or complaint, what-ever misfortunes came their way.

I thanked him sincerely for looking after Orlando, but he wasn't really listening; his mind clearly on something else. 'Lady Drusilla, as you know, I am never one to shirk my duty. And I must ask you, what is going on here?'

I stared at him, completely bewildered. 'I beg your pardon?'

He looked from Mr Reevers to me, and back again, in a way that left me in no doubt of his meaning. And I saw a muscle twitch at the corner of Mr Reevers' mouth. 'When I came across Orlando grazing by the track, I feared you had suffered an accident. Now I find you *alone* with Mr Reevers. What am I to think, ma'am?'

For a moment I was too dumbfounded to speak, but Mr Reevers quelled this insufferable little man with a single look. 'You forget yourself, sir. Lady Drusilla did suffer an accident, as you suspected, and I merely came to her assistance.'

'Ah, I see,' he acknowledged, unabashed. 'In that case---' And he frowned, as another thought struck him. 'But ma'am, what made you ride so far into the dense part of the wood?'

Again, Mr Reevers was equal to the occasion. 'Lady Drusilla saw a – um - a bird, I think you said, ma'am?'

He was standing slightly behind the parson, his expression clearly inviting me to enter into this farce, which I did with great relish. 'You can't have forgotten already, Mr Reevers.'

'Memory like a sieve, ma'am,' he confessed meekly. 'Let me think... was it a curlew?'

'A curlew?' the parson burst out in astonishment. 'In the woods?'

I shook my head, laughing. 'Not a curlew, Mr Reevers. A cuckoo.'

'Ah, I knew it was something beginning with a 'c'.' And the corners of his wide mouth turned upwards into a most engaging smile.

Mr Upton did not possess a sense of humour, but never missed an opportunity to air his knowledge. 'A curlew is a wading bird, Mr Reevers,' he announced, with a superior smile. 'Its habitat is always by water.' Mr Reevers listened in such apparent rapt attention, I had to bit my lip. 'The cuckoo, of course, does favour woodland areas. It is heard more often than seen. Lady Drusilla was indeed fortunate to see----.'

'I was,' I agreed. 'By keeping very still, I was able to watch it for some time.' After which it was a simple matter for Mr Reevers to relate how he'd inadvertently fired a shot, causing Orlando to unseat me.

I was still smiling as I rode home, for Mr Reevers, seeing the humour of the situation, had given way to it at once. Back at Westfleet, having explained what had delayed me, my aunt lectured me on the evils of riding unaccompanied by a groom, as I sometimes did. Which I endured in silence, gritting my teeth, and reminding myself I must not upset her.

A brisk walk round the gardens calmed me down, and when my aunt and cousin left to visit their friends, I went indoors to write down what I knew about Mr Saxborough's death. Finding Jeffel in the hall, I informed him I would be in the workroom if he needed me. Catching the faint look of surprise on his face, I admitted a little ruefully. 'Yes, I know, I have rather neglected it lately.'

'Very understandable, if I may say so, my lady.' Jeffel, a man of good sense, cheerful disposition and quiet efficiency, had been at the Manor for some twenty-seven years, and I could not imagine Westfleet without him. Tall and dark-haired, he had immense patience, as I remembered from my childhood, when he had never minded me pestering him, sometimes giving me piggyback rides around the hall if the weather was foul and father had gone out on business. But that had been a long time ago, and he said now, 'You'll find everything as you left it, my lady. And the windows were cleaned only yesterday.'

'Thank you,' I smiled.

But I didn't reach the workroom, for at that moment Giles, Thomas, and young Tom, came bowling up the drive in a gig. Being fond of them all, I was always pleased to see them. Once we were seated in the drawing room, Giles handed me a small package. 'We thought you might find this useful.' Hearing Tom's stifled giggle, I unwrapped it warily. Inside were several dock leaves. 'In case Orlando throws you into any more sting-ing nettles,' Giles chortled. And they all fell about laughing.

Half smiling, I commented dryly, 'I suppose it was foolish of me to expect any sympathy from you three.'

Wiping his eyes, Giles spluttered, 'What was it father said in his Will?' He clasped a hand to his forehead, making a pretence of thinking. 'Ah yes, I remember now. He said, you were the only female on the entire Island capable of riding his horses.' Mr Saxborough had settled a sum on money on his other godchildren, which would have meant nothing to me, as father's death had left me a very wealthy woman. As I learnt later, it was Giles's suggestion that I should choose a horse from my godfather's stables.

Thomas continued in the same bantering tone. 'The ques-tion must be asked Giles, were you wise to propose that kind of bequest to him?'

Ignoring their teasing, I said,' I'm very glad you did.' I'd coveted Orlando from the moment I first saw him, and

Thomas had insisted on giving him to me the day after the Will was read.

Giles smiled. 'He actually asked my advice. The first time I ever remember him doing so.' I caught the faint hint of sadness in his voice, for he had never been close to his father.

'Well, I couldn't be more grateful.'

He beamed at me warmly. 'I'll remember that when I need a favour.'

'A favour?' Thomas hooted in brotherly derision. 'When did you ever ask anyone for help?'

I joined in the laughter mocking Giles's legendary independence. 'Yes, Giles, do tell us. I should like to commit such a unique occasion to memory.'

Tom chimed in cheekily, 'You can't remember, can you Uncle Giles?'

Giles pretended to cuff his ear. 'Quiet, shrimp. There's nothing wrong with relying on oneself.'

'I'm not a shrimp.'

'Indeed, you are not Tom,' I agreed fondly. In fact he was almost as tall as Thomas, and rather handsome too, having inherited the Saxborough blue eyes and blond hair. Whereas Giles barely reached even medium height and had his mother's angelic looks, which combined with the Saxborough eyes and hair, gave him an almost girlish appearance. A sickly childhood having left him on the skinny side, he looked as if a gust of wind would easily bowl him over, leaving no outward indication of the iron resolve that lay behind those delicate features.

I'd noticed Tom was still limping slightly, and I asked when he was going back to school. 'Not until next term.' And he grinned. 'Dr. Redding said one hour at Winchester could undo all his efforts.' The day after Cuthbert's funeral, Tom had damaged his knee rather badly in a fall from a tree, when trying to extricate his kite. 'He won't even allow me to ride for another week.'

Giles ruffled the boy's hair. 'Still, he did say you can go sailing.'

'That's good news, Tom,' I encouraged.

His father said, 'He's to sit on the boat like a lady, and simply enjoy the sea air. And he'll do as he's told, if he wants that new fishing rod he's been pestering me to buy for his birthday.'

Before they left, Giles told me there had been no exchange of letters from my aunt and uncle on Saturday. 'That's three weeks now,' I said, a cold shiver running through me. 'My uncle's servant wasn't there, I suppose?'

He shook his head. 'Try not to despair, Drusilla. It so happens I'm acquainted with some people in that part of Normandy. I'll write to them. They might have heard something, you know how these things get about. Jacob, the man who collects your uncle's letters, is willing to deliver it.'

'I would be so grateful, Giles. But you must tell Jacob not to put himself at risk. My uncle wouldn't want that.'

'Jacob is a smuggler, Drusilla. He's used to taking risks. In any case, nothing may come of it,' he warned. 'It's just a chance, that's all.' I promised to pass the message on to my aunt, but she would know, as I did, what a very slim chance it was.

The only hope we could cling to, was that my uncle might be in hiding, although I didn't really believe it. I feared it was far more likely he was either dead, or in the hands of the revolutionaries.

3

Once the three Saxboroughs had driven off, I crossed the hall to the workroom, advising my butler, 'If anyone else calls Jeffel, I am not at home.'

'Very good, my lady.'

Taking one very deep breath, I went inside. Shutting the door, I leant against it, my senses instantly assailed by the old familiar smell of books, mixed with a faint hint of the sea from the fossils we had collected. I soon saw that everything was precisely where it had been on the night my father died. The room was free from dust, cleaned by the servants in the way father had directed, without disturbing what we were working on.

The fossil collection, which father had begun some thirty years ago, was displayed in waist-high cabinets across the width of the room, against the wall dividing the workroom from the library. In the centre was a long specially made table, constructed in sections; the tools and microscope father had used an hour before he died, were still at the end nearest to the fossil cabinets. Our desks, placed so that we faced each other, were beside the middle window to gain the best of the light, essential in an east-facing room.

In the darkest corner, well out of the morning sun on fine days, stood a tall bookcase, filled with father's favourite books, including a copy of his own, "The History of the Isle of Wight." The idea for this book had come to my father, Robert Davanish, Earl of Angmere, through his own love of the Island, and a desire to learn more of its secrets. A task he'd taken very seriously, wanting his book to be the most accurate and detailed ever written about the Island. This meant finding out the truth about everything from the tale of the immensely rich Isabella de Fortibus selling the Isle of Wight to Edward I, when on her deathbed, down to the rumours that the great grandmother of one of the Island's most respected men had been a rather ambitious parlour maid. The Island's powerful families naturally played a large part in its history; the story of William Saxborough being the most intriguing, and scandalous. And the one, I have to admit, I most enjoyed investigating. Father wrote the actual book, which had been very well received, and had an impressively long list of subscribers.

My job had been to record the Island's historical facts, and those of the great families, from Roman times to the present day, along with stories of shipwrecks and smuggling. And to help solve the mysteries we found.

I don't know how long I leant against that door, but eventually I forced myself to walk round the room, touching familiar things, before stopping in front of the charts that ran the length of, and were fixed to, the long inside wall opposite the windows. These showed father's first discoveries for a second book, on the Island's history before the Romans.

The shutters that usually covered the charts, keeping out the light, had not been pulled down on that last night, as we had meant to continue working after dinner, and the ink was already fading. Deciding I must make a start somewhere, I removed those sheets, rolled them carefully and stored them in a cabinet in case I ever decided to carry on with that venture.

The room felt decidedly chilly, and as I went to close the windows, I saw father's spectacles. He had put them on his desk before going to dress for dinner on that fateful December day, leaving them ready for use that evening; an evening he was never to see. I picked them up, blinded by tears, and slowly ran my finger round the metal frame, choking over the memories of those frantic searches whenever he mislaid them, and how, invariably, I was the one who found them.

Slipping them into his desk drawer, I closed the window with fingers that still trembled, wishing I'd never come in here, for I felt father's presence in a way that didn't happen in other rooms. And I knew exactly what he'd advise me to do in this situation; that I should simply get on with things.

Thus I took a fresh sheet of paper from a drawer, spread it out on the long table, securing each corner with fossils kept handy for that purpose. Selecting a new quill pen, I checked there was plenty of ink in the standish, and jotted down the sequence of events concerning Cuthbert's death, as I recalled them.

I took my time, wanting to be sure of including every tiny detail. My hand shook a little as I recorded how I had found his body, my writing becoming firmer when I moved on to the facts surrounding the incident. I noted I had not seen his horse; that Giles had found it later in a dense thicket with its leg broken, and had put it down himself. He had also gained Thomas's permission to remove the gate, so that when Marguerite went that way, she would not be reminded of how Cuthbert had died. Giles had always been very considerate of his mother's feelings.

I added that no-one knew who had closed the gate, and that I had found no fresh marks on it. A picture of what I had seen came into my mind; that for several yards in front of the gate, the mud had been much smoother. Yet, how could that be? People rode down the track every day. As I puzzled over it, the door opened, and Jeffel came into the room. Having told him I did not wish to be interrupted, I raised my brows at him in surprise.

'I beg your pardon for disturbing you my lady, but Mr Arnold would be grateful if you could spare him a few minutes on a matter of importance.'

William Arnold, the Island's postmaster and highly respected Collector of Customs, was based at Cowes. Now in his middle years, he had been a good friend to my father, and never bothered me over trivialities. On going into the library, his unusually grave expression made my heart sink a little, for the last thing I needed was yet another problem. Neatly dressed in breeches, a dark brown coat, white shirt and a plain cravat secured with a workmanlike pin, he bowed and greeted me with his usual quiet good manners, but refused my offer of refreshments, insisting he must not stay long.

I always had time for William Arnold. An agreeable man, who had been most helpful in supplying information about Island trade and shipping for my father's book; a copy of which father had given him for his own bookcase. Perhaps the most demanding of his many responsibilities was the detection of smuggling activities on the Isle of Wight. Unlike some in his position, he did not accept bribes to turn a blind eye to free trading. Nevertheless, a great deal of contraband was brought ashore unnoticed, there being too many landing places around the Island's coastline for his men to watch them all. He freely admitted too that he often sent up a prayer, when invited to a dinner party, that his host would not offer him smuggled brandy.

In exchanging the usual civilities I inquired after his wife, and he said, 'She's in good health, thank you, ma'am. The children keep her busy, of course, but she doesn't mind that, she tells me.'

I asked if he had recent news of John Delafield, one of Mrs Arnold's brothers, who had emigrated to New York some years previously, and he admitted sadly, 'Regrettably not. I'm afraid our correspondence has become somewhat lax of late, which is as much my fault as his. And I doubt he'll ever come home now he's acquired a rich American wife. Although I don't say as much to Martha, of course. She still misses him a good deal.' And he went on to explain the purpose of his visit. 'It grieves me to tell you ma'am, that my most reliable informant says Smith's farm is being used to hide smuggled goods.'

Jeremiah Smith was one of my tenants, and I had made it perfectly clear to him, as I had to them all, that my land was not to be used for smuggling purposes. That is, if they wished to remain my tenants. The laws governing smuggling were far from sensible, but while they remained in force, I would adhere to them. To find I was being disobeyed made me so angry I couldn't speak for a moment. A fact that did not escape my visitor.

'I can see you're as mad as fire ma'am, and so would I be if-------'

'I want him caught, Mr Arnold.'

He inclined his head. 'You can be sure I shall do my best, ma'am.'

Seething, I strode over to the window, staring unseeingly at the ox-eye daisies swaying in the breeze. 'When my father was alive, Smith wouldn't have dared to defy him. I imagine he thinks a woman is easier to fool.'

'No doubt he does ma'am, him being a man of little intelligence.'

Turning away from the window, I saw the understanding in his eyes, and apologised for my outburst with a rather shamefaced laugh. 'I'm afraid I was so furious I-----'

'Think nothing of it, ma'am. I don't, I assure you. Believe me, if every landowner was even half as co-operative, my job would be a good deal easier.'

I sat down again, calm enough now to think coherently. 'So what happens next? Will you search Smith's farm?'

He hesitated. 'Well ma'am, regrettably it's not quite as easy as that. These gangs naturally prefer farms close to the coast like Smith's, where contraband can be hidden quickly. Donkeys hauling kegs inland carries a greater risk of being caught. Mind you, houses and farms near the coast are the first places we look, so the hiding place has to be well thought out. We've found contraband hidden inside hayricks, under barn floors, in deep ditches, even buried in fields. But I have to catch Smith with the goods, and it might only be on his farm for a day or two. It would be easy if I knew where Smith's hiding place is, but my informant wasn't able to tell me.'

I nodded in sympathy, appreciating his difficulties. 'Well, I'll keep my eyes open, Mr. Arnold. I visit him frequently, and he's used to my poking into corners, asking awkward questions.'

'Ma'am, I applaud your sentiments, but Smith is a rogue and—'

'He's also extremely lazy, which is why I inspect his farm so often. And I might notice something.'

He paused, weighing up what I had said. 'In truth ma'am, I should be grateful for any information. But, we'll get Smith sooner or later, you can be sure of that.' And he got to his feet. 'If you'll excuse me ma'am, I must be about my business. I'm much obliged to you for your support in this matter.' After he'd gone, I sat thinking about Smith. He was both lazy, and greedy. Hiding contraband on his farm paid well, and required very little effort from him.

Smuggling was a fact of life on the Island, and many landowners were happy for a keg of brandy to be left by a rear door. The law hadn't stopped smuggling, nor would it when men earned more in one night's smuggling than in a week of working long hours on the land. When challenged by Mr Arnold's men at sea or by the Riding Officers ashore, they fought ferociously, for capture meant a long prison sentence, or five years pressed into the Navy, causing great suffering to their wives and children. Men who worked for the Revenue service were not popular with other locals, although Mr Arnold himself was highly respected in Island society. Even by those who regularly bought their brandy from smugglers.

Well, what other people chose to do was their business; as for Smith, he would regret the day he decided to disobey me.

I asked myself how father would have dealt with Smith, but had to admit it had not been the same for him as it was for me. Father had taught me how to run the estate, and it was a task I usually enjoyed. I had known all the tenants, apart from Smith, most of my life, Smith having lived at Cliff Farm for just five years. The others were decent, hard working people, and I had not expected any difficulties from them, or Smith, for that matter, following father's death. For, I kept their houses in good repair, dealt with any problems they had, showed genuine interest in them and their children, and believed them to be satisfied with their lives.

It was Cuthbert Saxborough who had warned me that, as a woman, I could not expect to control my tenants as my father had. And despite my protests, I knew most men agreed with him. Smith was clearly one of them. Well, he would soon learn how very wrong he was.

Not wanting to put Smith on his guard by storming down to his farm now, I decided to wait until morning, when I would be calmer. I returned to my notes on Mr Saxborough's demise, but I couldn't concentrate and eventually gave up. Needing something to take my mind off Smith, I decided to visit Marguerite Saxborough. I had called on my godmother virtually every day since she became a widow, for I loved her dearly, and an hour with her always left me smiling. It was exactly the tonic I needed right now.

When Parker, the Ledstone butler, ushered me into Marguerite's own personal drawing room, I found her reclining on a day bed, a pretty cap perched on her golden locks. Beside her, on a small table were medicines to cure every possible disorder, from smelling salts to an evil-looking potion for palpitations of the heart. She greeted me languidly, apologising for the curtains being drawn, but she had the headache. In fact, the curtains were only partially drawn. Her couch, positioned by the window, overlooked a formal garden and a particularly splendid fountain, and had an excellent view of the long drive that ran up to the house. And, more importantly, everyone who used it.

Scattered around the floor by the day bed, were several bandboxes full of letters and mementoes. As I sat on a chair beside her, she indicated the boxes in despairing fashion, saying distractedly, 'I'm so glad you're here, Drusilla. I don't know what I'm going to do. Giles says there isn't enough room at Norton House for everything I want to take.'

'I'm not surprised,' I teased affectionately, indicating the letters spilling onto the floor. Of the five houses belonging to the Saxborough estate, Ledstone Place was naturally the most splendid; Norton House, the finest of the rest, had been left to Giles in his father's Will, along with a sum of money in keeping with his position as the younger son. It was there he and Lucie would start married life, and Marguerite was to live with them.

The announcement of their betrothal had appeared in the 'Morning Post' shortly before Christmas, and I couldn't help thinking how different our lives had been back then. Before France declared war on us, and when Giles's father, and my own, had been alive.

It had been obvious from the start that Lucie and Giles were smitten with each other, and everyone, including Marguerite, had watched their courtship in delight. But, now, the prospect of moving made her say mournfully, 'I don't want to live at Norton House, Drusilla. I must go, of course. Only I know I shall hate it. Ledstone is my home and I want to end my days here, not in that horrid little cottage.' As Norton House possessed some fine reception rooms, several large bedchambers, and gardens that ran down to the beach, I had some difficulty keeping my composure.

What she really wanted, was for her and Giles to remain at Ledstone; but that was out of the question, Thomas had his own life to lead. Thus, I pointed out cheerfully, 'But you have always wished Ledstone had a view over the sea, and there is no better sight of the Solent than the one from Norton House.'

'That may be so, but *all* the rooms overlooking the Solent face North,' she complained petulantly, and shuddering at the prospect of having to sit in cold north-facing rooms for the rest of her days, pulled her shawl even tighter across her ample bosom.

I bit my lip firmly. 'To view the Solent from a south facing room, you need a house on the mainland.'

'What? And move away from all my friends?' Marguerite's eyes widened in horror. 'Besides, that would mean crossing that awful stretch of water.' Her whole body shuddered. 'And that, I have sworn never to do again. The last time it took eight hours and I thought I was going to die.'

'Then I'm surprised you wish to have a view of the water.'

'Oh, but the sea is so pretty to look at with all the boats bobbing about on it. Cuthbert often used to drive me to watch our brave sailors putting out to sea.' A tiny sob escaped her. 'Only that's all over now.' Impulsively she reached out and clasped my arm. 'Oh why did he have to jump that silly gate?' I didn't know the answer to that yet. In fact, there was only one thing I was absolutely certain of; that I would not stop until I had found out.

4

I comforted her as best I could, and after she had dried her tears, I tried to distract her mind from such thoughts by turning her attention back to the problem of the letters.

Gazing at the vast collection before me, I was convinced she had kept every letter she had ever received. 'Well, I won't burn Cuthbert's love letters, no matter what Giles says,' she announced in growing agitation.

Startled, I protested, 'I'm quite sure Giles doesn't mean-----'

'Or those from my parents, or my poor dear brother.'

'But you hated your brother.'

'Well yes, I did, when he was alive, ' she agreed cordially. 'Only now he's dead, I find I like him *much* better.' I struggled with myself before giving way to a fit of the giggles, for which I was gently chided. 'He was my brother Drusilla, however detestable. I won't throw his letters away. And if I keep them, then I must keep those from Cuthbert's brother too.'

I stared at her, convinced I hadn't heard correctly. Cuthbert's six sisters had all married gentlemen on the mainland; four of them, including Mr Reevers' mother, having since died, but I had never heard anyone mention a brother. 'Mr Saxborough had a brother?'

'Oh yes. Vincent was the youngest of them all, although I only met him once. He died when Giles was barely out of leading strings. Cuthbert never spoke of him after that, but he wouldn't want me to burn his letters. Nor those from my friends. Nor the invitations from my London season.'

No wonder Giles was concerned about having enough space at Norton House, which was less than half the size of Ledstone Place, if he had to house such items as five band-boxes of letters, mostly from long dead relatives. Persuading her to part with any of them would not be easy, but as most letters had been left unfolded and thrown into the boxes in haphazard fashion, wasting a great deal of space, I suggested, 'If it was all packed very carefully, I daresay they would fit into two bandboxes. Then you'd have three empty ones and----'

'Giles won't realise I've kept everything,' she exclaimed, clapping her hands together in delight. 'Drusilla, you are so clever. I would never have thought of that.' Not that she made any effort to do the task herself, being content to watch me first fold, then flatten all the letters. When everything fitted easily into two boxes, she beamed, 'Thank you, Drusilla. 'What should I do without you?'

I regarded her in some amusement. 'Get someone else to do it, of course.' An infectious chuckle escaped her, and she settled herself gracefully on the sofa, not in the least put out by my accurate assessment of her character.

Then, suddenly, she snatched up a card I'd placed in one of the bandboxes, hugging it to her bosom before showing me what it was. An invitation to her own wedding. Misty-eyed, she admitted candidly, 'Most people thought I married Cuthbert because he paid Papa's debts.' Since her husband's death, she had talked of him frequently. 'They were very considerable, it's true. But that isn't why I accepted him.'

As such barbaric arrangements did happen, I commented dryly, 'I'm very thankful to hear it.'

'I was quite pretty when I was young,' she ventured coquettishly.

'My dear ma'am,' I protested, 'you are far too modest. Giles said you had the whole of London at your feet.' I could believe it too, for despite a slight tendency to plumpness, she was still an extremely attractive woman.

'Well, it is quite true, so I shan't deny it. Even though I didn't have a penny to my name, I had several gratifying offers of marriage. I refused those who had no fortune, naturally.'

'Naturally,' I agreed, shaking with mirth.

'You may laugh Drusilla, but I was sick of being poor and always having to scrimp and save.' She pulled her shawl tighter round her shoulders, remembering the unheated rooms of her youth. 'Love is all very well, but it doesn't pay the bills, and above all else, I wanted to be comfortable. So I decided to find myself a rich husband. And that's when I met Cuthbert.'

At the mention of her husband, a solitary tear hovered precariously on the end of her eyelashes, a trick she once told me she had perfected when young. I could quite see how it would have affected her suitors. Occasionally, as now, she did it unconsciously.

'Cuthbert was just the man I was looking for. He was my father's age, of course, but he had a large fortune, and showered me with expensive gifts, so when he begged me to marry him, I accepted,' she confessed artlessly. 'And I have been perfectly content ever since, as you know.'

Indeed, Mr Saxborough's one saving grace, in my eyes, had been his devotion to his wife. But Marguerite's joyful tone soon evaporated as she remembered her present status. 'Only that is all at an end now.' She dabbed at her pretty violet blue eyes with a perfumed handkerchief. 'I don't want to leave Ledstone, Drusilla. How I shall bear it when the time comes I do not-------' She broke off on hearing someone approaching. Looking over my head her expression changed instantly from distress to joy. 'Giles -- I didn't hear you come in.'

'I walked in through your flower room, Mama.' This connected to Marguerite's personal drawing room, and she used it to arrange the flowers that decorated the whole house in the summer. The connecting door was open, for Marguerite loved the smell of flowers.

Giles greeted me cheerfully, although his faintly troubled expression suggested he'd overheard part of what she'd said, but she quickly showed him the three empty bandboxes, and he stared in astonishment, as well he might, for she never threw anything away. Seeing a question forming on his lips, she quickly fobbed him off by explaining, with exactly the right degree of wistfulness, that I had shown her how it could be achieved. Satisfied, he smiled at me gratefully.

I inquired after Thomas and he said, 'I've just taken him and Tom down to the yacht.'

'Again?' Marguerite burst out. 'That's the third time this week. Giles, you must speak to Thomas. He will ruin Ledstone if he goes on neglecting the estate for his own pleasures.'

'He's only making the most of the fine weather.' She frowned and he took her hands in his, reminding her gently, 'Ledstone belongs to Thomas now. He must be allowed to run it as he wishes. I cannot interfere. Just as I would not expect him to interfere if our positions were reversed.'

Marguerite clung to him. 'Oh Giles, if only they were.'

'You don't mean that,' he muttered tersely. And for one second his face revealed how much he wished it too. Quickly recovering himself, he joked, 'Why, I would have to be older than Thomas for that to happen, and think how old that would make you!' At which her eyes filled with such unspeakable horror I had to bite my lip firmly.

I thought it a pity estates weren't left to the son most suited to the task. For Giles had the caring attitude his father had lacked, besides a natural authority and a love of the land his brother did not possess. Thomas's natural charm made up in great measure for his slapdash ways, although Cuthbert had not seen it like that, grumbling that his son spent too much time idling his life away on boats. Cuthbert had left his land in excellent condition, and if Thomas continued to neglect things, Giles would not allow Marguerite to see how it affected him, for he was far too fond of his brother. Nor would he ever let her realise how deeply he minded leaving Ledstone. But I knew.

When I left Marguerite I was much more myself; a calmness I maintained on setting off for Smith's farm the following morning, accompanied by Mudd. John Mudd was of no more than medium height and build, with thick, dark brown wavy hair, and quite unremarkable in appearance, except for a pair of intelligent, deep nut brown eyes. He never indulged in tittle-tattle with other servants and I related what Mr Arnold had told me, asking him to keep an eye open for where Smith might be hiding contraband.

Cliff Farm was situated close to the chine at Hokewell Bay, and as we rode into the top end of the yard, Smith came out of his farmhouse. He was a large man, both in height and bulk. His mousy hair was unkempt, and his body, as could be ascertained from a considerable distance, was invariably unwashed. I did not like Smith, and he knew it, but he had ten children and a sensible, hard-working wife whose welfare did concern me. She and her two eldest sons did most of the work on the farm, and I did not believe she approved of Smith hiding contraband on my land. Greed had obviously overcome whatever common sense he possessed. The man had a sly, deceitful manner, but lacked the intelligence to use it to his advantage. Nor did he seem to understand that if he disobeyed me, I would find him out.

Thoughts that had me tapping my crop against the side of my boot as he slowly puffed his way up the slope of the farmyard towards me. He wasn't surprised to see me as I inspected the farm every month. I checked his outbuildings, fences, crops and the health of his animals, in my usual way before informing him everything seemed to be in order. 'Make sure you keep it that way.'

'You can rely on me, my lady,' he said obsequiously.

While Mudd saddled the horses, I warned Smith, as I also did every month, that my land was not to be used by smugglers, for he would have considered it odd if I deviated in any way from my normal behaviour. To my surprise, a faintly insolent expression crept into his eyes. 'I'd never do that, my lady. But you do right to keep away from smugglers. From what I hear, they don't like anyone interfering with their business. Doesn't matter who you are, they don't have any respect.'

Gazing at him in disbelief, I took a firm hold on my riding crop. 'Are you threatening me?'

'What me, my lady?' he said, feigning horror, his index finger pointing to his chest. 'I wouldn't do a thing like that. I don't hold with smuggling myself. But, there's no saying what your other tenants might get up to. With you being a lady, without a gentleman to protect you, and not knowing the evil ways of smugglers, I thought I ought to give you a friendly hint. I've seen what happens to people who get in their way.

Marking faces for life, pushing people off cliffs - terrible what they'll do for money. I wouldn't like anything to happen to you, my lady.'

I glared at him with loathing. 'No-one,' I said, tapping him sharply on the chest with my crop, 'no-one is going to tell me what I can or can't do on my own land, Smith. Not you, nor any of your smuggling friends. I won't have this farm used for smuggling purposes. Do I make myself clear?'

'Oh yes, my lady. Like I said, I wouldn't do that.'

'In that case, you have nothing to worry about, have you.' Mudd brought the horses then, and Smith stood watching us ride away, a smug smile on his face. A smile I vowed to wipe off as quickly as I could.

Once out of his sight, Mudd took one look at me and asked, 'Is something wrong, my lady?'

Seething, I told him what Smith had said. 'I shan't rest John, until that wretched man is under lock and key.'

'I'm afraid I saw nothing unusual, my lady. His ditches don't look as if they've been touched for years, the barn floor hadn't been disturbed, and I don't think he'd bury the stuff in a field.'

'I'm quite sure he wouldn't. Smith is far too lazy.' After we skirted round either side of a large puddle I told him, 'I think he hides the stuff in his pond.'

His eyebrows shot up. 'In the pond, my lady?'

'There's sediment a long way above where the water line is now, and we've had too much rain lately for that to have happened naturally.'

Mudd turned to me, a thoughtful look on his weather-beaten face. 'Well, the pond's deep enough, and it's nearer the coast than the farmhouse.'

'What surprises me is that he thought of anything so clever.'

'I doubt he did that, my lady. That'll be where he's been told to hide the stuff.'

'I hadn't thought of that,' I admitted, suspecting that kind of knowledge had come from his father, who had been involved in free trading for years in his younger days, and for all I knew, still was in some minor capacity.

My aunt and cousin spent the afternoon with Giles at Norton House to see what improvements were necessary. After dining together, Giles was to escort them home. So I dined alone and that evening, feeling rather restless, I walked through the orchard and then up the steep hill that led to the Downs, where I sat on the seat my father had placed there, enjoying the view.

Gazing down at the familiar old mellowed stone of the Manor, I thought how peaceful it looked. Rather as it must have appeared on the day my father first saw it. He had fallen in love with the Isle of Wight as a young man, seen this beautiful old manor house nestling at the foot of the Downs, yet within sight of the sea, found it was up for sale, and bought it. On his marriage, he'd added a light and airy south and west facing room for my mother, extended the dining room and kitchens, and built a new east wing, providing the house with a large yet cosy library, a spacious workroom for his many hobbies, and three extra bedchambers upstairs, making seven in all. Providing my mother with the perfect home, but sadly she died when I was three, giving birth to a son who did not survive an hour, and my father never totally recovered from her loss.

Westfleet Manor wasn't a house in the grand style of Ledstone Place, yet to my mind there was nowhere more beautiful on the entire Island. The house, half covered in green creepers that blazed a fiery red in autumn, exuded an air of peace and permanence. I loved everything about it, from the mullioned windows and wainscoting in the older part, to the wide sweeping staircase leading up from the hall. The manor was elegantly, yet simply furnished; every room welcoming and comfortable. I didn't mind in the least that it wasn't our ancestral home, or that we had nothing to compare with the Long Gallery at Ledstone with its impressive family portraits.

In the summer, I liked all the windows open, filling the rooms with the heady scents of honeysuckle, lavender and roses. In winter, the drawing room with its huge fireplace kept us warm on the coldest of days. Father and I had often sat there in the dark, the logs hissing and crackling, the flickering firelight casting great shadows on the walls as we talked far into the night. To me it was the perfect haven and I knew how fortunate I was to live here.

And I had no intention of allowing Smith to disrupt the smooth running of my estate. Recalling his bare-faced insolence, I got up and walked along the Down, trying to determine how best to deal with him. Deep in thought, I barely noticed the sea mist rolling in, as it often did here on the west coast, until I became aware I couldn't see more than a few yards in any direction. Having no idea how far I had walked, I stopped for a moment. I shivered, for it was chilly in the mist, and I had slipped out without a pelisse. Nor had I told the servants where I was going, having only meant to climb the hill.

It would soon be dark, and I wouldn't be able to see anything at all then. Giles would escort my aunt and cousin back from Ledstone before the daylight went, and if I wasn't there when they arrived home, and the servants couldn't tell them where I had gone, my already overwrought aunt would be absolutely frantic. I decided to walk down to a lower level, where I would recognise the houses.

It was then I first had the feeling I was not alone. I told myself not to be silly, that it was only the sheep, who roamed over the Downs. As I made my way downhill a stone rattled past me, making the hairs on the back of my neck stand on end. I tried to convince myself, not very successfully, that sheep disturbed stones too.

It was then I heard the unmistakable sound of footsteps, and swinging round on my heel, saw two vague shapes that were not sheep. I shivered again, but not from the cold, and called out, 'Who's there?' I cursed the quake in my voice, yet no-one answered, and the shapes faded back into the mist. My heart began to pound, for there was no better place to rob me; and if that wasn't their intention, as it would seem not to be, what did they want?

Determined to escape them, I lifted my skirts a trifle and ran along the track; then, where the mist seemed thickest, abruptly moved off it, going straight down the steep hillside. But I had forgotten fog makes the grass wet, and I found myself slipping and sliding down the slope, skidding and bumping out of control. I came to a halt near a road, gasping for breath, and feeling decidedly bruised. But, before I could get to my feet, two burly men seized me by my arms and lifted me up.

'How *dare* you!' I exploded. I knew all the men who lived locally: most were fishermen, who were also smugglers. The faces of these two men were darkened in the manner smugglers adopted, but I was sure I didn't know them. Neither of them spoke. Using their strength, and ignoring my desperate efforts to struggle free, they forced me over the road.

'Where are you taking me?' I demanded angrily. And then I saw. They were propelling me straight towards the edge of the cliff.

5

A vivid picture shot into my mind of Smith warning me that, those who got in the way of smugglers could end up at the bottom of a cliff. And I broke out into a sweat.

Kicking out at them, I yelled, 'Let me go, this instant.'

I should have saved my breath. At the very edge of the cliff, they lifted me up by my shoulders and feet, held me in mid-air so that I could see the tide swirling round the rocks below, and as they swung me back to throw me over the cliff I let out a blood-curdling scream. An image of my father flashed before my eyes, and then quite suddenly they dumped me on the grass. A voice, full of menace, warned, 'Stop interfering with things that don't concern you.' And they ran off into the mist without a backward glance.

Feelings of fury, terror, and relief, coming in such swift succession, left me gasping for breath, and when I tried to sit up the earth beside me lurched so alarmingly, I had to crawl away from the edge on my hands and knees. As I did so, I heard a horse thundering in my direction. The rider leapt off his horse, and knelt by my side, his eyes widening in horror.

'Lady Drusilla?' Mr Reevers blurted out in disbelief. 'My dear girl-- what happened? I heard a scream...... Has your horse thrown you again?' I tried to speak, only my lips were too dry to manage more than an unintelligible croak, so I shook my head. 'Are you hurt?'

'No,' I whispered, forgetting the bruises I'd collected when I skidded down the hill.

'Can you stand?' He took my hands in his, saying in concern, 'They're like ice.' As he gently helped me onto my feet I heard voices and shrank back. Mr Reevers eyed me thoughtfully. 'It's only Giles, with your aunt and cousin. We were escorting them to Westfleet, and came on the road because of the mist. I'd better speak to them.'

I held the reins of his horse while he did so, resting my head thankfully against the animal's warm neck. I heard the anxiety in their voices, but they said nothing, except to insist I take a horse and get home into the warm at once. Mr. Reevers escorted me the two miles back to Westfleet, sensibly refraining from asking questions, and having seen me into the house, hurried off to return the horse. In the hall I was greeted by a worried looking Jeffel.

'My lady,' he gasped, clearly shocked by my appearance. 'Your - your gown----'

'I was on the Downs and ----'

He looked at me, aghast. 'On the Downs, my lady? Surely, you weren't up there in the dark?'

I saw from the clock that I had been out almost two hours. 'I went for a walk and when the mist came down I lost my footing and fell down a slope. Then two men tried to rob me.'

Jeffel's face went white. 'My lady----'

'They ran off when they realised I had no money on me.' Explaining Mr Reevers had brought me home, I said, 'I shan't walk on the Downs at dusk again, you can be sure of that.' The troubled look changed to relief, and I smiled. 'What I really need now is a hot bath.' That brought him out of his daze, and he hurried off to give the necessary orders.

I enjoyed a long, reviving soak, the warmth restoring me to something approaching my normal state. Happy just to be alive, I even allowed Gray, my maid, to bully me into going to bed. When my aunt and cousin looked in later, I repeated the story I had told Jeffel, not wanting to add to Aunt Thirza's anxieties. She accepted my account without question, giving me a severe scold for behaving so foolishly.

Smith was behind the attack, I did not doubt that. He and his smuggling friends thought frightening me to death would stop me interfering in their activities. Thinking of how terrified I had been, I started shaking again. Every time I closed my eyes, I saw the sea swirling round those rocks. In that moment, I truly thought my last seconds had come.

I lay there for a long time trying to decide what to do about Smith. My first instinct was to turn him off his farm. But if I did that, his wife and children, who had done nothing wrong, would be forced to go with him, and they had suffered enough. Besides, if I took that course, Smith would escape punishment for his crimes, and I had no intention of allowing that to happen. I wanted Smith arrested and put in prison. That meant catching him with smuggled goods on his farm.

The best way to achieve that involved swallowing my pride for a time, and every feeling in me revolted, but it would be worthwhile in the end. And, with that thought on my mind, I finally fell asleep.

I woke much refreshed in the morning, and although not quite my usual self, I was determined to advise Mr Arnold of what I had seen at Smith's farm. My aunt and cousin were going shopping in Newport, and aware they would try to dissuade me from going out, I simply waited until they had left, when I informed the servants I meant to visit my old nurse in West Cowes.

I took Mudd with me, and when I told him the truth about the attack, the colour drained from his weatherbeaten face. 'Keep it to yourself, John. I don't want the whole house worrying. But I must find out who those smugglers were. I'm certain they weren't local men – the one who spoke didn't have an Island accent.' Besides, local smugglers knew I considered it my duty to obey the smuggling laws. Just as I saw that the extra money gained from smuggling made their lives, and that of their families, much more comfortable.

'I could ask my father. He knows most things that go on.'

'I would be grateful, John.'

On arriving in West Cowes, Mudd stabled the horses, while I spent a pleasant hour reminiscing with my old nurse, arriving just in time to avoid a heavy shower. On leaving her cottage, Mudd and I were threading our way through the narrow streets towards the waterfront, meaning to take the ferry across to East Cowes, where the Customs House was situated, when I saw Mr Arnold approaching from the other direction. He bowed and having exchanged greetings, I explained I was on my way to see him.

'Then I am glad I saved you a trip across the water, ma'am. There's a nasty nip in the air today.' A large wagon negotiating the narrow street, splashed mud in our direction, and he was instantly penitent. 'Forgive me, ma'am, I am forgetting my manners. Mrs Arnold would scold me something fearful if she saw me keeping you in conversation in the road.' And he insisted on escorting me back to the stables, so that I could tell him how he might be of service.

Walking up the street, with Mudd following, I inquired first after Mrs Arnold's health. 'She's very well, thank you, ma'am, though she's rather anxious about her brother in New York. It's six months since we heard from John Delafield.'

'Perhaps a letter has gone astray.'

'That's exactly what I said, ma'am.'

Turning into the wide alley that led to the stables, I told Mr Arnold about Smith's pond and the sediment that suggested a sudden drop in the water level. 'We've had far too much rain for that to happen naturally.'

'I wish everyone was as observant, ma'am,' he murmured, running a hand round his chin thoughtfully. 'So he's hiding the stuff in his pond is he.' I didn't mention I had been attacked, aware he'd do his utmost to apprehend Smith in any case. 'I'm most grateful to you, ma'am. Now we know where to look, we'll soon have him under lock and key.'

By the time we got back to Westfleet the clouds had disappeared, giving way to warm sunshine. My aunt and cousin were still out shopping, and I was sitting in the workroom thinking about what had happened when I visited Smith's farm, when a picture of him opening one particularly heavy gate flashed into my mind. He'd struggled to heave it across the ground, an action that had flattened the surface of the mud somewhat. It had reminded me of something at the time, but I couldn't recall what. Now, quite suddenly, it came to me. That was how the muddy track at the east gate had looked when I found Mr Saxborough's body. Smoothed somewhat by the shutting of the gate.

It was a minute or two, even then, before the true significance sank in. Before I realised what had been missing from that smoothed over mud. Hoof marks. If Mr Saxborough had jumped the gate, there should have been fresh hoof marks within that area. And there had not been. That could mean only one thing. The gate had been closed *after* his death.

I put my head in my hands and groaned at my own stupidity. Father had taught me that things weren't always what they seemed, yet when I found the gate closed, I'd assumed it had been shut when Mr Saxborough rode down the bridle path. For that was how it had looked. I'd accepted it despite being convinced he would never have jumped the east gate on that horse. How could I have been so blind?

I asked myself who could have wanted Cuthbert Saxborough dead? He'd made many enemies in his life, yet I couldn't think of one with the nerve, or the intelligence, to make his death look like an accident. I was still mulling it over when Mr Reevers called to see me.

Inopportune though his visit was, remembering his kindness the previous evening, I told Jeffel to show him into the library. Mr Reevers, looking every inch the gentleman in his riding breeches, dark blue coat and well polished boots, bowed when I entered the room and inquired if I had recovered from my ordeal.

'As you see,' I responded lightly. 'I am feeling much more the thing now.'

'Enough to take a walk in the garden?'

'By all means.'

I took a parasol, the sun having become quite hot, and on strolling into the walled garden, he indicated an arbour, suggesting we rest there. We had talked of general subjects up to this point, but now he urged, 'I should like to know what happened last night.'

'Certainly,' I said. And repeated what I had told everyone else.

The parasol shaded my face, which I hoped might help the situation, but this astute and observant man merely said, 'I understand you don't want to worry your aunt, and that tale will do well enough for her. But it won't do for me. I saw your face, and even in the darkness it was obvious to me you had suffered a severe fright—'

'Being set upon by two villains would terrify anyone.'

'True, but you are not the kind of female who is easily frightened. Nor one who screams and swoons for no reason.'

'I did not swoon,' I pointed out.

'No, but you couldn't stop shaking, could you.' He spoke with kindly understanding, and waited expectantly.

Watching a bee buzzing in and out the flowers of a tall fox-glove, I said, 'I'd rather not speak of it, if you don't mind.' Having made my wishes clear, I expected that to be the end of the matter, but Mr Reevers was not to be fobbed off so easily.

'I'm afraid, ma'am,' he said, in a perfectly amiable tone, 'that I do mind.'

'Well, really,' I muttered, snapping my parasol shut in a manner that conveyed my disgust. 'A gentleman,' I said, emphasising the word, ' would have taken the hint.'

Far from rising to the bait, he remained entirely unruffled. 'I shan't repeat it to anyone, if that is what's worrying you.'

I turned my head to look at him, wondering how he'd guessed this was my main concern, for I didn't want Smith alerted by some careless remark. 'How can I be sure of that?'

'I give you my word as a gentleman,' he said, poker-faced. I couldn't help but laugh, and he said, 'Besides, I don't want to leave the Island without -----'

'You're leaving?' News that, for no reason I could think of, left me feeling quite downcast.

'At daybreak tomorrow. Some urgent matters require my attention at home. I ought to have gone this morning.' And he cajoled, 'I wish you would tell me why those two ruffians were threatening you. I might be able to help.'

I stiffened a little, being accustomed to solving my own difficulties. 'I'm obliged to you, Mr Reevers, but I don't anticipate any more problems.'

He gazed at me meditatively, as if working out his next manoeuvre, making it clear he didn't intend to give up, even now. And I realised, in surprise, that he liked getting to the bottom of things every bit as much as I did.

A wry smile crossed his lips. 'Very well ma'am, but if you *should* be found dead at the bottom of a cliff one day, it would help the local constable if he knew who to arrest.' That made me laugh, despite the grave nature of his remark. It also made so much sense that I changed my mind and told him the truth.

A rose leaf fell on his sleeve and he brushed it off. 'What do you mean to do about Smith? Turn him off his farm?'

I shook my head, explaining I wanted Smith locked up. 'I shall let him think his friends have frightened me away.'

'You won't find that easy to swallow.'

I gave a grim laugh. 'No, indeed I won't. But it won't be for long.'

'I hope not.' He got up to take his leave and when I held out my hand to him, he lifted it to his lips. 'Keep away from smugglers, my dear. I rather fear those particular men mean business.' Bowing, he turned and strode off, and I found myself wondering if he was in the habit of addressing all young women as 'my dear.'

I didn't move at once, but sat in the arbour thinking about Mr Reevers, not having encountered anyone quite like him before. He was a clever man and had a sense of fun I liked. I suspected that he understood me very well, which was rather unnerving, for I could not say the same about him. There being rather more to him, I felt, than the face he showed to the world.

Later, back in the workroom, I tried to fathom out how Mr Saxborough had died. If he'd been thrown from his horse when the gate was open, then something must have been held across the track - possibly a rope. But, convinced though I was that Mr Saxborough had been murdered, I said nothing to anyone else, for I saw no way of proving it, as yet.

My uncle was always in my thoughts too, and I prayed Giles would soon hear from his friends in France. The waiting was hardest on my aunt, of course, and upon the servants who attended her. When, one morning, I found a housemaid in tears after my aunt had threatened to have her dismissed for humming while she worked, I decided it was time I took matters in hand.

Having reassured the housemaid, I suggested to my aunt that if she cared to refurbish the large south-facing bedchamber my father had used, it would be more comfortable than her north-facing room. She brightened visibly, but aware I found it difficult to change anything that had belonged to my father, she asked uncertainly, 'Are you quite sure, Drusilla?'

'Of course. It's a waste to leave it unoccupied.' We went to look at the room and watching her growing delight as ideas sprang into her head, I wished I'd suggested it earlier.

She proposed, 'Perhaps some bright yellow curtains and—'

I interrupted with a smile, 'Do whatever you want, Aunt.' Her taste in matters of fashion and furnishings was impeccable. It wouldn't stop her worrying, of course, but it would give her something else to think about. And, hopefully, the servants would be able to go about their duties without fear of being dragged into a mouse hunt, or being shouted at for humming.

6

In the midst of our difficulties, my friend, Julia Tanfield, held a party for her son, Edward, on his second birthday, combining it with young Tom's fourteenth which fell the following day. On the morning of the party, my aunt and cousin went to Ledstone to discuss wedding arrangements. And later Lucie and Giles were to escort Tom to Breighton House.

I wore a mauve riding dress and a wide-brimmed matching hat for the occasion, slipping two small birthday presents into the deep pockets of my habit. I had Orlando saddled, and set off in good time, my spirits lifted by the warmth of the sun. Leaving the Manor by the main entrance, I kept Orlando to a sedate trot as we approached the village of Westfleet, soon coming to the row of neat cottages built by my father for the estate workers. Windows and doors had been flung open to let in the sunshine, and shrieks of childish laughter emanated from the back gardens.

A little further on stood a pretty thatched inn, the 'Five Bells.' Barlow, the innkeeper, lounged in his doorway, a clay pipe in his mouth as usual, and as I stopped to exchange a few words with him, a duck followed by a dozen ducklings in single file, suddenly shot across the road in front of me, heading for the village pond. A sight that always made me smile.

Riding past the village green, two elderly men sitting outside the thatched cottages touched their forelocks, and I called out a greeting. The road then rose steeply up to the Norman church on the hill, with the parsonage some fifty yards beyond that, half way round a sharp bend. Enabling the parson and his wife to see everyone coming up the hill from the village, and giving them the opportunity to waylay those who didn't move past quickly enough. I swept up the hill, past the parsonage, and had almost reached the side road that led up the long steep incline to Breighton House, when the parson rode round the corner from the opposite direction. I groaned inwardly, aware that if I'd left home one minute earlier I'd have missed him altogether.

Good manners required me to stop and exchange the usual pleasantries, which led to my being forced to listen to a rambling account of how he had once again fallen victim to his old trouble. 'Only yesterday a nasty-looking boil broke out on my neck. Still, I mustn't complain.' A statement he instantly contradicted, and at such length, that the second he drew breath, I quickly excused myself on account of not wanting to be late.

He frowned and tutted. 'I must say ma'am, I consider it most inappropriate of Mrs Tanfield to include Tom in this merry making when he's in mourning for his grandfather.'

'We are hardly merry making, Mr Upton. It's merely an informal gathering. Tom is still a child and it seems a little harsh to deny him any recognition of his birthday.'

The lines of displeasure deepened on his face. 'His father is in London I believe ----'

'On estate matters, yes. Tom has permission to spend his birthday at Breighton House.' Not that it was any of his business, I thought.

'I dread to think what Mrs Saxborough would say if she knew of it.'

Irritated by his pompous attitude, I informed him a trifle abruptly, 'She not only knows of it, but has given her approval. She, at least, didn't want to spoil the day for him.'

'Well, I cannot approve ma'am,' he declared in a manner that showed he plainly believed himself to be above reproach on such matters. 'In fact I----'

Gathering the reins together, I cut him short. 'If Mrs Saxborough and his own father see no objection, I think it quite acceptable to go ahead. Now you really must excuse me.' And I rode off up the hill, muttering under my breath, 'Insufferable little man.'

I was still seething when I reached Breighton House, and barely noticed the magnificent views of the sea and surrounding countryside that I usually delighted in here. The house, square in shape, was constructed of Island stone, and had an inner courtyard, and a wide archway at the back leading to the stables. Built in the early part of the century by John Tanfield, Edward's great grandfather, a fine carriage drive swept visitors up to the front of the house. The welcome I received soon put me back into a sunny mood. Wade, the butler, showed me into the drawing room, where Julia greeted me, begging me to excuse her while she had a word with Wade.

In the four years since Richard Tanfield brought Julia back to Breighton House as his bride, we had become the greatest of friends. A redhead, with pale green eyes, Julia's face in repose was no more than ordinary; it was when she laughed, or talked animatedly, that she instantly became attractive. She was about five foot seven inches, with a well-proportioned figure, always beautifully dressed, having a flair for knowing exactly what would suit her best, and nimble fingers with which to copy the latest fashions for a fraction of the price, without anyone being the wiser. Something she did for enjoyment rather than necessity.

Richard, the younger of two sons, had embraced a life at sea, and at eighteen had come home to find his unmarried, dissolute elder brother was dead. Richard's inheritance, apart from the house, was no more than respectable, and he had remained in the Navy. A captain now, he had been on half-pay for much of his marriage, until the war began in February, when he had been given a ship. Feeling a sharp tug at my skirts, I looked down to find Edward beaming up at me. He held out his arms, shrieking with delight, 'Il-la.' This being his attempt at my name.

Scooping him up I gave him a big hug. 'Aunt to you, young man,' I said, laughing. 'Show a proper respect.' Sitting him on my lap, I saw a small, but growing stain on his shirt. 'What have you got there?' I asked suspiciously. Giggling, he removed a squashed beetle from his pocket.

Julia, watching him from the corner of her eye, broke off from speaking to Wade and groaned. 'Edward, couldn't you have kept clean just for one day?' With a long-suffering sigh she had him taken off to have his clothes changed, just as Lucie and Giles arrived with Tom.

Remembering his manners, Tom thanked Julia for inviting him to celebrate his birthday at her house. Edward's presence made for a great deal of informality, and the dishes set before us included all his favourite jellies, biscuits and little cakes, which he ate with great relish. I was amused to see Tom tuck into them too, finishing his repast with a gargantuan wedge of apple pie. Everyone had gifts for the boys. I gave Edward a small boat, and for Tom I'd settled on a penknife he had often admired. It had belonged to my father, and had a delicate ivory handle shaped like a serpent. I thought father would approve, as he'd always been fond of the boy. Tom sat fingering the penknife for some time, knowing what it meant to me.

'I don't know what to say,' he mumbled, looking up. 'I'll take good care of it Drusilla, I promise.' Then, in his good natured way, he took Edward off to sail the new boat on the small pond in the garden, while we all sat on the terrace in the sunshine.

Giles took the opportunity to announce he and Lucie were to be married on the twenty-seventh of October. 'We settled it this morning,' he said, squeezing Lucie's hand affectionately. 'And Mama and I move to Norton House in August.' He and Lucie talked blissfully of what the future held for them, and I prayed Giles would not let his love for Ledstone mar their happiness. If Thomas shirked his obligations on the estate, Giles would have to learn to live with the frustration. For there really was no alternative. Not for him. Glancing at Lucie, I noticed a distinct sadness in her eyes. Puzzled, I wondered what it meant.

Julia said, 'Good, that's you two settled. Now we need to find the right man for Drusilla.'

Groaning, I protested. 'You know perfectly well I don't mean to marry.'

'Nonsense. You don't want to end up a little wizened old maid, do you?'

'Little?' I gasped. 'It may have escaped your notice Julia, but I have to duck my head every time I come into this room.'

A small giggle escaped her. 'Well, all right, you may be not little, but----'

'I don't much care for wizened either, I might tell you.'

'That's because you're only twenty-six and cannot imagine yourself at seventy. If you had a husband, you'd take good care not to stoop. With you being so tall, you might easily allow yourself to do so, you know, and end up like that poor woman I saw in Portsmouth last month. Bent double she was, and had to use two sticks to get about. All she saw was the ground - she couldn't look up, poor soul. Never saw the sun unless she was sitting down.'

None of us believed in this woman's existence, for Julia had a vivid imagination, which she used to great effect whenever it suited her. We were all laughing so much, we barely noticed Tom bringing Edward back, until Edward, clutching his new boat to his chest, announced blissfully, 'I'se all wet.' In fact, he was soaked from head to toe.

Julia closed her eyes as Tom explained sheepishly, 'He couldn't quite reach the boat you see, and before I could—'

'Don't apologise Tom, please,' Julia sighed. 'I know *exactly* how it was. My son's chief aim in life is to see how many sets of clothes he can ruin in a day.'

Lucie exclaimed, 'Tom, you're wet too. Look at your shoes and stockings-------'

He glanced down at the waterline half way up his calf, acquired when he jumped into the pond to get Edward out. 'Honestly, it's nothing.'

'Oh Tom,' Julia burst out, instantly contrite. 'I'm so sorry. Come upstairs - I'm sure Richard's stockings will fit you. And we'll get your shoes dried in the kitchen.' Lucie offered to take Edward off to his nursery to be attended to, and I heard Julia say playfully, 'Now you can see what you're letting yourself in for.'

While they were out of the room, Giles told me he'd heard from his friends in Normandy. 'I'm afraid they know nothing of your uncle's circumstances.'

Finally understanding the sadness in Lucie's eyes, I said in dismay, 'I did so hope---'

'So did I, Drusilla. But all is not lost yet. They have promised to try to find out. Only it doesn't pay to be too inquisitive in France these days, so we must be patient.'

I nodded, asking rather despairingly, 'What did my aunt say?'

'She thinks, rightly I believe, that the Normandy estate is lost. She fears too that your uncle may already be dead. In which case, she insists the wedding must go ahead. She wants to see Lucie settled.' I saw the sense of that, and my aunt was a practical woman. Giles's friends might not learn anything, yet I found myself pinning all my hopes on this slender chance.

Staying calm was far from easy, and the weather didn't help. Twice in the next week great forks of lightning lit up the night sky, and violent crashes of thunder kept the entire household awake until the early dawn, leaving us all tired and irritable. My aunt fared worse than the rest of us, the lack of sleep heightening her fears for my uncle's safety.

'It's just this aw--awful uncertainty, Drusilla,' she burst out one morning, her voice breaking.

Gently I reminded her, 'Giles did say we must be patient.'

'I know,' she said in a choked voice, looking out at the torrential rain. She took a deep breath, forced back her tears, and began talking of her plans for her new bedchamber. Whatever her faults, I admired the courage with which she faced her uncertain future.

When the weather began to improve at the start of the last week in July, Giles called to say he was spending a few days with Mr Reevers. He kept his own small yacht moored on the Yar, often visiting his cousin, who lived on the mainland, near Lymington.

'He's finding life very difficult at present and he needs a friend.' As I opened my mouth, he shook his head at me. 'I can't explain. Better that he tells you himself. Besides, I'm beset with enough problems of my own. Like persuading Mama that Norton House cannot accommodate her entire wardrobe. She informs me nothing can be dispensed with, and we move next month.' He eyed me helplessly from under his long lashes. 'Will you talk to her, Drusilla? But for you she'd still have five bandboxes of old letters.'

'I'll try,' I said, guiltily refraining from mentioning I had not reduced the number of letters.

'I'll be back the day before our outing to Carisbrooke.' Lucie having expressed a desire to see the castle, Giles had arranged it, inviting my aunt and myself to join them.

When I called on Marguerite the next day she told me indignantly that Thomas had taken young Tom off sailing for a few days. 'Just as if he had no responsibilities at all. And he shows me no consideration whatsoever. He knew Giles was visiting Mr Reevers and I would be left on my own.'

'You have a house full of servants,' I reminded her gently.

'What use is that when I have no-one to talk to.'

'Well, I'm here now,' I said cheerfully. 'And I've promised to help you sort out your wardrobe while Giles is away.'

In the event I visited her every day, often accompanied by Lucie, but we failed to persuade her to throw away any of her clothes. She insisted, 'I might need them one day.'

Thinking of all the gowns that would never fit her again, I pointed out kindly, 'But you won't have space at Norton House for it all.' Tears filled her eyes, and she grew so distressed that Lucie suggested if all the items she no longer wore regularly were packed into trunks, she would find a place for them.

At which, Marguerite threw her arms round Lucie's neck. 'I knew you would understand. I can't bear to be parted from them, you see.'

On our way home, I asked Lucie where she would store these trunks. 'She'll need half a dozen at least.'

'I know,' she admitted cheerfully. 'But she was so upset I couldn't help myself. Perhaps they will go in the attic, and once the clothes are out of sight, she'll forget all about them.'

The day before Giles was due back, I was alone with Marguerite in her sitting room, trying to cheer her with the offer of some fine new roses, grown at Westfleet, which would be ready for planting at Norton House in the autumn.

She turned to me, her eyes brimming with tears. 'I know you mean it kindly Drusilla, and truly I am most grateful, but I cannot bear the thought of leaving my beautiful home.' Silent teardrops began to roll down her cheeks, and as she dabbed at them with a handkerchief, her butler came in with the day's post.

She turned her face to the window and I took the single letter from the salver, thanking him with a smile. He bowed and left the room again, apparently oblivious to Marguerite's tears. The direction on the letter was inscribed in large flamboyant writing. A hand I had seen fairly recently, although I could not immediately recollect where.

Marguerite quickly dried her tears, for she loved to receive letters, especially from her London friends who kept her up to date with all the latest scandals, fads and fashions. When I handed her the letter, she commented eagerly, 'Now who can this be from? The writing looks familiar, but I can't think who-----'

'You could try opening it,' I suggested amiably.

'Are you sure you don't mind? I own I should like to.'
Eagerly she broke the seal and opened the single sheet. Glancing first at the signature at the bottom, her eyes widened and a startled exclamation escaped her. Blood drained from her face, and she fell back against the cushions in a swoon, the missive fluttering from her grasp on to the floor.

Seizing the smelling salts from the table where she kept her medicines, I waved it vigorously under her nose. As she began to recover her senses, I bent to pick up the letter. The signature was one I had seen before, and I saw then why my godmother had fainted.

For the letter came from a dead man. Or to be precise, from a man my godmother had for some twenty years believed to be dead.

7

When Marguerite opened her eyes and saw the letter in my hand, she shuddered, and the greyness of her face made me say, 'I'll ring for some brandy.'

As I reached for the bell-pull, she grasped my wrist. 'Please don't. It would choke me.' She pulled her shawl tightly round her shoulders as if cold. 'I don't suppose I imagined it, did I?' she whispered in forlorn hope. 'The signature I mean.'

I shook my head, for the writing was perfectly legible. Handwriting I had seen when helping Marguerite sort out her five bandboxes of letters. Those signed 'Vincent' were from Cuthbert's brother.

'I thought you said Vincent was--------'

'Dead?' She shivered. 'He was, Drusilla, I swear. Cuthbert told me so. And he couldn't be wrong about such a thing, could he?'

'It would seem he must be,' I murmured dryly.

She fell back against the cushions and wailed, 'Whatever am I to do?'

'You could read the letter,' I suggested in an encouraging tone.

'Must I? He's bound to want something. He always did.' She begged, 'You read it, Drusilla.' She reached for her smelling salts in readiness. Already this year, she had lost her husband,

and would soon lose the home she loved. To her, this letter, from so unexpected a source, could only mean bad news.

The letter had been written from a hotel in New York, and was dated 7th June 1793. The sevens being crossed in the French style. Flattening the sheet, I read it to her.

My dear Marguerite,

I cannot tell you how deeply saddened I was to hear of my brother's unfortunate accident. A friend in London supposing, rightly, that I would wish to be informed of this unhappy event, sent me the cutting from the 'Morning Post,' and I have thought of little else since. Believe me, I cannot adequately express to you my deep sense of shock and bereavement.

When I took up my pen to offer you my most sincere condolences, I found myself thinking of Ledstone for the first time in years. The house holds so many happy childhood memories for me, that I was suddenly overwhelmed by a longing to see my old home once more before I die. For I am no longer young, my dear Marguerite, and there cannot be many years left to me. As for the quarrel that estranged me from my family, that ceased to be of consequence long ago.

I am a widower now alas, but my son Piers gives me great joy. For the past year we have been travelling together in America, an unforgettable adventure that ends on the first of July when we sail home on the 'Carolina.' This being the most modern and comfortable ship we can find, for Piers suffers badly from sea sickness. God willing, we should arrive in England some time in August. After our long absence abroad, some urgent matters require my personal attention in London, but we hope to make a short stay on the Island in September, before returning to our villa in Italy.

I will write again when we reach London, but we shan't impose on the family at Ledstone, being quite content to put up at the George in Yarmouth. My kind regards to Thomas, whom I understand has a young son, and to your own dear Giles.

Vincent had signed his name with a flourish, and folding the sheet, I gave it to Marguerite. 'It is a very proper letter, don't you think?'

'Yes, but he shouldn't be writing to me when I thought he was dead.'

Laughter rose in my throat. 'He obviously doesn't know you believed that.'

'Well, he should have known,' she insisted resentfully, without explaining why. Unfurling a pretty French fan Giles had brought back from his travels, she began to employ it absently.

Deeply curious about the family quarrel Vincent spoke of in his letter, I asked if she knew what had caused it. Snapping the fan shut, she leaned forward, eagerly confiding, 'It was all rather dreadful really, Drusilla. He eloped with an actress.'

That, I agreed, did make her totally ineligible. 'Was she very pretty?'

Marguerite considered, her head to one side. 'I only saw her once. Her face was red and blotchy from crying, which made it difficult to tell, but she did have the most beautiful honey coloured hair. Cuthbert described her as ravishing, and I imagine she must have been, or Vincent would not have run off with her. But Cuthbert was furious with Vincent for bringing a woman of her class to Ledstone.'

I could picture the scene all too easily. 'When did this happen?'

'Twenty-six years ago. I remember particularly, as Giles was only a few weeks old. When Vincent announced his intention of marrying the girl, Cuthbert warned that such a marriage meant exile, for a woman of that class would find herself ostracised by Island society. Nor could he expect financial assistance if he was determined to ruin himself. But Vincent wouldn't listen, he was in love, he said. The arguments made my head ache so abominably, I was forced to retire to my room. In the morning, Vincent and the girl had gone,' she declared with remembered relief, 'And Cuthbert said we were never to speak of his brother again.'

I saw how that had come about, but one thing still puzzled me. 'I don't understand why you thought Vincent was dead.'

'Well, despite Cuthbert saying he wouldn't help his brother, about a year later Vincent wrote asking for a loan. There was a child then----'

'Piers?'

'Yes. They were living in the most squalid lodgings, but Cuthbert said Vincent only had himself to blame.' She shivered, thinking of freezing rooms. 'I persuaded Cuthbert to send money for the baby's sake. But Vincent kept asking for more. Then, after about five years, the letters suddenly stopped. When another year passed without a letter, Cuthbert said Vincent must be dead.'

'I see why he thought that,' I admitted. 'But what of the child?'

'Cuthbert said the boy was better off with his mother, and by then we had no idea where Piers was living, and nothing to recognise him by except a lock of his hair.' She pointed to the two bandboxes full of her old letters, which stood in a corner ready for the move to Norton House. 'I expect it will still be in there somewhere.'

We searched the bandboxes and she found the right letter, removing the blond lock. 'How soft it is,' she sighed, holding the hair against her cheek. 'I have a lock of Giles's hair that is very similar.' And instantly justified her hoarding instincts.

'Now do you see why I wanted to keep my letters? Whenever Cuthbert persuaded me to throw something away, I always found a need for it the very next day.'

The lock of hair was cut on the boy's fourth birthday, according to the accompanying letter which Marguerite gave me to read. Vincent had written that Piers had a fever, and the doctor advised the boy needed decent food and lodgings free from damp, neither of which Vincent could afford. He wrote,

'*I beg of you to help me Cuthbert, for Piers is as much a Saxborough as your own son, but with none of his privileges. I wonder how long your sickly Giles would survive in the conditions in which we live. Piers, at four years of age, bears a remarkable resemblance to the portrait of your good self that hangs in the gallery at Ledstone. The one Mama had done when you were five. His hair, as you can see from the lock I have enclosed, is blond, like so many of our ancestors. He is fortunate in having his mother's beautiful eyes and charming nature, being a prettily behaved child who can recite any number of nursery rhymes.*

This, inevitably, was followed by a request for funds. Marguerite encouraged me to peruse the letters, and I found many such requests, along with appeals to be given a house on the Ledstone estates. Cuthbert had sent money to please Marguerite, who would have been greatly upset by the truth of Vincent's barbed remark that Giles would not survive the conditions Piers was forced to endure. Besides, financial help could be kept secret. Allowing Vincent to return to Ledstone meant Cuthbert's public acceptance of Vincent's marriage, which he would never have agreed to.

'But surely,' I said, 'if Vincent had died, his widow would have written to inform you.'

'Cuthbert said the girl was merely an actress, and very likely couldn't write.' It wasn't an unreasonable assessment, but I suspected Cuthbert wanted to believe his brother was dead. Well, plainly, Vincent was very much alive. But, why had he given up this easy source of income when, according to his last letter, he'd couldn't pay the doctor treating his son's fever?

Marguerite suggested, 'Perhaps he had a run of good luck. Vincent was a gambler, and Cuthbert used to say fortunes were won and lost at the gaming tables.'

I shook my head. 'I cannot believe it's that simple.' And suggested light-heartedly, 'Perhaps he will tell us.'

'Well, I intend to ask him,' she stated with unusual resolution. 'If Vincent means to show his face at Ledstone after all these years, I think I'm entitled to an explanation.'

'They may not bother you at all. You'll be at Norton House long before they arrive.'

Her mood instantly brightened. 'So I shall. I hadn't thought of that.'

It was the first favourable reason she had found for moving, and I made the most of it. 'It will be for Thomas to invite them to Ledstone. You and Giles need do no more than hold a dinner party.'

She eyed me speculatively. 'Do you really think so, Drusilla?' But the gloom soon descended again. 'Very likely Thomas will be off sailing somewhere, and then Giles and I will be forced to entertain them at Norton House. And I do so detest tripping over unwanted guests at every corner of the house. But we cannot allow them to stay at the George. Think how people would gossip. Still, at least Vincent is a widower now. After all, no-one would expect me to entertain a common actress.'

Nevertheless, I couldn't help wondering what Giles and Thomas would make of it when they returned home. Would they object to a visit from the black sheep of the family?

On riding home Mudd told me his father believed Smith was involved with a vicious gang of smugglers from Guernsey, but he didn't know their names. I said, 'Don't worry, John. Smith will tell us fast enough when he's arrested. He won't take all the blame himself.' A day I prayed wasn't too far away.

What with Smith, the mystery of Mr Saxborough's death, visiting my godmother, keeping an eye on my aunt, and dealing with household and estate matters, I had no time to think about the outing to Carisbrooke castle, but I looked forward to it and woke early on the day itself.

The deep lilac full skirted driving dress I planned to wear, hung up ready, its matching wide brimmed hat on a chair close by. Julia had taken me to a new establishment in Newport, owned by a woman who had the sense not to frown at my height, or fuss over me because I was wealthy. A woman who quickly appreciated I simply wanted fashionable clothes that suited me, and would enjoy wearing. On this occasion she had excelled herself, for on showing me this material I had instantly fallen in love with the softness of it, and knew I would feel not only comfortable but rather dashing in it too.

Springing out of bed, I ran my fingers along those delicate folds before going to draw back the curtains. At the sight of a cloudless blue sky, I eagerly threw open the casement window, savouring the delicious warming scents of this glorious morning. The servants were up and the kitchen door obviously open, as I could hear the clattering of pots and pans, and the occasional burst of laughter. Westfleet Manor had always been a happy house; for father and I believed in showing appreciation to those who looked after us well.

Giles should have returned from visiting Mr Reevers yesterday, but as he hadn't called to see Lucie last night, I assumed he'd arrived later than expected, and I had almost finished breakfast when Jeffel came to tell me Giles was here. 'Oh good,' I said. 'Ask him to join me, would you.' I was alone as usual, my aunt and cousin not having left their bedchambers yet. 'And Jeffel, see Miss Lucie is informed.' I smiled up at him. 'She was a little worried when he didn't call yesterday.'

'That's only natural, my lady,' he responded warmly. Lucie was a favourite with Jeffel, for she loved listening to his fund of stories about the pranks Giles had got up to as a boy.

Giles soon joined me, his dark coat enhancing his blond hair and intelligent blue eyes. He grinned boyishly. 'I came early in case you thought I'd forgotten.'

I rolled my eyes at him, for Giles never forgot a thing. 'Would you like some coffee?'

'Please.' He eyed the breakfast fare with interest. 'I must say that ham looks delicious.'

Inviting him to help himself, I poured him some coffee. 'Haven't you eaten this morning?'

'Yes, I had breakfast with Mama.' Announcing it as if he did so every day.

For a brief moment I was speechless. 'Your Mama never leaves her bedchamber before ten.'

'Ah - well, I'm afraid I caused her some anxiety last night.' Explaining in between mouthfuls of ham, 'I didn't reach Ledstone until after six this morning.'

I blinked in surprise. 'Why was that? It was calm enough yesterday-----'

'It wasn't the weather. I had some business to attend to which took much longer than I'd expected, and when I got back to my yacht I'd missed the tide. I didn't dare go to sleep in case I missed the next one too.'

'No wonder you look tired. Would you rather we postponed the outing?'

'Good heavens, no. I feel fine.' Having finished the ham, he picked up his coffee cup. 'The weather is perfect and I would hate to disappoint Lucie.'

Drinking his coffee he said, in answer to my questions, that Thomas and young Tom were still away, but were expected back before he and Marguerite moved to Norton House in ten days time. And that Mr Reevers was resolving his difficulties in the only way possible, although he refused to say what those troubles were. When I spoke of Vincent's letter, he broke in, his face faintly troubled, 'Let's discuss that later. There's something I must tell you before the others come down to breakfast.' He hesitated briefly, as if choosing his words with care, when the door opened and Lucie came in. Murmuring under his breath that he'd tell me later, he jumped up to greet the woman he adored.

Leaving them alone, I longed to know what Giles had been going to tell me, but I didn't get another chance to speak to him before we set off for Carisbrooke.

Aunt Thirza, seating herself in the open carriage, happily squashed up her skirts to make room for Lucie and Giles, only protesting when I climbed up to take the reins. 'Really Drusilla, you might let Mudd drive us. You always rattle on much too fast.'

I counted to ten under my breath, found it wasn't nearly enough, and tried to imagine instead what it would be like if she lost her voice for a whole week. Or even a day. This highly agreeable vision softened my mood almost at once, allowing me to concentrate entirely on keeping the horses at a steady pace. For I enjoyed driving, and as Giles was with us, we had no need of a groom.

The journey was pleasant and uneventful, and despite her concerns over my driving, Aunt Thirza seemed happier than at any time since my uncle's letters had stopped. The sunshine had clearly put her in a good mood, which pleased me as I wanted her to enjoy the day.

Once the horses were stabled, we strolled up to the castle, which was looking its best in the bright sunlight. Lucie particularly wanted to see the building where Charles 1st had been imprisoned for nearly a year, before being taken to London to stand trial and eventual execution. Here she eagerly examined the window through which the King had meant to escape by squeezing through the bars. Then, after letting himself down to the courtyard using a rope, a gaoler had agreed to help him over the wall, where horses waited to take him to a ship.

'A wise man,' I said, ' would have ensured he could squeeze through the bars before the attempt began. Especially as it was the only thing required of him.'

Aunt Thirza instantly censured, 'Drusilla, you are criticising a man who was our sovereign.'

Even Lucie thought I judged him too harshly. 'He checked his head would go through, and assumed his body would too.'

'Not a wise assumption, when his life was at stake. Research should always be thorough.'

Giles commented, 'You would think that, Drusilla. That's how you approach problems yourself. But a King is used to having things done for him.'

'Yes, but surely he realised it was *his* head they would chop off if he failed?' I said.

Lucie said, 'You know so much about it all, Drusilla, I feel quite ignorant.'

Aunt Thirza instantly bristled and I said quickly, 'I like history Lucie, just as you love sewing. I can tell you all about this castle, but I couldn't sew a neat hem, not even if my life depended on it.' That made Lucie smile, and Aunt Thirza nodded in approval.

Lucie said, 'If the King had escaped, would he ever have reached France?'

'If smugglers can cross the channel,' Aunt Thirza declared, 'so can a King.'

Giles pointed out, 'Smugglers are inconspicuous, ma'am. A King is not.' He seemed rather subdued, which wasn't like him at all, and I put it down to tiredness.

His betrothed asked, 'Do you know any smugglers, Giles?'

'Everyone on the Island knows people involved in the trade.'

'I am thankful to say I do not,' my aunt pronounced predictably. 'Nor do I think it wise for you to do so either, Giles.'

Giles, anxious to maintain the harmony of the day, suggested we take a walk around the ramparts. The seventy steps made for a strenuous climb, but when my aunt and cousin stood admiring the view, I was able, at long last, to ask Giles what he'd meant to tell me this morning. Drawing me further away from the others, he murmured softly, 'I have news of your uncle.'

The tone of his voice implied it was not good news, and fearing the worst, I turned to look at him, my heart hammering. 'Is....is he....?'

He shook his head. 'He's in prison. In Normandy.' I closed my eyes in relief. For it meant there was some hope, when I had feared there might be none at all. 'The friends I told you about have a contact at the prison. It seems your uncle is being moved to Paris soon.'

'Paris?' I repeated in alarm. Many of the worst atrocities occurred in Paris, and the thought of my dear uncle being in that violent city filled me with horror. 'Can anything be done to get him out? I don't care what it costs.'

'I'll do all I can, you know that,' he said, but could not hide his unease. 'Your uncle may not have a title but he owns an estate, and to the sans-culottes that makes him an enemy of the people. Anyone caught helping him escape would forfeit his own life.'

Thinking of what a man of my uncle's class would suffer in a prison run by the revolutionaries made me shudder. He wasn't one of those hated aristocrats who treated their employees worse than their animals. Charles Frere behaved with decency and humanity in his dealings with those who worked for him. But, as in all revolutions, the good were tainted by their association with the bad, and had to be eliminated. And, as Giles was gently insinuating, it might not be possible to save him.

'Do you realise Giles, we've been laughing and joking about King Charles's attempts to escape, and how he lost his head, when my uncle is in prison and might--------' Unable to go on, I turned away from my aunt and cousin, fearing they would realise something was wrong.

The strain he'd felt today showed fleetingly on his face. 'Yes – I found that — difficult.'

'I thought you were rather quiet.'

He glanced across at my aunt and cousin. 'I should have told them this morning, but they were so looking forward to the outing, I couldn't bring myself to do it. It seemed so heartless.' I understood, for I would have done the same thing myself. 'I'll ride over in the morning, as if I've only just heard. One day can't make any difference.' A decision I agreed with wholeheartedly.

Giles had arranged for us to partake of light refreshments at an inn on the way home, and we drove off under a blazing sun, the air so still I could hear every word of the lively discussion that ensued on all we had seen. But none of it sank in; all I could think of was my uncle.

Although I kept the horses to a sensible pace, the carriage swayed a little as we rounded a particularly sharp bend, bringing a severe scold from my aunt. 'Do slow down Drusilla, or we shall all end up in a ditch.'

Giles, ever the diplomat, assured her I had never overturned a carriage in my life. 'We'll be at the inn in five minutes, ma'am. I think some refreshment will ....'. His voice trailed away, and we all became aware of a horseman riding towards us at breakneck speed.

Recognising the man, I brought the carriage to a halt at the side of the road and turned to Giles. 'Were you expecting your groom?'

Mystified, he shook his head, and jumped down from the carriage. 'What the deuce is he doing on Merrydown?' This horse, Giles's favourite, had been ridden so hard steam rose from the sweat on its flanks.

Leatherbarrow was head groom at Ledstone; a quiet, sensible man, who was not easily ruffled. To see him upset and agitated, which he plainly was now, filled me with foreboding. Hurriedly dismounting, he uttered a breathless, 'Thank goodness I found you, sir.'

Giles took a step towards him, asking fearfully, 'My mother---'

'No, sir. She is --- safe.' Leatherbarrow's voice was distinctly unsteady. The horse nudged his arm and he automatically settled the animal with a calming hand. Then, visibly taking a deep breath, he said, 'There's been a terrible accident, sir. Mr Thomas and young master Tom--' He stopped, as if searching for the right words.

'*Go on*,' Giles urged. 'What sort of accident? Are they badly hurt? For heaven's sake, *tell* me.'

'Sir ---' Leatherbarrow lifted his shoulders in resignation, for there was no easy way to say what he must say. 'I'm afraid they're dead, sir.'

8

'Wh-a-a-t?' Giles uttered the word on a long disbelieving gasp, as if he must have misheard. And he stood, stupefied, his eyes fixed on Leatherbarrow. Waiting, as we all were, for the groom to retract his words. For, surely, such a terrible thing was not possible. When he remained silent, Giles hissed insistently, 'They *can't* be-----'

His groom's voice shook. 'I'm afraid it's true, sir.' With a helpless gesture of his hands, he said quietly, 'I'm very sorry, sir.'

We knew then there was no mistake. Yet still we stared at the groom, all of us quite motionless, too stunned to take it in. Lucie gave a little sob, and my aunt, white-faced and shaking, clutched the side of the carriage.

Giles demanded, his voice trembling, 'What happened?'

Leatherbarrow automatically moved his horse so that a cart could pass. 'They drowned, sir.'

I whispered, 'What - both of them?'

Leatherbarrow glanced up at me. 'Yes, my lady.' Another sob escaped Lucie, and my aunt took her hand in comforting fashion as Leatherbarrow went on, 'The local Riding officer found Mr Thomas's body at Hokewell Bay, close to the village. Master Tom was a few hundred yards further round the bay.' Having delivered the terrible news, the groom awaited instructions. But, numbed with shock, not one of us moved, or spoke.

Leatherbarrow urged, 'Mrs Saxborough begs you to come at once, sir.' Still no-one moved, and he said, his voice heavy with meaning, 'She's very - distraught, sir.' Giles passed a hand across his forehead, as if by doing so he could somehow gather his wits together.

I asked, in a strained voice I barely recognised as my own, 'How did it happen Leatherbarrow? Was the yacht wrecked?'

The groom raised his eyes to mine. 'I think it must have been, my lady.'

Giles demanded savagely, 'What do you mean by that?' I had never heard him speak so harshly before. 'Is there no wreckage?'

'None that I know of, sir.' He went on quietly, 'The Riding Officer found nothing else.' Giles gripped the side of the carriage, his knuckles white. 'Mrs Saxborough sent me to find you, sir.' The urgency in the groom's voice left us in no doubt as to the effect of this second tragedy on my godmother. 'They are taking the -- the bodies-- up to Ledstone.'

Giles looked up at me with so much pain in his eyes I caught my breath. After a moment, I managed to say, 'You must go at once, Giles.'

Lucie, who had been weeping silently, added her voice to mine. Giles looked round at us all, somehow remembering his manners, even at such a time. 'But that will leave you unescorted.'

Whereupon my aunt, who never went anywhere without an escort, said in a resolute voice, 'Your concern does you credit Giles, but this is an emergency. We shall be quite safe.'

Leatherbarrow suggested, 'If you take Merrydown sir, then I can ---'

I broke in, 'Escort us home. That is very sensible, Leatherbarrow.' And I indicated he should sit beside me.

Giles climbed into the saddle, gathering the reins with hands that were visibly shaking. After glancing round at us all, he rode off, and I drove on towards Westfleet. Whereas the conversation had flowed easily before, now no-one spoke, once I had made sure Leatherbarrow had told us everything he knew. The inn where we were to have partaken of refreshments soon came into sight, and I sent Leatherbarrow in to explain we couldn't stop. After which, I hurried on, determined to reach home as soon as possible.

My aunt no longer complained at being shaken up by the speed at which we were travelling, nor did she comment when I asked Leatherbarrow to tell Giles I'd come to Ledstone as soon as I had changed my clothes. Or when Lucie said she would accompany me, except to insist that Mudd went with us.

Two thoughts came unbidden into my mind then. That Giles was now Mr Saxborough of Ledstone Place, and a very rich man. And that my godmother would not have to leave her home after all.

To own Ledstone and marry Lucie would give Giles everything he could ever want, not that he would have admitted it. Being certain, as I had been, that it would never happen.

After all, if Thomas succumbed to some disease, there was always young Tom, full of youthful vigour, who would marry in a few years and produce a family. Now that wouldn't happen. I thought of the polite, kind-hearted Tom and his great zest for life. A boy everyone liked. I recalled the party Julia had organised for his birthday, and his delight in the penknife I'd given him. Tears misted my eyes, and I quickly blinked them away, aware I must get my passengers home safely. Afterwards I remembered very little of that drive, thinking only of what was happening to the Saxborough family.

Leatherbarrow had said the tragedy was 'a terrible accident.' That was how Cuthbert Saxborough's demise had been described too. And Thomas was as expert on a boat as his father had been on a horse. A parallel I found profoundly disturbing.

I brought the carriage to a halt in front of the house, where my aunt and cousin alighted. Driving round to the stable yard, one look at Mudd's face told me the appalling news had already reached Westfleet. Leatherbarrow returned to Ledstone on the horse Giles had ridden over on this morning, and I told Mudd to saddle Orlando and Lucie's horse, and to be ready to accompany us in fifteen minutes.

Up at the house, Jeffel's countenance mirrored the shock that was on all our faces. 'Miss Lucie says you are going to Ledstone, my lady.'

'As soon as we have changed. I can't tell you when we'll be back, I'm afraid.'

For once his usual composure had deserted him, and he couldn't quite control the emotion in his voice. 'Please tell Mr Giles how sorry all the Westfleet servants are, my lady.' Many of them had known Giles all his life, and he was a popular visitor. For he wasn't above stopping to chat with even the lowliest scullery maid, and he always rewarded any little service done for him with a warm smile.

Promising to pass on their condolences, I caught a glimpse of myself in the hall mirror, ashen-faced and tense. With an effort, I remembered the house still had to be run and said, 'Mrs Frere will be staying here, Jeffel. I don't know if she will want dinner. She might prefer.....'

'Don't you go fretting about Mrs Frere, my lady. We'll look after her.'

After my father's death it was kindness that had overset me the most, and so it was now. My aunt's frequent criticisms of the servants did not make her popular with them, but she was *my* aunt and the only way they could help me at present was to attend to her needs. Uttering a choked, 'Thank you,' I rushed off to change into a black riding habit.

Minutes later Lucie and I hurried out to the waiting horses, and I said, 'You go to Ledstone with Mudd - I'll be along later.'

'Why?' she asked, bewildered. 'Where are you going?'

'To the beach. To see if any wreckage has been washed up yet.'

The cliff was much lower at Hokewell than further round the bay, the hamlet itself being too unsightly to encourage visitors, which suited the local smugglers. Although the long curving sweep of the coastline from Hokewell to Dittistone in the distance was a delight to the eye.

On the low cliff top, a cluster of grim-faced villagers stood watching Thorpe, the local Riding Officer, meticulously searching the area, and as I tethered Orlando, I asked if anyone had seen anything. But no-one had. Thorpe, one of four Riding Officers patrolling the coastline of the Island, was particularly zealous in carrying out his duties, and therefore hated by the local populace. He willingly showed me where he'd found Thomas's body, and explained, 'I was riding to Dittistone to visit a friend, but I always keep an eye open for anything unusual, even when I'm off duty. You wouldn't believe some of the things they get up to, ma'am. Submerging the stuff offshore with a heavy weight and retrieving it with a grapnel when it suits them. Or they'll bury the contraband in the sand and recover it later. And that's what I thought it was when I first caught sight of something on the beach. Only when I got closer did I realise it was a body.' He turned to me with genuine sadness. 'You can imagine how I felt when I saw it was Mr Thomas.'

No words could convey my own feelings, so I simply said, 'What did you do then?'

'I sent one of the locals to fetch the parson. Him being the proper person to tell the family at Ledstone Place. Only he'd left for Newport an hour earlier. By chance, the constable was in Hokewell, and he came down straightaway. He went as white as a sheet when he saw Mr Thomas, and then someone came running along the cliff saying there was another body.' He shook his head sorrowfully. 'I don't mind telling you ma'am, I could have wept when young master Tom was brought up from the beach. The constable was fair trembling at the thought of having to break the news at Ledstone. I was thankful I didn't have to do it, especially when I heard Mr Giles had gone to Carisbrooke for the day, and only Mrs Saxborough was at home.'

I asked him if the yacht could have foundered on the underwater ledges that ran along this part of the west coast. As many ships, large and small, had done over the centuries. Removing his hat, he scratched his head. 'I don't see how, ma'am. It was calm last night, and Mr Thomas knew this coast like the back of his hand.'

After requesting Thorpe to inform me of anything that did come ashore, however insignificant, I went on to Ledstone. The stable yard was eerily quiet; no cheerful chatter, or grooms whistling as they went about their work, and I handed Orlando over to Mudd, who told me the parson had arrived a few minutes ago.

Parker already had the door open, and relieving me of my crop and riding gloves, he spoke in a low, urgent tone. 'Thank heavens you've come, my lady. Mrs Saxborough has been asking for you this past hour or more.'

His face told me the full extent of my godmother's distress. 'Is Miss Lucie with her?'

'She is, which Mr Giles was very thankful for, what with the parson insisting Mrs Saxborough needed spiritual guidance. If you'll forgive me for talking plainly my lady, we all know what she thinks of him,' he observed, raising his brows eloquently, and speaking in the confidential manner of a trusted servant who had watched me grow up, and could still remember scolding me for sliding backwards down the Ledstone banister rail.

'Indeed,' I murmured, as I removed my hat.

'Mr Giles took Mr Upton into the library, and that's why I had the door open. It wouldn't do for the parson to find out other visitors were allowed, when he was not.'

I half smiled. 'Then I shall be very quiet, Parker. Tell me, has the doctor been sent for?'

'Yes, my lady.'

'Good.' I glanced up the wide staircase. 'I take it Mrs Saxborough is in her bedchamber?'

He sighed. 'She retired there the moment the news came - just like when we heard of Mr Saxborough's accident. The servants are all in tears. None of us can believe it.' Almost overcome himself, he swallowed hard. 'I didn't know what to say to Mr Giles when he came in.'

'None of us knows what to say, Parker,' I assured him sadly.

I walked up the stairs, tapped softly on the door of my godmother's bedchamber, and went in to find her propped up in bed by a mass of pillows, quietly weeping. The room was filled with the aroma of roses from her favourite perfume, and the curtains were half drawn. Lucie sat beside the bed and as I closed the door, Marguerite held out her hand to me, sobbing,

'Drusilla, thank goodness you're here. I never meant it, you know, not for a moment.'

'I'm sure you didn't,' I agreed soothingly. Not knowing what she was talking about, I lifted an inquiring eyebrow at Lucie, whose infinitesimal shake of her head suggested it was not significant. In fact, uppermost in my godmother's mind was regret for a remark she'd made in my hearing not long ago.

'I did say I wished Giles could inherit Ledstone, because it would be so very much more comfortable,' she confessed, mopping her eyes with a perfumed handkerchief. 'But I would never have said it if I'd known Thomas and his poor boy were going to drown.'

'Of course you wouldn't have,' Lucie said. She knew instinctively how to calm her, and did so with very real affection. Giles had chosen his bride wisely, for this sweet child would never come between him and his mother.

'And I *know* I said I didn't want to leave Ledstone. But if spending the rest of my days in those cold, draughty rooms at Norton House would bring Thomas and young Tom back, I would gladly do so. Even if a chill on the lungs carried me off, as it very soon would do.'

We did all we could to pacify her, but still the tears flowed, and suddenly she clutched my hand. 'Drusilla, I'm frightened.'

'There's nothing to fear---'

'But there is,' she cried, her voice rising hysterically. 'Don't you see - everyone I love is being taken from me, one by one. First Cuthbert, and now Thomas and his poor boy.' She shook visibly, as she voiced her greatest fear. 'Next time it could be Giles----' Breaking into such heartrending sobs I decided to ask Dr Redding to look in on her.

Marguerite had been fond of Cuthbert, in her way, for he doted on her. As for Thomas and young Tom, she accepted rather than loved them. Not worrying over their welfare, yet wishing them no harm. But, Giles was a different matter. He was the only person she had ever really loved in her entire life. As long as he was safe, she could survive any other catastrophe.

Going to fetch Marguerite a clean handkerchief I saw Dr Redding riding up to the house, and while he was with my godmother I quietly slipped into the back parlour where the bodies were.

The curtains were drawn, and a single candle burnt on the mantle shelf above the fireplace. I found myself shivering, even though the room was warm, but I had come to see the bodies for myself, and this was my only chance. Picking up the candle with an unsteady hand, I crossed to where they lay, pulling back the covering sheets before my courage failed me.

9

When I found Cuthbert Saxborough's body, I had not been prepared for the sickness in my stomach, or the sense of disbelief. And nor was I now. Thomas's face was white, the skin on his neck sagging into folds of icy coldness, and I was filled with a deep sadness. But it was the sight of young Tom that upset me most. Touching his cold cheek, I wept unashamedly. I had always been fond of him, and to see him lying there with the air squeezed out of his lungs, when at fourteen he should have had his whole life before him, filled me with a sense of utter helplessness.

Hurriedly drying my eyes, being aware Dr. Redding might come in at any minute, I looked for any clue as to what had happened. It wasn't easy to see by candlelight, but to open the curtains seemed wrong, and I worked as best I could under the dim, flickering flame. Their clothes were full of sand, their shoes and stockings missing. Thomas had a few coins in his pocket, but I saw no signs of violence, just a few superficial marks probably caused through being washed up on the beach. The Saxborough ring, which Thomas had worn proudly since the death of his father, was missing, and I presumed Giles had removed it for safe keeping.

Dr Redding came into the room just as I was replacing the sheets. An intelligent bachelor of about thirty, rather good looking with dark brown eyes and hair, he relied largely on common sense in his dealings with patients. On seeing me, he stood stock-still in the doorway, an expression of horror on his face. 'Forgive me ma'am, but this is hardly the place for a lady.'

'No, and I can't offer you any sensible explanation, except that I wished to see the bodies for myself.'

His countenance relaxed at this, and shutting the door, he set his bag down on a chair. 'After an accident of this kind, some people do find a sight of the bodies helps them accept the truth.' He ran a hand distractedly through his dark hair. 'To be truthful with you ma'am, in this case, I have some difficulty in believing it myself.'

He promised to inform me of his conclusions, and told me he'd given Marguerite a sleeping draught. Realising the examinations might take some time, I went up to my godmother to find the sleeping draught had already taken effect. Lucie sat by the window, looking out at a sea mist that was beginning to engulf the garden. I had entered the room so quietly she didn't realise I was there until I touched her arm, and when she turned her head I saw her face was wet with tears.

Drying her eyes, she whispered, 'I can't stop thinking about Thomas and young Tom. It's so unfair Drusilla, they both had everything to live for.' It did not seem to have occurred to this sweet child that Ledstone, with all its riches, now belonged to Giles. When it did, I thought, it would sadden her greatly that so much wealth should come to them at such a cost.

Lucie suggested we took turns to sit with Marguerite, offering to do so first. Returning downstairs, I asked the housekeeper to prepare rooms for Lucie and myself, before going into the library to write an explanatory note to my aunt. Walking down to the stables through the thickening mist, I sent Mudd home with the note, instructing him to return in the morning.

Going back to the drawing room to await Dr. Redding, and wandering restlessly about the room, I happened to glance up at the much prized painting of William Saxborough, with his second wife and seven daughters. William, the family's most famous ancestor, was also the most notorious, having supposedly murdered his first wife, although father and I failed to find any real proof when researching for his book, which after two hundred years wasn't surprising.

But Thomas and Tom had died only this morning; surely it would be easier to find out the truth about them. Looking into William's evil eyes, I soon turned away, convinced they were mocking me.

When Dr. Redding returned he begged my pardon for keeping me waiting, saying Giles had asked a lot of questions. 'Most of which will be in your mind too ma'am, I imagine. But first I should tell you that, in my opinion, drowning was the cause of death in both cases.'

I drew a deep breath. 'You are absolutely certain?'

'As far as I can be. I found no signs of violence.'

'I see,' I said, sinking into the nearest chair. 'Can you say how long they were in the water?'

He pursed his lips. 'It's difficult to be precise, but living here, I've seen many drowned men, and I would say it wasn't more than an hour or two. They were probably washed up at high tide, which I gather was soon after four.' Opening his bag, he handed me a further sleeping draught for Marguerite, should I consider it necessary. 'I'll call again tomorrow morning.'

I asked if he believed Thomas and Tom had died as a result of an accident, and he glanced at me thoughtfully. 'You mean bearing in mind what happened to Cuthbert Saxborough?'

'That is what I mean, yes,' I acknowledged, appreciative of his quick understanding.

'Well, it has the appearance of an accident ma'am, but I wouldn't like to commit myself, without knowing how, or why, they came to be in the water. Finding the answer to that, I am glad to say,' he said, firmly shutting his bag, 'is not part of my duties.'

After he'd left the house, Parker advised me Giles was still engaged. Not with the parson, who having been told Mrs Saxborough was sleeping, had left long ago. But there were arrangements to make, the coroner to inform, and now Thorpe, the riding officer, was with him.

So I took a brisk walk around the grounds, although the eerie quietness of the mist made everything seem even more unreal. But there was nothing unreal about those two bodies. Dr. Redding said Thomas and his son had drowned. I did not doubt it. Nor did I doubt that Cuthbert Saxborough had broken his neck when thrown by his horse. But what had caused Cuthbert to be thrown? Had the gate been closed after his murder, as I believed? And how had Thomas and Tom come to be in the water?

As for Giles, this terrible happening would change his life, making him a man of great importance on the Island. But it would be a long time before he stopped grieving for Thomas and young Tom.

When I returned to the house, Giles was awaiting me in the drawing room, and he instantly rose to his feet, thanking me for looking after Marguerite. Once we were both seated, he began to talk of the tragedy. 'I don't understand how it happened, Drusilla. There hasn't been a storm, and no boat was ever kept more seaworthy.' He passed a hand across his eyes. 'Even though I have seen the bodies, and touched them---' Faltering, he looked down at his hands, struggling to control his voice as it broke up. 'I still cannot believe they are really dead.'

Before I could speak, Parker came in to set out a cold collation. 'I took a tray up to Miss Lucie first, as your ordered, sir.'

'Thank you.' He looked up at his butler, the faintest of smiles touching his lips. 'I see cook has put out some ham.'

'She thought it might tempt you to eat, sir.'

Thoughtfulness that so nearly overcame Giles it was some moments before he could trust himself to speak. 'Thank cook for me, Parker. I should be grateful if you would convey my gratitude to all the servants for the way they have kept the house running today.'

As Parker quietly closed the door behind him, Giles turned to me with a rueful smile, 'Would you believe, I'm famished. Isn't that extraordinary?' He picked up a plate. 'Can I help you to something?' Giles, first and foremost a gentleman, never forgot his manners. Only then did I realise how hungry I was too, gratefully accepting a plate of cold meats and a glass of wine. Giles went on, 'Thorpe tells me you went down to the beach yourself.'

'Yes,' I said, cutting into a thick slice of beef. 'To see if there was any wreckage.'

'Thomas wouldn't have foundered on the ledge, Drusilla.'

'I can't believe it either, but it must be considered.'

Mechanically he went on, as much to convince himself as me. 'Thomas knew every inch of that ledge, and in any case, the sea was like a mill pond last night. I should know, I was almost becalmed coming back across the Solent.' Giles twisted the stem of his glass in his fingers, swallowed what was left of his wine, and placed the empty glass on the table. 'I just can't think what could have gone wrong. Unless — unless Tom fell overboard in the darkness------'

'And Thomas jumped in to rescue him, you mean?' For they were both strong swimmers.

He lifted his shoulders. 'It's the only thing I can think of.'

'Surely he would have tied a line to his waist first? Unless it came adrift.'

Giles refilled his wine glass. 'Thomas was careless about many things, but the life of his son wasn't one of them. He would have made doubly sure the line was secure. Anyway, there was no line attached to his body.'

'Nor the mark of one round his waist.'

His eyes flickered in surprise. 'How do you know that? Did Dr. Redding tell you?'

'No. I looked for myself while the doctor was with your Mama.' Giles choked on his wine, and as he stared at me aghast I said, 'I thought I might see something that explained the accident.'

For a moment he gazed at me in disbelieving silence. 'And did you?'

I shook my head. 'I did notice Thomas wasn't wearing the Saxborough ring, but I presume you removed that for safe keeping.'

'Me?' Giles touched the middle of his chest with an index finger. 'No, the ring was missing when I saw Thomas.' Reminded of the bodies, he shuddered. 'Thorpe said the ring wasn't on T-Thomas's f-finger w-when—' He sat staring into his glass, biting his trembling lip, striving to regain control. Eventually he said, as if it was of no consequence, 'It must have fallen off in the sea.' He looked up at me. 'Dr. Redding was kindness itself. He said that in his experience, misfortunes have a nasty habit of coming together.'

'There is a good deal of truth in that.' Gently I reminded him of fishermen drowned at sea, some families losing more than one son on the same night. But those kind of mishaps, where a man was swept overboard in bad weather, or a boat was lost in a sudden squall, were more likely to be witnessed by other fishermen, and so could be explained. I was quite certain no witnesses to this tragedy would be found.

Pushing back his chair, he stood up. 'If you'll excuse me Drusilla, I must look in on Mama.' I reminded him the doctor had given her a sleeping draught. 'I'd forgotten that. Still, I would like to see her for myself.'

Giles adored his mother, and watching him go out the door, his shoulders hunched with exhaustion, my heart went out to him, for Giles was very dear to me. We had grown up together, and I knew him inside out. I understood how his mind worked and what was important to him; I was familiar with his kind ways, his courage, humour, thoughtfulness and honesty. A gentle man in every sense, he had a great respect for all living creatures. Even as a child, he had carried spiders outside rather than squash them.

Glancing at the clock, I saw it was almost ten. Was it really only this morning that we had set out for Carisbrooke?

That night I sat with Marguerite, promising to call Lucie at four, and pointing out to Giles he would be more useful to his mother when she was awake. I kept a single candle alight, for she was very restless; tossing and turning, and muttering in her sleep. Then, just after one, when I was about to give her the extra sleeping draught, she fell into a deeper sleep. I rested on the day bed, from where I could watch for any change, and found myself thinking that at this time last night, Thomas and young Tom had been alive. Yet, within an hour or two, they had drowned on the calmest of nights.

How could such a thing have happened? I considered every possibility I could think of, as father had taught me to do. Could Giles be right? Could Tom have fallen overboard? Or had the yacht struck a rock, or collided with another boat? I desperately wanted it to be an accident, but in my heart, I already knew that it wasn't. And that conviction so absorbed my thoughts that even the news of my uncle slipped my mind.

10

An eerie silence descended upon Ledstone that night as thick curtains of mist and fog drifted in from the sea, enveloping the walls of the old house. By morning not even the seagulls could be heard calling to each other, as if the birds themselves were mourning the loss of the two fine Saxboroughs lying in the small back parlour. Neither Marguerite nor I stirred until well after seven, when Lucie rushed in, her face flushed with guilt. 'Why didn't you wake me?'

Rubbing my eyes, I set my feet on the floor, quietly explaining that Marguerite had passed a tolerable night, and I had eventually fallen asleep myself. My godmother sat up drowsily, puzzling briefly at our presence, before her memory returned, whereupon she sank back onto her pillows with a despairing groan. Almost at once we heard a gentle knock on the door, and Giles came in. Joyfully Marguerite held out her arms to him, and as he hugged her, Lucie insisted I went down to breakfast.

Being glad to stretch my legs, I retired to the bedchamber I was always given when staying here; known affectionately as the Royal suite, this being where Queen Elizabeth would have slept if she'd kept her promise to William Saxborough to visit Ledstone. The sight of that delicate leaf pattern on the walls and the prettily embroidered bed hangings in rose pink and cream, always relaxed me, and it did so even on this dreadful morning. I rang for some hot water, and refreshed by a thorough wash, I changed into the clean morning gown and stockings I had brought with me, pulled a comb through my hair, and went downstairs.

Giles joined me when I was on my second cup of coffee, saying Lucie had told him I'd slept a little last night.

'Unlike you,' I murmured, for he looked utterly exhausted. 'Did you sleep at all?'

He shook his head and sat staring at his plate. 'I feel so guilty.'

'Guilty? What do you have to be guilty about?'

He gave a short, harsh laugh. 'Think about it, Drusilla. How often do you imagine I wished Ledstone was mine? I've always known exactly what I would do here. And now--------' He turned his hands upwards in a gesture of helplessness, his blue eyes full of anguish.

'I know,' I murmured compassionately, putting my hand on his arm.

I saw precisely how it was. Yesterday, shocked and grief-stricken at the loss of Thomas and Tom, he'd had no time to think of anything except how to deal with the things that follow any tragedy. It was only later, lying awake in bed, he'd recalled those times he'd dreamed of owning Ledstone. Never expecting it to happen, nor wanting it to if it cost the lives of those he loved. But being human, he'd sometimes indulged the daydream to the point of deciding how he would run Ledstone if it was his.

I tried to put this into words, pointing out, 'Every younger son has thoughts of that kind.' In truth I was far more worried about what was happening to the Saxborough family, and I told him so plainly. 'Giles, I want you to promise me you will take the greatest care of yourself. At least until we know how Thomas and Tom died.'

He gazed at me in utter astonishment. 'Drusilla, are you suggesting someone is trying to kill off the whole family? That's utter nonsense........'

'Is it? Since April your father, brother and nephew have all died.'

'That doesn't mean there's a conspiracy. I agree father was foolish to jump the east gate on a nervous horse, but he's fallen off there before, as we all have. He was just unlucky. Whereas Thomas and Tom were probably lost in some freak accident. But I promise you nothing is going to happen to me. I never do anything without thinking it out first. You, of all people, should know that.' That was true. Even as a child he hadn't embarked on any seemingly reckless exploit without planning what to do if it went wrong. But that didn't stop me being anxious.

I saw little of Giles in the days that followed. While Lucie and I cared for Marguerite, he dealt with the funeral arrangements, the necessary legal matters, assisted with the official inquiries into the accident, and received those who came to offer their condolences and pay their respects to Thomas and Tom.

On the second morning, Mr Arnold came to tell me, most apologetically, that he couldn't spare anyone to watch Smith at present, as all his men were out searching for wreckage from Thomas Saxborough's yacht. It was the duty of the Customs service to help in the aftermath of a shipwreck, but as everyone knew, it wasn't only Mr Arnold's men who might be of assistance. In fact, Giles had ridden down to Hokewell straight after breakfast that first morning to offer the local smugglers a reward for any information. He knew these men well, and very little went on at sea that they weren't aware of, or wouldn't hear of through other smugglers.

Later, quite by chance, I overheard Leatherbarrow telling another groom that Giles hadn't found a single smuggler at Hokewell. Every man had been out since daybreak searching for wreckage. A sign of their loyalty to Giles, and a gesture so filled with kindness, it almost overset me again. I guessed Jackson was behind it. A giant of a man, with a black tangled beard that gave him a fearsome appearance. Useful for a smuggler, this being the reason he grew it, I suspected, for I had seen him many a time with his children, and no man had a gentler disposition.

When Giles was a boy, Jackson and the other smugglers had happily filled his head with tales of how they fooled the Riding Officers. Things he'd repeated to me, in a voice that ached to be part of it all. How they showed a signalling light in one bay, fooling the Riding Officer into keeping watch there, while the goods were brought ashore elsewhere. Stories of horses' hooves being covered in sacking, to avoid leaving a trail directly to the smuggled goods, while old horseshoes on sticks marked out a track for the Riding Officer to follow, in the opposite direction.

Giles had loved these yarns, and willingly helped the smugglers. Once he saw the Riding Officer concealing his men along a route smugglers used to transport kegs. Guessing information had been laid, he ran like the wind to warn them, and watched as each revenue man was found and silently bundled away. When the Riding Officer finally realised what was happening and tried to escape on horseback, he was speedily unseated. The horse was sent packing, and although the Officer ran to the beach, the kegs had gone. It was no wonder the smugglers wanted to help him now. I smiled to myself, remembering how Giles had longed to go on a smuggling run, for their lives seemed so much more exciting than his.

Giles had been a sickly child, and everyone from his parents down to his nurse, mollycoddled him on account of his poor health. He found his own way of dealing with it, by persuading them he was well, even when he was not. So that no-one would stop him doing the things he enjoyed.

Whenever I went beyond the grounds of Westfleet as a child, Mudd always accompanied me, and if Giles was with us, Mudd allowed him to do things that would have had my godmother reaching for her smelling salts, had she known. Scrambling down crumbling cliffs, climbing trees, riding bareback races across the Downs. Things Giles revelled in, which Mudd considered only right for boys, and which I enjoyed too. How much simpler life had seemed then, I sighed.

Damp and dreary weather added to the atmosphere of gloom at Ledstone Place in the days leading up to the funerals. Rain lashed unrelentingly against the windowpanes of Marguerite's bedchamber, saturating lawns, sweeping in torrents across the gardens on a strong south westerly, battering the last few foxgloves to the ground, and ruining entire drifts of ox-eye daisies and marigolds. Water dripped everywhere, from gutters and trees, forming puddles on paths, lawns and flower beds. The smell of damp earth and rain permeated the whole house, the air feeling so chilly, that Giles ordered the fires to be lit, for it felt more like late October than the first week of August.

Marguerite began to improve during the day, but at night her fears for Giles's safety flared up again, despite all our efforts to comfort her. She suffered one terrible nightmare; in which

Giles was swept out to sea by a huge wave and lost, leaving her so distressed I almost sent for the doctor.

On the morning of the inquest, Giles barely quibbled when I insisted on going, but I learnt nothing of any consequence from these proceedings. The local constable had no new evidence, Thorpe gave a coherent account of how the two bodies had been found, and Dr. Redding confirmed his opinion that drowning was the cause of death. Giles affirmed when he'd last seen his brother and nephew alive, stating they were both strong swimmers. Mr Arnold said that, despite a thorough search, no wreckage had been found as yet, and the weather that night had been fair, with calm seas. A witness testified as to when the yacht left Yarmouth, and a seaman Thomas had employed on occasion, stated the yacht was always kept in perfect condition.

The Coroner made the point that even the most experienced of yachtsmen could misjudge a situation, and it seemed probable that sometime during the night in question, for reasons unknown, Thomas and his son had become separated from their yacht in the darkness, and consequently drowned. There being no evidence to suggest this was anything other than a tragic accident, the jury brought in a verdict of 'Death by Misadventure.'

On the day of the funeral, Marguerite came downstairs for the first time, keeping to her drawing room, where Lucie and I looked after her. She cried unashamedly as the funeral procession made its way down the drive and out the gate towards the church. Lucie's tears were silent, as were mine, but I prayed none of us would ever experience another day as heartrending as this had been.

The service was followed by a cold collation at Ledstone, and everyone of note on the Island attended, including the

Governor, Mr Orde. I'd expected to see Mr Reevers, until I learnt from Giles that his cousin was in London, and unaware of what had happened.

Lucie and I went home a few days after the funeral, promising to visit Marguerite frequently. Lucie stayed until the afternoon, but I left after breakfast, and as I came down the staircase I saw Mr Reevers handing his hat to Parker. He strode swiftly across the hall, taking my hands as I stepped off the last stair, and holding them a trifle longer than was strictly necessary.

'I came as soon as I could,' he said, his face grave. His eyes rapidly surveyed my face. 'My poor child, you look positively haggard.'

I managed a rueful smile. 'You have such a way with words, Mr Reevers.'

A faint chuckle escaped him. 'I do beg your pardon. I simply meant you have obviously had a harrowing time of it.'

'No more than anyone else.' And remarked, 'Giles will be glad to see you, I know. He's with his mother at present.'

'In that case, I won't disturb him.' Explaining I was going home he insisted on escorting me outside. Parker opened the door, and we walked out, stopping short of where a groom was waiting with Orlando. He asked quietly, 'Do you know how Thomas and Tom came to drown?'

'No, but Giles has offered five hundred pounds to anyone who knows how the accident happened.'

'Five hundred?' His eyebrows shot up. 'Well, that should do the trick, if anyone does know.' He paused. 'Perhaps another vessel ran into the yacht in the dark.'

'But wouldn't they have stopped to pick up Thomas and Tom?'

'Smugglers might not. Especially if they were French.'

A blackbird landed on the roof nearby and began to sing. 'I hadn't thought of that.' And I asked if he was making a brief visit.

'That depends on Giles. I'll stay as long as I can be of use to him.'

'He may well be glad of your company when his uncle and cousin arrive.'

He stared at me, puzzled. 'Which uncle and cousin is that, ma'am?'

'Of course,' I said, 'with you being away, you won't know about Vincent.'

'Vincent?' he repeated, bewildered.

'Cuthbert's brother. Didn't your mother tell you about him?'

His brow furrowed in deep thought. 'Oh yes, I remember. He ran off with some dancer.'

'Actress.'

'Actress, then. But, surely, he died years ago.'

'So everyone thought. Only it appears he isn't dead, after all.'

Mr Reevers gazed at me in astonishment. 'Not dead?'

I explained about Vincent's letter, and that it had arrived the day before the yachting accident. 'In fact while Giles was staying with you,' I said. 'Vincent and Piers mean to visit Ledstone shortly. I hope you don't object to meeting the black sheep of the family?'

He didn't answer immediately, and when he did speak, it was a rather indistinct, 'Not at all.' The news had clearly shocked him, but then it had astounded us all.

On the way home, I considered his suggestion that a French smuggling vessel could have run into Thomas's yacht. But there were a number of possible theories, any one of which could be right. What was lacking was real evidence; without which we'd never learn what really happened.

Then, as I rode across the Downs, I saw a boy flying a kite. He was about Tom's age, and for one second, thinking it was him, I raised my hand to wave, until I remembered that Tom would never fly a kite again. I thought of all the other things he would never do again, and of the life he should have had. And my heart ached for him.

On reaching Westfleet, I entered the house by a side door, going straight up to my bedchamber. Here I sank into a chair, savouring that familiar smell of freshly polished wood, and allowing the feel of my own home to fill me with all its time-worn comfort and ease. I had not been this tired since the death of my father, and I even allowed my maid to coax me into taking a long bath scented with lavender, before I finally went downstairs.

Jeffel greeted me with pleasure, assuring me there had not been any problems during my absence. Which, if true, was the longest period my aunt had ever gone without upsetting anyone, but even she said that the servants had been very good. I told her all that had occurred at Ledstone, including the details of Thomas's Will, which left everything to Tom, and in the event of Tom's death without issue, to Giles.

When I asked how she had occupied herself, she said, 'I finished the curtains for my new bedchamber. Which reminds me Drusilla, what happened to your father's clothes? I haven't come across so much as a handkerchief.'

'They're in the small bedchamber.' I'd had them moved about a month before my uncle's letters had ceased, thinking he could use them if he had to leave France in a hurry. Many emigres arrived with little more than they were wearing, and not much money either.

My uncle was a couple of inches shorter than my father, but had much the same build, and the clothes could be altered to fit. Now I feared they would never be needed. I knew I ought to tell my aunt he was in prison, but I couldn't bring myself to do it, excusing my cowardice on the grounds that it would be better if she read the actual letter from Giles's friends herself. In a few days I would mention it to him.

That afternoon, when Aunt Thirza took the carriage to Ledstone to bring Lucie home, I went into the workroom to write down the few facts I had about the yachting tragedy. First though, I wrote a note to Mr Arnold asking him to inform me personally of any wreckage found. He might raise an eyebrow on receiving such a request, but he would do it, without question, knowing I would not have asked without good reason.

After I'd sealed it with a wafer, and given orders for Mudd to deliver it, I heard a slight movement, and saw the kitchen cat sitting in my father's chair, grooming herself. 'You scamp,' I chuckled, going over to smooth the soft tortoiseshell fur. 'I bet this isn't the first time you've sneaked in here either.' Jess began to purr loudly, so clearly begging to be allowed to stay in this blissful haven, that I laughed out loud.

'Oh, very well. Just as long as you don't disturb me, mind.' Jess, recognising the tone of surrender to her desires, curled up and went to sleep. Meanwhile, I noted when Thomas had set sail, what the weather had been like, when and where the bodies were washed up, the fact that no wreckage had been found yet, what the Riding Officer and Dr. Redding had said, and that no-one had reported seeing the yacht while Thomas was away.

Wandering across to my father's desk, I leant against it, absently smoothing the sleeping cat, as I considered the various ways a boat could founder. Jess, annoyed at being woken, hissed in warning, her claws unsheathed. She certainly knew what she wanted, and went all out to get it. Laughing, I moved away and found myself thinking that, if the three Saxboroughs had all been murdered, then the man responsible was going all out to get what he wanted too.

It crossed my mind fleetingly, that finding a live murderer wasn't the same as collecting facts about someone long dead, and assembling them in the correct order, as I had been accustomed to do. This murderer, having killed twice, would not hesitate to do so again, if I found out who he was. And I gave an involuntary shiver, remembering the two bodies I'd seen in that small back parlour at Ledstone Place.

But why had Cuthbert and his two immediate heirs been murdered? Did someone have a grudge against the family? Or was it all to do with money and position? Going back to the chart, I drew up the Saxborough family tree, starting with the notorious William. Married twice, his wives had only produced daughters. He'd had one brother, whom he loathed, and rather than allow him to inherit, he made provision for the inheritance to go through the female line, if necessary.

Which, I concluded, meant Mr Reevers, the son of Cuthbert's eldest sister, was Giles's heir at present. It wasn't until I began writing down the names of Cuthbert's six sisters that I thought of Vincent. And saw how his being alive changed everything. For, until Lucie and Giles had children, Vincent and Piers came between Giles and Mr Reevers. Something neither Mr Reevers, nor Giles, were aware of until after Thomas and Tom had died.

Hardly a week had passed since the arrival of Vincent's letter, yet I knew a good deal about him from his earlier communications. I've always had a good memory, and I recorded what Vincent had written of his wife and son, their health and appearance, and about his own impecunious state at that time. And that now he could afford to travel in America for a year with his son. Details that helped me see the family as a whole.

I noted where the men of the family were at the time of the two incidents. Giles had been riding on the estate when his father died, and sailing back across the Solent when Thomas's yacht foundered. Mr Reevers had sailed to London the day before the two bodies were found, but where he was when Cuthbert died, no-one knew. Vincent and Piers had been either in America, or crossing the Atlantic, and still being at sea, would not yet be aware of the yachting tragedy. Having included every fact I could think of, I waited until the ink had dried and then fixed the chart of events to the wall, with the family tree next to it, and stood looking at it for some time.

Lucie joined us for dinner as planned, but only pecked at her food and was so subdued that the instant the servants left the room, I demanded to know what was wrong. But it was Aunt Thirza who answered, her bosom heaving with indignation. 'I met the parson's wife on the way to Ledstone, and she had the temerity to ask if, in the circumstances, Lucie meant to cry off from the wedding.'

'Cry off?' I repeated, astounded. 'What circumstances are you talking about?'

Lucie looked up, her lip trembling. 'Drusilla, they are saying that Giles - that he -'

My aunt cut in, 'There is speculation that Thomas and Tom did not die as a result of an accident. And that Giles had a hand in it------' That completely took my breath away, and while I struggled to find my voice, my aunt went on worriedly, 'It's most unfortunate Giles was at sea that night.' I recalled that after visiting Mr Reevers, a delay in a business matter had caused him to leave later than planned.

'He was seen mooring his boat in Yarmouth early that morning,' Lucie whispered.

'It's being said,' my aunt went on, a tremor in her voice, 'that Giles paid smugglers to make the deaths appear accidental.'

I burst out angrily, 'That's a monstrous suggestion.'

Aunt Thirza could not hide her concern. 'It's all over the Island, according to Mrs Upton.' The parson's wife loved nothing better than spreading rumours.

'The thing is, Drusilla,' Lucie whispered, 'Giles *is* friendly with the local smugglers. And last night--'

'It's absolute nonsense,' I said, 'as you -----.'

My aunt cut in, 'What Lucie is trying to tell you is that-----' Her voice shook, but she forced herself to go on. 'Last night, Giles was seen giving money to smugglers.'

I opened and shut my mouth twice before any words came out. 'Who saw him?' I managed at last.

My aunt shook her head. 'Mrs Upton said it was common knowledge.'

'What does Giles say?'

'He wasn't there when Mama arrived. He'd gone to Newport on business,' Lucie said, with tear-filled eyes, and my heart went out to her. Preparing for her marriage should have been a happy period in her life. Not a time of tragedy, worry, and now this awful rumour. Nor did she know her father was in prison. And I wondered why it was that troubles always seemed to come together.

I tried my best to calm her fears, but she was still upset. 'How could anyone think Giles capable of such a wicked thing?'

'People who know him won't think it,' I said, with quiet conviction. 'The truth is, with Giles coming into his inheritance in such a way, there was bound to be a good deal of wild gossip.'

Aunt Thirza said, 'That's exactly what I told Mrs Saxborough.'

'Wha-at?' I stared at her in horror. 'You told my godmother about these rumours?'

Aunt Thirza's lifted an eyebrow in surprise. 'Of course.'

'Oh Aunt, how could you? Just when she was beginning to calm down too.'

My aunt was bewildered. 'But she was bound to hear them.'

'How?' I was absolutely seething. 'She hasn't gone out since the accident, and she refuses to see any visitors at present but ourselves. Who would have told her?'

'If I had a son, and such rumours were circulating about him, I would wish to know.'

Tossing my napkin onto the table, I pushed back my chair. 'Yes, but you are not Marguerite Saxborough.'

Aunt Thirza sniffed. 'I think it unwise to shield Mrs Saxborough from the truth. Naturally, I told her the rumours were nonsense. No person of sense would believe Giles had anything to do with it. If they were murdered, it's far more likely to mean the start of a Revolution in England. And that's what I told her.'

I closed my eyes and groaned. After what was happening in France, this was precisely what many people, including Marguerite, did fear.

I was so angry, that for one very brief moment, I asked myself why it was that, if a murderer was indeed at large, he had failed to choose my aunt as a victim.

11

Giles came over later and put our minds at rest by explaining the men in question had been out from dawn to dusk every day searching for wreckage from Thomas's yacht. 'I gave them some money because they hadn't worked since the accident. Most have families to feed and I couldn't let them be out of pocket on my account.'

So that was how it had happened. Someone had seen him do it, and jumped to the wrong conclusions. How easily rumours were started.

Before he left I had a word with him urging quietly, 'Giles, oughtn't you to tell my aunt and cousin about my uncle?'

'I will. As soon as the contact at the prison finds out what the actual situation is.' I swallowed hard, thinking of what my uncle must be suffering, and the awful fate that could lay ahead of him. 'Don't despair, Drusilla. He's alive, and that's what matters.'

It was just like Giles to remain optimistic. Yet each day my uncle spent in prison brought him closer to facing trial, and for someone of his class there would be only one verdict. It was also typical of Giles that in the midst of the worst tragedy in his own life, he'd still found time to think of Lucie's father.

Now he'd become Mr Saxborough of Ledstone Place, a man of fortune and immense influence in the Island, he soon set about implementing the reforms he considered essential. Increasing the pay of his employees, improving the servants' quarters, and living conditions of his tenants. Giles had seen how the worst members of the French aristocracy had forced their dependants to live in hovels, to bake their bread in the estate ovens, paying an inflated price for the privilege, uncaring of whether they or their children starved as a result. Cuthbert Saxborough had not gone to those lengths, but Giles, unhappy with the way his father treated his servants and tenants, had added that touch of humanity missing from Ledstone for fifty years.

Not everything was as easy to resolve, however. The five hundred pounds reward, a fortune to virtually every Islander, remained unclaimed. Yet someone must know how Thomas and Tom had died.

I happened to call on Marguerite shortly after she received the expected letter from Vincent, which she passed to me with a sigh. It was quite short, and had been written a week earlier, on board the 'Carolina.' Dated the 14th August, it read:-

My dear Marguerite,

Our ship docks in London in the morning after six long weeks at sea. My poor Piers has had a terrible time of it, being laid low with the most awful sea sickness.

Once I have dealt with my business affairs in London, and Piers has recovered his strength, we will come down to the Island. I am so looking forward to seeing you all. You, my dear Marguerite, will I am sure be every bit as beautiful as I remember. When I left England Giles was just a baby, of course, and Thomas a happy-go-lucky boy of fifteen, much the same age as his own son must be now.

We expect to cross the Solent in about two weeks and will put up at the George in Yarmouth.

He ended in the usual way, signing his name with the same flourish as before. When I handed it back to her, she said in a faltering voice, 'Vincent doesn't know about Thomas and young Tom.' Her bottom lip began to tremble. 'However am I to tell him-----'

'His man of business in London will do that. Or that friend he spoke of in his first letter - the one who sends him news of the family. It was in all the newspapers.'

She began to look more hopeful again. 'Perhaps when he hears the news he'll decide not to come. He must realise how devastated we all are.'

I thought that unlikely, for there could be no objection to visits from close family members at such a time, and Vincent had crossed an ocean in order to see his birthplace one last time. Marguerite, resigned to her fate, warned that no-one should expect her to enjoy it, for visitors always wore her down.

Glancing out the window, she suddenly grabbed my arm in agitated fashion, pointing to a figure riding up to the house. 'Who is that? Oh dear, where are my spectacles?' And frantically began searching the table bearing her medicines and the latest fashionable journals. Slightly short-sighted, she refused to wear her spectacles in the company of anyone outside the family and myself.

'It's all right,' I said, recognising the horseman. 'It's only Mr Arnold.' Her spectacles had fallen on the floor and having picked them up, I handed them to her.

'Mr Arnold?' Putting on her spectacles, she looked out the window. 'So it is. I suppose he wants to see Giles.' But Giles was out on the estate, and when Parker came to inquire if Marguerite would receive the visitor instead, she threw up her hands in resignation. 'Oh very well.' And quickly hid her spectacles in the table drawer.

After exchanging the usual pleasantries, Mr Arnold took a letter from his pocket, explaining it was from John Delafield, his brother-in-law in New York. 'There's a passage I believe will interest you, ma'am. If I may read it to you?'

Puzzled, she murmured politely, 'By all means.'

He unfolded the sheet. 'It is dated the 10th of June, and my brother-in-law says, *Early in February I met a most interesting gentleman staying at the house of a friend, here in New York. My intention was to write to you then, but some pressing business matters demanded my attention, and then - well, to be truthful, it slipped my mind, and you know how time flies when you are busy. Still, better late than never. This gentleman went by the name of Mr Vincent Saxborough.*"

'Vincent?' Marguerite echoed in surprise.

Mr Arnold nodded, smiling. 'I understand he is visiting Ledstone shortly, and I thought you would like to hear of this encounter, and he read on,

'*Mr Saxborough seemed a most agreeable gentleman, conducting himself with an ease of manner that could only please. His views in male company were those of a man of sense, while his undoubted charm made him a great favourite with the ladies. His clothes were of the finest, he was clearly quite at home in the very cream of society, and I soon discovered, (though not through him) that no hostess in town considered her dinner party complete without him. Which I could well understand, for he has a most amusing way of relating a story. His son, Piers, a rugged looking* young man, was rather quiet, but it was clear he greatly admired the American way of life.

Of course, with so unusual a surname, I asked Vincent if he was related to Mr Cuthbert Saxborough, and you can imagine my surprise when I discovered they were brothers, for I had no idea Mr Saxborough possessed a brother, had you? We talked at some length then, and on several other convivial occasions in the following weeks, before he and his son left New York to see something of the south.

Quite by chance I bumped into Mr Saxborough a few days ago, when I learned he and his son had enjoyed several agreeable weeks of southern hospitality. He told me the sad news of his brother, and how it had made him think about Ledstone, which led, as such thoughts often do as one grows older, to a wish to see his boyhood home once more. I gather they leave for England at the beginning of July. Thinking of the old country made me realise I hadn't written since January, which is very remiss of me. Still, I was sure you would be interested to hear of my encounter, and I can only say that it shows what a small world it is in which we live.'

Mr Arnold folded the letter again. 'The rest is family news, ma'am.'

Marguerite thanked him for his kindness, and when he left a short time later, she sighed, 'Mr Arnold meant it kindly, I know, and I am glad Vincent has made something of himself, but I still wish they weren't coming here. It will be most awkward.'

I couldn't help feeling sorry for Marguerite. She'd had so much to contend with this year.

The following afternoon, I was talking to Aunt Thirza in the drawing room when Mr Reevers called to inquire if

I cared to ride out with him. He was impeccably dressed in riding breeches, a well-cut dark green coat, and top boots, and accepting his offer politely, I left him chatting to my aunt, while I sent a message to the stables and went to change into a riding dress. For some reason I couldn't quite explain, I found myself wishing I could wear my bright blue habit, which suited me particularly well. But that was out of the question as I was still in mourning for my father.

Putting on my hat and gloves, I collected my riding whip, and went downstairs again, where my aunt instantly commanded, 'Mudd will go with you, Drusilla.'

Before I could speak, Mr Reevers quickly reassured her. 'I'm delighted to see you believe in observing the proprieties, ma'am. Frankly I find the behaviour of many younger people these days leaves much to be desired.'

It was as much as I could do to keep a straight face, and the moment we reached the courtyard, I burst out in amusement, 'Do you always pander to the wishes of older ladies?'

'Always,' he insisted, his eyes gleaming wickedly. 'And not only the older ones either.' I shook my head at him, laughing.

A few minutes later, as we picked our way along a very muddy Manor Lane towards the Downs, with Mudd following at the correct distance, Mr Reevers said, 'I wanted to tell you, I may be coming to live on the Island? Giles has most generously offered me Norton House.' I was so surprised I couldn't think what to say. 'My own house is being sold in order to settle the debts my father left when he died earlier this year.' I looked at him in dismay, realising what it must mean to him, but he simply shrugged. 'I knew he had debts, of course, but not the extent of them. He'd always dismissed them as insignificant,' he said, unable to hide the irony in his voice. 'In fact the sale will only just cover them. Fortunately, I have no family obligations to worry about. My father was a widower, all my sisters are married, and I have no brothers.'

Feeling I should say something, I uttered a totally inadequate, 'It must be very difficult for you, Mr Reevers.'

A wry smile twisted his lips. 'The dice falls the wrong way for us all at times, ma'am. I hope to find some other way of restoring my fortune.'

I wondered how he could possibly resolve such a devastating, and unforeseen, financial hardship, but he didn't refer to it again. Instead he challenged me to a race across the Downs, and seemed not at all put out when I won. Riding along at walking pace, waiting for Mudd to catch up, Mr Reevers asked if Smith had been dealt with yet.

'Unfortunately not. Mr Arnold's men are too busy looking for Thomas's yacht.'

'And no-one is watching Smith?'

'No, so I shall have to be patient. Which,' I admitted ruefully, 'is not something I am good at. My father said I was far too impulsive, and I know it to be true, though I do try not to be.'

'You run the estate yourself?'

'Father taught me how, and generally I enjoy it. My other tenants are honest and hard-working. Naturally they have their problems, as we all do.' As I went on to elaborate, I caught sight of two women walking towards the Down and instantly urged, 'Let's canter on.'

He raised his brows. 'When Mudd is not even in sight? Really ma'am, you shock me. What would your aunt say?'

'Oh, never mind that,' I muttered brusquely. 'That awful Mrs Upton is coming this way.'

'The parson's wife?'

I nodded. 'She's the one who spread those ugly rumours about Giles giving money to smugglers, and if I have to speak to her I will almost certainly be extremely rude.'

His lips twitched. 'It's too late, I'm afraid. They've seen us. If we ride off now, with Mudd nowhere to be seen-----' he let the sentence hang in the air, and I groaned.

Mrs Upton's eyes were gleaming as she and her companion approached us. 'Lady Drusilla, how pleasant. And Mr Reevers too.' As he returned her greeting, she looked around for a groom, and seeing no-one, asked archly, 'Is Mudd not with you?'

Mr Reevers said pleasantly, 'Lady Drusilla dropped her handkerchief and he's gone to fetch it.' At that moment, Mudd came into sight, and when he reached us, Mr Reevers asked if he'd found my handkerchief.

Mudd blinked, but being familiar with my opinion of the parson's wife, took in the situation at a glance. 'No sir. I think the wind must have taken it.'

'Very likely,' Mr Reevers agreed, and addressing Mrs Upton, casually remarked, 'I saw Mr Upton the other day riding through the woods with a rather pretty redhead. Is she a relative?' Choking, I somehow turned it into a coughing fit. He looked at me, his eyes dancing. 'Are you all right, ma'am?'

I nodded, not trusting myself to speak, but Mrs Upton didn't notice. She was staring at Mr Reevers. 'There's no red-head in our family, sir. Are you sure it was Mr Upton?'

'Quite sure. No doubt it was all perfectly innocent, but that doesn't stop people tittle-tattling, does it, ma'am.'

This episode left me feeling very much in accord with him, but my happy mood suffered a severe setback later that day when Mr Arnold sent me a note expressing his regret that urgent and pressing commitments prevented him setting a watch on Smith for the next few weeks.

I called on Julia the following day, riding the short distance unaccompanied, but she was out. From her hilltop property I could see Smith's farm quite clearly. His pond was situated half way between the farmhouse and the fence separating the farm from the coastal area beyond. On a dark night it wouldn't take long to move contraband off the beach and onto my land.

As Mr Arnold couldn't have the farm watched at present, I decided to call on Smith myself, ostensibly to ensure he was keeping my land in good order, as was my habit. Some inner instinct did urge me to stop and think it through first, but I ignored it. After all, what could possibly go wrong? If there was clearly contraband hidden in his pond, I could call in Thorpe, the Riding Officer. If there wasn't, I would try again another time. The truth was, I wanted Smith under lock and key, and I'd waited long enough.

Cliff farm was only a mile from Breighton House, and the dismay on Smith's face when I rode into his farmyard led me to hope I had called at exactly the right moment.

'You seem surprised to see me, Smith.'

'Oh no, my lady. I just didn't expect to see you alone. Not after that accident I heard about.'

I fixed my gaze on him. 'What do you know of that?'

'Only what I was told,' he said, affecting horror. 'That you were set upon one night. It must have been a nasty shock.' I didn't answer, informing him instead that I'd come to see round the farm. 'Shall I put Orlando in the stable, my lady?'

'No, I shall ride. You can walk.' The further away he was, the better I liked it. The wind was swirling round the court-yard, and the stink from his clothes and body was truly ghastly. I turned Orlando's head towards the barn. 'Let's get on.'

I inspected his stables and outbuildings, his sheep and cattle, and the few crops he grew. The pond, despite being in a dip, had recently overflowed onto the field, although the water level was now well below the top again, which told me it had been used to hide contraband very recently. I said nothing, pointing out instead that a nearby fence needed repairing.

'I'll see to it at once,' he promised. As I was about to leave, he said, 'Best keep out the way of those smugglers, my lady. Don't want you falling foul of them again.'

An unmistakable smirk settled on his features; and that, combined with the fact that I would have caught him red-handed if I'd called a day or two earlier, made me so angry I completely lost my temper. Furious at such barefaced insolence, I urged Orlando towards him, my riding whip raised in my hand. Fear swept away his smugness, and as he backed off, I turned Orlando sideways, pinning Smith up against the farmhouse wall.

'You once informed me smugglers don't like interference,' I said, my voice shaking with rage. 'Well, no-one meddles in the way I run my estate.'

I rode off then, aware I had let my temper run away with me, but too angry to care. Smith considered all women to be weak, even one in my position. I had seen enough bruises on his wife to know the kind of bully he was. But when I calmed down, I had to admit I had not acted sensibly. For, he now knew the attack on the cliff had not frightened me, as he had believed. Nor had I caught him hiding contraband on my land, which had been the whole purpose of my visit.

But that wasn't the end of my troubles, for on arriving back at Westfleet, I found my aunt sitting in the blue room, some sewing on her lap, a threaded needle in her hand, staring out of the window, so deep in thought she wasn't aware I had come into the room.

12

'Are you all right, Aunt?' I asked in concern.

Startled, she jumped. 'Oh, Drusilla. I didn't see you.' Hastily she applied herself to her sewing again, but observing how her hands trembled, I sat beside her and asked what was wrong. She turned to me, the lines of anxiety etched more deeply than ever. 'I'm so afraid I'll never see Charles again,' she burst out, choking back a sob.

Horrified, I protested, 'Oh no, you mustn't think that. We would have heard----'

She swallowed hard. 'That's what Lucie says, but I'm not so sure.'

Lucie, who walked in at that moment, was so concerned about her mother she stayed at home the next day, instead of going to Ledstone. She sent Mudd with a note to Giles, explaining the situation, and received a reply, in which Giles promised to come over later.

'Obviously, he can't bear to be apart from you for even a day,' I teased, bringing a rosy blush to her cheeks.

'I do consider myself most fortunate,' she murmured, her eyes shining. Frankly, so did I. Giles would make her the perfect husband; few men were as unselfish, kind and thoughtful as he was.

That morning we spent a pleasant hour or so in the music room. Lucie played the piano and sang delightfully, and I often wished I had her skill, for while it was an occupation I enjoyed, my own efforts were rather indifferent. My aunt loved music, but there had been little time lately for such pleasures. Today, however, Lucie and I sang a duet, and I even persuaded my aunt, who had no voice at all, to join Lucie for a simple song. After which my aunt and I sat back listening to Lucie playing some of her mother's favourite pieces. The effort was well worthwhile, for it cheered my aunt no end.

But Giles didn't ride over as promised, instead he sent a groom with a message telling us the exciting news that Vincent and Piers had arrived, and inviting us all to spend the following day at Ledstone for the purpose of meeting the visitors. Lucie, although disappointed that Giles had not come over, couldn't wait to see the newcomers for herself.

'After a whole year spent in America, they must be bursting with thrilling stories of every kind,' she said, her eyes shining with excitement.

My aunt, who still thought Giles should not entertain the black sheep of the family at Ledstone, indulged her daughter for once. 'I'm sure it will be most agreeable.'

I believed it would indeed be agreeable, provided Vincent did not have the same patronising manner towards women as his brother. I knew very little of America, except what I had read in the newspapers, and the occasional item of interest in John Delafield's letters related to me by Mr Arnold. I had visited France and Italy, but couldn't imagine travelling as far as America when it meant spending six weeks at sea, and often longer, just to reach New York. But I was as eager as Lucie to hear what it was like there.

In his letter, Vincent had mentioned making a brief visit before returning to his home in Italy. Giles did not expect them to stay more than a week, which would certainly please my godmother, with her dislike of unwanted visitors.

I dressed with great care for the occasion the following morning, lightening the bodice of my gown with a silver leaf-shaped brooch I was very fond of, which had belonged to my mother. Lucie always looked pretty whatever she wore, and my aunt settled for her favourite dove grey.

The three of us set off for Ledstone at a sedate pace, with Mudd in attendance, for my aunt would never ride anywhere without a groom. There was an air of expectation in our small party, for although Aunt Thirza did not approve of the visit, even she was curious. As for Lucie, her eyes were round with excitement at the prospect of meeting the man who had, as she had put it, given up everything for the woman he loved. 'I can't wait to meet him,' she sighed, clearly expecting someone dashing and handsome.

A notion my aunt swiftly rejected, telling her not to be so foolish. 'Mr Saxborough must be well over fifty, and will very likely wear spectacles.'

Lucie's face fell, and I hid a smile. Evidently romantic heroes did not wear spectacles. I suggested that if Piers had inherited his father looks, she'd have an idea of Vincent's appearance when young, which made her eyes light up again.

But when Parker ushered us into the drawing room, we saw that Piers was several inches shorter than his father, and of a much stockier build. He had the blond hair of his Saxborough ancestors, whose portraits hung in the Long Gallery, although his eyes were gray rather than blue, and I remembered how Vincent had said, in one of his old letters, that

Piers had inherited his mother's eyes. As for his features, they could only be described as ordinary.

Vincent, on the other hand, was of my own height, his grey hair dressed in a fashion that added to his elegant appearance. His face was lean, his eyes intelligent, and thankfully his manner bore no resemblance to his brother's, being both distinguished and pleasant. And, I noted, he did not yet wear spectacles.

Piers had a rather abrupt way of speaking, and while he responded civilly when Giles introduced him to us, he did not look as if making our acquaintance would add to the enjoyment of his day. His eyes too, held an expression I couldn't quite fathom out at first. Then Vincent said something to Marguerite that made her laugh, and when Piers glanced at him, I realised what it was. Contempt. As if he strongly disapproved of Vincent being pleasant to the family who, in his opinion, had treated his father so badly.

If Vincent was aware of this, he gave no sign of it. He appeared completely at ease, behaving as if he had remained within the bosom of his family for the past twenty-five years, and had merely returned from a long trip abroad.

His clothes were of the finest quality, his bow was faultless, as were his manners. After the introductions had been made, I watched him escort my aunt to a comfortable chair and set it so that the sun, which had just come out, was not in her eyes.

When introduced to Lucie, he held her hand longer than was strictly necessary, exclaiming, 'Enchanting.' In a way that made the child blush. He turned to Giles, saying, 'You're a very lucky fellow.'

'I'm well aware of that, Uncle,' he said, smiling at Lucie in a way that made her blush again.

Vincent sighed. 'Mind you, if I was twenty years younger........'

Marguerite chided in mock reproach, 'Vincent you mustn't tease Lucie so.'

Her voice was both warm and coquettish, and I stared at her in disbelief, remembering how she had dreaded this visit. But Vincent possessed an effortless charm, especially with women. Even Aunt Thirza was not immune to it. And I wondered if this was how he had lived all these years. Captivating rich middle-aged women in his engaging fashion and perhaps relieving them of some of their wealth. Yet, his answer to a question Lucie put to him a little later, suggested this wasn't so.

Encouraged by Vincent's comment that she was far prettier than any young lady he had seen in America, Lucie inquired in her musical voice, 'Have you been travelling in America for pleasure, Mr Saxborough?'

He inclined his head. 'Fortunately I am able to indulge myself these days. It wasn't always so, as I'm sure you know.'

'Oh, I know very little....' And she flushed in confusion at having uttered anything so brazen. Luckily my aunt failed to notice, being engaged in a one-sided conversation with Piers.

'Well, I spent several years in a rather impoverished state, until I joined a friend in a business venture which became highly profitable.'

When Lucie asked what kind of business it was, my aunt became aware of the conversation, and quietly admonished, 'Lucie, it is rude to pry into a gentleman's business affairs.'

'I am obliged to you, ma'am,' Vincent responded courteously. 'But young people are naturally curious I find, and I am quite happy to answer. With your permission, of course.' Which left my aunt no choice except to accede graciously. 'I made my money from gambling. For many years I ran a gaming club in Paris.' Lucie's mouth fell open, and Vincent leaned back in his chair, quite unruffled by the stunned silence that followed. 'I do not shock you, I trust?' Lucie hastily assured him he had not, but her eyes said something quite different. 'And I owe it all to Cuthbert.'

'Cuthbert?' Marguerite blurted out, astonished. As well she might, for he had not been in the habit of giving his money away.

'Yes. If you remember, I wrote quite frequently when I first went abroad. Money was tight then, and he helped me out. I make no bones about it, you see. But when this business opportunity arose, I grabbed the chance to make a success of my life. I promised Cuthbert that if he funded me in this venture, I would never ask him for another penny.'

Marguerite said happily, 'So that's why you stopped writing. But I still don't understand why Cuthbert imagined you were dead.'

He gazed at her, utterly stunned, then he began to laugh softly, as if it was a huge joke. 'So he thought I was dead, did he?' Removing an expensive enamelled snuff box from his pocket, he flicked it open, taking a pinch of the contents before remarking, quite unperturbed, 'I didn't know that. He gave me a large sum to invest in the business, and I promised never to bother him again. So I didn't. That was the agreement.' He glanced round at us all, admitting artlessly, 'I imagine he didn't expect me to keep my word. Understandable I suppose. I had made that particular promise before. Several times,' he ended with a chuckle.

My aunt stiffened visibly at this revelation, and I quickly changed the subject. 'Do tell us what you thought of America, Mr Saxborough.'

He looked across at me, his blue eyes twinkling merrily. In fact, far from being embarrassed at the situation he was in, I suspected he was enjoying himself hugely.

'I liked it, Lady Drusilla. The Americans are a most friendly people. How many evenings did we dine alone, Piers?'

'Very few, Papa,' he said dutifully in his deep, rather monotonous voice.

'All the English people we met wanted news of home, and when I said we were returning to Italy by way of London, you will not believe how many letters were entrusted to us. I saw to their safe delivery while Piers was recovering his strength, except for a letter from John Delafield to a Mr & Mrs Arnold, who--—'

'Mr Arnold?' Lucie interrupted, in surprise. 'The Customs Collector?'

Vincent turned his head to look at her. 'You know the gentleman?'

'A little, but Giles and Drusilla have known him for years.'

Vincent glanced at Giles. 'In that case, I should be most obliged if you would furnish me with directions to his house.'

Giles nodded. 'Certainly. Or you could give it to a groom to deliver.'

'I could, yes. But John Delafield spoke of the Arnolds with such affection, I feel I almost know them, and to be truthful, I have a great curiosity to meet them for myself. It will also allow me to answer any concerns they have about Mr Delafield's health, appearance, and family. All the little details one longs to hear about when separated for years from loved ones.'

Just as he had been separated from his family, I thought. Yet I could detect no bitterness in his voice. Just a simple understanding of what it was like to be in that position. As if he could recall what it had once meant to him, but that its importance had faded over the years.

Attempting to bring Piers into the conversation, I asked if he'd enjoyed his visit to America as much as his father. Before Piers could open his mouth, Vincent answered, 'What young person wouldn't - it is a young country, after all.'

'Come, Mr Saxborough,' Aunt Thirza broke in graciously, addressing Vincent. 'Let your son speak for himself.'

Vincent inclined his head. 'I must warn you that he, like all young people nowadays, has opinions I cannot agree with. Still, that is the way of the world, I suppose.'

Piers did not seem particularly discomforted by this remark. In fact, he had shown very little emotion of any kind so far. Except boredom. I suspected he cared nothing for his ancestral home, and had only come to please his father.

Nevertheless, on the subject of America, and their system of government, Piers was surprising eloquent. 'Rank counts for nothing in America. Everyone is equal, and a man is judged by what he achieves, not by his title or------'

Vincent cut in, 'That's true up to a point. What has taken the place of rank, is money. In America, if you have money, you can be as equal as you like.'

Marguerite fingered the expensive brooch she was wearing. 'Money has always been vitally important to *my* comfort.'

Lucie and I exchanged speaking glances, and as I stifled a laugh, so the door opened, and Mr Reevers came in. He apologised for keeping everyone waiting, as he had been at Norton House, and hadn't realised how late it was. With the gathering now complete, Parker announced nuncheon was served.

All the best silver had been laid out, the chandeliers sparkled, and pretty arrangements of sweet peas and Marguerite's favourite roses were placed on the table and around the room, filling the air with their soft summer fragrance. Smiling to myself, I recalled my godmother's determination not to put herself out for these unwanted visitors. Of course, the servants had done the actual work, she had only given the order, yet the fact she had bothered to do even that much, told me that she liked her visitors. Or one of them at least.

My godmother sat at one end of the table, with Giles at the other. So that she would not be obliged to talk to my aunt or Piers, she had placed them to the right of Giles. Conversation was of a lively but general nature while the servants were in the room, Vincent entertaining us with stories of their travels, proving himself to be, as Mr Delafield had described in his letter, an amusing raconteur.

The nuncheon consisted of various cold meats, the turkey being particularly delicious. There were cold pies, of pheasant and pigeon, along with a vast array of salads, cheese cakes, apricot tarts, an orange cream, a blancmange, and various fruits, including a whole pineapple. It was altogether as convivial a meal as I could recall. Even Aunt Thirza seemed to be enjoying herself, and when Giles mentioned that Mr Reevers was to be his groomsman at the wedding, she spent some time enlightening that gentleman on his forthcoming duties.

At one point I turned to Piers, and searching for a suitable topic to discuss with him, asked if he was fond of riding.

'I like to be out in the fresh air,' he said. 'Riding, walking or sketching.'

'Well, the Island offers many excellent subjects. Although I've never been able to do them justice myself.'

'You sketch, ma'am?'

I smiled faintly. 'I have tried, but the sad truth is, I cannot draw. I'm sure you will do very much better.'

'Perhaps,' he said, and became silent again. I asked which London hotel he'd stayed at, and he replied, 'Grillons, ma'am.'

'I hear it's a excellent hotel,' I commented, hoping to draw him out.

'Yes. Everything is of the finest.'

There was a hint of sarcasm in his voice, which puzzled me. Vincent seemed unaware of it and said, 'While we were there, my friend who keeps me informed of events in England, showed me the newspaper accounts of the yachting accident ----' His voice began to break, and he put a hand over his eyes. 'Forgive me – I—'

Lucie's soft heart was touched. 'There is nothing to forgive, Mr Saxborough.'

'Dear child,' he murmured, still distressed. 'I could not believe it, you see. First my brother's accident, and then Thomas-----' Reaching for his glass, he drained it. 'Not that I knew Thomas well. He was away at school when Cuthbert and I quarrelled. Poor Cuthbert,' he sighed. 'I always hoped that one day we would be on good terms again. And now it's too late.' When he looked up, I saw tears in his eyes. 'Still, he did reach his three score years and ten, whereas Thomas cannot have been more than ---' He stopped and calculated.

'He was just forty,' Giles sighed.

'That's only thirteen years younger than myself. I had not realised.' He shook his head sadly. 'His son too. A mere boy, with his whole life before him. And to die in such a way.'

Every line on Vincent's face was etched with sorrow, unlike Piers, who seemed not to care one jot, either for those who had died, or the family members still living on the Island. It wasn't so unreasonable when he'd never known any of them. He obviously felt out of place here, and I suspected, if he had any say in the matter, they would not stay long at Ledstone.

After nuncheon, Marguerite, my aunt and Lucie announced their intention of retiring to her sitting room to discuss wedding arrangements. Giles looked at me, 'What would like to do, Drusilla?'

Knowing he and Mr Reevers were taking Vincent and Piers on a tour of the estate, I said cheerfully, 'Come with you, of course.'

Vincent was rather taken aback. 'Do you not intend to join the other ladies?'

I shook my head. 'I would much prefer to ride.'

'But are you not a little fatigued after your nuncheon?'

I smiled. 'It is not eating I find tiring, Mr Saxborough, but inactivity.'

When the men went off to change into riding clothes, I murmured to Marguerite, 'You seem to be getting on famously with Vincent.'

'Well you see Drusilla, he makes me laugh. And nothing is too much trouble for him.'

'What you mean is, he spoils you.'

She giggled. 'Yes. Isn't it wonderful!'

I went up to the room allotted to the Westfleet ladies, to put on my hat. This was soon accomplished, and picking up my riding gloves and whip, I was taking a short cut via a rather dark corridor when I almost bumped into a servant. He bowed, mumbled an apology and would have walked on, if I hadn't stopped him.

'I don't know you, do I? Are you new here?' He looked to be in his early twenties, tall and slim, with fair hair, and was very neatly dressed.

'I'm Wistow, your ladyship. Mr Vincent's valet.'

'Oh I see,' I smiled. 'I should have guessed.' I asked how long he had been with Vincent, and on learning it was five years, commented, 'Then you were with him in America?'

He admitted it, and I asked if he'd enjoyed the experience. 'It was most interesting, but I am happy to be back in England again.'

'You have family here?'

'In London,' he said. 'A father and a sister.'

He spoke particularly well for a man of his years and station, a fact I casually mentioned to Vincent while we waited for the others to join us in the hall. 'Oh yes, he's a most superior being. I have to pay him a quite exorbitant salary to prevent him going elsewhere.'

'Really?'

'His father is one of the most sought after valets in London ma'am, and Wistow was trained by him. He's quite indispensable to me.'

Everything about Vincent, the clothes, the expensive valet, his confident manner, all pointed to him being a very rich man. And none of that would have happened, I reflected, if Cuthbert hadn't assisted him in the beginning. I was glad for Marguerite's sake that Cuthbert had done at least one thing in his life to help someone else.

13

The other gentleman soon joined us and from a remark Piers made, it became clear he preferred shooting to riding round the estate. Giles, ever the good host, said he would take a gun out with Piers, if Mr Reevers and I accompanied Vincent.

'Unless,' he suggested to Vincent, 'you wish to go shooting too.'

Piers sniggered. 'Papa does not care for sport.'

'Very true,' Vincent agreed affably. 'I should like to see the estate, however.'

Mr Reevers offered, 'I'll take Piers shooting, Giles. I could do with some practice.'

Observing the look that passed between Giles and Mr Reevers, and aware that Giles enjoyed shooting, I urged, 'Why don't you both go? I should be happy to accompany Mr Saxborough.'

Giles protested politely, but as I knew Ledstone almost as well as he did, and Vincent had grown up here, he soon gave way. That being settled, the others headed for the gun-room. As Vincent and I waited for the horses to be brought up from the stables, I inquired casually, 'You do not care for shooting, Mr Saxborough?'

'No, Lady Drusilla. I have never enjoyed the sight of blood. Either human, or animal. It may not be quite the thing to make such an admission, especially to a lady, but I once had to be revived with sal volatile after witnessing a horse being put down.'

I hardly knew what to say. Few men would openly confess to what most people would consider a weakness, at least not on so short an acquaintance, yet he had done so with that same lack of awkwardness he had shown in taking up his natural place at Ledstone Place again. I saw he was watching me in amusement.

'I could have made up some excuse as to why I do not shoot, but a discerning woman like yourself would have quickly seen through it. I believe you and I both prefer plain speaking. 'Amused by his quick and accurate reading of my character, I countered, 'Mr Saxborough, I have watched you captivate my godmother, behave with fatherly charm to Lucie, and in a suitably serious manner with my aunt. Tell me, is there any kind of woman you cannot beguile?'

Vincent threw back his head and roared with laughter. 'My dear Lady Drusilla, it is that very diversity in women that I find so fascinating. And a lady as intelligent and refreshingly honest as yourself is a rare joy.'

Smiling, I shook my head at this amusing and charming man, whose company I was already beginning to enjoy, and as we toured the estate, I took the opportunity to ask about his wife.

'I lost her when Piers was four,' he sighed. 'She nursed Piers through a fever, then fell a victim to it herself. She was gone within a week. I believe I would have followed her but for-----' He broke off and brushed a hand across his eyes.

I murmured softly, 'Piers must have been a great consolation to you.'

Composing himself, he said, 'I had him educated in England as his mother wished. By then, thanks to the money Cuthbert sent me, I was well on my way to becoming a rich man.' And he acknowledged, 'I have much to be grateful for.'

When we reached the place where the East gate had been, he gazed down the long straight track, as if picturing his brother riding along it on that fateful day. I said nothing about the gate being closed after Cuthbert's death, as I had no real proof.

Vincent turned to me. 'So you found him, ma'am. A nasty shock for a lady.'

'A nasty shock for anyone, Mr Saxborough.'

'Most ladies of my acquaintance would have swooned on the spot.'

I pointed out reasonably, 'That would not have helped the situation.' Remarking casually that I had never fainted in my life.

'Never, ma'am?' he repeated, raising his brows in surprise. I laughed. 'People who faint are invariably taken off to lie down upon their beds, and I wouldn't like that at all. I might miss something important. In any case I had to get word to Ledstone.'

He nodded . 'What happened to Cuthbert's horse? Has it been sold?'

'It got caught up in a thicket and broke a leg. Giles had to put the poor thing down.'

'Giles eh?' He shuddered. 'He's a braver man than me. I would have sent a groom to do it.'

As we rode slowly up the track, he said, 'This has been a dreadful time for my family. Still, Giles is an excellent young man. He and Lucie will bring the Saxboroughs about again.'

Arriving back at the house, we joined the others in the drawing room, where Giles remarked that Piers was as fine a shot as Mr Reevers, or himself. As Giles was an expert, I eyed Piers with respect.

Giles, who had arranged an outing for my aunt's birthday on Friday, invited Vincent and Piers to join us. He hoped to distract my aunt from worrying about my uncle, at least for a short time, and wanting to intrigue her, had refused to say where we were going. When Vincent tried to prise the information out of him, I laughed. 'He won't tell you, Mr Saxborough. Giles never divulges secrets.'

With the time of the expedition settled, Giles and Lucie wandered off together, Marguerite began to talk animatedly to Vincent, while my aunt seemed set on dragging Piers out of his shell. At which point Mr Reevers begged me to accompany him to the Long Gallery to enlighten him about the family portraits. 'Frankly ma'am, I can't tell one ancestor from another, and Giles says you know more about them than anyone.'

On reaching the Long Gallery, he first pointed to a picture of a tall, blond-haired man in doublet and hose. 'He's a rum looking character, I must say. Who is he? Some local villain?'

I laughed. 'I must beg you to show some respect, Mr Reevers.' And I indicated the ring on the man's finger, given to him by Queen Elizabeth, along with the Ledstone estates. 'This is your most revered ancestor. The one who built Ledstone Place. You must have seen the painting of William in the drawing room, the one with his wife and seven daughters----'

'The man with the evil eyes? Is that William? I wouldn't like to meet him on a dark night.' He peered closely at the painting in front of him. 'He doesn't look so bad in this one.'

'He was much younger then.'

'Before he did away with his first wife eh?'

'Oh, so you do know something about your forebears.'

'Everyone in the family knows about William.'

Hearing voices, we looked round to see Giles and Lucie coming towards us. When Lucie saw which ancestor we were looking at, she gave an involuntary shiver, and I couldn't resist teasing, 'Did Giles tell you why William rid himself of his first wife?'

'Well - no,' she admitted uncertainly, glancing at him.

'He's afraid you wouldn't marry him if you knew,' I said, tongue-in-cheek.

Giles was grinning and Lucie looked from him to me, her cornflower blue eyes every bit as innocent and enchanting as her nature. 'Whatever do you mean, Drusilla?'

'Well, it was on account of her only producing daughters,' I explained, trying to keep a straight face. Mr Reevers choked back a laugh, but Lucie's eyes widened with horror that any man would murder his wife for such a reason.

Giles squeezed Lucie's hand. 'I'll be more than delighted with seven daughters, if they're all as beautiful as their mother.'

She smiled up at him, her cheeks flushed pink, then turned to me. 'How did William get away with it?'

'According to William she died of a fever on a visit to France, but there's no tombstone in the village where he said she was buried, nor any record of her death that father and I could find.'

Lucie's eyes grew rounder. 'You went there?'

'Father believed in getting to the truth.' So did I for that matter. 'That's why the book took us so long.'

Her hand flew up to her mouth. 'Is it all in his book?'

Smiling indulgently at her, I nodded. 'I did mean to read it, truly I did. Whatever must you think of me?' One look at Giles's face told me what he thought of his future wife.

Amused, I said, 'I think you would rather read a novel.' Adding affectionately that it would be very boring if everyone liked the same things. 'Still William's plan misfired. His second wife produced another three daughters.' Directing them to a painting of all seven girls, I recounted that two had died in childhood, one of consumption at twenty, and one in childbirth. 'Only one survived beyond forty.'

Lucie said, 'I suppose people didn't live so long in those days.'

'Not when William was around,' Giles declared in jocular fashion. 'But his descendants were a dull lot. All very law abiding.'

She looked so cast down, Mr Reevers teased, 'In my opinion, ma'am, one murderer should be quite sufficient for any *respectable* family? Two would seem a trifle excessive.'

An infectious giggle escaped her, then she asked me wistfully, 'Are you certain they were all honourable, Drusilla?' When I nodded, she looked so disappointed, I murmured provocatively, 'Well, unless you count Giles's plan to become a smuggler.'

Instantly Giles said, 'If we're ever short of money, I could always--------' Laughing, Lucie pushed him playfully and he caught her within his arm, smiling down into her eyes. And I thought I had never seen two happier people.

We studied the more interesting portraits of William's descendants. His pretty granddaughter who married a lord; his great, great, grandson, Cuthbert's father, who wore a black patch over the eye he lost after a bizarre accident with a barrel of a gun, and the portrait of Cuthbert with Marguerite, Thomas and Giles, painted about twenty years ago. It was a good likeness of Cuthbert in particular, the artist having captured the expression of unapologetic superiority I had seen so often on his face.

Giles and Lucie were soon chucking over a picture of his great Aunt Imelda, who bore an uncanny resemblance to one of the horses in the Ledstone stables. Mr Reevers went to see what they were laughing at, while I moved on to a portrait of young Tom, done two years ago. Tears misted my eyes as I thought of how cruelly his life had been cut short, and I knew I wouldn't rest until I found out the truth about his death.

Returning to Westfleet later, I studied the charts in the workroom, but saw no answers to the questions in my mind. If only I'd known then what I needed to look for.

In the morning, Lucie went to Ledstone for the day, while my aunt and I had a long discussion about the wedding arrangements. That afternoon, shortly after my aunt had gone to visit a friend, Mr Reevers called, inviting me to go riding. I accepted happily, for riding with a man who did not treat me as if I was made of china, or needed a rest every ten minutes, was a rare pleasure. Mudd accompanied us, and riding up Manor Lane to the Downs, I inquired civilly after the Ledstone visitors, remarking that my godmother seemed to be enjoying Vincent's company.

'Well, she has certainly stopped referring to him as the black sheep of the family.'

'Ah, but black sheep are never boring. Unlike some worthy relatives.'

Mr Reevers arched one of his bushy eyebrows provocatively. 'Are you thinking of any worthy relative in particular?'

I choked at the implied reference to my aunt, and saw his eyes were brimming with laughter. It was odd how things has changed between us. That disastrous start, where his carelessness had caused me to land in those nettles, was all but forgotten. I couldn't say when I had started to like him, or even why I did, except there was a strength of character in his face I hadn't noticed in the beginning. And he made me laugh. An all too rare quality. Most men I met seemed not to possess a sense of humour.

After a brisk gallop over Luckton Down, we returned by way of the coast in the direction of Dittistone. Riding along the cliff top at Hokewell Bay, I mentioned this had been my father's favourite beach, and he asked if I still went there.

'I do,' I said, 'though not as often as before.'

The tide was well out, and he glanced at me. 'Would you do me the honour of walking with me on the beach? Or would your aunt disapprove?'

'She would insist on Mudd attending us.'

'Would she,' he murmured in a droll tone. 'Ah, but someone has to look after the horses.'

He dismounted and handed the reins to Mudd, before turning to assist me. Leaving the horses to Mudd's care, we walked towards the chine behind Smith's farm, where Mr Reevers inquired, 'Are you able to clamber down, or shall I carry you?'

I remarked lightly, 'What would you do if I took you up on your offer?'

He smiled down at me, an amused glint in his eyes. 'Frankly, I'd be in the suds! But as you know the beach well, I felt fairly safe. And I was counting too on your dislike of being treated as a helpless female.'

I laughed, enjoying this lighthearted banter. 'Are you always so barefaced?'

'Oh yes. Always.'

Scrambling down the steep chine without mishap, we were walking along the firm sand when I bent to pick up a stone. Turning it over, I threw it away, and he asked what I had been looking for.

'Fossils,' I explained. 'My father collected them. I keep them in the workroom.'

A gull landed on the sand in front of us, and as it took off again, squawking, he said, 'I wish I'd known your father. Giles said he was the most fascinating man he'd ever met.' Giles had told me that too, and it filled me with pleasure. 'But why did he live here instead of his ancestral home?'

Since my father's death, most people had avoided speaking of him in my presence, although I had often longed to do so. Whether Mr Reevers understood that or not, it was hard to tell, for his face expressed nothing but polite inquiry. Thus I strolled along the wide stretch of sand, enjoying the feel of the fresh sea air on my face, as I had so often in the past, explaining that father had detested the situation of his family seat, and the cold, damp winters that went with it.

'He loved Westfleet and the Island, and when he became Earl of Angmere shortly after my mother died, he refused to leave it to live in a place he loathed. I was his only child, and convinced he'd never marry again, he invited his heir, a brother, with five sons, to live there. As father said, it would be his one day anyway. Which, of course, it is now.'

'Your father must have been a most unusual man.'

'I think so, naturally. In fairness, I should tell you he was wealthy enough to do precisely what he wished.'

'And is this a good place to collect fossils?'

I nodded. 'Particularly after a storm-----'

'A storm?' he repeated, puzzled.

'Heavy seas sometimes dislodge fossils from the crumbling cliffs.' I told him of the odd looking bones we'd found a year or two ago after a particularly violent storm. 'Father said they didn't belong to any animal he'd ever seen.'

We were walking fairly close to the cliff face, and he glanced up at it. 'I must say it looks decidedly unsafe.'

'I have seen pieces fall, but not often.'

'Well, that's a relief,' he grinned. 'By the way, I found a copy of your father's book in Giles's library. It's a pity you couldn't find out how William Saxborough murdered his wife, but----.'

'It was too long ago, and he'd covered his tracks well. If it had happened recently, we might have resolved it.'

He eyed me thoughtfully. 'Would you have wanted to do that?'

'Oh yes. I like solving puzzles.'

'Then it's as well you weren't around at the time. Murderers have a nasty tendency to do away with people who find them out.' William Saxborough was long dead, but the man who had killed three Saxboroughs was very much alive, and the thought of what he might do sent a shiver up my spine. Mr. Reevers went on, 'Was there an official investigation?'

'Yes, but it failed.' The wind blew a strand of hair across my face, and I brushed it away. 'Just as today's investigation is failing - to find out what happened to Thomas and young Tom, I mean.'

'Nor will they,' he said, 'if French smugglers were involved.'

The wind had turned blustery in the last half hour, and a sudden fierce gust tore the hat from my head. Just as it began to bowl along the beach, Mr Reevers grabbed it. Brushing the sand off as best he could, he returned it to me. 'Shall I fix it back in place again?'

His audacity made me gasp. 'You will do no such thing.'

'You needn't be afraid I will hurt you with the hatpins. I know how to fix them.'

'I have no doubt of *that*,' I spluttered, and glanced up at the cliff top.

'Mudd can't see us, if that's what is worrying you.'

'It isn't,' I retorted shortly.

'Why look up then?'

His eyes softened into that intimate look he'd begun to adopt when we were alone, and I opened my mouth to put him firmly in his place, when a movement in the distance, close to Hokewell village, caught my eye. 'Good gracious, isn't that Piers Saxborough? What on earth is he doing?'

14

Piers held a long stick which he kept pushing into the sand, in the manner of a Riding Officer searching for kegs buried by smugglers. The beach itself was deserted, and he obviously thought he was alone, but we could see what Piers plainly couldn't. A group of angry villagers gathering on the cliff top. Piers might be a gentleman, but smugglers were no respecters of rank when their livelihood was at stake.

'Oh dear,' I murmured, half in amusement. 'There's barely a man in Hokewell who isn't involved in free trading. Perhaps we should intervene---'

'Must we?' Mr Reevers drawled lazily. 'I should infinitely prefer to watch. Of course, if you like the fellow —'

'It's not that. Only he is Giles's cousin-----' I looked at him, remembering Piers was his cousin too, but at that moment Piers, realising he was no longer alone, hurriedly left the beach, leapt onto his horse and galloped off. 'How very odd. Why on earth would Piers want to test the sand?'

Mr Reevers shook his head, still grinning. 'Who knows?' he said as we made out way back to the horses. 'But if he carries on doing it, he'll end up in a ditch one dark night. A wise man would stick to sketching.'

I raised my eyebrows at him. 'Have you actually *seen* any of his sketches?'

'I saw one purporting to be of Dittistone Bay,' he admitted, grimacing. And drawled, 'One can only hope his technique will improve.'

'You shouldn't mock—'

'Shouldn't I?' He smiled down at me. 'You, of course, with your obsequious nature, would naturally admire his drawings.'

I choked. 'How do you know what my nature is?'

'My dear girl, I knew that within five minutes of making your acquaintance.'

I lifted my chin. 'I wish I might say the same of you, Mr Reevers. And I am not 'your dear.''

'No. But that could easily be remedied.'

I uttered a kind of spluttered gasp, and looking up, saw his eyes were full of laughter. 'You should be more cautious, Mr Reevers. I might have taken you seriously.'

His expression softened. 'Might you?' He gazed sidelong at me, and I stiffened instantly, uncertain of where this was leading. A muscle twitched in the corner of his mouth. 'Ah, but I was quite certain you would not. You see I had the pleasure of meeting Julia Tanfield the other day, and she informed me you don't mean to marry. So I knew I was perfectly safe.' And he grinned wickedly at me. I should have been shocked I suppose, and I should certainly have delivered a sharp rebuke, but it was all I could do not to laugh out loud.

Riding back to Westfleet with Mudd in attendance we spoke of ordinary things, and after bidding him farewell, I walked into the house still smiling to myself. Apart from Giles and my father, I'd never met another man who laughed at the same things as I did. But now when I met Mr Reevers in the company of others, I found myself glancing in his direction if something amused me, aware he would find it diverting too.

Hearing voices coming from the drawing room I went in to find my aunt and cousin had both returned. But Lucie was close to tears, and on seeing me she burst out, her lip trembling a little, 'Drusilla, Giles has to go away.'

'Go away?' I repeated. 'Where to?'

'London. He has to attend to some legal matters - a letter came this morning.'

'Can't his attorney come to the Island?' I asked.

'He could, but Giles wants his wedding clothes made in London. So he means to do both together.'

'Very sensible,' my aunt commented.

'He's going the day after tomorrow,' Lucie declared forlornly. 'While the weather seems settled.'

I reminded Lucie, 'Well, it's only seven weeks to the wedding.'

'I know,' she sighed, trying to resign herself to Giles being away for three or four weeks.

I reminded her of the exciting day ahead of us tomorrow, this being my aunt's birthday outing, which knowing Giles, would be planned down to the tiniest detail. He'd promised to be at Westfleet at eleven, so I was a little surprised when he arrived half an hour early. Luckily I was ready, and was arranging some flowers in the drawing room when Jeffel ushered him in. As I told him, my aunt and cousin were still dressing, and he nodded, as if that was what he had expected.

'I came a little early on purpose, Drusilla,' he said, crossing the room to where Jess, the kitchen cat, had settled herself against the mullioned windows to bask in the sunshine. Smoothing her gently, he went on, 'I wanted a word with you in private.'

'With me?' Suspecting this concerned my uncle, my heart lurched in alarm.

He didn't answer, for Jeffel had reappeared with some refreshment, and observing the confection on the plate, Giles commented in blissful anticipation, 'Ratafia biscuits.' A response that brought a gratified smile to Jeffel's lips. 'Cook had just finished making a batch, sir.' Giles was a favourite with the Westfleet servants, and his addiction to ratafia biscuits well known to the indoor staff. Cook, in particular, thought Giles far too thin.

'Truth to tell, Jeffel,' Giles admitted, seating himself opposite me, 'Westfleet's ratafia biscuits are lighter than those at Ledstone. But for heaven's sake don't repeat that or my cook will leave our service in a huff, and my mother will never speak to me again.'

Jeffel's usual professional demeanour instantly softened. 'I'm sure nothing could ever stop Mrs Saxborough speaking to *you*, sir.'

When my butler had left the room, I objected jokingly, 'Stop buttering up the servants, Giles. If Jeffel repeats your remark to cook, I can expect an immediate demand for an increase in pay.'

'And very well deserved it would be,' he said, taking another biscuit. 'Aren't you going to try one? They really are delicious.' He brushed a tiny crumb from his riding breeches, but seemed loathe to say what he wished to speak to me about.

Unable to bear the suspense any longer, I asked fearfully, 'Have you news of my uncle?'

He shook his head. 'No, it's nothing like that.' I didn't know whether to be glad, or sorry, but he began to wander round the room, picking up books and putting them down again, before he finally stopped by the fireplace, resting one foot on the fender. Eventually he said, 'The truth is Drusilla, I want to beg a favour of you.'

I burst into laughter. 'No wonder you look so uncomfortable.' Giles had always been fiercely independent. He might ask me to do some kindness for his mother, but never for himself, as this favour clearly was. 'How many days have you spent looking for some way to avoid asking my help?'

He gave a wry chuckle. 'No more than four or five, I swear.' Adding ruefully,'How well you know me.'

I thought I understood what this favour was. 'Your Mama will have Mr Reevers to look after her, and Vincent and Piers to entertain her, but I'll happily keep an eye on her while you're away.'

Giles employed his most angelic smile. 'I would be most grateful.'

'It's such a loathsome task, I'm amazed you dare ask me,' I mocked softly. 'Your Mama being the tartar she is.'

He laughed appreciatively. 'Well, actually, that isn't the favour. I knew you wouldn't mind visiting Mama. Drusilla, I need someone I can trust to relay a message to Leatherbarrow.' Whenever Giles sailed to London, he sent Leatherbarrow home with the yacht, until it was required.

'Wouldn't it be wiser to keep him with you this time? Your Mama would feel easier in her mind if she knew you weren't alone.'

'I won't be alone. My valet goes to London, naturally.'

'You know perfectly well what I mean, Giles. Leatherbarrow would offer some protection when you are out and about.'

'Not you too, Drusilla. Mama can hardly bear to let me out of her sight for fear of something happening to me,' Giles sighed. I made no comment and he continued, 'You know better than anyone what Ledstone means to me, but I never expected to inherit the estate. I wish with all my heart that

Thomas and young Tom were alive, but they're not, and nothing I can do will change that. Ledstone is mine now, and when Lucie and I are married, I shall have everything a man could possibly want. Do you imagine I would risk losing all that? I promise you nothing is going to happen to me.'

There being no answer to that, I asked, 'What is this message you want me to deliver to Leatherbarrow?'

'Only to let him know when I want the yacht.'

'I always thought you wrote to your Mama.'

'I did at one time, but a messenger is quicker. Only I don't want Jacob walking up to the stables in full view of the house.' Visitors on foot always came down the quarter mile long drive. 'It's rather awkward with Vincent and Piers being here. But it's not just that - the thing is, Mama misses very little of what goes on at Ledstone.'

That was very true, yet I couldn't see what his difficulty was. 'I don't understand, Giles. Isn't Jacob the man who collected my uncle's letters in France?'

'Yes, but he didn't bring them up to the house. I met him in the village.'

I frowned at him, puzzled. 'Giles, why don't you want your Mama to see Jacob?'

'Well — he is rather fearsome looking, and she's still worried sick over these silly rumours connecting me with smugglers.' He turned up his hands in appealing fashion. 'It's only tittle-tattle, but I don't want anything upsetting her while I'm away.'

'Couldn't you find someone more suitable?'

'I haven't had time, what with everything else, and Jacob is reliable.' What he'd said sounded plausible enough, yet I had the distinct feeling he had not told me everything, and that I would not approve of whatever it was he had omitted.

'Where does Jacob live?'

'He comes from Blackgang.'

I stared at him in horror, for some of the most notorious smuggling gangs were to be found at Blackgang. Remembering his childhood longing to join the smuggling fraternity, my heart began to pound. Surely he could not be so foolish. I swallowed hard. 'How far are you involved with these smugglers, Giles?'

He threw back his head and roared with laughter. 'I shan't be arrested by Mr Arnold and hauled aboard the revenue boat along with a keg of French brandy, if that's what you mean. Smugglers are used to carrying messages, that's all. In their business they have to be discreet and quick.'

Again that was perfectly credible. Jacob had certainly proved his worth in the matter of my uncle's letters. Yet there was something about Giles's manner I found disturbing. Disturbing, and vaguely familiar. It took me a moment or two to realise what it was. There was an air of suppressed excitement about him and it reminded me of the times when, as children, we had crept out at night to watch the smugglers. His eyes had sparkled with the thrill of it all then, and for one brief second I had seen that same look again.

All our lives we had shared problems, laughed at the same things and confided in each other. I had never kept anything important from him, and I'd always assumed it was the same with him. His love for Lucie meant we saw less of each other, as was only natural, yet when we did speak, there had been nothing in his manner, before today, to suggest he had stopped confiding in me. I didn't know when, or why, that had happened. Only a certainty that it had.

Looking at him, I saw he was totally in command of himself again, his eyes showing only a slight anxiety as he awaited my answer. 'Of course, I'll help,' I said. It was only a small favour designed to spare his mother any more worry. He thanked me, and I asked how we were to know if news came of my uncle.

'Radleigh will look after Ledstone while I'm away. He'll pass on any information.' He hesitated, knowing I thought my aunt and cousin should be told my uncle was in prison. 'Leave it one more week would you, Drusilla? If nothing's changed by then, do what you think best.'

'All right,' I agreed. And aware Marguerite would worry about him even more when he was in London, I urged, 'Try to set her mind at rest, if you----'

'I've already done so, Drusilla. I told her that dealing with solicitors and tailors in London is much safer than riding a horse round the Island.'

I nodded, praying he was right. I just wished I didn't feel so uneasy.

15

My aunt and cousin joined us then, ready for the outing. Giles at once admired Aunt Thirza's birthday presents; a lace shawl from Lucie, and a book of poems I had given her, before handing her his own gift, a bottle of French perfume. I raised an eyebrow at him, realising it must have been smuggled, but he only grinned, and she was too delighted to ask how he'd come by it.

We soon set off for Ledstone Place, where the gentleman came out to greet us. Vincent, elegantly attired in a dark green coat and fawn riding breeches, was his usual charming self, but Piers, who was in his favourite maroon, seemed particularly morose. As I slipped from the saddle, Mr Reevers came over to greet me, looking very dapper in a light blue coat. I was not surprised to learn Marguerite was still in her bedchamber, as she was never on time for anything.

The grooms walked our horses and while we stood talking, Giles suggested to Piers that he take his sketch book, there being excellent opportunities for drawing today. When Piers went to fetch it, Vincent told us, 'I'm afraid my son is not at his best today. He has a touch of earache. Something he suffered from rather badly as a child.'

Aunt Thirza, of course, knew exactly how to cure this painful condition. It involved the use of an onion, and while

Vincent listened courteously, Mr Reevers murmured to me under his breath, 'Should I procure an onion for Piers do you think? I have a strong desire to see what he would do with it.'

I made a sound between a choke and a splutter. 'Have you no sense of decorum?'

'None whatsoever. I thought you knew that.' And I had to bite my lip to stop myself laughing.

When Piers returned, Giles announced we were going to Allum Bay, and I saw Aunt Thirza's eyes lit up. She had, on occasion, expressed a desire to visit this unusual place, and I smiled gratefully at Giles, amazed that with so much else on his mind, he should have recalled her wish.

Five minutes later my godmother appeared, dressed in a stunning black riding habit and a very dashing hat. Looking round at us all, and employing her most dazzling smile, she inquired with perfect innocence, 'Oh dear, have I kept you waiting?'

Everyone assured her otherwise, Giles assisted her onto her horse, and with Vincent riding beside her, we set off down the long drive. Marguerite being a nervous horsewoman, we rode the four or five miles in a very leisurely fashion. Dismounting at the top of the steep cliffs that led down to the bay, Marguerite announced this was as far as she meant to go. 'For no matter what anyone says, I simply cannot clamber down that dreadful cliff.' Giles, having anticipated this, insisted on staying with her, and spread some thick rugs, brought for that purpose, on the ground.

The descent to Allum Bay was extremely difficult, but my aunt was determined to achieve it. Vincent, at his most gallant, urged, 'Do take my arm, ma'am. We can't have you injuring yourself.' Progress was naturally slow, none of us saying much, as we concentrated on negotiating the long descent to the beach.

I had always been impressed by the coloured sands here. They were mainly yellow, white, red, black and green, which as I explained to my aunt, were most vivid when seen in sunshine after heavy rain. Piers settled himself on a rock with his sketch book, and while the others admired the sands, I searched for fossils, having the good fortune to pick up what appeared to be a tooth. It was so large, I couldn't think which animal it had come from, and put it in my pocket to look at later.

My aunt, moving well back from the cliffs to gain an overall view of the colours, stood on some big stones covering the shingle, so near the water's edge I called out, 'Be careful, Aunt. Those stones are slippery.'

Alarmed, she headed back towards the cliffs, and began collecting samples of the different colours, attacking the sands with such vigour that Mr Reevers warned her of the danger of cliff falls.

'It would seem no part of this beach is safe,' she smiled, aware he was teasing her, and went on putting the samples into the small containers brought for that purpose.

Vincent spoke nostalgically of the fine time he had here as a boy pretending to be a smuggler, and after glancing at Piers's sketch, murmured to me, 'I'm afraid his command of the craft is sadly lacking. Still it keeps him happy.'

After Piers had finished his sketch, and my aunt had seen all she wished to, we started on the long, steep climb back. When my aunt reached the top and saw the picnic laid out ready, she announced she was absolutely famished. Amid the general laughter, we settled ourselves comfortably on the rugs, eagerly tucking into the delicious spread Marguerite had

ordered. Cold meats, pies, hard boiled eggs, tomatoes from
her greenhouse, a delicious cheese, followed by apple pie and
fruit, washed down with Giles's best wine.

Resting in the sunshine after this delectable repast, I took
another look at the fossil I'd found on the beach. Watching
me, my aunt sighed, 'You already have a room full of fossils.
Surely you cannot need any more.'

Vincent commented, 'I didn't know you collected fossils,
ma'am.' I didn't answer at once, as Mr Reevers had spoken
at the same time, wishing to see the tooth. As I handed it to
him, Giles explained to Vincent that fossil hunting had been
my father's hobby. 'What Drusilla particularly enjoyed was
helping with his "History of the Isle of Wight."'

To my surprise, Piers said, 'There's a copy in the library at
Ledstone. It has everything I---'

'If you assisted with that, Lady Drusilla,' Vincent intervened, eyeing me with respect, 'I must congratulate you.'

Giles said, 'Drusilla listed the known facts of each historical event on large sheets of paper, which were fixed to the
walls of their workroom, so that every detail could be seen at
a glance. It was most impressive I can tell you.' Somewhat
embarrassed, I insisted it was simple common sense. And as
everyone had now examined the tooth, I put it back in my
pocket.

Mr Reevers smiled lazily at me. 'That's because you have
a logical mind, Lady Drusilla. Do you have plans for another
book?'

'One day, perhaps,' I answered vaguely.

At which Lucie blurted out in surprise, 'Oh, but I thought
— I mean, you are working on something, surely. You always
seem to be in your workroom lately.'

I'd thought Lucie's head was too full of wedding plans to notice what I was doing, and the last thing I wanted was for attention to be drawn to the information on my wall charts. But she'd aroused everyone's curiosity now, and they all looked in my direction, expecting me to tell them exactly what I was doing. And, in that moment, I couldn't think of any explanation that wasn't an outright lie. I'm not averse to stretching the truth, or even twisting it a little, but I have never been able to lie convincingly. So, foolishly, I hesitated.

Giles gazed at me thoughtfully, but said nothing. The other gentlemen waited politely for me to answer. My aunt, however, was not so reticent. 'Surely Drusilla, there can be no need for secrecy.'

Somehow I collected my wits together. 'I suppose I take after my father. He didn't tell anyone he was writing a book until he was certain he could make a good job of it.' Both those statements were true, and I hoped they would all assume I *was* working on another book, but didn't want to talk about it yet.

Vincent flicked open his snuff box and took a small pinch of snuff with his fingertips. 'I wish I could write a book, I must say. You're a very clever woman, ma'am.'

'Oh yes,' Lucie declared eagerly. 'Drusilla is the most intelligent person I know.'

Instantly Giles threw up his hands in mock despair. 'I had hoped you wouldn't discover that until *after* we were married.'

Once the laughter had died down, Marguerite gazed fondly at her son. 'What Lucie meant Giles, is that Drusilla is the cleverest *woman* she knows.'

By the time we reached Westfleet that evening the fine weather had begun to break, and it soon became clear we were in for a severe gale. Aunt Thirza said she was thankful it had not come in earlier and spoilt the day, as she had not enjoyed herself so much in months.

That night, listening to the wind rattling the leaded windows of my bedchamber, I finished the last few pages of the novel Julia had lent me, and being still wide awake, wondered if my book on fossils could tell me anything about the tooth I'd found. The book was in the workroom, and the servants had gone to bed, but as reading often helped me to sleep, I slipped on my dressing gown, picked up the candle, and shielding it from draughts with my hand, tiptoed down the creaking staircase as quietly as I could. When I opened the workroom door, I heard a slight movement, and almost instantly, the candle was knocked out of my hand. I shrieked, the candle holder struck the floor with a clang, and a shadowy figure dashed across the room, and out of the door that led to the garden.

Instinctively I ran after him, but the darkness and the howling of the wind made it impossible to see or hear anything. Going back indoors, I was lighting the workroom candles when Jeffel, wearing a dressing gown over his night attire, came to see what all the commotion was about. I told him somewhat breathlessly, 'I came down to fetch a book and disturbed a burglar.'

Jeffel peered at me anxiously. 'Are you all right, my lady?'

'Just a little shaken. Still, I shook him too. He fled like a frightened rabbit,' I said, indicating the workroom door.

Taking a lighted candle, Jeffel carefully inspected the door. 'He picked the lock, my lady. I can see a scratch mark that wasn't there yesterday.'

There were no bolts on this particular door and I asked Jeffel to fit some in the morning. 'A new lock would be advisable too.'

'Very good, my lady.' He pushed a cabinet in front of the door, in case the burglar came back later, and mopping his brow, asked if I'd seen the man.

I shook my head. 'It was too dark.'

'I'd better check if anything is missing, my lady.'

While he did so, I looked round the workroom itself. Only then did I notice that the shutters covering my wall charts had been raised, revealing every scrap of evidence I had gathered about the murders. The purpose of the shutters was to keep out the light, not to conceal what was recorded; so there was no lock. And I had closed them myself, barely an hour since. Jeffel returned, reporting all was well, and I asked him to fix good strong locks to the shutters too.

My aunt and cousin came into the room, and it all had to be explained again. While they were naturally anxious, the man had long gone, and there being nothing we could do now, we went back to bed. Here I reflected on the sheer chance that had taken me down to the workroom at that particular moment. If I hadn't done so, would I ever have known an intruder had been in the house? If he'd managed to lock the door again and pulled the shutters over my wall charts, I wouldn't have suspected a thing.

By morning the gale had abated to a breeze, and immediately after breakfast I decided to tackle the estate accounts, which I had rather neglected lately. I sent a message to the stables telling Mudd I wouldn't need him before eleven, and repaired to the library, settling myself at my writing desk. But instead of concentrating on the accounts, I kept thinking about last's night incident. Then twice in the next fifteen minutes my housekeeper asked to see me, Jeffel came in to inform me the carrier had brought a large parcel for Lucie, and that having found bolts in the house, he could fit them now, if convenient.

I decided if Jeffel was going to start hammering in the workroom, the accounts could wait. I would ride down to Hokewell Bay, where I could walk undisturbed, and sort out the thoughts running through my mind. It was not yet nine o'clock, and none of the family was up, thus after sending a message to the stables for Orlando to be saddled, I wrote a note for my aunt, saying I'd gone down to the beach to see if last night's heavy seas had dislodged any fossils from the cliffs.

Strolling down to the stables, I remembered I'd told Mudd I wouldn't need him until eleven. The groom saddling Orlando, touched his cap and said Mudd was out exercising a horse, but was expected back any minute. The beach being only a five minute ride from Westfleet, I took the reins, instructing the groom to tell Mudd to come down to Hokewell Bay when he returned.

On reaching the bay, I tethered Orlando to the gate at the back of Smith's farm, where Mudd could take care of him. There was no sign of Smith or anyone else on the farm, and walking down to the beach, I looked up at the cliff face, observing last night's high water mark was several feet above my head. Perfect for dislodging fossils. I searched automatically, making slow progress along the beach, my mind on the break-in. This, I was sure, had came as a result of my hesitation at Allum Bay the previous day. When I had stupidly made it all too obvious I was working on something I didn't want to talk about.

There was nothing of any significance on my charts, just generally known facts, and background details which helped me to see the situation as a whole. I had not included my theory of how Cuthbert Saxborough might have died, as it was only guesswork. And I didn't have a theory about the yachting tragedy. I believed the intruder had simply wanted to find out how much I knew. Now he'd seen how little that was, perhaps he would be satisfied. For one thing was certain; I had no evidence that would lead me to his identity.

By the time I started to retrace my steps the tide was well on its way in, the strongest waves coming to within ten feet of me. I stopped briefly, to examine a piece of dislodged cliff, but there were no fossils in it, and I had barely moved on half a step, when something extremely heavy struck my right shoulder. And for the first time in my life, I lost my senses entirely.

When I came to, I was face down in the sand. A sandfly landed on my nose, and when I brushed it away, an agonising pain shot through my right shoulder. The throbbing made me feel nauseous, and I lay still until it had subsided. The chunk of cliff that had knocked me senseless was close by, and it had grass on it, signifying it had become dislodged from the cliff top. After a gale, I had seen small pieces fall down the cliff, but nothing this size. Nor had I been struck by one before.

My face was turned towards the sea, and I was trying to work out how to get up without fainting, when a particularly ferocious wave raced up the beach drenching me with freezing cold water. That cleared my muzzy head, and in relief I remembered the message I'd left for Mudd. When he saw the state of the tide, he would come looking for me. The way the servants fussed was a nuisance at times, but now I thanked heaven for it. Gingerly lifting my head to look for Mudd, I saw what my stupefied brain had forgotten, and I groaned. The high cliffs were impossible to climb, and I could only get off this beach by way of Hokewell chine, at which point the cliff jutted out some thirty yards nearer the sea than where I was now. To reach safety, I had to get round that first. But, if the tide had reached me here, then the water would already be two or three feet deep where the cliff jutted out. And there was no sign of Mudd.

I couldn't understand why he hadn't come. Even if my message had been forgotten, Mudd would have seen that Orlando was not in his stable, and asked where I had gone. Glancing up at a watery sun, I judged from its position that it must be about two hours to nuncheon. No-one else at Westfleet would worry about me until then. By that time, I thought it highly likely I would be dead.

16

Gritting my teeth, I leant on my good elbow, and gradually got up onto my knees, just as a second chilling wave crashed over me. The beach lurched alarmingly, then a wave smacked into a nearby rock, throwing ice cold water into my face, and the swaying stopped. Using the cliff as a support, I slowly inched my way upwards, shivering from the drenching and the south westerly breeze.

Gasping and cursing, I stumbled along the beach for what seemed an eternity, holding my shoulder in a vain effort to stop the excruciating pain, hampered by sea-soaked skirts and freezing water surging around my legs. By the time I reached the point where the cliff jutted out nearer the sea, the breakers smashing against it sent spray ten foot up into the air. Thirty yards stood between me and the safety of the next beach, but it might as well have been thirty miles.

I leant against the cliff, teeth chattering uncontrollably, watching wind whipped waves rising majestically into gigantic curling breakers that hung in mid air, before crashing in a swirl of foam that swept to the foot of the cliffs and round my ankles. As each wave receded, the fierce undertow tore savagely at my legs, seeking to drag me into the sea.

All along the beach I had prayed it wouldn't be necessary to swim. I was a poor swimmer at the best of times, and I didn't know if I could stay afloat with a shoulder that had me screaming with pain. But I only had two choices. I could swim. Or I could stay here and wait for the waves to smash me to pulp against the cliff. I began to laugh a little hysterically at having to choose between being battered to death, or drowning. The first meant certain death, the other gave me a very slim chance. It was an easy decision.

I had once seen my father bowled over by the force of a wave, and these were only moderate, for the gale had abated. I had often marvelled at the might of those thundering breakers, but looking at them now, my mouth went very dry.

Sitting on a rock, I dragged my riding boots off by wedging them, one at a time, between two rocks and pulling my foot out. Removing my stockings, I lifted the voluminous skirts of my riding habit and tied the saturated cloth round my waist as best I could, to stop the wet material hindering me in the sea. Taking a deep breath, I waded into the water, ignoring the towering waves slamming against the cliff. I turned my back to two huge breakers, somehow keeping upright, and before the next one reached me, launched myself towards and through it. But the wave struck the cliff near me, flew up into the air, and a jet of water shot straight in my mouth.

Choking, I reached for the sand, but I was already out of my depth, and the sea closed over my head. Kicking frantically upwards, I broke through the surface, gulping, gasping, spluttering. White froth from the wave tops hit me in the face, only there was no going back now, and that calmed me. Using what little stamina I had left, I threw everything into getting beyond the jutting out cliff. Turning parallel to the coast to keep the cliffs in view, I swam on my left side kicking hard with my feet, thrusting my left arm forward, and barely moving my right.

Slowly clawing my way along, I was a fraction past the middle of that jutting out cliff, when a giant wave crashed over my head. With my back to the breakers, I hadn't seen it coming. As I went under, a huge press of water propelled my body inexorably forward. I tried kicking upwards, but it was useless. There was a roaring in my ears, and I knew I couldn't hold my breath much longer. Not that it mattered; I was about to be splattered against the cliffs.

At the precise moment I thought my lungs must burst, my left knee scraped against something firm. Then my head broke through the surface. I was kneeling on sand. In front of me the beach led up out of the chine. I had missed the cliff by a whisker. I staggered up onto my feet, reeling and gasping, taking great gulps of fresh air into my starved lungs, savouring the glorious flavour of salt on my lips. It had never tasted so good. My shoulder felt as if it was on fire, but I no longer cared. I was alive.

Untying my skirts, I waded towards the water's edge, stepped on a sharp stone, lost my balance, and fell backwards into the water. I saw the next wave rise to a dizzy height above me, felt the fierce undertow dragging me back into the sea, and as I clutched desperately at the moving sand, the wave crashed over my head, choking me.

As the sea receded, I heard a shout, and with my last ounce of strength I lifted my head to see a man galloping down the beach towards me. Bringing his horse to an abrupt halt, he leapt off, and without stopping to remove his boots or coat, Mr Reevers plunged into the water, scooping me up as if I was a lightweight, murmuring, 'Oh, my dear girl,' with more agitation that I thought him capable of. I had never been held so close by a man before, although I did not think of that until later.

Carrying me up onto the beach, he looked at me with such intensity I whispered, a little frightened, 'What is it?'

He gave a harsh laugh and muttered, 'I thought you were dead.'

Setting me down carefully on a large rock, he removed his jacket and placed it, with great gentleness, round my shoulders. It was warm from his own body and I snuggled into it gratefully. I expected him to ask what had happened, but all he said was, 'Can you ride?'

'I th-think s-so,' I said through chattering teeth. 'Where's Mudd?'

'He'll be here any minute.'

While he hurried off to fetch Orlando, I looked at the waves still crashing relentlessly onto the shore, and knew I would never watch them again without shuddering. Not if I lived to be ninety. Mr Reevers came back with Orlando, helped me to my feet, and when he cupped his hands, I put a foot into them, not caring that it was bare. He levered me onto my horse, but landing in the saddle jarred my shoulder, and I winced out loud. 'Hold on, my dear,' he said softly, handing me the reins.

He mounted his own horse, and as we made our way out of the chine I saw Mudd riding towards us like a demon. When he was close enough to see how wet and bedraggled I was, his face turned ashen.

'I'm all right, John,' I managed to say as he came to a halt. 'Except for my shoulder. There was a cliff fall.'

Mudd opened his mouth to speak, but Mr Reevers intervened. 'Fetch the doctor, Mudd. I'll see Lady Drusilla safely home.'

Mudd looked from him to me. 'Yes sir,' he said. And galloped off.

Every movement sent a searing pain through my shoulder, and I could not ride above a walking pace. In a halting voice I told Mr Reevers what had happened, and he muttered savagely, 'You're lucky to be alive.'

He explained how he'd called to see me, only to find everyone from home. 'Your aunt and cousin had just left on a mission to check the sheets at the inns where some of the wedding guests will be staying. A groom accompanied them, of course, but whether he was guarding them, or the innkeepers, I can only guess.' I managed a weak chuckle, and he said, 'Then I learned you had ridden out on your own and—'

When I tried to speak, he interrupted, 'Don't say any more. Save your strength. One of your grooms said you'd left orders for Mudd to join you, but he still wasn't back. I was just leaving to look for you when Mudd returned. His horse went lame, and he'd had to walk three miles home. When the groom gave Mudd your message, and told him how long you'd been gone, he went white. He shouted at the poor man for not going with you, and raced off to saddle a horse with what I can only describe as feverish speed.' I smiled dutifully, aware he was trying to take my mind off the pain. 'As you saw, he almost caught me up. He must have ridden like the wind.'

I whispered, half smiling, 'Mudd never loses his temper.' Thinking he'd made that part up.

'I assure you ma'am, that he did. And it was quite a sight, I can tell you.'

He went on to talk of trivial matters. 'Knowing your interest in Piers, you'll be pleased to hear his ear is a little better this morning,' he said, in a light bantering tone. 'As for myself, I should have gone out shooting with Giles today. I have been practising a good deal lately, and hoped to outdo him. When he told me a problem on the estate required his immediate attention, naturally I accused him of inventing an excuse to avoid pitting his skills against mine. But that sort of thing never works with Giles. He only grinned at me and said tomorrow would do as well. So I decided to go for a ride, and came to see you, believing it would be far more enjoyable if I was accompanied by a beautiful woman.'

I gave a weak chuckle. 'You should have asked Lucie then.'

He put his head to one side for a moment, as if giving that his grave consideration. 'I did think of that, but lovely though she is, she's not at all in my style.'

When we finally reached Westfleet, Mr Reevers lifted me from my horse and carried me inside, where I was greeted by more shocked faces. First the servants, and shortly afterwards from my aunt and cousin, on their return. Everyone made a great fuss, which I bore with unusual patience, for many times that morning I had thought I would never see any of them again.

That afternoon Mr Reevers came over with Giles and Vincent, and when Giles saw me reposing against a pile of cushions on the drawing room sofa, he teased, 'I never imagined the day would come when I'd find you acting the invalid.'

Vincent protested, 'Oh come now, Giles. Do show a little more compassion. Lady Drusilla has been through a terrible ordeal.'

Giles stood smiling, his hands resting on the back of a chair. 'If I know Drusilla's servants, she will already have had her fill of being fussed over.'

I laughed, and begging them to be seated, admitted that was true. 'But I don't mean to complain. I'm only too aware how lucky I am to be here at all.'

Vincent said in agreement, 'Life is so uncertain, is it not? You only have to look at what has happened to my family to realise that, ma'am. But no bones broken I hear.'

'No. My shoulder is severely bruised, and I must rest for a week. Dr. Redding informs me I have been most fortunate.'

'Indeed. And I must beg you to forgive me for being blunt ma'am, but I for one would rest easier in my bed if you refrained from riding out alone in future.'

'I have already promised my aunt not to do so,' I admitted.

This brought a faint smile to Mr Reevers' lips, but Giles was much more forthright. 'I'm very glad to hear it, Drusilla. Although you must have been very worn down to agree to it.'

In fact I'd decided it would be by far the wisest course, having realised something very odd about the incident. I had, on rare occasions, seen small pieces of cliff falling, but had stood back, warned by them ricocheting against the sloping cliff face. The chunk that had knocked me out had grass on it, which meant it had come from the very top. Yet, I'd heard nothing, suggesting it had not struck any part of the cliff on the way down.

The other fact I reflected on was that I had tethered Orlando to the gate at the back of Smith's farm. After losing my temper with Smith, I had been on my guard, fully expecting trouble, but a week had passed without any repercussions, and I'd assumed he'd seen sense at last. It seemed I was wrong. Smith must have seen Orlando, walked along the cliff top and tried to kill me.

Giles, who was sailing to London on the afternoon tide, went to make his farewells to Lucie, and half an hour later I watched the gentlemen ride off together.

I recovered from my ordeal quicker than expected, helped by the warmth and comfort of my own home. My shoulder still protested at any sudden movement, and for a night or two I slept somewhat fitfully, keeping upright against a mass of pillows. Dr. Redding had suggested I rest for a week, but three days of languishing on a sofa was as much as I could stand, despite the kindness of my many visitors. Julia, Vincent and Mr Reevers came every day, and even Piers accompanied the gentleman on one occasion.

On the fourth day, my shoulder being much improved, I decided to go for a gentle ride. I strolled down to the stables, and as Mudd saddled the horses, so Mr Reevers rode into the stable yard. On seeing Mudd tightening the girth on Orlando's saddle, he arched an eyebrow at me.

I looked up at him, smiling ruefully. 'Yes, I know, but if I stay on that sofa one more hour, I shall go mad. I'm only going to Hokewell. With Mudd, of course.'

He inclined his head. 'May I ride with you?'

'If you wish, but you'll find it very dull, I'm afraid. I shan't go above a walk.'

'So I assumed.'

I used the mounting block to ease myself into the saddle, after which Mudd got up onto his horse, reached down for a spade standing against a nearby wall, and laid it across the saddle in front of him. Mr Reevers turned to me and raised his brows. 'Wouldn't a pistol offer better protection?'

Laughing, I explained, 'I want to see if a piece of earth can fall from the cliff top without hitting anything on the way.'

He studied me thoughtfully for a long moment. 'Yes, I see.'

Even at a walking pace we soon reached the cliff top, and he helped me to dismount. Mudd tethered the horses safely, while Mr Reevers went down to the beach. When he reached the right spot, I told him to stop. Mudd had already prised a chunk of earth from the crumbling cliff top with the spade, and I directed him to let it drop as if it had fallen naturally.

It bounced down the sloping cliff face, with bits flying off, and Mr Reevers called out, 'I heard that all right. Try a bigger piece.' Again it struck the cliff, and Mr Reevers shouted he was coming back. On reaching us, he directed Mudd to cut another large piece. 'Now,' he said, once Mudd had done so, 'let's see what happens if I throw it.'

It hit the ground without touching the cliff face at all, and my voice trembled slightly as I asked, 'Mr Reevers, when you were on the beach, standing close to the cliff, could you see me up here?'

He turned to me and shook his head, an inscrutable expression in his eyes. 'Who knew you were here that day?'

'No-one. But, as you saw, I rather stupidly tethered Orlando to the gate at the back of Smith's farm.' And I explained how I came to lose my temper with the man. 'I informed him no-one was going to dictate to me what happened on my own estate.'

'Which told him those two ruffians who dragged you to the cliff edge didn't scare you off.'

'Yes,' I said, full of regret. 'Smith must have walked along the cliff top and waited for the right moment.'

'I see. So, what will you do now?'

'I intend to have Smith arrested, of course.'

He hesitated, then said, 'Villains tend to develop some nasty habits when provoked.'

'I'm not afraid of Smith.'

He turned and looked me straight in the eye. 'If you want to stay alive, I strongly advise you to keep out of this business.'

17

Having suffered no ill effects from my short ride, I tried a gentle canter across the Downs the following morning, and felt only a few minor twinges. When I got back, my aunt and cousin were just leaving for Ledstone Place, where they were to spend the day deciding on the new furnishings for the bridal apartments.

I changed out of my riding habit, and had just gone outside for a stroll round the garden when I saw Julia walking up the drive. She was alone, and I had barely greeted her when another visitor appeared. Mr Upton.

'Do try to smile, Drusilla,' Julia murmured, glancing at my face. 'Or he'll think you don't want to see him.' I stifled a laugh, and I was wondering how quickly I could escape from the parson, when Vincent and Piers rode into view. 'You're very popular this morning,' Julia teased.

She had not met the Saxborough gentlemen before, and after making the introductions, I invited them all into the house, where we repaired to the drawing room. Jeffel brought suitable refreshments, and in response to my visitors' solicitous inquiries into my health, I assured them I was much improved.

Mr Upton, never one to lose an opportunity to moralise, addressed the Saxboroughs in his pompous way, a false smile on his lips. 'I'm afraid I had to scold Lady Drusilla for venturing out without her groom in attendance.' Wagging a finger at me, he declared, 'These little accidents only happen when you flout the conventions, ma'am.'

Thankfully, Vincent already had the measure of the man. Lifting an elegant quizzing glass to his eye, he studied Mr Upton in obvious concern. 'My dear sir, is that a boil starting on your neck?' The parson's hand flew up to what was no more than a pimple, and I choked. Vincent warned, 'Better have that seen to, or the next thing you know it will need lancing.'

I smiled gratefully at Vincent and his eyes twinkled in understanding. A faint suggestion of something other than boredom crossed Piers' face, and Julia, having smothered a giggle, advised Mr Upton, 'Mr Saxborough is right. Besides, you must look your best for the wedding.'

The parson retorted, 'Frankly ma'am, I am in two minds about officiating at this marriage. I do not approve of what I can only describe as, undue haste, in the matter. Considering the sad losses the family has suffered, August of next year would be a more appropriate date. When the full period of mourning is over. Many of my parishioners have expressed the same sentiments.' He looked across at Vincent and Piers. 'Do you not agree, gentlemen?'

Piers gave an indifferent shrug, while Vincent removed his snuff box from a pocket, flicked it open, and took a pinch, before saying, 'Young people like to get on with things, and I believe they are right. Life must go on.' Shutting his snuff box, he put it back in his pocket. 'But if that is your opinion sir, perhaps you should allow someone else to conduct the marriage service.'

As I said to Julia later, after all three gentleman had departed, 'I thought Mr Upton was going to have a seizure.'

Julia giggled. 'So did I. I must say I was quite taken with Vincent Saxborough. Such a charming man.' After a slight hesitation, she said, 'I met Mr Reevers the other day, and thought him exactly the sort of man to appeal to you. He's taller than you too.'

'Must a husband always be taller than his wife?' I mused. 'I might fall in love with someone six inches shorter than myself.'

She shook her head at me, laughing. 'Don't be absurd, Drusilla. You're far too sensible.' I opened my mouth to speak, but she intervened, 'Yes, I know, you don't intend to marry. But you have never yet been in love. That changes everything, believe me. And if Mr Reevers isn't quite in your style, there's always Piers.'

'Or Vincent,' I countered, tongue-in-cheek.

Her eyes gleamed for a brief moment, until she realised I was leading her on. 'Now you're being ridiculous. He must be twice your age.'

'At least,' I agreed, chuckling merrily. 'Still, we shouldn't discount him altogether. He might be my last chance. I shall depend upon you to tell me which one I should choose. Though I'd rather it wasn't Piers, he's too morose.'

'He was quiet, wasn't he. But I expect he's shy, and that wouldn't suit you at all. Still, there's nothing retiring about Mr Reevers.'

'My godmother doesn't like him,' I pointed out, as if that settled the matter.

She shook her head at me in despair. 'You're a hopeless case, Drusilla.'

'I rather think I am. I'm afraid I value my independence too much and no man, I fear, could live with that.'

I spent the afternoon in the workroom and having recorded the details of the break-in, I sat thinking about the cliff-fall. Twice now Smith and his friends had tried to stop me interfering in their smuggling activities, but I did not intend to let them get the better of me.

I felt well enough to ride to Ledstone the following morning, where I saw Leatherbarrow was back and learnt Giles had enjoyed an uneventful trip in favourable weather. Up at the house, Marguerite exclaimed joyfully, 'Drusilla.' And held out her hands to me. 'At last. I have missed you so very much.'

As I calmed her fears about the cliff-fall incident, a sudden burst of heavy rain, rapidly lowered the temperature. Marguerite pulled her shawl tightly round her shoulders, grumbling, 'This rain will ruin my roses, and Mr Reevers has put an end to what little comfort I have left.'

'Why? He seems a perfectly civil gentleman.'

'Civil he may be, but I cannot like him.' Adding fretfully, 'I wish Giles hadn't asked him here.'

'Someone must look after the estate while Giles is away,' I said cheerfully. 'And he wants to see if Norton House will suit him.'

'Perhaps he won't like it. I don't see how anyone could, when all the best rooms face north.'

I changed the subject, talking of the wedding, and an hour later, I was about to leave when Mr Reevers walked in. Bowing, he inquired after my health.

'I am very much better sir, as you can see.'

Nodding, he smiled at me in a way that made my heart give a sudden lurch. I was so unprepared for this strange event, that I babbled rather incoherently that I would walk down to the stables now the sun was out. When I accepted his offer to escort me, Marguerite looked from me, to Mr Reevers, and back again, grappling with the unthinkable suspicion that I actually liked him.

On going outside, Mr Reevers stopped to admire the view. A flight of steps led from the stone terrace to a lawn, where a peacock was preening its feathers. Beyond the lawn a path ran downhill through some oak trees to the lake.

'It is a breath-taking sight, isn't it,' I said. 'William Saxborough planted those trees.'

'He wasn't all bad then.'

'I don't believe anyone can be totally evil.' He raised his brows in quizzical fashion and I went on, 'What I mean is, evil men cannot spend their whole lives being wicked. They might be perfectly amiable most of the time, be fond of their wives and children, and hold any number of sensible views that you and I might agree with.'

'Do you really think so?' he murmured doubtfully, as we walked towards the stables. 'Tell me, just how many truly evil men are you acquainted with?'

I choked back a laugh, for his eyes were dancing. 'None, I hope. But—'

'You disappoint me.'

He brushed a hand over some lavender bushes, filling the air with perfume. 'Wonderful stuff, lavender.' And he turned back to gaze at the house. The original red brick building, built in the sixteenth century, had been added to twice, the result being distinctly pleasing to the eye. 'I can see why Giles loves this place. What man wouldn't be content to live out his life in such beautiful surroundings. Giles is a lucky fellow.'

Observing more black clouds forming I said I'd better be on my way before it rained again. He looked up at the sky, stating confidently, 'It won't rain in the next half hour.'

'You cannot possibly know that.'

'True,' he admitted with a grin. 'But I am fairly sure. As a sailor I am accustomed to reading the weather.'

'Oh,' I said in surprise, unaware he had an interest in sailing. 'What kind of a yacht do you have?'

'A very small one.'

'Is it capable of crossing the channel?'

'It is.' And he murmured provocatively, 'Should you have a desire to go there.'

I retorted with some severity, 'That is not what I meant, as you very well know.'

'No, I was afraid of that.' And he deliberately heaved a sorrowful sigh.

I didn't go straight home. Fancying a longer ride, I went past Westfleet up onto Luckton Down. Strangely enough it didn't rain for half an hour, as Mr Reevers had prophesied, but soon after I was caught in a succession of heavy showers, returning home soaked to the skin. Unfortunately, I entered the house just as my aunt was crossing the hall, and had to endure a severe scold on my foolishness in staying out in the rain, especially with an injured shoulder.

My aunt's moods were very up and down these days. On her birthday trip to Allum Bay, she had seemed almost carefree. But every time she read of yet another gruesome atrocity in France, she sank into despair, convinced she would never see my uncle again. I tried to be patient, all too conscious of what she was going through, and of my own guilt at not having told her my uncle was in prison.

I'd promised Giles to wait a week before doing so, in case news arrived from his friends in Normandy, and tomorrow that time would be up. But the strain of this enforced wait, and my awareness of the distress it would cause when I did speak, meant my patience was at a particularly low ebb.

Thus, when at dinner my aunt again condemned my foolishness in getting soaked, warning that she knew of at least three people who had ended up in the churchyard through riding in the rain, I completely lost my temper.

'In that case Aunt, if I should contract an inflammation of the lungs and be carried off, you will have the satisfaction of knowing you were right. And you may have your warning carved on my tombstone.'

Lucie, striving to keep a straight face, quickly applied herself to a dish of apple compote, while my aunt, in opening her mouth to speak, caught her breath and choked on the piece of peeled pear she was swallowing. At which moment Jeffel unexpectedly entered the room, and Aunt Thirza, determined to maintain her usual composure in front of him, turned an interesting shade of puce.

Jeffel, who appeared not to notice, informed me, 'Mr Arnold has called, my lady. He asks if you could spare him a few minutes.'

'What, now? At this time?'

'Yes, my lady. I believe it is a matter of some importance.'

Aunt Thirza, recovering from her encounter with the pear, ordered, 'Tell him we're at dinner, Jeffel.'

Jeffel inclined his head respectfully, but addressed his response to me. 'I did inform Mr Arnold you were at dinner my lady, but he asked me to say he believes you would wish to see him.'

'In that case, kindly inform Mr Arnold I shall be with him directly.' Jeffel bowed and left the room, and I put my napkin on the table, saying, 'You must excuse me, I'm afraid.'

Over the years, I could recall one or two highly distinguished visitors whom Jeffel had kept waiting while we finished dinner. Mr Arnold, however, was not a man to waste my time, or his, on a trivial matter, and Jeffel, who missed nothing that went on at Westfleet, had judged I would wish to see him. I crossed the hall in some apprehension, wondering what could have happened, for he would not have considered even the arrest of Smith a matter of great urgency.

When I entered the library, Mr Arnold rose from his chair, bowed and greeted me with an abject apology for interrupting my dinner. He wore breeches, a neat, serviceable riding coat, and mud spattered boots. Assuring him I had finished my meal, I urged him to be seated.

He took a seat, but refused any offer of refreshment. 'I mustn't stay, Lady Drusilla. But I knew you would wish to see this.' Taking a small box from his pocket, he handed it to me.

Opening the box, I gasped, for the item inside was extremely well known to me. A beautiful ring, consisting of a large square emerald surrounded by diamonds, which I had not expected to see again. Thomas had worn the Saxborough ring ever since the death of his father, but it hadn't been on his finger when his body was found, and like everyone else, I had thought it lost in the sea.

18

'Where did you find it?' I whispered, looking up at him.

'On the body of a man taken up from Dittistone Bay this morning.'

I suddenly felt very breathless. 'Do you know who he was?'

'A free trader, ma'am. French by his clothes. Likely he fell overboard in that squall last night. In foul weather, on a pitch black night, he'd have very little chance of being picked up again.'

'No,' I agreed. 'But the ring? Where was it?'

'On a particularly stout chain round his neck, hidden under his thick clothing.' He added, 'One of the revenue boats found him in the cave.' The cliffs at Dittistone were of chalk, and the cave, though not large at its entrance, ran back a long way, and could only be investigated at low water. 'They got him out just before noon, discovered the ring, and brought the body back to Cowes.'

'I see.' Taking the ring out of the box, I gazed at it, mesmerized, conscious only that this changed everything. Here, at long last, was real evidence. Proof that Thomas and Tom had been murdered. I looked up and said quietly, 'The ring must have been stolen before Thomas went into the water.'

'Yes,' he agreed, shaking his head in sorrow. 'I've thought of nothing else since I left Cowes. I imagine the yacht was boarded by a gang of French smugglers, the man found today being one of them.'

'If they only wanted the ring, why didn't they just take it? Why murder two innocent people?'

He gave a little shrug of helplessness. 'The French are a law unto themselves these days, ma'am. With the Saxboroughs being members of the class the revolutionaries are busy eliminating, I fear they simply threw Thomas and his son overboard.'

I closed my eyes momentarily, trying not to think of what Thomas and Tom must have endured. Putting the ring back into the box, I returned it to him. 'I should like to see this man.'

His brows flew up in horror. 'Ma'am, I—'

'I must know who he is. If-----'

'Forgive me, but it would serve no useful purpose.' He put the box carefully into his pocket, hesitating a little before saying, 'To be blunt, he suffered such a severe buffeting against the walls of the cave last night I doubt his own mother would recognise him now.'

I groaned. Nothing in this business was easy. 'Surely, there must be something that would identify him.'

'I found nothing, I'm afraid, ma'am.'

Collecting my wits together, I asked, 'You have seen him yourself?' He inclined his head and looked down at his hands. 'Did he have anything in his pockets?'

'A small number of French coins.'

'Nothing else?'

'Not a thing, ma'am. I made a thorough search.'

'Yes, of course.' I did not doubt it.

'He was of medium height and build, with black hair. His clothes and boots were what any French fisherman or smuggler might wear. Dr. Redding, who examined him, says his death was caused by drowning.'

So this man had stolen Thomas's ring, put it on a strong, thick chain, and kept it hidden, knowing he must wait until it was safe to sell it. A man who knew how to bide his time, but who had been caught out by a squall and lost his life. It was, I supposed, justice of a kind.

When I thanked Mr Arnold for his frankness, he said, 'There is one other thing, ma'am. Obviously I recognised the ring, but I had to ask Mrs Saxborough to confirm it officially. In fact, I have just come from Ledstone. She understood that the ring, being evidence, could not be returned to the family yet.' He hesitated. 'But I must confess to you ma'am, she did not realise the true significance of this discovery. She took it to be a simple matter of theft, and----' He ran a finger round the inside of his collar. 'You will think me a coward ma'am, and rightly so, but I hadn't the heart to enlighten her, not after all she has suffered this year. I'd hoped Vincent Saxborough would be there, but he and his son are enjoying a convivial evening with friends in Ventnor. Mr Reevers was also out, and as Mrs Saxborough does not find him agreeable, perhaps he's not the best person to—' He broke off awkwardly, then said, 'The situation must be explained to her. I have no right to ask it of you ma'am, but--------' His expression was one of hopeful entreaty. He wasn't a man to shirk his duty, but coping with a distraught woman shedding copious tears was another matter entirely.

'I'll ride over this evening, Mr Arnold.'

'I am most grateful,' he said, his brow clearing, and stood up to take his leave, patting his pocket to make sure the ring was still there.

After Mr Arnold had left, I returned to the dining room and told my aunt and cousin the devastating news. They stared at me dumbfounded, Lucie turning so white I thought she was going to faint. Crossing to the sideboard, I poured a little brandy into a glass, which she took with shaking hands, sipping it slowly, until her colour began to return.

My aunt, herself rather pale, became concerned over Marguerite's reaction to the appalling news, and when I repeated what Mr Arnold had said, she nodded. 'Yes. She will listen to you, Drusilla.' She looked out of the window at the sky. 'I should go before it rains again.' Going up to my bedchamber, I rang for my maid, who packed an overnight bag, while I changed into a riding habit.

I took Mudd with me, and told him about the ring. 'John, could Mr Thomas have stumbled on some French smugglers picking up illegal goods?'

'No-one worries about smugglers, my lady.'

'French spies then. Or revolutionaries?'

'You don't believe that no more than I do, my lady.'

His face was grave and troubled. 'No, you're right. I don't.' But father had taught me to consider every possibility, however remote, and I wanted to believe Thomas had seen something he shouldn't; something utterly unconnected with his family, and had been murdered as a result. But Mudd was right; in my heart, I knew that wasn't what had happened. If Thomas had come across smugglers going about their business, he would have bought a keg of brandy off them. He had been very partial to brandy.

So, why had they been killed? Certainly not for a ring that could be easily snatched from Thomas's finger. There had been no signs of violence on the bodies, yet Thomas and Tom, both strong swimmers, had drowned on a calm warm night in late July. I did not want to think about how that had been achieved.

Who had wanted to make murder look like an accident? No gang of French smugglers would go to that much trouble. But if I could find the name of the dead smuggler, it would lead me to the gang he worked with, and eventually, to the truth. Full of hope, I said, 'We'll go by way of Hokewell, John. I must speak to Jackson.' If anyone could discover the identity of the dead smuggler it was another smuggler.

I found Jackson tending his garden, and when I explained what I wanted, he asked respectfully if the reward Giles had offered still stood. 'It does,' I promised, knowing it was what Giles would wish. 'And I'll double it if you give me the names of every man in that gang.' I asked if it would be difficult, what with the war and everything, but he shook his head.

'French free traders don't care about the war, my lady, or the revolution. They're only interested in money. I'll do my best, I can promise you that. I might cheat the government out of a bit of tax, but I don't hold with killing. Mr Thomas was a proper gentleman, and there was no finer boy on the Island than Master Tom.'

When I reached Ledstone, I saw Marguerite considered the appearance of the ring as good news. 'Now Giles will wear it, like all his ancestors. Of course, I gave Mr Arnold a sum of money for the man who found it. If he hadn't spotted the ring, it would have been buried with the man, and lost for ever.'

Dittistone churchyard was the last resting place of men from many distant places, whose ships foundered on the underwater ledge. Or when, as last night, a smuggler had fallen overboard and drowned. It was common enough, and soon forgotten. I sat listening to her chatter, understanding Mr Arnold's difficulties all too well. Taking a deep breath, I explained how the smuggler must have acquired the ring.

She stared at me, her voice rising in alarm, 'Are you saying Thomas and young Tom were murdered because of the ring?' She didn't want to face the truth, and who could blame her. Tears clung precariously to her eyelashes, her shawl clutched tightly across her bosom.

'It is worth a great deal of money,' I pointed out, as if agreeing with her conclusion.

Her bottom lip wobbled, but even then she interpreted it in her own way. 'At least it will stop those silly rumours about Giles. The smugglers he knows are English, not French.' Her tone implying that no-one in their right senses had anything to do with the French. Luckily she had never been a deep thinker, but I was thankful Giles had arranged for Jacob to bring his message to Westfleet. Jacob wasn't French, but Marguerite would still be greatly agitated if a fearsome looking smuggler walked up the drive at Ledstone.

As the reality of the murders sank in, she begged me not to leave her alone at Ledstone that night. I thought of Mr Reevers, Vincent and Piers, and the servants in the house, but agreed without hesitation, thankful I'd brought my night attire with me.

I said, 'There's bound to be an official investigation.'

'Then Giles must come home at once.' This was a conclusion I had also come to. As head of the Saxborough family, his place was here. 'Leatherbarrow must go to London tonight, Drusilla. Will you write a letter explaining? Giles will listen to you.'

I agreed willingly, but crossing to my godmother's writing desk, a thought struck me. 'I had better warn Leatherbarrow first---'

'Why?' she demanded petulantly. 'He'll do as he's told.'

'Yes, of course he will, but he'll need the yacht, and I don't know the state of the tide. If I speak to him now, he can make his preparations while I write the letter.'

'Oh very well,' she said, reaching for the bell-rope.

'No, don't ring. I'll go down to the stables myself. I want a word with Mudd too.'

'All right, but don't be long. I shan't have a moment's peace until Giles is safely home again.'

Walking down to the stables, I came across Mudd first. He had just finished grooming Orlando, and I sent him to inform my aunt I wouldn't be home tonight. 'Come back in the morning, John. After breakfast will do. There's no hurry.'

'Very good, my lady.'

He went to saddle his horse, and walking on I found Leatherbarrow brushing mud off the legs of one of Giles's hacks. On seeing me, he stood upright and touched his cap, smiling. 'Good evening, my lady. The weather's------'

I interrupted, 'Leatherbarrow, how soon can you leave for London? Mrs Saxborough has a urgent letter for Mr Giles.'

Blinking, he stared at me fixedly for a moment. He still held the brush he'd been using, and without speaking, he put it down very slowly, as if thinking. Calling to a couple of stable lads, he told them to continue with the grooming.

He still did not answer me, and I presumed he was working out when the tide would be suitable. But on turning to me again his face bore an impassive expression, of the kind I did not associate with Leatherbarrow. Whatever was troubling him, it wasn't the state of the tide.

I lifted an eyebrow in inquiry, and he said quietly, 'May I show you the new colt, my lady?' Assuming he wished to speak to me alone, I walked across to the paddock with him, well out of earshot of the grooms and stable boys.

As I dutifully admired the colt, I said, 'Out with it, Leatherbarrow. Is there something wrong with the yacht?'

'No, my lady.' He hesitated. 'May I respectfully ask if this letter is really urgent?'

Obviously he suspected this was one of my godmother's fancies, but that still didn't explain his reluctance to obey orders. 'Yes, it is,' I replied. 'In fact, I mean to write it myself.' I told him why, explaining how the Saxborough ring had been found.

Staring at me in horror, he reached out to the paddock rail, as if to steady himself. 'But why -- why did the Frenchies have to kill them?'

'I don't know why, Leatherbarrow. I wish I did. But the news will be all round the Island soon, and Mr Giles cannot stay in London when two members of his family have been murdered. His place, as head of the family, is here. You do see why he must come home at once.'

'Yes, my lady, I do.' He shifted from one foot to the other, and turned a troubled face to me. 'The problem is, my lady, Mr Giles isn't in London.'

19

For several seconds I was speechless. 'What do you mean, he's not in London?' The unsteadiness in my voice clear even to my own ears. 'Where is he, Leatherbarrow?'

Avoiding my eyes, he answered awkwardly. 'I don't rightly know, my lady.' This I did not believe. If anyone knew where he was, that person was his groom. Leatherbarrow had been entrusted with the task of keeping him safe, ever since the five year old Giles had been caught clambering onto the back of his father's favourite horse.

Leatherbarrow was a tall man, and stronger than his wiry frame suggested, having once carried his young charge two miles home after a fall from a tree had severely twisted Giles's knee. He was a dependable and discreet servant; so discreet, that if he had known where Giles was, he would have delivered the letter without mentioning Giles wasn't in London.

The light was fading fast, and the grooms and stable lads returning to their quarters cast no more than a cursory glance in the direction of the paddock.

'You must have some idea, Leatherbarrow.'

The groom looked down at his feet, clearly uncomfortable, and mumbled, 'I don't rightly know what to say, my lady.'

'Very well, let's start at the beginning. Last week you left Yarmouth and sailed to London.' He didn't answer, and I persisted, 'You did go to London, didn't you?' He hesitated, then gave a slight shake of the head. I gazed at him, puzzled. 'Was there was a change of plan?'

'No, my lady.' And he said guardedly, 'Mr Giles does mean to go to London later, that I do know, but I can't say where he is now.'

'Can't? Or won't?' I asked in a gentle tone. The groom shifted from one foot to the other, clearly not knowing how to answer, and I urged, 'Under normal circumstances Leatherbarrow, I shouldn't dream of asking you to break a confidence, but there is nothing normal about what is happening now. I simply cannot tell Mrs Saxborough that you don't know where he is.' I didn't need to explain why. Every servant at Ledstone knew how she fretted over Giles. 'Nor can I concoct a story that will satisfy her, unless I know the truth. You do see that, don't you.'

'Yes, my lady, I do,' he sighed.

'At least tell me where you left him.'

'Begging your pardon, my lady, but that won't help you.'

'Allow me to be the judge of that.'

With considerable reluctance, he obeyed. 'He's in France, my lady.'

'France?' I gasped, utterly taken aback. I took a long deep breath. 'Whereabouts in France?'

'He went ashore in Normandy, my lady.'

'Where precisely?'

'It's a remote spot on one of the beaches, well away from any village.'

The manner in which he spoke made me say, 'You speak as if you've been there often.'

'Not often, my lady.'

'But you have left Mr Giles at this place before?'

He covered his face with his hands. 'He'll skin me alive.'

'I promise you he won't,' I assured him kindly. 'I'll explain I gave you no choice. How long has this been going on.' He hesitated, and I said, 'You may as well tell me now, Leatherbarrow.'

He looked at me and whispered. 'Since he came down from Oxford.'

'Four or five years?' I spluttered. The years before the outbreak of hostilities, when he'd travelled abroad for pleasure. Preferring to cross the channel in his own yacht, mooring at one of the bigger ports. Or so he'd told me.

We were still standing by the paddock, and I hoped Leatherbarrow wouldn't notice I was using the upright post beside me as a support. 'What did he do on these visits to France?'

'I don't know, my lady. He wouldn't say. Only I wasn't to tell anyone where I left him.'

My throat suddenly felt very dry, and I went on a little shakily, 'What happens when you arrive at this beach?'

'There's always a Frenchie waiting with a horse, my lady.'

'This Frenchman,' I said apprehensively, gripping the wooden post tightly. 'The one with the horse. Is - is he a smuggler?'

'I believe so, my lady.' I closed my eyes, but it was dark now, and I doubted he noticed. 'When he wants to be picked up, he sends Jacob with a message.'

I swallowed, recalling the casual way Giles had asked me to do him a favour. 'Only this time Jacob will come to me.'

For the first time Leatherbarrow relaxed. 'So I understand, my lady,' he grinned.

I thought for a moment. 'When the message comes, you'll pick him up from Normandy and sail on to London?'

'That's it, my lady. He says his business there won't take more than a week and I'm to wait for him.'

In desperation I asked, 'Leatherbarrow, doesn't he even hint where he's going to in France?'

He wavered. 'Not normally, my lady.'

'Only this time he did?' A small groan escaped him. 'Come on Leatherbarrow, I must know.'

After a moment, he said, 'I suppose it won't do no harm now.'

I was of the opinion it would do me a great deal of good. The thought of Giles alone in a hostile country run by a bunch of uncivilised cut-throats, where mobs ran riot in the streets, and one unwise remark could mean arrest and execution, made the hairs on the back of my neck stand up. Why had he taken such a risk? He was getting married in a few weeks. What could be so important? And then an awful thought struck me.

Barely able to get the words out, I whispered, 'Does it concern my uncle?'

Even in the darkness I caught the slight fluttering of his eyelids. 'It seems he's in a prison in Normandy, my lady.'

I ran my tongue round dry lips. 'Yes, I know that.'

'He's being moved to Paris early this week, and Mr Giles said once there, he'd never get out alive.'

My voice shook as I asked, 'Has —has he gone to rescue my uncle?'

He looked at me helplessly. 'Yes, my lady.' Now I understood the sparkle in Giles's eyes, and why he'd left in a hurry. But how could he actually enjoy risking his life?

I didn't ask what crime my uncle was accused of, for the bloodthirsty tyrannical Committee of Public Safety had swept aside the kind of truth and justice we were accustomed to in England. Those who dared to criticise the revolution, or suggest life had been better under the monarchy, were silenced by the guillotine. If Giles was caught trying to rescue my uncle, justice would consist of a sham trial and swift execution.

'Are you all right, my lady?' Leatherbarrow inquired worriedly. Swallowing hard, I reassured him, and asked if anyone else knew where Giles had gone.

'Oh no, my lady. Mr Giles won't have spoken of it. He says the only sure way to keep a secret is not to share it with anyone else.' I smiled grimly, remembering Giles had once said the same thing to me, and asked how the rescue was to be achieved. 'By stopping the coach on its way to Paris. He said one prisoner wouldn't warrant much in the way of guards. And he could have Miss Lucie's papa safe on the Island in a few days.'

I groaned. 'Didn't he stop to think what it would mean to Miss Lucie and Mrs Saxborough if he was captured or killed?' My godmother, for one, would never recover from such a blow.

'I did try to make him see sense, my lady. But it's a long time since he took much notice of anything I said. And you know what he's like once he makes up his mind.'

'Indeed, I do,' I muttered with feeling.

'I begged him not to go risking his life, but he said there was no risk, because he and this Frenchie had it all worked out.' He owned anxiously. 'I wish he hadn't gone, my lady, and that's the truth.' I gave a shiver, for even as we spoke, Giles might be in prison, or dead. And there was absolutely nothing we could do, except wait. And pray.

I couldn't help admiring his courage, although he wouldn't have seen it like that. Indeed, I knew exactly how it had been. Giles, discovering Lucie's father faced certain death, saw a chance to save him, and had not hesitated. The possibility of failure probably hadn't entered his head, as he would have planned everything with his usual thoroughness. Yet, how could anyone be safe in France when the King himself had been forced to climb the steps to the guillotine?

I returned to the house intending to tell Marguerite that Leatherbarrow couldn't leave before morning because of the tide, praying I could think of a better excuse overnight. I found Mr Reevers sitting with her, and she greeted me with relief, her eyes begging me not to leave her alone with this man again. He sat on the other side of her and could not see her expression, but she could not quite keep her dislike of him out of her voice. 'I was just explaining to Mr Reevers why Leatherbarrow is going to bring Giles-----'

Mr Reevers intervened, 'Frankly ma'am, I consider it both unnecessary, and unwise, to send Leatherbarrow on such an errand.'

'Unwise?' I repeated, puzzled.

'Certainly. Giles will instantly rush home and seek out these French smugglers himself. In my opinion, men who would kill a man and a boy for the sake of a ring, no matter how valuable, are not to be trifled with.'

Marguerite gave a cry of alarm. 'Oh no. That's just the sort of thing Giles would do. Drusilla, I absolutely forbid you to write to him.'

I assured her I would naturally abide by her wishes. Thankful to have that problem solved so easily, I eyed Mr Reevers with some curiosity, for while Giles might well act in the manner he had said, I had the oddest feeling he had another, quite different, reason for not wanting a message to be sent.

That night at Ledstone the weather remained calm, and when I retired to my customary guest bedchamber, the only sound I heard was an owl hooting nearby. But my fears for Giles kept me awake, and in thinking of it all, I suddenly saw he might have another reason, apart from the joy it would bring Lucie, for wishing to reunite my uncle with his family, and I laughed softly to myself.

If my uncle did not survive, Giles would insist on my aunt making her home at Ledstone, but as she did not get on well with Marguerite, such an arrangement would cause endless friction. If, however, my aunt and my uncle were reunited, they would set up home together elsewhere, enabling Giles and Lucie to start their married life without that kind of discord. As he naturally wished to do. And Giles had always found a way to get what he wanted. As a child, he'd learned not to confront a situation head-on when a subtle approach achieved the result he wanted. True, he wanted to get my uncle out of prison, but the secondary benefit would not have escaped him.

I was up early as usual the following morning, and walking down to the stables before breakfast, told a relieved Leatherbarrow that my godmother had decided not to send for Giles. If people considered that odd, then her fear that he'd go after the murderers himself would do very well as an excuse. Everyone would understand that.

As breakfast would not be served for half an hour, I went for a stroll to get some fresh air. I climbed up the steep incline that ran from the edge of the rear gardens onto a small plateau, from where there was an excellent view of the house, stables and gardens on one side, and the parklands on the other. It was a short, if arduous climb, and as I stood at the top regaining my breath, I heard the sound of a galloping horse. Glancing in the direction of the parklands, I soon recognised the rider. It was Mudd. And he was heading for the stables at breakneck speed.

I frowned. Why was he in such a hurry? And why had he come so early? I had distinctly told him to come after breakfast. On reaching the stables he leapt off his horse, passed the reins to a groom, and start to run towards the house. My heart began to pound, for Mudd never ran. My first thought was that he had news of Giles. That something had gone terribly wrong.

I began to make my way down the hill, and when Mudd saw me, he stopped and looked up. Although he didn't speak until I reached him, I saw he was beaming from ear to ear. 'My lady, there's wonderful news. Miss Lucie's papa is home. He turned up at Westfleet in the middle of the night.' I closed my eyes momentarily, overcome with relief that my uncle was no longer in the hands of the revolutionaries. And if he was safe, then surely Giles was too.

'The Frenchies had him in prison, but he escaped,' Mudd went on, still grinning. 'He came over on a smuggling run, his face blackened with gunpowder, just as if he was a common smuggler. Miss Lucie said she didn't recognise him at first.'

Giles had wanted my uncle out of France quickly and quietly. A smuggling run was fast, and he would have paid the men well. As the wonderful news sank in, I was filled with so much joy I could not trust myself to speak. I brushed away a tear and Mudd, who missed very little, merely said, 'I felt a bit tearful myself, my lady. Cook said most of the servants were crying too.' I laughed a little shakily, and he went on, 'Cook said it was the Frenchies who ought to be locked up, and not a God-fearing gentleman like Mr Frere.'

With a slightly watery chuckle, I pointed out, 'My uncle is half French.'

'Yes, my lady, but cook said he was half English too, and as far as she was concerned, that was the only half that counted.'

Laughing, I regained control of my emotions. 'How does my uncle look, John?'

'I haven't seen him myself, my lady, but Miss Lucie says he's very thin and rather weak.' Then choosing his words with care, went on, 'Mrs Frere charged me with a message. She would be obliged if you would return home as soon as possible.'

I stifled a chuckle, guessing her actual instruction had been to insist I came home at once. 'I shall, of course,' I said, eager to see my uncle for myself. 'As soon as I've breakfasted and taken leave of Mrs Saxborough.'

In the event it was over an hour before I left. Having had breakfast, I sent for Marguerite's maid who, on my instructions, roused her mistress. On entering my godmother's bedchamber I found her propped up against the pillows, her nightcap askew, trying to shield her eyes from the sunlight streaming in through the window.

Sleepily she grumbled, 'Whatever is the matter, Drusilla?'

Drawing up a chair beside her bed, I sat down. 'My uncle has escaped from prison in France,' I explained cheerfully. 'He arrived at Westfleet last night, so you see I really must go home at once.'

She tried hard to take it all in, but was never at her best in the mornings. 'Your uncle was in prison? How on earth did he escape?'

'I don't know yet. I haven't spoken to him. I'll come back later and tell you all about it.'

Her face brightened at that. 'You promise?'

'Of course.'

As I stood up to go, she asked me what time it was. The clock on the mantle shelf over the fireplace was one Giles had brought home from Paris a few years earlier, but she couldn't see the hands on the clock face without her spectacles. When I told her it wanted a mere three minutes to eight, a look of such horror crossed her face that I left the room laughing. As I closed the door, I heard her instruct her maid to draw the curtains again as she refused to get up at such an unreasonable hour, even with guests in the house.

Looking in at the breakfast parlour, I found Mr Reevers enjoying a substantial plate of ham and eggs. 'Please don't disturb yourself,' I said quickly, as he started to rise from his chair. 'I only came in to take my leave.'

'Are you going home this minute? Won't you have some breakfast first?'

'I've already eaten, thank you.' And I told him the good news.

He leant back in his chair, a thoughtful look on his face. 'Came back on a smuggling run eh? These free traders have their uses, I must say.'

I agreed that, on this occasion, they certainly did. But recalling what he'd said last night, I blurted out impulsively, 'Mr Reevers, would you tell me—' and hesitated, trying to frame my question diplomatically.

His eyes softened into an expression that made the colour rise in my cheeks. 'Stuck for words ma'am? I don't mind what you ask me.'

Annoyed at the effect he was having on me, and the fact he was aware of it, I snapped, 'Yes, but will you give me a straight answer?'

'If I can.'

'Why don't you want Giles home?'

He blinked at me in surprise. 'For the reason I gave Mrs Saxborough. If Giles knew those French smugglers had murdered Thomas and young Tom, he wouldn't hesitate to go after them.'

I knew he was right, but I said, 'Is that your only reason?'

A slight smile played on his lips and he shook his head.

20

My heart sank. I desperately wanted him to be a man with high principles. To be honourable and incorruptible, and I was so afraid that he wasn't. I took a deep breath. 'Will you tell me the other reason?'

'If you insist. If Giles comes home I won't have an excuse to stay here, and I don't want to leave the Island at present,' he murmured a little huskily. And he smiled up at me in a way that left me in no doubt of his meaning. I wasn't able to answer him, as Vincent come into the room at that moment. Having told him the good news, I simply took my leave, saying I was eager to see my uncle.

Wanting a quiet word with Leatherbarrow, I walked down to the stables, where one look at his face told me he'd heard the good news. I smiled. 'Mudd told you, I suppose.'

'Yes, my lady. I was never more thankful. I just wish Mr Giles was out of France too.'

So did I, but I said, 'Don't worry. He's bound to send word for you to bring the yacht any day now.'

When I explained Giles's part in it all to Mudd, as we rode home, he merely said, 'He always was a daredevil, my lady.' We skirted our way round some sheep, and Mudd asked thoughtfully, 'Why didn't Mr Giles come back with them?'

'I doubt he ever meant to. It wouldn't do for Mr Saxborough of Ledstone Place to be caught on a smuggling run.'

Mudd chuckled. 'I see what you mean, my lady. Especially with them being Frenchies.'

'French?' I gulped, swallowing hard. 'The smugglers were French?'

'So Miss Lucie said, my lady.' Then I remembered the French smuggler who always met Giles on that beach in Normandy. No doubt he had arranged it.

Some gulls swept across in front of us, making Orlando toss his head, and Mudd said, 'When I think the danger Mr Giles was in, my lady, well — I would have been shaking in my shoes. Only I swear he actually enjoys it.'

'Indeed,' I agreed sardonically.

'I expect he had it all worked out, like he did as a boy. I remember him clambering down a cliff to get his kite and telling me I needn't worry because if he'd fallen, there was a wide ledge half way down that would have saved him. And there was too.'

'Clambering down a cliff is very different from helping my uncle escape from France,' I remarked dryly.

'Yes, my lady, I see that. What I mean is he wouldn't have gone down the cliff if the ledge hadn't been there.'

'There wouldn't have been a ledge to save him in France,' I pointed out.

'No, my lady. But he'd have something in mind if things got difficult.'

A sudden breeze sprang up and I filled my lungs with the refreshing salty tang of the sea. 'You may well be right, John. When Mr Giles returns I mean to ask him.' That wasn't all I meant to ask him either.

I stopped for a moment, and easing myself in the saddle, gazed out to sea towards France. I couldn't see the coastline from here, of course, nor thankfully, was I ever likely to hear the screams of those suffering the terrors and barbarities of the bloody revolution that had been going on there for four long years now. The thought of so much bloodshed sent icy cold shivers up and down my spine, for if those jackals got their hands on Giles they would tear him apart.

Having explained Jacob would inform me when Giles was ready to come home, I said, ' I never imagined the sight of a smuggler arriving at Westfleet would be a cause for celebration John, yet no man would be more welcome at this moment.'

Arriving back at Westfleet, I dismounted outside a side door and handed Orlando's reins to Mudd. Hurrying inside, I found the whole household in a state of euphoria.

Jeffel greeted me, grinning from ear to ear. 'Isn't it the most wonderful news, my lady,' he burst out exuberantly. 'If only you had been here last night. I opened the door, you see. It was well after midnight, and I took a poker with me, just in case. I didn't recognise Mr Frere, I'm afraid. I thought he was a smuggler, what with him being in old clothes and his face all black with gunpowder. 'What do you want, my man,' I says to him.' My butler shook his head, chortling at his own mistake. 'Then he said, 'Don't you know me, Jeffel?' Of course, when I heard him speak, I knew he wasn't any smuggler, but I didn't know *who* he was, even though I held the candle up close to his face. Not everyone who speaks like a gentleman is honourable, as I'm sure I don't need to tell you, my lady. When he told me his name, naturally I let him in then.'

'I'm glad to hear it,' I said, laughing. Jeffel couldn't have been more thrilled if it had been his own uncle who'd escaped from the French. Nor did he begrudge my aunt such happiness despite her occasional, unwarranted criticisms of the way he carried out his duties.

'Well, my lady, you can't be too careful. I mean, no respectable person knocks on the door after midnight. By this time, the whole household was awake. Cook came out, and when she realised it was Mr Frere, she dashed off to the kitchen to get him something to eat, and to heat some water for him to wash his face. He was chilled to the marrow too, but we soon got a nice fire going in the drawing room.' He broke off from his tale, lowering his voice to a confidential tone. 'I should warn you, my lady, that he looks a little gaunt, having been stuck in a French prison all these months.' Returning to his normal voice, he went on, 'Then Mrs Frere and Miss Lucie came down to see what the commotion was about, and for a moment, even they didn't recognise him.'

'I don't suppose they did,' I conceded, with a watery smile.

'Mrs Frere sent for Dr. Redding at once, in spite of Mr Frere saying it could wait until morning. But the doctor insisted he didn't mind a bit being hauled out of his warm bed on such an occasion as this. And he says there's no lasting damage done, or any disease.'

'That is good news,' I said, relieved. 'Where is he now, Jeffel?'

'Oh, do forgive me, my lady. Here I am chattering on, and you'll be wanting to see Mr Frere for yourself. They're all in the blue room, I believe. Mr Frere said he wanted to be somewhere in the light, what with it always being dark in his prison cell.'

Thanking Jeffel, I went through the drawing room into the blue room, stopping in the doorway. They had not heard me approach, and were sitting on the far side of the room by one of the big windows. I stood quite still for a moment, gazing at my uncle, who sat beside Aunt Thirza, with Lucie at his feet. Despite Jeffel's warning, I was greatly shocked by the sight of the hollow-eyed, white-faced, haggard man before me. So unlike the slightly plump, contented uncle I'd always known. I wasn't surprised Jeffel hadn't recognised him; I would not have done so myself.

I was grateful to have a moment to school my face into an appropriate expression, before I walked into the room, smiling. Seeing me then, he got up slowly, a beam of pleasure on his thin face, and I, abandoning all pretence of calm, threw my arms round his neck. 'Uncle, I cannot tell you......' The rest of my words caught in my throat and I stood for several moments hugging him in grateful silence. Releasing me, he kissed me on both cheeks, and took my hands in his. I tried not to notice how bony they were.

'I am extremely glad to be here, Drusilla my dear,' he said, his voice a little feeble. 'Have you heard how I turned up in the night looking like a smuggler?'

'Yes. Jeffel told me.'

My uncle gave a weak chuckle, and I urged him to sit down again. Although obviously very worn down after his long imprisonment, he was in high spirits. 'I thought he wasn't going to let me in, you know. Mind you, once he realised who I was, he couldn't do enough for me. In fact he stayed up half the night, fussing over me like a mother hen.' He turned to my aunt, saying, 'All the servants have been wonderful, haven't they, my dear.'

My aunt nodded. 'Yes, they were very good.' She spoke in a subdued tone, and although I could see she was very happy, she said very little all the time I was in the room, which I put down to her being badly shaken by my uncle's appearance.

As if aware I was watching her, she looked up at me, a curious mixture of pain and joy in her eyes. 'Your uncle has had a terrible time, Drusilla. He's been in prison, you know.'

Jeffel appeared at that moment with an extra blanket to keep my uncle warm, and returned a moment later with a bowl of sustaining soup cook had made especially. Savouring the delicious smell of it, my uncle begged Jeffel to thank cook, and having tasted the soup, pronounced it to be best he'd ever tasted.

'Mudd says you escaped,' I said, when he'd finished this repast.

'Oh, it wasn't any of my doing, I'm afraid. Some friends in France bribed a guard at the prison with a very large sum of money. And then paid smugglers to bring me to the Island.'

Lucie asked curiously, 'Who were these friends, Papa?'

'The Chevaliers. A father and son. People I became friendly with after you and your mother left France. I was lonely, and they were kind enough to invite me to dine quite often. You would like them, I know. I shall repay the money, of course, just as soon as I'm on my feet again. They risked their lives to save me, a debt I can never hope to repay.'

Lucie put a hand on her father's arm. 'They must be very brave, Papa. I should like to meet them, to thank them personally.'

'When this dreadful revolution is over, you shall.'

It was a plausible enough story, and one which my aunt and cousin seemed to have accepted without question; and which I would have done too, if I had not known better.

My uncle said that the estate in France was totally lost. 'But I have been exceedingly lucky to escape, as I don't need to tell you.'

For myself, I was content just to listen to the sound of my uncle's voice, and revel in the joy of the day. Even the sun put in an appearance, and we enjoyed its delicious warmth, refusing to move until the bell rang for dinner. My aunt, who always dressed for dinner no matter what had happened, declared she had no intention of doing so today. For once we found something to agree on, and indeed, the whole house seemed to radiate with happiness.

I woke later than usual the following morning, having slept more soundly than I had in weeks. I dressed hastily, urging my maid to be quick with my hair, as I was anxious to see how my uncle was. Going downstairs, I was surprised to find him alone in the breakfast parlour.

'Ah, Drusilla. Good morning,' he beamed. 'Your aunt is not yet awake, and it seemed a shame to disturb her.'

'Shouldn't you be resting too?'

He shook his head. 'Sleep was one thing I wasn't short of in prison. There wasn't much else to do.'

Lucie had not risen yet either, and after a simple breakfast, we walked very slowly down to the walled garden, settling ourselves on the seat in a pretty rose arbour, sheltered from the wind. My uncle turned his face up to the sun, closing his eyes in blissful appreciation, and I was struck even more by the hollowness of his cheeks, and the wasted paleness of his skin. But Dr. Redding's recommended diet, and cook's special egg custard, would soon put the colour back into his cheeks, and I was sure he would be well enough to play his part at Lucie's wedding.

When a small cloud obscured the sun, he opened his eyes, and I remarked casually, 'That fable about how you escaped from France will do for everyone else Uncle, but that isn't what happened, is it.' He threw me such a startled look, I laughed. 'Tell me, did Giles hold up the coach on the road to Paris, as he planned?'

He sat bolt upright in the seat, his eyes suddenly alert. After a moment, he said, 'I didn't realise you knew, Drusilla. Giles didn't mention it.'

'Didn't he?' I said, feigning surprise. 'Well, he probably didn't think it important. He and I have always been very close, you know. He meant to overpower the guards, with the help of some Frenchman.'

He eyed me in a calculating manner for a second or two before answering. 'Giles doesn't want it known, Drusilla.'

I nodded. 'That's why I didn't mention it before. Tell me, is he safe? Did everything go according to plan?'

He hesitated, then seemed to make up his mind. 'Giles was well when we parted. But they held up the coach before it reached the prison, not afterwards.' I wondered aloud what had made Giles change his plans, but he didn't know. 'They tied the guards to a tree in the middle of a wood, after borrowing their uniforms. Naturally when I saw two guards waiting to take me to Paris, I assumed they were revolutionaries. I didn't recognise Giles, not having seen him since he was a child.' Father and I had occasionally stayed at my uncle's house when they lived in London, but they had only visited the Island twice; when I was seven, and again when Giles was at Oxford.

My uncle went on, 'I don't mind telling you Drusilla, I thought my last hours had come.' For a brief moment the anguish he'd felt at that time showed in his face. Then he relaxed and put his hand over mine. 'Still, that's all over now, thanks to Giles. But for him, I should have joined those poor souls imprisoned in Paris.' Tears glistened in his eyes. 'I will never be able to repay him.'

Giles had changed all our lives for the better. For now my uncle would walk down the aisle with Lucie on his arm, as a father should. My aunt and uncle would set up home again, allowing Giles and Lucie to start their married life in the way he desired. An added benefit, achieved without anyone being the wiser.

I asked where Giles was now, but he didn't know. 'I expected him to return with me, but he said if the revenue cutter stopped the boat, it wouldn't do for him to be caught with a gang of French smugglers.'

'But it was all right for you,' I said, amused.

'Better that than the guillotine.'

This method of execution, brought into use the previous year, had been invented by a man called Guillotin, as a means of despatching condemned prisoners in a swift, humane manner. My uncle explained to me how the victim was tied to a plank and pushed into position, whereupon a sharp blade plummeted earthwards, severing the head, which dropped into a basket. First used on common criminals the previous August, a machine had been set up in the place du Carrousel, where three prominent royalists had soon lost their heads.

'Whenever some important person was guillotined, the prison guards were only too eager to give me the news,' he said. 'Not that I am important, but those ruffians think all landowners are rich.' I shuddered at the thought of him suffering this terrible fate, and he put a comforting hand on my arm. 'Don't upset yourself, my dear. I've lost my estate, but I still have my life, thanks to Giles. Believe me, I could not wish for a finer son-in-law.'

Thankfully, the loss of his estate had not left him totally penniless. 'The proceeds from the sale of our London home are still with Coutts bank,' he said. 'I wanted something to fall back on if I failed to make a success of the French estate. It will be enough to buy a modest house, smaller than before of course, as we shall need some capital to live on. But we will have enough.' A proud man, he was telling me, in his own way, that he had no intention of being a drain on the resources of either Giles or myself.

Crossing his ankles in leisurely fashion, he turned his face up to the sun again, and we sat for a while in companionable silence. I don't know where his thoughts were, but mine were all with Giles, and I looked up to find my uncle watching me. 'What's bothering you, my dear?' he asked in concern.

'Oh, I was just wishing Giles would hurry home.'

He didn't say anything for a minute or two, then murmured, 'Drusilla, I must confess there is something I haven't told you.'

21

I turned to my uncle in alarm. 'What haven't you told me?'
'Giles had some business to attend to before he came
home.'

'Business? In France?' The Ledstone Place estates had no
business interests outside the Island that I'd ever heard of.

He nodded. 'That's what he said.'

Unable to even guess at what he was doing only increased
my fears for his safety. But I hid these anxieties as best I could
during what was otherwise a very happy time at Westfleet.
A steady stream of callers kept me busy, wanting to hear of
my uncle's dramatic rescue first hand, but he wasn't strong
enough to receive visitors yet, as I explained to Mr Arnold
when he looked in briefly on his way to dine with a friend in
Dittistone.

'I thought that's how it would be ma'am, but I couldn't
pass the door without saying how happy Mrs Arnold and I
were to hear the wonderful news.' I thanked him and he went
on soberly, 'May I ask - is it true that he came over on a smuggling run?'

I admitted it somewhat ruefully. 'You must forgive me
Mr Arnold, if I don't, in this instance, condemn the use of
free traders.'

He inclined his head. 'If it meant saving the life of a loved one, I would gladly deal with the devil, ma'am. Nor do I expect your uncle to betray those who helped him. But,' he went on a trifle awkwardly, 'they were *French* smugglers......'

'As was the man who stole the Saxborough ring, you mean?' Again he inclined his head. 'That has been on my mind too, but there must be many such gangs, I imagine, and I'm afraid my uncle could not tell you anything, even if he was willing. He said he was blindfolded before going on board, kept below during the run, and the men who rowed him ashore all had blackened faces.'

'I can't say as I'm surprised, ma'am. Smugglers don't give anything away to strangers.' And he soon went on his way.

I continued to smile upon all such visitors, even the parson and his wife. To them, and anyone who asked, I repeated the story my uncle had invented, keeping it as vague as I could. He was greatly touched by the messages I passed on from people he'd never met, promising to thank them personally when he was stronger. Meanwhile he was savouring the simple pleasures of life again. Being with his family, enjoying the sustaining broths Dr. Redding had prescribed, sitting in the sun listening to the birds, watching the bees and butterflies, and laughing at the antics of Jess who pounced on everything that moved.

The happiest sight for me was to see my uncle strolling slowly through the gardens with Aunt Thirza's hand tucked into one arm, and Lucie's into the other. And I left them to enjoy the pleasure of each other's company whenever I could.

On one such morning, when they went for a walk, I added to my charts the details of how the Saxborough ring had been found. And sat thinking about how Thomas and young Tom had died. When a local fisherman drowned, his body could come ashore quickly, or it might not be found for days, or weeks, and often not in an area where he was known. Yet the two Saxboroughs had been washed ashore within an hour or two of drowning, on the west of the island where everyone knew them, and in a state where they could be identified. It was all too easy, too convenient. As if the bodies were meant to be found.

Had they been drowned first, I asked myself with a shudder, and put on the beach to make it look as if they had been washed up? If so, where was the yacht?

And why had the smuggler stolen the ring? Had he done so against orders, greed overcoming all else? Father had taught me that things weren't always what they seemed; but in this terrible affair, nothing was what it seemed. Mr Saxborough's death appeared to be caused by jumping the east gate; Thomas and his son drowned, presumably when their yacht foundered. 'Accidents' planned and carried out with meticulous care. Plans spoiled, it would seem, by the greed of one French smuggler.

Had these smugglers murdered Cuthbert Saxborough too? If they had done so, why hadn't they taken the ring then? Why wait until they had killed two more Saxboroughs? That made no sense at all. But then none of it made any sense.

In the morning the spell of fine weather gave way to a ferocious gale, and I groaned in despair, conscious it would delay Jackson's attempts to contact French smugglers, and prevent Jacob appearing with a message.

It didn't rain, but the violence of the wind whipped the seas into such a tumult that for three days no boat was able to cross the Solent, leaving us without newspapers, or letters, to tell us what was happening outside the Island.

On the third day, the gale finally blew itself out. That evening Julia had asked me over for a cosy chat, and before leaving home I strolled round my garden inspecting the damage caused by the gale. The gardeners, having cleared the fallen branches, were tidying up shrubs and flowers as best they could after so severe a battering, but sadly many were past saving, and as I rode over to Julia's, the wind began to get up again. I didn't take Mudd with me for so short a distance, but told him to come over at ten to accompany me home, and in the event I was very glad I did so.

Once Edward had been taken off to bed, I told Julia about my uncle's escape, which she listened to goggle-eyed.

'Well, that is something exciting to tell Richard in my next letter.' With a sigh, she added, 'I must tell him about the Saxborough ring too.' Tears welled in her eyes, and she quickly brushed them away. 'I keep thinking about Tom - he was such an agreeable boy, with so much to look forward to, and he never had a life at all.' When I mentioned there was still no sign of wreckage from the yacht, she suggested, 'Perhaps the French took it to use for smuggling.' I sat staring into the fire for a moment, not having thought of that.

Around ten Julia sent a message to the stables, where Mudd was waiting. The wind had increased in the past hour, and as I looked out the window at the swaying trees, thinking we were in for another gale, I noticed a faint light bobbing about in the distance. Pointing it out to Julia, I asked what she made of it.

'It's probably smugglers,' she said without interest. As we stood watching, the light suddenly disappeared. 'Oh well, it's gone now,' Julia said.

'Yes, but it was near Smith's farm and he's been hiding smuggled goods on my land. This could be my chance to catch him red-handed—'

'You're not going down there at this time of night, surely.'

'It's my property, Julia.'

'I really don't think you should go. Smugglers don't take kindly to interference - not from anyone.'

'Don't worry, I'll keep well out of sight. If smuggled goods are being taken on or off my land, I'll send for the Riding Officer.' I hoped it wouldn't be too difficult to find Thorpe at this time of night.

Julia walked out the house with me, and as I took Orlando's reins from Mudd and climbed into the saddle, she urged, 'Take good care of her ladyship, Mudd. Come back here if you need help.'

There was enough moonlight for me to see my groom's eyebrows shoot up, and when I told him what I'd seen and that I intended to find out if Smith was involved, he gazed out towards the coast and said respectfully, 'I can't see a light, my lady.'

'No, it's gone now, but it was there.'

Waving goodbye to Julia, we set off down the drive and headed for the coast, but on reaching the cliff top, there was still no sign of the light. The south westerly wind was strengthening rapidly, breakers thundered onto the shore, and then the moon emerged from behind a cloud, and I saw what the darkness had kept hidden. A small brig, driven into Hokewell Bay by the gale, was listing badly. I guessed it had struck the underwater ledge that ran along this part of the coast, and that the light I'd seen had come from this vessel, before it began to heel over.

Ferocious, towering waves, whipped up by the wind, smashed into the stricken ship, sending columns of spray hurtling high into the air. Thinking of the men on the brig, I shouted above the wind, one hand clinging to my hat, 'John, fetch Mr Thorpe. I'll get help from Smith's farm.'

'He'll be at the inn this time of night, my lady.'

'His sons might be home. They'll be of more use than their father.'

As he galloped along the cliff top, I leant down to open the gate at the back of Smith's farm, walked Orlando through, closed the gate and cantered up to the house. Riding past the pond I saw the water overflowing onto the surrounding grass. I'd caught Smith with smuggled goods at last. But I didn't stop. The men on the brig were fighting for their lives.

Reaching the farmhouse, I rapped on the door with the top of my riding whip, but did not dismount. Smith opened it, tankard in hand. When he saw me his eyes widened, and he quickly wiped his mouth with the back of his hand. I wrinkled my nose in disgust, for his clothes were filthy, he stank of ale, and he wouldn't be much use if he was drunk.

'Where are your sons?' I demanded.

'Well, the young ones are in bed, and my two eldest are out courting.'

I groaned inwardly. 'Well, you'll have to do. You have a rope on the farm?'

He eyed me warily. 'All farmers have ropes, my lady.'

'Fetch it then. And come with me.'

'Why? Where are we going?' When I told him about the brig his face lit up. 'I'll fetch my coat, my lady. We can't let those poor devils drown can we.' It wasn't the sailors he was thinking of, as I well knew, but the cargo they carried, and how much money he could make.

I had never seen him move so fast. He was outside in less than a minute, and ran off to the barn, quickly returning with a long rope.

'What do you use that for?' I asked.

'I always has a good rope my lady, in case of shipwrecks,' he told me innocently. 'What with me being so near the coast.' I had no doubt he used it for hauling tubs up the cliff, but I said nothing. He looked up at me, a hint of slyness creeping into his voice, 'My wife's sending one of the boys to the village to rouse the good folk there, so there's no need for you to stay, my lady. What I mean is, there'll be things not fit for you to see. Dead bodies aren't a pretty sight.'

'Don't waste your breath, Smith. I've no intention of going home.' He glowered and protested, only quietening down when he saw I meant what I said.

I didn't tell him I'd sent Mudd to find the Riding Officer, fearing he would refuse to come, for Thorpe would stop any looting of cargo. I made Smith keep up with me as I rode back across the farm, going just fast enough to force him to run, still carrying the heavy rope.

When we reached the cliff top he was gasping for breath, and I stopped for a moment. The wind, still increasing in strength, nearly tore my hat off. The ship was leaning at a perilous angle now, being pounded by monstrous seas. As I watched, one wave bigger than all the rest sent it clean over on its side.

Moonlight illuminated things I will never forget, and would have given much not to see. Men struck by pieces of wreckage, others jumping into the water, or engulfed by gigantic breakers, and worst of all, the piercing screams carried to us by the gale.

Smith yelled above the wind, 'This is no place for you, my—'

'I told you before, I'm staying.'

'You shouldn't be out alone this time of night.'

I stared down at him. 'Are you threatening me?'

'Not me, my lady. I'm just thinking of your safety.'

I didn't answer him. There was something red in the sea about half way between the ship and us. I shouted, 'There's a man in the water.' I pointed, and saw from his face that he'd spotted the man too. 'Come on,' I urged. 'Let's get down to the beach.'

The chine at Hokewell Bay was almost directly behind Smith's farm and we were soon on the sands. Orlando was used to the beach, and the thundering of the waves didn't worry him. He wouldn't let me down. Smith was a different matter, yet he was the only hope this man had. I would do what I could, but I didn't have a man's strength, and that's what was needed here.

As we hurried along the beach Smith drew my attention to two bodies floating face down in the water. We couldn't help them, and if they had tried to swim ashore and failed, what chance did this other man have?

I ordered Smith to give me the rope, and he handed it up, quite unconcerned. I tied one end round the pommel of my sidesaddle just as Smith, who was watching the breakers, yelled, 'There he is, coming in on a wave.'

This was what I had been hoping for. Only as everyone who lived on this coast well knew, the wave might bring him in, but the savage undertow would just as quickly drag him back out again. I'd heard many tales of men who thought themselves safely on shore, only to be viciously drawn back into the sea and never seen again. It had almost happened to me too, after Smith felled me with that piece of cliff.

Now this man was fighting for his life as I had done, and I was determined he would survive. I gave Smith the other end of the rope, urging him to tie it round his waist. 'When the wave brings that man in,' I shouted, 'grab him.'

'Me?' he gulped, his eyes almost popping out of his head. 'I c-cant. The undertow will get me. I'll drown.'

'Not if you tie the rope securely. Orlando will pull you back if you get into trouble.'

He began to bluster, 'But - but - I'll have to take my shirt off, and that wouldn't be seemly in front of your ladyship.'

'This is a crisis Smith, and I am willing to put up with it.'

He stood there, ashen-faced in the moonlight, wringing his hands. 'I can't do it by myself. I can't.'

'You won't be on your own, Smith. I'm here.'

He was visibly shaking, but he didn't try to run off, knowing I would stop him. 'If you don't help this man he'll drown like the others.'

Smith turned to me, his eyes stretched wide with terror. 'I don't care if he drowns. He's nothing to me, is he. I've got a wife and ten children to feed. I'm not going in that water.'

'For once in your life Smith, do something useful. You won't drown. Orlando and I will keep you safe.' He watched the breakers thundering relentlessly onto the beach, looked back at me, and quite suddenly, his legs buckled under him, and he sank onto the sand in a crumpled heap. He had fainted.

He was safe enough for the minute, and slipping from the saddle, I picked up the coil of rope Smith had dropped, and walked Orlando close to the water's edge, where terrifying, mountainous waves crashed onto the sand with such force I could feel the power of them through the very soles of my feet. Orlando whinnied a little in alarm, and I put my head against his to calm him.

As the next big wave rose and rushed towards us, I gazed out past it to where I'd last seen the man swimming. The wind kept blowing my hair across my face, but I caught a brief glimpse of red, losing sight of him once more as the next wave began to draw itself up to a terrifying height. I glanced up at the empty cliff top, wishing Thorpe would make haste, and as the sea receded, walked a yard or two forward on the wet sand.

My skirts, already sodden from the spray, clung to my legs and the wind had finally claimed my hat, sending it flying toward the cliffs like a large exotic bird. I waited anxiously, moving my feet constantly to stop them sinking into the wet sand. The wave began to curl over at the top, slowly at first, before racing forward at a frightening speed, sweeping the man in. I knew I only had this one chance to save him.

The terror I'd felt when I'd almost drowned on this beach, the despair, the bursting lungs, were all so vivid in my mind, I ran a little further into the foaming sea, and as he hurtled forward, I threw the rope towards him with every ounce of strength I possessed. Turning quickly, I hastened back to the water's edge, still clinging to Orlando reins.

Somehow the man caught the rope, and he hung onto it, even when the savage undertow strove to drag him back into the sea. Hundreds of little stones and shells rocketed past him through the wet sand into the bottom of the next breaker, but the instant that wave began to curl over, I walked Orlando slowly away from the sea, pulling the man safely onto the shore.

The seaman lay on his back gasping for breath, his chest heaving. Kneeling beside him, I rolled his body over, and when he finally stopped coughing and spluttering, I helped him to sit up. He began thanking me volubly in French, speaking far too quickly, the wind whipping away much of what he said. Father had not had a flair for languages, and having educated me himself, French was not my strong point either. I looked back out to sea for more survivors, and the man shook his head at me, using a word I recognised.

'Mort?' I repeated, and he nodded. I thought they probably were all dead, as he said; it was incredible that anyone had survived at all.

He started talking again, and I was trying to make sense of it when Mudd and Mr Reevers galloped onto the beach. Mr Reevers, having bumped into Mudd on his way home, had come to help. 'Thorpe's not far behind with his men.'

'It's too late I think,' I said. 'This Frenchman says all the others are dead.'

Mr Reevers glanced at the two bodies, then at Smith, a perplexed expression on his face. 'Isn't that your bad tenant?'

'Regrettably,' I admitted.

'Is he hurt?'

'No. He fainted.'

At which point Smith came to with a groan, sat up, scratched his head, looked at the sea, remembered why he was there, and leapt up. To stop him running off, I directed him to take Orlando up to the top of the beach and look after him.

When the Frenchman began talking again, Mr Reevers answered him in fluent French, before turning to me. 'He says you saved his life.'

'I threw him a rope, that's all. Fortunately he held on to it.'

Eyeing me thoughtfully, he looked at the breakers crashing onto the sand, and said, 'He wishes to express his gratitude.'

'Tell him I was glad to do it.' He was a Frenchman, and our enemy, but I could not have stood by and watched him drown.

The Frenchman told Mr Reevers the captain had been washed overboard by a huge wave. The brig had come from

Bordeaux, and was breaking up when he left it. He thought the cargo, French wine, would be lost too. Not the news Smith hoped to hear. Nor was that the end of Smith's troubles on this night, although he didn't yet know it.

Heavy clouds began to obscure the moon just as Thorpe came onto the beach with eight men, all carrying flaming torches. I quickly apprised him of the situation, and he asked the Frenchman a few questions, with Mr Reevers's assistance. The man was shivering uncontrollably now, and Mr Reevers said to Thorpe, 'If I take him back to Ledstone, you can interrogate him in the morning.' This being agreed, Mr Reevers explained it all to the sailor, then bowed in my direction. 'Your servant, ma'am.'

Only then did I become conscious that my clothes were saturated, and my hair a mass of knotted tangles. Mr Reevers must have noticed too, but all he said was, 'I hope to see you soon in happier circumstances.' Climbing into the saddle, he reached down and hauled the Frenchman up behind him as if he weighed no more than a baby.

When I told Thorpe I believed Smith had smuggled goods in his pond, his eyes gleamed with satisfaction. 'Is that so, ma'am?' He glanced towards my tenant, cowering further along the beach. 'I must keep watch for bodies or cargo coming ashore. Still there's no reason why I can't deal with Smith first.' He smiled, a look of understanding in his eyes. 'Would you like to witness what happens, ma'am?'

'I would,' I returned emphatically. I was wet and shivering with cold, but I had waited a long time for this moment, and I had no intention of missing it now.

Thorpe beckoned to Smith, who reluctantly led Orlando over. As I took the reins, the Riding Officer told Smith, 'I'm going to search your farm for contraband.'

'What now?' I could hear the panic rising in his voice.

'Yes,' Thorpe said. 'Right now.'

'B-but it's too dark. And the moon won't come out again, if that's what you're thinking. It's clouded right over. Best come back in the morning.'

'You're forgetting my men have come equipped,' Thorpe said, indicating the flaming torches.

'But you need them here. Saving lives is what you should be doing. Lives is more important than tubs of brandy Mr Thorpe, even if they are Frenchies. Besides, I haven't got anything hidden on my farm.'

'In that case, you have nothing to worry about, have you.'

Smith whined, 'It's all right for you, but I've got to get up early in the morning.'

'Then the sooner we start the better.'

22

Thorpe called his men together, left two on the beach to watch for bodies or cargo coming ashore, before leading the others up the chine and through the gate on to Smith's farm. I followed on horseback, accompanied by Mudd. Smith, although concerned by this development, wasn't as anxious as I'd expected, convinced perhaps that no-one would think of looking in the pond. But when the Riding Officer headed straight for it, I thought Smith was going to faint again. Thorpe's men circled the pond, holding the flaming torches aloft to give the best light, at which point Smith gave up protesting his innocence.

'Who informed on me?' he demanded angrily. 'I've a right to know.'

Thorpe glanced at me, and I said, 'You've forfeited whatever rights you had Smith. But you may as well know -- I informed Mr Thorpe.'

'You?' he gasped. 'But - how - ' I told him what I'd noticed about his pond, the sediment being higher than it should have been, that the water was sometimes quite low, yet at other times it overflowed, which it was doing now.

'It was quite simple really,' I said, not bothering to hide my satisfaction. 'I warned you what would happen if you disobeyed me.' He glared up at me, sullen and uncommunicative now. 'Still, you needn't worry about your wife and children. They will do very much better without you. And it's not just hiding smuggled goods you have to worry about. Attempted murder is a capital offence, and- ------'

'Murder?' he echoed, startled and alarmed. 'That had nothing to do with me. It was those Guernsey smugglers who threatened to throw you over the cliff. I didn't know anything about that until----'

'I'm not talking about that. When I was on Hokewell beach you knocked me out with a chunk of cliff and I nearly drowned.'

I heard his sharp intake of breath. 'You said that was an accident----' I explained why I knew it wasn't and his voice rose with fear. 'That wasn't me, I swear.'

'Do you really expect me to believe that? I left Orlando tied to your gate.'

He stared at me, his face a ghastly white. 'I didn't know that.'

I shrugged with indifference, for Smith was an habitual liar. Turning to Thorpe, I expressed my sincere thanks and left him to get on with his job. Smith was still protesting his innocence when Mudd and I rode off. Even in the darkness, I could see Mudd was grinning.

'I do believe you enjoyed that, John.'

'Well, my lady, it was the look on his face when he learnt you had spotted the stuff was in the pond,' he chortled.

'Yes, I found that rather satisfying myself.'

'If I may so my lady, his lordship himself couldn't have handled it better.' I thanked him, for there could be no higher praise. But riding back along the cliff top, I looked out at the wrecked French brig, and thinking of the men who had drowned, Smith's arrest did not seem quite so important.

Those seamen were our enemies, yet they all had families; mothers, wives, children.

Dismounting outside the front door, I handed Orlando over to Mudd's care and went indoors. The hall clock showed it was after one, the candles were low in their sockets, and everyone, except my butler, had gone to bed. He had fallen asleep in a chair, and I gazed at him in fond amusement, for in general he didn't fuss, yet he would never retire to bed until I came home.

When I called his name softly, he woke immediately, jumping up in some confusion. 'I didn't hear you come in, my lady.'

I smiled at him. 'You shouldn't have waited up, Jeffel. You knew I had Mudd with me.'

'Yes, my lady, but I wouldn't have had a wink of sleep. Why, you might have been set upon and robbed.'

Refraining from pointing out he'd managed to doze in an uncomfortable hall chair while waiting for me, I explained briefly about the shipwreck. Horrified though he was, he couldn't hide his delight that I'd caught Smith out. 'You'll be better off without him, my lady. He always was a trouble-maker.'

Catching a glimpse of myself in the hall mirror, I saw my hair was a mass of tangles, and there was a large salt tidemark on my riding dress. When I began to shiver again with the cold, Jeffel insisted on making me a warming drink of hot milk and brandy. I drank it with relish, feeling better for it. I wouldn't let him call my maid, as it would have taken her an hour to sort my hair and I was exhausted. Going to my bedchamber, I simply peeled off my damp clothes, slipped on a warm nightdress, and climbed into bed. As I drifted into sleep, I wondered what my father would have made of tonight's exploits, and decided he would have approved.

The following morning the wind had moderated to a gentle breeze, and it was raining steadily. I badly needed to take a bath, and by the time the servants had brought up enough cans of hot water, and my maid had washed and untangled my hair, half the morning had gone.

I went downstairs to join my aunt, uncle and cousin for, what was for me, a late breakfast. By then they knew of the shipwreck, although I didn't mention my part in it until my aunt had poured herself a cup of coffee and buttered some toast. She listened in silent approval at first, but the instant I said I'd gone on to the beach, the storm clouds began to gather. I played down my part in the French sailor's rescue, but even so, she burst out, 'For heaven's sake Drusilla, you should have left that to the men. Why, your petticoats must be utterly ruined.' To which even my uncle laughed heartily.

Fortunately, I was saved from a further rebuke when Jeffel came in to inform me Mr Arnold had called, and was awaiting me in the library. I found him standing, gazing out at the garden, and when he turned and bowed, I remarked that the garden was in a sorry state, the gale having ruined the flowers.

'Actually I was admiring your greenhouse ma'am,' he said, as I begged him to be seated. 'I built a small one for Mrs Arnold a few years back. She's very proud of her geraniums. Especially those she grew with seed from America.'

'How fortunate you are to have a relative living in America,' I observed, smiling. Jeffel came in then with refreshments. It was getting on for eleven, and while I didn't require anything, I knew Mr Arnold would have breakfasted hours ago. My visitor accepted a glass of wine and a freshly baked biscuit, before answering, 'I was saying to Mrs Arnold the other day that it must be eight years since her brother went to America. She soon corrected me mind, as wives do. It's ten years, not eight, she said, as if I should have known all along. Of course, she wishes John Delafield was here with us. She worries about him, especially when months go by without a letter from him.' As I sympathised, he accepted another biscuit. 'Still, I mustn't keep you talking about my family, ma'am. I came to thank you for your help in capturing Smith, and to assure you he is safely in custody.'

'Did he tell you who paid him?'

'No, ma'am. To be truthful, I doubt he knows who runs the gang. I'd dearly love to get my hands on the men in charge, but they're too clever by half to get caught.'

He told me the French brig had completely broken up, more bodies had come ashore, but none of the cargo, which he thought was lost. I advised him I also wanted Smith charged with attempted murder, explaining about the men who had attacked me in the mist, and how Smith had knocked me senseless at Hokewell Bay with that piece of cliff. He asked me a number of questions and promised to see it was dealt with in the proper manner.

After Mr Arnold had gone, I gave some thought as to what to do about Smith's wife and ten children. Crossing to the shelf where the estate records were kept, I took down the book in which I recorded the details of all my tenants, including the names and dates of birth of the children. Turning to the pages concerning Smith, I saw his eldest son would be twenty-one in three months time. He was a polite, sensible young man, quite unlike his father. Whenever I went to the farm, he and the brother closest to him in age were always hard at work, yet he was rather young to take on the tenancy.

I mulled the situation over for some time before coming to a decision, and wanting to inform the family of it immediately, I rode over to the farm straight after nuncheon, accompanied by Mudd. The rain had stopped by this time, although the skies were still leaden. I found Daniel, the eldest boy, mending a fence. He glanced up as I approached, an anxious look on his face. Putting the hammer down, he touched his forelock.

'I've got everything in hand, my lady. We'll manage very well without my father, if you'll let us stay.' And he pleaded, 'You won't turn us out, will you?'

I smiled. 'No, I shan't do that.'

He let out a long sigh, releasing all his pent-up strain. 'I won't let you down, my lady, I swear.'

'No, I don't think you will. If you do well here, I shall transfer the tenancy to you on your twentyfirst birthday. Provided you look after my land properly, and don't allow it to be used by smugglers, it will remain in your name.'

His eyes lit up, and as quickly clouded again. 'But when my father comes out of prison—?' 'Even then,' I assured him. In any case, Smith would be given a lengthy sentence for hiding contraband. I didn't mention he'd also tried to murder me, as I had no proof, and the family had already borne more than enough.

When we went back to the farmhouse to speak to his mother, she sent the younger children out to play, and begged me to be seated before daring to look at her son. His beaming face told her all was well, and I repeated to her what I'd told Daniel, conscious of the strain in her eyes and the bruises on her face.

Tears threatened, and she sank onto a chair, taking a minute to compose herself before owning, 'I've been that worried, my lady. What with Daniel being so young, I didn't know what was to become of us all.' But her mood quickly began to lighten at the prospect of life without her drunken bully of a husband. 'There'll be no more smugglers made welcome on this farm, my lady, you can be sure of that. My boys and I will see everything is done as you would wish.'

She hesitated a moment, and then said, 'When Jeremiah eventually gets out of prison, he'll want to come back here-------'

'No, I'm sorry, but I cannot allow that, Mrs Smith. He must find somewhere else to live.'

She looked at me as if I'd just handed her a bag of gold. 'You won't change your mind will you?' she asked worriedly. Smiling, I promised I would not, and left soon after, thankful that problem was solved, and that it had brought some happiness to that long suffering family.

Mudd and I rode down to the cliff top to see what was left of the brig, but the tide had covered it. The wind had eased off, the waves were significantly calmer; the only reminder of what had gone on here last night being the men salvaging wood from the wreck.

Luck was truly on my side that morning, however, for on making our way back to Westfleet we witnessed a scene I would never forget. We had just slowed to a walk to negotiate the steep descent from the Downs into Manor Lane, at which point we had an excellent view of the whole lane. It was ankle deep in mud from this morning's rain, and deserted, apart from the parson, who had reached the far end where the road dipped sharply downhill into the village.

Local boys often used this slope as a mud slide in wet weather, and had obviously done so today. For we saw Mr Upton take a few tentative steps down the slope, and almost at once slip out of control, lurching forward a little, then equally unsteadily backwards, waving his arms about as he tried to save himself. For one brief moment he seemed to regain his footing, until a sudden gust of wind upset that delicate balance, causing him to fall onto his derriere, skewing sideways as he slid slowly down the hill.

As he flailed about at the bottom, trying to get back on his feet, a farm cart came past, splattering him liberally with mud. The driver of the cart jumped down, assisted Mr Upton to his feet, and tried to help him on to his cart, no doubt meaning to see him safely home, even though it was only a short distance. But the parson's boots must have been caked in mud, for his foot slipped on the step of the cart, and he fell face down in the mud. By now I was laughing so much I couldn't speak, and Mudd was little better.

'We shouldn't laugh, my lady,' he chortled, making no effort to hide his own mirth.

'No ---- and I wouldn't,' I gasped, holding my sides. 'If only he wasn't so full of his own importance.' When I related the tale over dinner even my aunt laughed heartily, having fallen out with Mrs Upton through that lady's scandalmongering over Giles giving money to local smugglers.

Lucie then began speculating on how much longer Vincent and Piers would stay on the Island. 'It's more than three weeks since they arrived. And they only came for a week.' We had seen very little of them, as Vincent was enjoying visiting all old friends and haunts.

My aunt sniffed. 'It was a mistake to entertain them at Ledstone. Giles should have let them put up at the George, as Vincent undertook to do in his letter. He won't find it easy to get rid of them now. Vincent may seem charming, but in my experience black sheep never change their spots, and----'

she stopped, staring at us in bewilderment as we all fell about laughing. 'What have I said?'

Lucie mopped her eyes, still gasping for breath. 'Black sheep don't have spots, Mama.'

My aunt blinked at her, and then smiled. 'Oh well, you know what I mean. The thing is, Vincent's presence could spoil the wedding.' She turned to my uncle. 'Charles, you must speak to Giles about it.'

'My dear,' he protested mildly, 'I do not think---'

He was not allowed to complete the sentence. 'He's not obliged to invite them. Vincent chose his own way of life and-----'

I cut in, pointing out reasonably, 'Aunt, the wedding is still four weeks away, and I doubt he'll stay that long. After a year in America Vincent must find Island life very flat. I'm quite certain Piers does.'

Lucie agreed. 'He never looks as if he's enjoying himself. Vincent's quite different though.'

'Is he just as you expected?' I asked, smiling at her.

'Oh yes.' A heartfelt sigh escaped Lucie. 'He's exactly the kind of man who would give up everything for love.'

My aunt gave another sniff. 'You'll notice he very soon forgot such nonsense when he ran out of money.'

My uncle turned to her, his eyes twinkling, 'I don't recall money coming into the conversation when I made you an offer, my dear.'

'It wasn't my place to discuss money,' she said, her expression softening. 'My father dealt with such matters, as is only right and proper.'

'So, if I had been penniless would you have refused my offer?' he ventured in a jocular tone.

'If you had been penniless Charles, you would never have made me an offer. Let alone suggest I exchange my comfortable home for some flea-ridden hovel.'

Chuckling, my uncle slapped a hand across his knee. 'No, you're quite right. I should never have dared!'

'I meant Charles, it would not have been the act of a true gentleman. And that is something you have always been.'

There was an unaccustomed tremble in her voice, and I watched in astonishment as a faint flush rose on her cheeks. Although I knew she was fond of my uncle, I'd always assumed her marriage had been one of convenience. I tried to picture her as a young girl in love, as it seemed she must have been once, but my imagination refused to stretch that far. Yet she was right about my uncle. He was a kindly man, who despite treating those who worked for him with humanity and decency, had still lost everything to the Revolution. And, but for Giles, would have forfeited his life too. Not that my aunt knew that, of course. Nor did Marguerite, thankfully.

That evening I sat in my workroom going over the events of the day. With Smith arrested, his farm was now in good hands. My uncle was regaining his strength, and having taken his first ride since arriving at Westfleet, had come home with some welcome colour in his cheeks. Paddy, the horse I'd had saddled for him, was a quiet, placid animal, just what my uncle needed at this point in his recovery. Accompanied by my aunt and cousin, he had taken a gentle outing along the coast, and had announced his intention of riding up on the Downs next.

In the midst of these pleasant thoughts, my uncle put his head round the door. 'Are you busy, Drusilla? Or would you care for a game of chess?'

I smiled at him. 'Of course I'll play. My turn to win, I think.'

He laughed. 'Not if I can help it.' But this being one of those rare days when everything went right for me, for once I did win.

In the morning my uncle again went riding with Aunt Thirza and Lucie, while I visited one of my tenants. Approaching Hokewell on the way home, I reflected, as I had many times before, that even in the sunshine, the village had an ungodly appearance. Visitors to the Island did not linger here, and I could understand why. Riding through the village and out on to the stretch of road that led to Westfleet, I was about to break into a gallop when a large, burly fellow suddenly emerged from behind a tree and hailed me.

His seafaring clothes were far from clean, but it was the unkempt black beard and large scar running down the left side of his face that gave him a menacing appearance. If this was Jacob, the messenger, I thought, as I brought Orlando to a halt, no wonder Giles didn't want Marguerite to see him. He touched his forelock, and I gazed down at him, trying to hide my dismay at his appearance. 'You have a message for me?'

He grinned up at me, displaying a large gap in his upper front teeth. 'Mr Giles said to tell that frosty-faced old coot, Leatherbarrow, to meet him at the usual place at daybreak the day after tomorrow.' And turning on his heel, he strode off.

Ignoring the manner of the message, I called after him. 'Wait.' He stopped, and looked back at me. 'Is that all?' I demanded.

'It is. Mr Giles never says more than he needs to.' And he went on his way.

This last remark puzzled me. If Jacob merely told Leather-barrow when to bring the yacht, what did it matter how much Giles said? Secrecy was essential after my uncle's rescue, but Jacob's comment implied Giles always wanted his messages kept quiet. Or was I reading too much into a simple remark?

Nevertheless we went straight to Ledstone, by way of Manor Lane and the Downs, where I urged Orlando into a gallop. Clattering into the stable yard at Ledstone, I dismounted just as Leatherbarrow emerged from the stables, and I was easily able to pass on the message.

The relief on his face was palpable. 'I'll set off at once, my lady. The tide will be about right in two hours.'

'Won't you be missed?' I asked in concern.

He shook his head. 'Mr Giles always leaves strict orders that I'm to keep his yacht in good order while he's away. I work on it sometimes when he's home, sleeping on board for a few nights, then no-one thinks it odd if I do so when he's away.'

'I see,' I said thoughtfully, recalling occasions when I had commented on Leatherbarrow's absence and had been told exactly that. Giles, as always, had every tiny detail worked out.

Passing on the message lifted a great weight from my shoulders. Giles was safe and well, and would soon be back home. I had not admitted, even to myself, how very worried I had been.

Catching sight of my godmother strolling alone in her garden, I went to join her. 'Drusilla,' she exclaimed gaily, holding out both hands to me. 'How delightful. When I saw someone riding towards the stables, I was afraid it was that dreadful Mr Reevers.'

Laughing, I returned her greeting. 'What has he done to upset you now ?' I inquired, as we walked past the house to her rose garden.

'He seems to have taken over the whole estate, making the decisions, just as if—'

'Giles did ask him to look after things while he was away.'

She sniffed. 'Yes, I suppose so. Oh, I do so wish Giles would come home. At dinner I have to converse with three gentlemen, two of whom I detest.' She eyed me speculatively. 'You wouldn't care to dine with us tomorrow----?' She stopped and put a hand to her mouth. 'Oh I forgot, the gentlemen are all dining with the Arnolds tomorrow. Come the day after -- Friday. And bring Lucie.' I assured her, quite truthfully, that I would be delighted, and felt certain Lucie would too. She relaxed, only to beg a moment later, 'You won't change your mind will you?'

I went off into a peal of laughter. 'Of course not. I shall enjoy it.'

Reaching her rose garden, we sat on one of the long seats, and I complimented her on the brooch she was wearing. 'Is it new? I don't remember seeing it before.'

'Well, actually, Vincent gave it to me.'

I blinked in surprise. 'It looks rather expensive.'

She giggled, pleased. 'I imagine it is. He wanted to show his gratitude for Cuthbert's help all those years ago. He brought it all the way from America you know.'

Removing the brooch, she handed it to me. It was delicately made in the shape of a heart, fashioned in diamonds and rubies in a gold setting, the workmanship of the highest quality. 'It is truly beautiful,' I said, a trifle enviously, as I returned it to her.

She pinned it back onto her dress. 'I think so, and I do love pretty things. Whenever Cuthbert came back from London he always brought me some little trinket.'

I started to laugh. 'My dear, dear godmother, you do not possess anything as trifling as a mere trinket. Pearl necklaces, gold bracelets, rings and brooches galore, even a diamond tiara, but-----'

'I have been lucky haven't I,' she admitted artlessly. 'Cuthbert gave me the tiara after Giles was born. I'd always wanted one, and he was so thankful I'd come through the birth safely he said I could have anything I desired.'

'That was a little rash of him, wasn't it. You might have asked for something out of his reach.'

'Oh no. I've always been quite sensible you know, Drusilla.' I bit my lip, struggling with myself briefly; 'sensible' was not a word I had ever associated with my adored godmother. When I gave way to a peal of mirth, she giggled. 'Oh well, perhaps not always, but I knew how to go about getting what I really wanted.'

I choked. 'Now that, I do believe.'

A word of encouragement soon had her relating how she came by most of her jewellery, and I was still listening, wrapped in admiration, when Vincent came to join us. I welcomed him with a smile. 'Have you come out to enjoy the sunshine?'

'One must I think Lady Drusilla, we see so little of it here,' he said, executing an exquisite bow.

Marguerite patted the place beside her, and Vincent obediently sat down. 'I have some good news,' she told him. 'Drusilla and Lucie are to dine with us on Friday.' He responded with all his usual charm, pulled an elegant gold box from his pocket, flipped it open, and took a pinch of snuff, listening attentively as my godmother promised, 'I shall order a lemon tart especially for you, Drusilla. Then I can be sure of your company, even if it rains.'

'With a lemon tart on offer, you can be sure of my company even if it snows.' I had been talking for well over an hour, and when I stood up to take my leave, Vincent insisted on escorting me to the stables.

He chatted in his engaging way about how much things had changed at Ledstone since his childhood, and as we strolled back past the house, I noticed Piers sitting in the library, his back to the window, industriously writing. He was wearing one of the maroon coats he favoured, which showed off his blond hair to advantage, and I found myself thinking it a great pity Piers did not possess his father's charm and impeccable manners. Or perhaps, I reasoned charitably, he was one of those people who found it easier to express his feelings in a letter. I didn't know if that was true, but today I was ready to think the best of anyone, now I knew Giles would soon be home.

I decided to watch Leatherbarrow sail out of Yarmouth, aware I would feel even happier once I had seen him go on his way. Riding through Dittistone we passed the cottage where Mudd senior lived, and my groom said his father was asking around about the dead French smuggler.

'He knows some of the Frenchies, my lady.'

'That is good of him, John,' I said, for as Jackson had told me, a mere war did not appear to interfere with the serious business of smuggling. 'Does your father speak French?'

'He's picked up a smattering over the years, my lady. I remember him bringing back a French newspaper once, thinking I could read it to him. Of course, being in French, I couldn't make head nor tail of it.' And he chuckled merrily.

'He never did understand why I could read English, but not French.'

He shook his head, still grinning, and I recalled how, when I was six, father had caught me trying to teach Mudd the words in one of my books. I had been told to stop pestering the poor fellow and leave him in peace. But Mudd said I wasn't pestering him, and he'd always wanted to read. Father, a great believer in helping people to improve themselves, offered to teach him. Mudd, a quick learner, was soon reading books and newspapers, but turned down father's suggestion that he could find a more rewarding career, insisting there was nothing more rewarding than working with horses. Ever since that time, all our newspapers were passed on to Mudd. Despite Aunt Thirza's warning that it didn't do for servants to get above themselves.

Soon we were climbing the rise, from the top of which were some excellent views. Hills rolled majestically to the east, while ahead lay the Solent, where on a day like this, there would be vessels of all sizes to be seen, from fishing boats to men o' war fresh out of Portsmouth Harbour, to ships bound for America and other distant parts of the world. I didn't expect to see Giles's yacht yet, realising Leatherbarrow was probably still making his way out of the river Yar.

Just before the top of the rise, passing a track that led to Dell Farm, I saw a movement out of the corner of my eye. Stopping abruptly, I turned Orlando into the narrow tree-lined track. Some twenty yards ahead of me, on a patch of grass, lay an inert figure. Kneeling beside him, holding a hefty piece of stone aloft over the man's head, was Mr Reevers. I recognised the unconscious man instantly. It was Leatherbarrow.

23

For a moment or two I felt sick. Then, resolutely urging Orlando forward, I ordered Mr Reevers to drop the stone at once. But even as I spoke, Mudd brushed past me, pushing my horse under the trees, where my hat became caught up in the overhanging branches. Muttering angrily about interfering servants, I disentangled myself, to find Mudd had placed himself between Mr Reevers and myself.

'Best do as her ladyship says sir,' he advised impassively.

Although badly shaken by the scene in front of me, I insisted, 'I will deal with this, John.'

Mr Reevers put the stone down, and raising his head, met my gaze squarely. 'Yes, I can see how it must look,' he murmured, in unruffled understanding. 'But the fact is I was on my way to Norton House when I heard a horse whinnying in distress. I turned off the road and found Leatherbarrow exactly as he is now. This stone was beside him, and I was checking it for blood when you arrived.'

'I see,' I whispered, more relieved than I cared to admit.

Leatherbarrow hadn't moved, and his face was deathly white. 'Is he alive?' I asked apprehensively.

'He's still breathing, but badly hurt, I believe. He needs a---'

'Yes,' I broke in, and said to Mudd. 'Find Dr. Redding and---.'

Mudd looked at me in horror. 'I can't leave you here, my lady.'

Mr Reevers spoke with quiet authority, 'Your concern does you credit Mudd, but whoever attacked Leatherbarrow has gone now. Lady Drusilla will be quite safe with me.' Mudd looked at me for approval and I gave it, urging him to hurry, and to tell the doctor we were taking the groom to Dell Farm.

He rode down the track, turned towards Dittistone where the doctor lived, and with one quick anxious glance back at me, galloped off. Mr Reevers, still kneeling beside the groom, removed a pistol from the pocket of his riding coat, put it on the ground, took off the coat and tucked it round the unconscious man. 'We must get him into the warm quickly. Where is this farmhouse?'

I pointed towards a small copse. 'About a hundred yards down the track on the other side of those trees.'

He nodded, picked up the firearm, and I watched in utter disbelief as he pointed it in my direction, and walked towards me. 'You know, a sensible woman would have ridden straight past,' he said softly. 'Or sent her groom to investigate.'

As he stood beside Orlando, his white shirt ruffled by the breeze, I gaped at him, too shocked to speak. I couldn't believe this was happening. Every instinct I possessed had told me to trust this man. He watched me intently with cold eyes, waiting for me to answer, but I couldn't. My mouth was too dry.

'Don't you have anything to say?'

Running my tongue round my lips, I whispered, 'Mudd knows-------'

'Yes, but you would still be dead. And a story about Leatherbarrow's attacker returning is easily concocted. Sending Mudd away was foolish.'

'He'll be back soon.'

'But not in time to save you. You should never leave yourself unprotected,' he murmured, levelling the pistol at me.

Desperately glancing towards the road, I tried gathering the reins, only for Mr Reevers to shake his head at me. 'I shouldn't. You'd never reach the road. Believe me, there is no way you can escape.'

Orlando, sensing my increasing distress, shook his head and whinnied. Mr Reevers, instinctively reassuring him, took his eyes off me for a split second, and I lashed out with my riding crop, sending the pistol flying through the air and out of his reach. Quickly urging Orlando sideways, I knocked Mr Reevers to the ground, seized the pistol I had taken to carrying with me lately, and pointed it at him with a surprisingly steady hand.

Mr Reevers got to his feet and brushed himself down. 'Very neatly done, ma'am. I must congratulate you, ' he said, employing his most disarming smile, and he took a step towards me. 'Stay where you are.'

He eyed me somewhat ruefully. 'I didn't realise I was that convincing,' he said. 'Yes, I know what you're thinking, but the truth is quite different. Forgive me for being blunt, but rushing straight into this kind of situation, as you did, is highly dangerous. I wanted to show you where that could lead, because next time you might not be so fortunate.'

'I - I don't believe you.'

'I can see that. It is true, nevertheless. Murderers do not stop to chat with their victims. If I had attacked Leatherbarrow, you would already be dead. I would only have waited until Mudd was out of earshot. I beg of you to take more care in future, Lady Drusilla.' He glanced down at the groom. 'We must see to Leatherbarrow. I'll stay------'

'No, you go. I'll stay here.'

His lips curled into a faint smile. 'Very well.' He lowered his voice. 'I told Mudd the assailant had gone, but he could be hiding in those trees. Leatherbarrow has a tidy sum of money on him, and I may have disturbed the man before he could take it. Please, be careful.'

Collecting his horse, quietly grazing under a tree, he rode off down the path to the farmhouse. Dismounting, I picked up the firearm from the ground, knelt beside Leatherbarrow and waited.

My hands were shaking, for I simply didn't know what to believe, and if Mr Reevers had lied, as I very much feared, then he wouldn't come back.

It was, therefore, a considerable relief to see him returning with three of the farmer's strapping grown-up sons. Between them they carried Leatherbarrow to the farmhouse, where they put him between clean sheets in one of the bedchambers. Within minutes Dr. Redding arrived, Mudd having found him at home for once. While the doctor was making his examination, I went outside to speak to Mr Reevers, determined to clear the air between us, but Mudd, who was waiting with our horses, told me he'd gone back to Ledstone. 'He said he couldn't do anything more here my lady, and thought to save you the unpleasant task of telling Mrs Saxborough the bad news.'

I was grateful for that, although he might have waited to hear the doctor's verdict first. Still, my godmother was easily alarmed and it was better that he recounted the incident in his calm, rational manner, before she heard a garbled version from anyone else. It was also one less problem I had to deal with, the most worrying of which was how to bring Giles back from France.

It would be simple enough if I knew where he was, as I could go in Leatherbarrow's place. But Leatherbarrow had spoken only in vague terms of a lonely spot on the Normandy coast, and locating Giles on the vast stretches of beach along that north coast would be impossible, unless I knew where to go. Going back indoors, I suddenly realised someone else did know. Jacob. The smuggler who'd brought the message.

Ten minutes later, the farmer's wife, a plump, sensible woman in her middle years, came into the room followed by the doctor, but my heart sank when I saw how grave he looked.

'Well ma'am, I have done what I can for Leatherbarrow, but the blow he received was a severe one.' He put his bag on the kitchen table. 'The attacker used a large stone, you said?'

'Yes, about twice the size of my hand.' I asked how long it might be before Leatherbarrow regained consciousness, if he was to recover.

He pursed his lips in thought. 'Impossible to say with any certainty, ma'am. Possibly not for a day or two, but he must on no account be moved again.' I nodded, having expected that. 'He'll be in excellent hands here.'

Mrs Ward, the farmer's wife, bobbed a curtsey. 'There's my two daughters and myself, your ladyship. We'll do all we can, you can be sure of that. I've known Will Leatherbarrow all my life, and there's not a finer man on the Island.'

'No, indeed,' I agreed.

'It'll be those murdering Frenchies who did this,' she burst out, her eyes filled with hatred. 'The ones that did for poor Mr Thomas and his boy. If I could get my hands on them, I'd make them wish they'd never left their heathen country.' I said quietly that I understood how she felt, and thanked her for allowing her daily life to be cut up, promising she would be suitably recompensed.

As Dr Redding and I walked out the house together he owned, 'In truth, there's very little I can do, but I've left instructions that I'm to be called if there is the slightest change. In any case, I'll look in again later today. What puzzles me is why he was set upon so violently. Was he robbed?' I shook my head, repeating what Mr Reevers had said about the groom having money in his pockets.

The doctor frowned. 'I can't see any local man being responsible. Leatherbarrow is too well liked, but I must say it has not been a good year for those who live at Ledstone Place.' Collecting his horse, he said the constable at Dittistone ought to be informed of the assault. I promised to see it was done, and he nodded. 'Well, if you'll excuse me ma'am, I must be on my way.'

Mudd led Orlando over to me, I climbed into the saddle, arranged the skirts of my riding habit neatly, and rode back up the track, stopping at the place where Leatherbarrow had been attacked. Leaving Mudd to look after the horses, I made a thorough search of the area. Although I already knew I would not find anything. A frustrating lack of evidence surrounded the deaths of the three Saxboroughs, and I was quite certain the attack on Leatherbarrow was connected with those murders.

As for Mr Reevers, I didn't know what to believe. A quick thinking man like him could turn most circumstances to his advantage. But one piece of his advice I did intend to take. I meant to be much more careful in future. And not only of dangerous situations.

Riding down to Dittistone to speak to the local constable, I told Mudd what the doctor had said about Leatherbarrow. 'When we reach Westfleet, I want you to go and see Jacob---'

'Jacob, my lady?' he repeated, as if he'd misheard.

'Yes. He lives at Blackgang.' Jacob's dark, menacing looks were well suited to that lawless village. 'Ask Jacob where Mr Giles will be waiting for Leatherbarrow. Then I can go in his place.'

Mudd's eyebrows shot up. 'Not on your own, my lady, surely?'

I had sailed with Giles occasionally, but had never liked being cooped up in a small space and I knew nothing about navigation. 'I'd prefer you to accompany me, but it's not an order. You may remain here if you wish.'

'As if I would, my lady,' he retorted indignantly.

Smiling, I thanked him, although I had known what his answer would be. 'Well, if you're sure. I mean to take Mr Giles's yacht, but we'll need a seaman with us. Someone who knows the Normandy coast, and who can be trusted not to talk about the trip.'

'My father knows the French coast like the back of his hand. He'd come like a shot.'

'Ask him then John, if you please.'

In Dittistone he stopped at his father's cottage while I spoke to the constable, who set off at once to make his own inquiries. Frankly, I did not expect him to make any progress.

Mudd was waiting outside when I left, and told me his father was very willing to come with us. As we rode past the church and village green, with its cluster of cottages, I asked Mudd why he'd pushed me under a tree when we first saw Leatherbarrow.

'I beg your pardon, my lady,' he began awkwardly. 'Only it looked as if Mr Reevers was attacking Leatherbarrow, and I promised his lordship I'd - er - try to see you didn't come to any harm, when he was no longer here.'

A lump came into my throat, for it was so exactly what my father would do, that I could almost hear him saying it. I swallowed hard. 'When was this?'

'About a year ago, my lady. When he was coming up to fifty. He said his own father had died at that age, and I think it was on his mind. In any case he said, he wouldn't be here for ever, and er - well, that's about all, I think---' and his voice trailed away into an embarrassed silence.

'I see,' I murmured dryly, knowing exactly what he'd left unsaid.

Father had not liked me to ride alone, his view being that, if I had an accident, it might be two or three hours before anyone was aware of it. I thought he was worrying unnecessarily, but to please him I had taken Mudd with me after that.

After father's death, however, I had reverted to my old ways, riding alone sometimes on short journeys and on my early morning rides. Until the incident with the cliff fall; since when I had not gone out alone, apart from the occasional mile long trip in daylight to see Julia. But, I was unaware of my father's concerns over his health. He hadn't mentioned any problems, and was rarely ill. In fact, on the morning of the day he'd died, he'd raced me to the top of a hill. He had been slow to regain his breath, but I hadn't thought anything of it at the time.

Mudd interrupted my thoughts. 'This trip to France, my lady,' he said worriedly, as we reached the Downs. 'What his lordship would have said about that, I dare not think.'

I looked at him. 'Knowing what I do John, what would he have said, do you think, if I then did nothing?'

He had no answer to that, and parting company at Manor Lane I went home, while he rode on to Blackgang. When I walked into the house a few minutes later, the look of relief on Jeffel's face made me smile.

'Oh dear, am I late for nuncheon?' I saw by the hall clock that I was, by almost an hour. At the sound of my voice, my aunt, uncle and Lucie came hurrying into the hall, and I told them only that Leatherbarrow had been attacked. Lucie, unaware Giles was in any danger, showed a natural warm-hearted concern for a servant she liked. My aunt began asking questions, and as she and Lucie were naturally looking at me, they did not notice my uncle's ashen face.

Catching him alone later, I said someone else would fetch Giles once we knew where he was waiting. I didn't say I was that someone, nor do I think that occurred to him, but he was very worried about Giles being stranded. 'I'll never forgive myself if anything happens to him, Drusilla.'

After nuncheon I went for a stroll in the garden to think of a way to explain why I was going away for a few days without taking my maid, when I saw Mudd returning. Walking over to the stables, I met him half way across the cobbled yard.

'Did you find him, John?'

'No, my lady. His wife said he wouldn't be back until tonight.'

I groaned. 'Where has he gone for heaven's sake? Did she tell you?'

'She said he was out on one of the fishing boats.'

'Something to do with smuggling no doubt.'

'I expect so, my lady.'

I stood thinking for a moment, and he waited for me to speak. 'We can't go to Normandy without knowing where Mr Giles is. We'd never find him. If you speak to Jacob tonight, we'll leave first thing in the morning.'

'Very good, my lady.'

That evening I played chess with my uncle in the library, and it was after nine when he, having won the deciding game, joined my aunt and cousin in the blue room, while I stayed to read the newspaper. I had barely picked it up when Jeffel came in to say Mudd wished to see me. I nodded. 'Send him in, please Jeffel.'

I saw from Mudd's face that the news was not good. 'Jacob was at home this time, my lady, but he doesn't know where the rendezvous is.'

'Doesn't know?' I echoed, dismayed. 'But he must.'

'He waits at a French inn, and Mr Giles sends him his orders there.' I closed my eyes in despair, cursing Giles and his secretive, meticulous planning. 'What will you do now, my lady?'

I sighed. 'I don't know, John. I'll think about it and let you know in the morning.'

After he had gone I studied a map of Normandy, looking for what Leatherbarrow had described to me. An isolated beach well away from any village. But, there were numerous such places along what had to be hundreds of miles of coastline. Leatherbarrow obviously had to know the rendezvous, but Jacob did not need to, so Giles hadn't told him.

I accepted I could not go, yet it wasn't a decision I made easily, for I felt that, somehow, I ought to be able to do *something*. Yet it was Giles who had made that impossible, and only my knowledge of him, and how he planned things, stopped me giving way to despair.

At that moment, my aunt, uncle and cousin, came in to say goodnight. At present, my uncle, on Dr. Redding's advice, retired to bed promptly at ten, and glancing at the library clock I saw it was almost that now. Aunt Thirza and Lucie soon left, but my uncle lingered for a few minutes, quietly urging, 'Try not to worry about Giles. He's no fool, my dear.'

'I know,' I sighed. But that night I had a terrible nightmare in which Giles was trying, singlehandedly, to fight off a horde of sans-culottes on a French beach.

When my maid drew back the curtains in the morning, the house was engulfed in thick fog, and going down to the stables after breakfast, I could see no more than a yard ahead of me. Which, as I said to Mudd, would have stopped us going to France this morning in any case, and made me feel marginally better.

Nor was there much sense in going out riding until it cleared, and I spent the morning in the workroom. Writing down how Leatherbarrow had been attacked, and thinking about the way Mr Reevers had acted.

The fog hung around well into the afternoon, at which point I rode over to Dell Farm, but Leatherbarrow was still unconscious, and I began to fear the worst. I slept badly that night and awoke again at daybreak, thinking of Giles waiting in vain on the beach. Jumping out of bed, I drew back the curtains to find an overcast sky, but the fog having completely gone, I went for a long ride before breakfast.

This being the day we were dining at Ledstone, Lucie and I, accompanied by Mudd, called in at Dell Farm on the way, learning from Mrs Ward that Leatherbarrow was showing signs of coming round.

'That is good news,' I said in huge relief, as she led the way up to his room.

'The doctor thinks it will be a day or two yet before he regains his senses properly,' she warned, opening the door of the bright bedchamber at the back of the house. A jug of fresh flowers stood on a table beside the bed, next to a basket of fruit, which Mrs Ward announced proudly, Mrs Saxborough had brought up herself.

I responded appropriately, and looking at Leatherbarrow detected a slight improvement in the colour of his face, but he did not open his eyes, and we soon left promising to call again the next day.

At Ledstone, Marguerite awaited us in the family drawing room, the gentlemen not yet having joined her, and she was delighted to hear Leatherbarrow was on the mend. 'I took a basket of fruit for him, you know.'

I smiled. 'Yes, we saw it.'

'Well, when he does comes round, I thought fruit might tempt him to eat. I find I can often manage a grape or two when I'm not feeling quite the thing, and I know Giles would want me to do everything I can for his groom.' She looked up at me. 'I've hardly slept these last two nights, thinking about it all. Still, there is one good thing to come out of it. I have rid myself of Mr Reevers.'

24

'What do you mean?' I gasped.

'He's gone to London to see Giles.'

'London?' And without thinking, burst out, 'But Giles isn't-----'

When I stopped, Marguerite gazed at me, puzzled. 'Isn't what, Drusilla?'

'Isn't likely to be in London much longer,' I said quickly, gathering my wits together.

Lucie gave me an odd look, but my godmother accepted my explanation without question. 'Oh well, he's gone anyway. When he told me about Leatherbarrow, I said how worried I was by what was happening at Ledstone. And I have been Drusilla, ever since the Saxborough ring was found round that smuggler's neck, and we realised poor Thomas and Tom had been murdered. Giles is ignorant of it all, and he should be told. He ought to be here. To tell the truth, I was in tears, and Mr Reevers said I was quite right. Which did surprise me, because we don't usually agree on anything. He insisted on leaving at once, promising me Giles wouldn't go after the murderers now, not with the wedding being so close.'

I stared at her, conscious only of a sinking feeling in my stomach. 'He left the same day?' She nodded happily. 'Within half an hour, on account of not wanting to miss the tide. He took Giles's boat too, it being much faster than his. I must say two whole days without that dreadful man has---' she stopped, for the door opened and the gentlemen came into the room.

They bowed, Vincent's graceful bearing sharply contrasting with his son's perfunctory civility, and the usual pleasantries had barely been exchanged when Parker came in to announce dinner was served. The dinner was good, as were all meals arranged by Marguerite, but I was too stunned by Mr Reevers's sudden departure to appreciate either the food or the conversation. As I sat toying with the piece of pie on my plate, puzzling over why he'd gone now, when he hadn't thought it necessary before, I became aware my godmother was speaking to me. Looking across at her, I forced a smile, and asked what she had said.

'I wondered why you hadn't tried the lemon tart, Drusilla,' she murmured. 'I had it made especially for you.'

I smiled. 'It looks absolutely delicious.'

She gazed at me in concern. 'Are you feeling quite the thing? You're very quiet tonight.'

Reassuring her, I tucked enthusiastically into a portion of the deliciously tangy tart, just as Lucie ask Piers how he liked the Isle of Wight now. To my surprise, he answered at some length. 'The coastal scenery interests me most,' he said. 'I hadn't realised how much the sea erodes the cliffs. At Blackgang I was told the edge of the cliff where I stood could be gone by next year.' He seemed to be making an effort to be civil, Lucie having hit on a subject that intrigued him, for there was no sign of his customary surliness.

Resolutely thrusting all other thoughts from my mind, I encouraged, 'If you come back next year, you'll see for yourself how much it has changed.'

'Perhaps I will.' And he almost smiled. 'I have been reading your excellent book on the Island, Lady Drusilla----'

'My father's book, Mr Saxborough.'

He inclined his head. 'Yes, of course. I had no idea there had been so many shipwrecks.'

'The coast, especially here on the back of the Island, can be really treacherous. Three American ships were lost on the underwater ledge in one year alone, and a French sloop was smashed to pieces under the cliffs at Dittistone.'

'Foreign ships, in bad weather,' he commented. 'It doesn't happen to local fisherman--- '

'In severe weather it can happen to anyone. At the end of May, the revenue cutter ran aground when chasing smugglers during a gale and was damaged beyond repair. '

Piers asked, 'Has the cutter been replaced?'

I nodded. 'By the 'Swan III.' ' And I explained the importance of the boat in Mr Arnold's fight to reduce smuggling on the Island. 'Some years ago, his official request for a fast cutter being turned down, he and one of his brothers-in-law funded one with their own money. Sadly it foundered in a gale within a month, and the Commissioners of Customs finally agreed to provide a replacement.'

Piers asked several questions about the Customs service, until Marguerite beseeched, with her most entrancing smile, 'Oh do let us speak of something else. Talking of boats always makes me feel queasy.' Everyone laughed, and we dutifully changed the subject.

I invited Vincent and Piers to call at Westfleet now that my uncle was well enough to receive visitors, and they promised to do so soon. The more I saw of Piers the less I liked him, but I couldn't leave him out of the invitation. Vincent, on the other hand, was a charming man, and exactly the companion Marguerite needed at this time. Like many a rebellious youth, he had become a man of sense in his mature years. He teased her fears away with kindness and patience, filling her days with amusing and interesting conversation. She would miss him when he went back to Italy, but she had the wedding to look forward to, the joy of living at Ledstone with Giles and Lucie, and the prospect of grandchildren.

Vincent, having visited all his old haunts and the friends from his youth, spent most of his time at Ledstone now. Which suited Marguerite perfectly, especially as Piers was invariably out touring the Island, usually with a sketchbook in his saddlebag. When the gentlemen rejoined us after dinner, Lucie asked Piers if she could see some of his sketches, but he insisted they were not fit to be shown in company.

At which my godmother declared, 'We're all family here, Piers. Well, Lucie soon will be, and Drusilla has always been like a daughter to me.'

Still he shook his head, until Vincent said in some amusement, 'I think you must fetch them, or you will offend the ladies.'

'If you insist,' he muttered abruptly, and left the room without a backward glance.

'I'm bound to own Piers is right,' Vincent admitted. 'He cannot draw. He hopes that, with perseverance, he may improve.'

Piers returned shortly with several sketches, all of coastal scenes, but his tendency to include every rock on a beach gave his drawings an unbalanced appearance. Nevertheless, I commented diplomatically, 'I admire anyone who can draw. I gave up the attempt by the time I was fourteen.' Lucie, in her kind-hearted way, found something to appreciate in them all, and my godmother said everything that was proper.

I suspected Piers used his sketching as an excuse for getting out of the house. The amiable pursuits enjoyed by his father, of genteel conversation with Marguerite, a stroll in the gardens, or a sedate carriage ride round the estate, were far too slow for a young man, and I imagined he would be thankful to leave the Island.

That evening, back at Westfleet, when everyone had retired for the night, I sat in the library puzzling over Mr Reevers's swift departure. I couldn't understand why he'd left for London in such haste. And I couldn't forget how I'd seen him bending over the groom, stone in hand. Or that awful moment when I thought he meant to shoot me. Nor could I help thinking of his desperate financial situation, or that, at the time of the murders, he must have thought himself next in line to inherit Ledstone, after Giles.

Yet he was also Giles's friend, entrusted with the care of Ledstone, and Giles's judgement was normally sound. So Mr Reevers might have been trying to warn me of the consequences of rushing impulsively into dangerous situations, and perhaps he had gone to London, believing it was time Giles returned. But what would he do when he discovered Giles wasn't there?

I kept mulling it all over in my mind, but the more I thought, the less sure I became of anything. There were too many uncertainties; too many questions I couldn't answer. Some of the more worrying thoughts kept me up for a long time gazing unseeingly into the waning library fire. At one point, I went into the workroom to look at the details I was sure of, for it was always useful to remind myself of irrefutable facts. But, as I was to find out much later, one fact I believed to be a cast iron certainty, couldn't have been more wrong.

The wedding was only three weeks away now. By then, I would surely know who was involved in the murders. A thought that made me tremble. For, while I wanted to know the truth, I was becoming increasingly afraid of what that truth might be.

Visiting Dell Farm the following morning, I found Leatherbarrow had regained consciousness at last, but it was another fortyeight hours before he was capable of answering questions. He was propped up in bed with several pillows, with a clean bandage round his head, his face white and strained. 'How are you feeling, Leatherbarrow,' I asked, sitting on the chair beside the bed.

'A bit weak my lady, but Mrs Ward said her chicken broth will soon set me to rights.' He glanced at the empty bowl on the bedside table. 'That's the third helping I've had today.'

He spoke in a way that made me ask, 'Do you like chicken broth?'

'Oh yes, my lady,' he answered, a little hesitantly.

'Only not three times a day?' He smiled rather sheepishly, and I said, 'I'll get Dr. Redding to speak to Mrs Ward. She'll listen to him.' He thanked me, and I asked if he felt up to telling me about the day he was attacked.

'All I remember is leaving Ledstone, my lady. After that - well - I've tried to think, but my head's so muzzy. The doctor says it will come back to me in time.' Concentration was obviously difficult, and not wishing to tire him, I did no more than ask where he was supposed to meet Giles. 'He wouldn't be there now, my lady. He told me he wouldn't wait more than a day. People notice strangers and he couldn't risk someone reporting him.'

This eased my mind more than I could say. I had wondered what Giles would do if the weather made it impossible for his groom to get to Normandy in time. I was sure he'd have some contingency plan, for Giles always did, and it was that hope I had clung to after Leatherbarrow's attack.

Even so, I put the obvious question, 'How will he get home?'

'That's what I asked him.' And he mumbled drowsily, 'He said it was better I didn't know.' His eyes were drooping, and having first made sure the blankets were well tucked in, I left feeling almost light-headed with relief.

I had a word with Dr. Redding as I'd promised, and when I saw Leatherbarrow the next morning, he thanked me profusely. 'Are you still getting the broth?' I asked, smiling.

'Yes my lady, but I've also had an orange and an apple peeled for me this morning.' His memory had still not returned, however, nor did it do so while he remained at Dell Farm.

On my way home, I rode into Hokewell to see Jackson, in the hope he had news of the dead French smuggler who'd stolen the Saxborough ring. I had called several times recently without finding him in, but today I saw him walking towards his cottage. He looked round on hearing the sound of a horse, and stopped to wait for me.

'I'm glad I've seen you, my lady,' he said, touching his forelock. Lowering his voice, he went on, 'I've just come back from France and I was coming up to the house later. It isn't good news, I'm afraid. None of the Frenchies I've spoken to know who the man was.'

My heart sank, for this had been my only real hope of finding out. 'Had they heard about Mr Thomas and Master Tom?'

'Yes, my lady, they all knew. These things get about like wildfire. But not one of them saw anything that night, nor have I heard as much as a whisper as to who did it. I'll keep asking, but I think the dead man must have come from a part of France we don't go to.'

'Yes, I see.' It was impossible to hide my disappointment, and all I could do was urge him to keep trying. I'd had such high hopes of Jackson. Someone must know something, and it was human nature to talk about things, no matter how secret.

Nevertheless, life carried on as usual, and with the wedding being so close now, I set in motion a great flurry of activity to ensure the house was spotless. Ordering the preparation of guest bedchambers; furniture to be given an extra polish, carpets to be thoroughly beaten, as well as the meticulous cleaning of spare crockery and glasses. The gardens too had to be immaculate, a supply of extra wine glasses for the wedding breakfast had not yet arrived, and Lucie's last minute fittings had to be squeezed in.

Dr.Redding continued to be pleased with my uncle's progress.'He'll soon be his old self again,' he told me one morning. 'Oh, by the way, Leatherbarrow returned to Ledstone yesterday.'

I raised my eyebrows in surprise. 'So soon?'

'It was his choice. He won't be fit enough to resume his duties for some time, but the poor fellow was fretting at Dell Farm. He said the women never gave him a moment's peace with their infernal fussing.'

'I can imagine,' I said, with a chuckle. 'Mrs Ward is a good, kind-hearted woman, but she does have a reputation for liking everything to be just so.'

'Leatherbarrow may not have liked her fussing, but he owes a great deal to her nursing skills.'

'Indeed he does.'

Later that day, going to Dell Farm to thank Mrs Ward, I learnt Marguerite had handsomely recompensed her for the trouble she had been put to. And after some persuasion, she accepted the sum of money I had brought with me, when I suggested it might come in handy for her first grandchild, expected shortly. I admired the dresser one of her sons had made, and a pretty drawing her youngest daughter had done of the farmhouse. Two kittens, belonging to the farm cat, scampered into the room, only to be quickly shooed out again. One of her sons came in covered with dirt from his exertions on the farm, and he too was sent packing in much the same manner, for daring to present himself in that state before a visitor. I was still smiling at this episode as Mudd and I made our way back to the road.

I decided to ride up onto Hodes Down, above Dittistone Bay, to enjoy the magnificent view, only to find the coast shrouded in mist, as often happened in this area, even when the sun was shining inland. The ships that were visible, made slow progress in the light wind, and as I rode down the hill towards the bay, I caught sight of Piers talking animatedly to some local fisherman. Intrigued by this unusual show of fervour, I kept out of sight until he had ridden off, and when I spoke to the fishermen they were only too eager to tell me about it. 'That gentleman, Mr Giles's cousin,' one man said, touching his forelock respectfully, 'ought to know better than to ask a lot of tom-fool questions.'

'Such as?' I invited pleasantly.

'How much we earn in a week? And was it was enough to live on?'

A fisherman with ten children muttered, 'And did we find other ways to make money?'

'If he goes on asking those sort of questions,' said another man indignantly, 'someone might take offence, if you get my meaning, your ladyship. No disrespect to you, of course.'

I said with quiet authority that I understood perfectly, and that they could safely leave the matter in my hands. Relief showed in their faces, and I inquired if Piers had said anything else.

'Well, he did ask old Harry if he approved of what was happening in France,' one man said. A statement that made his companions grin. I looked around, but old Harry had disappeared, probably into the inn further round the bay. A well-known local character, he spent most of his spare time at the inn, and the rest running messages for the free traders to earn enough money for his drop of ale.

'What did Harry say?' I asked, amused.

'Well, your ladyship, he said all foreigners were heathens, and nothing the French got up to surprised him.'

I laughed, wondering what Piers had made of that. He'd ridden off in the general direction of Ledstone and I decided I had better warn him that asking smugglers how they earned their money was not very wise. I gave Mudd permission to visit his father in Dittistone while I did so, if he wished. Something I often did when I visited Ledstone.

When I arrived, Parker informed me that both Piers and Vincent were in the library. On being shown in, I found the two gentleman sitting by the window in quiet conversation. Both rose and bowed, but only Vincent was smiling.

'Lady Drusilla, how delightful.' I apologised for interrupting them, but Vincent swept such concerns aside. 'We were not discussing anything of consequence.'

Piers set a chair for me, and I thanked him with a smile, but his own features remained impassive. His manners, as usual, were correct, but purely mechanical, without any of Vincent's natural warmth. Mr Reevers had described Piers as boorish, which I considered particularly apt. Yet, when the subject under discussion interested him, he was capable of adopting a perfectly amiable manner, as he had proved when Lucie and I dined at Ledstone.

I took the chair offered, and came straight to the point, grateful for Vincent's presence, as it made my task easier. I turned to Piers with a polite smile. 'Please don't take offence at what I am about to say. Only I feel I must offer you a friendly word of warning.'

For a second his eyes flickered with anger. 'Indeed?' he murmured stiffly.

Vincent was aghast. 'I do trust Piers hasn't offended you in some way, ma'am?'

'No, not at all.' And I explained that, as most local fishermen were also smugglers, they were suspicious of outsiders asking questions about how they earned their money

Vincent slapped his thigh, roaring with laughter. 'If that's what you've been doing Piers, you'd better watch out, or you'll find yourself trussed up like a chicken and left in a ditch.'

'Yes,' I agreed seriously. 'Or be found with a knife in your back.'

Vincent whistled. 'As bad as that? It's so long since I lived here, I'd forgotten how these smuggling gangs work.' He looked across at his son, anxious now. 'Well, my boy, I----'

'Yes Papa,' he cut in abruptly, and fixed his eyes on my face. 'May I ask ma'am, how it came to your notice that I talked to these men?'

'I have lived on this Island all my life, and the local people know they can come to me with their problems, or to Giles when he is here. Any stranger asking questions makes them uneasy. Even if he is a gentleman.'

A rare smile crossed his lips. 'I hadn't realised, ma'am. I was interested in how well they were able to live, but I see I must be more careful. I am obliged to you, ma'am.'

I rose then, saying I must pay my respects to my god-mother before I left. Vincent insisted on escorting me, but Piers remained in the library, where he had a book he wished to read. As we walked along the corridor I said, 'I hope Piers will take my warning seriously, Mr Saxborough.'

'Oh, he will, I assure you. He means no harm by it. In fact he's the same wherever we go. Always asking questions. Piers likes to get the feel of the place, to talk to the local people. It helps him with his sketching, he says. Our year in America affected him profoundly. He believes in a classless society, and is greatly concerned for the welfare of the lower classes.'

Marguerite's eyes lit up as we entered her drawing room. 'Drusilla, how delightful. Come and sit by me. I have something wonderful to tell you.' Smiling up at Vincent she announced joyfully, 'I have finally persuaded Vincent to stay for the wedding.'

'That is good news,' I agreed, for he would be a decided asset at the wedding breakfast.

Vincent seated himself and said, 'Marguerite insisted on it, and I was delighted to accept. Piers is pleased too, as he hasn't yet finished exploring the Island.'

Marguerite clasped her hands together and implored, 'If you made your home on the Island, Piers could spend all his time exploring.' Vincent shook his head, a half smile on his lips, and insisted such a scheme wasn't possible.

I stayed for another half an hour, and riding through the parklands on the way home, told Mudd the reason Piers had given for his behaviour, as I wanted to see his reaction. 'It seems Mr Piers was concerned for the fishermen's welfare, John.' I encountered such a look of disbelief, I burst into laughter. 'No, I don't believe it either. But may I ask why you don't?'

'Well, my lady, the grooms at Ledstone say when Mr Piers comes back from a ride, he hands over his horse without so much as a smile, let alone a word of thanks. He doesn't ask them what they think of the French.'

He hadn't asked me either. In fact, he had not asked my view on any subject. He was always tolerably civil to me, but I had the distinct impression he considered a woman's opinion of no importance. And I wondered how he justified this flaw in his vision of an equal society.

In one respect, he reminded me of Cuthbert Saxborough. Not in his features, or build, for I could see no resemblance there; it was more to do with the harshness in the eyes. The kind of look I associated with those who considered other people's feelings to be of no consequence. Cuthbert, with all his power and riches, had never concerned himself with the sensitivities of those who served him. Yet, he'd had an authority about him that came from his breeding. Something Piers did not possess, and without it, he seemed even more heartless.

But then something happened that took my mind off Piers completely. As we rode back to Westfleet that afternoon, Mudd told me his father had met a man who said he knew how Thomas and his son had died.

25

Mudd told me the news when we stopped to rest the horses on top of the Downs. 'This man lives in Gosport, my lady.' Gosport, a growing town on the mainland, was just across the harbour from Portsmouth. 'He heard about the five hundred pound reward, and says he knows the men who murdered Mr Thomas and master Tom.'

'Does your father think he's genuine?'

'He doesn't know, my lady. But this man said he had proof.'

'Proof?' I repeated, hope growing in my voice. 'What sort of proof?'

'He wouldn't say. My father was at an inn quietly asking around about the dead Frenchie, but no-one could tell him anything. This man waited until my father left, then caught up with him in the alley. Said he didn't want to be overheard.'

So this man was taking a risk. He wanted the money, but was scared of being found out. And that lifted my hopes even more. 'How am I to contact him?'

'At the inn in Gosport where my father met him.' He didn't tell me why his father had gone to Gosport, and I didn't ask, mindful that it probably involved smuggling. 'But he won't be there again until next Wednesday.'

'Wednesday?' I reiterated in dismay. This was only Thursday. Six days, I thought, bursting with impatience.

'What sort of inn is it, John?'

'My father says it's an alehouse, my lady. The sort of place frequented by common sailors.'

I frowned. 'Clearly I cannot go there then.'

'No, my lady.'

Detecting the faintest suggestion of relief in his voice, I suppressed a smile. It was, however, sheer common sense. For, if I walked into such an inn everyone would stare, and this Gosport man would never approach me. Not even for five hundred pounds. Mudd's father had not been out of place there, yet such was this man's fear of being seen speaking to him, he'd only done so out in the dark alley.

Mudd said, 'I could go, my lady.'

'Yes,' I conceded thoughtfully. Mudd could do so. 'How are you to recognise him?'

'I'm to sit at the table nearest the door at seven o' clock.'

I bit my lip, still hesitating. 'Are you sure you want to do this, John?'

'Yes, my lady, I am. Mr Giles or Mr Reevers would go if they were here, but they're not. Whoever murdered Mr Thomas and Master Tom tried to kill Will Leatherbarrow too. And Will and I have been friends a long time.'

'In that case I'll work out what we should do.'

In fact, an idea was already forming in my mind. In the first place, I was determined to speak to this man myself. I wanted to hear what he said, to see his face when he spoke, to make my own judgement on whether he was being truthful. And I needed to see the proof he said he had.

But finding a way to do this wasn't my only problem. I could not stay in Portsmouth without an escort. When father was alive, we always put up at the 'George' in the High Street, and as my maid was terrified of the sea crossing, I left her at home. Therefore, no-one would be surprised if I arrived without her, but I could not go accompanied only by my groom. In the end, however, my problem was solved far more easily than I could have hoped.

Walking round the gardens later that day trying to find a solution, I saw my uncle coming towards me. He was already a different man from the one I had welcomed home last month, having filled out with good Island cooking. He smiled as he approached, and offered his arm to me. 'Drusilla, my dear, may an old man accompany his pretty niece on her walk?'

I laughed. 'You are not old, neither am I pretty. But I should be delighted to walk with you.'

We strolled up past the house, through the long border, into the orchard, enjoying some warm sunshine. 'Your aunt is too busy with wedding preparations to take the air, and being outside has become one of my greatest pleasures since I came out of prison. I used to wonder if I would ever do so again.'

I put my hand on his arm in reassurance. 'Well, you needn't ever fear prison again.'

'Thanks to Giles,' he murmured, and glanced at my profile. 'You're not still worried about him, are you? From what Leatherbarrow said I'm sure Giles knows what he's doing.'

In truth I was still a little anxious, but I shook my head. 'Uncle, there may be a chance to find out who murdered Thomas and young Tom.' And I repeated what Mudd had told me.

He gazed at me speculatively. 'And you want to go to Gosport.'

It was a statement, not a question, and I smiled warmly at him. 'I knew you would understand. I intend to go somehow. But how? I cannot see ------'

He squeezed my arm. 'Well, all you need is an escort, surely?'

'Yes, but there's no-one I can ask, and I cannot go alone. Yet, go, I must. Mudd will be with me, of course, and can arrange for me to meet this man in a more suitable place. But-----'

'You must be properly accompanied, Drusilla. Quite apart from reasons of propriety, it would be most unwise to meet this man attended only by your groom.'

'I realise that. Only I cannot see-----.'

'There's a perfectly simple answer, my dear. I will go with you.'

'You?' I blurted out, aghast.

'Yes. Why not?'

'But----

'No buts, Drusilla. Today I rode into Yarmouth, and I still have enough energy to walk with you.' He reminded me that he'd driven my aunt to Newport, ridden to Ledstone to meet Vincent and Piers, and even enjoyed one or two gallops on the Downs. 'I am quite strong enough to cross the Solent and go with you to meet this man in Gosport.'

It was an offer I longed to accept, but a trip to Portsmouth was far more tiring than anything else he'd done, and I hesitated. 'I don't know, Uncle.'

'Drusilla, I owe my life to Giles, and if I can help find out who killed Thomas and his son it would repay a little of the debt I owe him.'

In the end I capitulated, it being the only solution to my problem. For all his eagerness though, a trek across the Island to Cowes, followed by a sea crossing to Portsmouth would exhaust him, and for that reason I suggested, 'I think we should leave on Monday, stay the night at Cowes, and cross over to Portsmouth early on Tuesday.'

He smiled at me gratefully. 'That sounds an excellent plan for an old man like me.' I didn't tell him the other scheme I had in mind. In fact, I had no intention of mentioning it at all, if I could help it, until the very last moment.

Sitting in the sunshine, we concocted a story for our projected trip that would satisfy my aunt. An innocuous shopping expedition seemed best, and thankfully she was far too busy organising the wedding to think of coming with us. As she'd already told me the hat I'd purchased for the wedding made me look dowdy, I simply said I'd decided she was right, and I meant to buy something better.

My uncle was keen to acquire a good pair of riding boots from the excellent man my father had patronised, admitting that the ones he'd had made on the Island pinched a trifle. Aunt Thirza reminded him she'd said all along they were poorly fabricated, although she was rather doubtful about the wisdom of him making such a trip. But my uncle insisted it would do him good, and a stay of three nights in Portsmouth allowed him plenty of time to rest.

When I told him about Piers' encounter with the Dittistone smugglers, he was highly amused, but clearly the incident had worried Vincent, for he called at Westfleet the following afternoon to speak to me about it. Jeffel ushered him into the drawing room, and as he bowed I thought how distinguished he looked in his sky blue coat and fawn breeches. Once seated, he said he'd had a serious talk with his son.

'The trouble is ma'am, Piers is a little naive. Still, I've made the situation very clear to him, and I am persuaded he won't so much as look at a smuggler again. I'm much obliged to you for taking the trouble to warn him. Not everyone would bother.' Before I could answer, he said, 'Now that's off my chest, might I accept your kind invitation to show me round your gardens? If it's not inconveniencing you, ma'am'

I smiled. 'I should like nothing better.'

But as I stood up, Jeffel came in to inform me Mr Arnold wished to see me. 'He has another gentleman with him, my lady. A Captain Kettlewell.'

Vincent gave a loud gasp. 'Did you say Captain Kettlewell?'

Jeffel inclined his head. 'Yes, sir.'

I asked Vincent, 'Do you know the gentleman?'

'If it's the same man, and with such a name I imagine it must be, I know him very well.' I directed Jeffel to show them in, and to bring suitable refreshments.

After Jeffel had left the room, Vincent removed his snuff box from his pocket and flicked it open. 'Are you acquainted with the captain, ma'am?'

'I've not yet had that honour,' I said, watching him take a pinch of snuff. 'But Mr Arnold is on friendly terms with many of the captains whose ships call at Cowes.'

Vincent rose as the two gentlemen entered the room. Captain Kettlewell, a jolly man, in his middle years, stopped in his tracks when he saw Vincent, and in a booming voice, acquired through years of giving orders on board ship in every kind of weather, burst forth, 'By all that's wonderful!' He strode eagerly across the room, a wide smile on his face, and wrung Vincent's hand heartily. 'Mr Saxborough, how are you, sir?'

'Very well, as you can see,' Vincent answered with obvious pleasure. Glancing in my direction, he murmured courteously, 'You must allow me to make you known to Lady Drusilla Davanish.'

The captain turned to me, instantly begging my pardon for his rudeness in not greeting me on entering the room. A tall man, with weather-beaten features, he had a rather large girth which creaked when he bowed.

'The truth is ma'am, I never thought to have the good fortune to meet up with Mr Saxborough again.' Smiling, I assured him I understood perfectly how it was.

Mr Arnold stood quietly watching, a broad grin on his face. Jeffel came in with a tray then, and I invited the gentlemen to be seated. 'You'll take a glass of wine, Captain?'

'I'd be glad to, ma'am. Nothing like wine to sharpen the appetite.'

As the wine was poured, Mr Arnold explained, 'We're on our way to visit Captain Wilson at Dittistone ma'am, so we mustn't stay long.' Captain Wilson, who had retired from the sea a year before, loved nothing more than to entertain officers whose ships brought them to the Isle to the Wight.

Once the glasses were filled, and Jeffel had left the room, I looked from Vincent to Captain Kettlewell, murmuring politely, 'I take it you gentlemen are old friends.'

'I like to think so,' the Captain chortled. 'Mr Saxborough and his son were passengers on my ship when we left New York at the beginning of July. It took us over six weeks to reach London, but I wish it had taken twice as long, for I have never enjoyed a voyage more. Mr Saxborough, as I expect you have discovered ma'am, has an endless fund of stories, and he kept us so well entertained that conversation round my dinner table has seemed very flat ever since. Very flat indeed.'

'You are too kind sir,' Vincent murmured modestly.

The captain drank a little wine before asking Vincent, 'Tell me, is your son with you?'

'No, he's gone off on an expedition of his own. You know what these young men are. He'll be sorry to have missed you, Captain.' And suggested hopefully, 'Perhaps another day?'

The captain heaved a sigh of regret. 'I only wish it was possible, sir. But my ship lies anchored in Cowes roads at this moment, and we're bound for New York on the morning tide if this weather holds, which I have to say I think it will.' He paused. 'Are you making a long stay on the Island? If you should still be here when---- '

Vincent shook his head. 'I'm afraid we leave for Italy next month.'

'In that case, please convey my respects to your son, and tell him how sorry I am to have missed him.'

'I'll do so gladly, Captain.'

Mr Arnold, who had been sitting quietly, took the opportunity to explain the reason for his visit. 'I thought you'd wish to know ma'am, that Smith's trial is to be held next month.' It was typical of him to bring the news himself rather than send a messenger, and I thanked him for his thoughtfulness. 'Don't give it another thought, ma'am. It wasn't out of our way.' He glanced across at Vincent. 'Whereas Mr Saxborough went very much out of his way to show Mrs Arnold and myself a great kindness, bringing us a letter from my brother-in-law, John Delafield. Taking the trouble to deliver it personally the day after he arrived on the Island. You may imagine how grateful we were.'

Before I could speak, Vincent said to me, a little embarrassed, 'It was nothing I assure you. To be truthful ma'am, Mr Delafield talked so fondly of his family, I felt I almost knew them, and the letter gave me the perfect excuse to meet them. Since then, we have become the best of friends, for I found they were all as kind and welcoming as he had described.

Even Miss Susan Delafield was just as I had imagined her; a delightful, if shy, young lady.' Mrs Arnold's sister had lived with the family for some years.

Mr Arnold acknowledged, 'She is a delicate creature I'm afraid, and easily upset by the slightest thing. We still tease her about the time she kept her clothes on all night during a hurricane, for fear of being blown out into the street in her night attire.' He chuckled a little as he recounted the tale. 'John wanted her to join him in America, but frankly, I doubt she could stand the voyage. I've even known her to become a trifle queasy taking the short ferry ride from West to East Cowes in rough weather.'

Captain Kettlewell said bluffly, 'It takes some folk that way. As Mr Saxborough here knows only too well. His poor son suffered very badly.'

'He was ill?' Mr Arnold inquired politely.

'Seasick,' the Captain pronounced heartily, in the manner of one who had never suffered a moment's queasiness in his life.

Vincent sighed. 'He turned green the minute we slipped anchor.'

'Mind you, it was a rough passage for summer,' the Captain said. 'But no son could have been better cared for, I promise you. They occupied the two most comfortable cabins on the ship, and Mr Saxborough looked after the young man himself. I had his meals brought to the cabin, which is always best, I find, in such cases. He encouraged his son to eat, to play cards, or to read, and take a turn round the deck with him when it was quiet.'

'Luckily,' Vincent said, 'I seem to have an iron constitution.'

Mr Arnold finished his wine and put his glass down. 'Well, we must be on our way I'm afraid Lady Drusilla, or

Captain Wilson will wonder what has become of us.' Vincent expressed the hope he would see Mr Arnold again soon, before turning to heartily shake the captain's hand once more.

After Jeffel had shown Mr Arnold and the captain out, I took Vincent on a tour of the gardens as promised. Walking out onto the terrace and down the steps, he told me what a delight it was to see Captain Kettlewell again.

'No-one could have been kinder to my son than he was on our long voyage. In fact, if we had sailed with him when we crossed to America last summer, I wouldn't have had so much difficulty in persuading Piers to return home. The captain on that ship was most unsympathetic, and seven weeks is a long time to be at sea under those circumstances.'

'Indeed it is,' I agreed, looking across at him. 'You didn't wish to stay in America?'

'Not for ever, ma'am. If I had been happy to do so, I think we would still be there, but I prefer to spend my last years in my Italian villa.'

A pleasant hour was spent touring the gardens, which he much admired. At the top end of the orchard, we climbed the steep path up the hill, and stood looking down at Westfleet laid out below us. 'This is one of my favourite spots,' I said. 'It's the only place I can be certain no-one will disturb me.'

'Perfect indeed,' he agreed. 'I have a similar hideaway in the grounds of my villa in Italy, where I sit and enjoy the sunshine.'

After he had taken his leave I went into my workroom, where I noted down every detail I'd learned since Leatherbarrow regained consciousness, including the information about the man from Gosport.

When I'd finished, having a spare half an hour before going to dress for dinner, I set about sorting out my father's desk. He had been a tidy man, and deciding what to throw away and what to keep, was not difficult, except in the sense that destroying anything of his was hard for me. But it had to be done, I could not live in the past.

I had almost finished, when I came across a piece of paper on which he'd written a reminder to himself. *'Solving a mystery is often a matter of asking the right question.'* Something I had obviously failed to do. I studied every scrap of information again very carefully, trying to work out what I could have asked, and hadn't. But I still could not see anything I had missed. Not then, or after dinner, when I tried again. Yet it *was* there, as I was to discover much later.

26

My impatience at having to wait six days before meeting the Gosport man had soon gone; in fact as we were to leave on Monday, I barely had time to prepare for the trip, acquire the money I needed, and make my plans for the crucial meeting.

Nor could I leave without saying goodbye to Julia and my godmother. Thus, after breakfast on Saturday, I walked over to Breighton House in the sunshine, carrying a basket of Westfleet's best apples. Julia, who was out in the garden with Edward, greeted me with delight, thanking me for the apples. Sitting in an arbour, watching her son run about the garden, she asked if Giles was back yet.

When I shook my head, she declared, 'Surely it's time he was. Has Lucie heard from him lately?'

'She had a letter today.' Letters had come for Lucie and Marguerite regularly, presumably written in advance, and sent by the valet awaiting Giles in London. Edward came running up then, wanting to play 'all fall down,' as he put. 'Very well, young man,' I said, 'but may I point out I have a lot further to fall than you.'

He responded with a gleeful, 'Il-la fall down too.'

Which, as I dryly remarked to Julia, showed a lamentable shortcoming in her son's character, if he wanted to play Ring-a-Ring-a-Roses in order to see me fall from a great height. But, when he put his little hand into mine, I found I couldn't resist. After the three of us spent a very tiring ten minutes chanting and falling down, Edward chased off after a red admiral, allowing me to tell Julia of my expedition to the mainland, and my official reason for going.

She immediately nodded her approval. 'Very wise, Drusilla. That hat does nothing for you. Indeed, I cannot imagine why you bought it. You wouldn't have done either if I had been with you. Why, I could make you a better one myself. In fact, I will if you like.'

I smiled a little ruefully. 'That would have been perfect, but my uncle ought not to go to Portsmouth on his own. In any case, I haven't been off the Island in over a year.'

She began to chatter about the best place to buy a hat in Portsmouth, but I was only half listening. All I could think of was that at long last I might find out who had murdered the Saxboroughs.

Awaking on Sunday to blue skies and warm sunshine, I enjoyed a gallop across Hokewell Down before breakfast. Tiny wisps of cloud floated against the blue sky, and slowing Orlando to a walk, I turned my face up to the sun, stopping to enjoy the view of Hodes Down, which with those sheer chalk cliffs running steeply down to Dittistone Bay, was at its most breathtaking on such a day. A man o' war began making its way round the headland, a majestic sight with its sails billowing in the soft morning breeze.

In this war, much depended on the success of our Navy; and it was vital to the Isle of Wight, with our position leaving us vulnerable to invasion. Yet, up here on the Downs, it was hard to believe that anything other than the bleating of the sheep, the sound of horses galloping, and the shrieking of gulls, could ever disturb the peace of our Island.

Orlando gave a snort, eager to be off again, and I talked softly to him, running my hand down his neck affectionately, rather enjoying the pungent aroma of horses mixed with that of the sea. After today it would be at least a week before I could be up here again, and I would miss it. Yet I couldn't wait to meet the Gosport man.

I had told no-one how I meant to achieve this, and I knew father would have been horrified. But now he was no longer here, I had to make up my own mind. Thinking of the way young Tom's life had been cruelly cut short, I knew I was doing the right thing, and I turned Orlando towards home.

That afternoon, I visited my godmother, finding her talking to Vincent in the rose garden. The instant she saw me she clapped her hands in pleasure. Patting the place beside her, she urged, 'Do come and sit down, Drusilla. Vincent was just telling me about Italy.' He sat opposite, on a seat Marguerite had placed there purposely, as in her view, three or four people sitting in a straight line made conversation difficult.

When I asked Vincent how long he'd lived there, he said, 'About five years. After the gaming club was sold, I spent some time travelling and when I came across this charming villa, I knew at once I would be happy there.'

'Did you never think of returning to England?'

'My dear Lady Drusilla, England to me means Ledstone and this Island. And my home was barred to me.' He spoke without bitterness, as if it no longer signified. 'No, better by far to stay abroad.'

Marguerite touched his arm in sympathy. 'If you had written to Cuthbert, and told him your business venture was a success, I'm sure he would have relented.'

He inclined his head. 'Perhaps I should have written, but pride you know--' And he shrugged.

My godmother knew as well as he did, that his choice of wife was the real stumbling block, but she answered without thinking. 'You should never let a silly thing like pride stand in the way of something you really want.' She turned to me for support, 'Should he, Drusilla?' Marguerite was never intentionally thoughtless of the feelings of others, but I rested my hand briefly on her arm, hoping she would heed the warning. She glanced at me puzzled, and I answered with a good deal of constraint, that judging what other people should do was never as simple as it seemed.

Vincent responded gratefully. 'I knew at once you were a person with superior understanding, Lady Drusilla. But, if I had known Marguerite as well as I do now, I believe I would have swallowed my pride, no matter how difficult I found it. Still, we are what we are. To one's own self be true.'

'Yes,' I said. 'That is something I heartily agree with.'

Marguerite looked from me to Vincent, her voice eager. 'It's not too late, Vincent. Won't you reconsider returning to the Island? If only Giles hadn't offered Norton House to Mr Reevers. Still very likely he won't want it, and then you-----'

Embarrassed, Vincent protested, 'No, no. You are too good, but it is impossible----'

'Why? I see no reason.'

'Giles might not like it,' he pointed out.

'Why should he object?' She appealed to me. 'Do add your voice to mine, Drusilla. We cannot lose Vincent again, now he has returned to us.'

In the weeks since Vincent's arrival, Marguerite had blossomed to a degree I had never seen before. His presence so brightened her life, she told me later, that it helped her forget the terrible events of this year, and her worries about Giles. I understood how she felt, for I enjoyed Vincent's company myself. His conversation was invariably amusing and always interesting. It was no wonder Captain Kettlewell missed his presence at the dining table; he was an asset at any social gathering.

I asked. 'Have you considered living on the Island again, Mr Saxborough?'

He leant back in his seat, drew his snuff box from a pocket, and flicking it open, took a pinch, before answering, 'At one time perhaps, but not now. I have become too fond of my villa in the sunshine. I'd forgotten how wet and windy this Island can be. Then I have my son to consider. He has no wish to settle in England, and I could not bear to be parted from him for long.'

'No, indeed,' declared Marguerite, as he returned the snuff box to his pocket. 'That is something I do understand.'

I inquired, 'Where is Piers today?'

'Out exploring again.'

'If he grows to love our Island,' Marguerite appealed ingenuously, 'then will you stay?'

Vincent lifted his shoulders. 'Who knows.'

Satisfied she'd set his thoughts in the right direction, she asked if Piers was making any progress with his sketching. Vincent wrinkled his nose. 'Not in my opinion, I'm afraid. I find them too mathematical, but then I have always been a romantic. He's gone to Blackgang today. I warned him to keep away from that dreadful place, but he takes no notice of anything I say.'

Marguerite sighed. 'So it is with all young people, I find.' The mention of young people inevitably led Marguerite back to the wedding, and she revealed excitedly, 'My gown has arrived at last, Drusilla. You must see it before you go home.'

'I can see you ladies have much to discuss,' Vincent said, rising to his feet, 'and I have some letters I really must write, so if you'll forgive me-----'

Watching him stroll back to the house, Marguerite said wistfully, 'I'm sure Vincent would stay if Giles hadn't offered Norton House to Mr Reevers.' Her mouth formed into a pout. 'Do you think that awful man will want the house, Drusilla?'

'I imagine so. If it solves his financial problems.'

'Well, I wish he'd address his problems in some other way. I don't want him at Ledstone, or on the Island.' She twisted her handkerchief unconsciously. 'I can never tell what he's thinking. Nothing shows in his face--- whereas I always know what Vincent is thinking.'

As we walked back to the house, I teased, 'And to think you once said a Yarmouth inn was quite good enough for Vincent.'

'Yes, I did, didn't I,' she admitted artlessly. 'Still, how could I know he would be so perfect a companion. When I think how Cuthbert treated him, I could sink with shame. But Vincent says he forgave him long ago. He understands, you see. In fact, he admits that if Piers wanted to marry someone quite unsuitable, he would try to prevent it.'

'Age brings wisdom,' I surmised.

'He is wealthy too. Which makes everything so much more comfortable.' When I reminded her he'd made his money from gambling, she dismissed that with a wave of her hand. 'He gave that up years ago. Anyway what does it matter how he made it? The important thing is that he's no longer poor.'

I teased, 'A highwayman might say as much.'

'Don't be so provoking, Drusilla. That is entirely different. People who gamble do so by choice, no-one forces them to risk their money. And what else could Vincent have done? As a gentleman, he wasn't qualified for any kind of occupation. Luckily everything has worked out very well for him.'

'So it would seem,' I murmured.

'His clothes come from the top establishments, his valet is most superior, and he treats the servants generously. They all like him Drusilla, and indeed he is truly the gentleman. He's a charming companion, and Giles likes him too.'

Eager to take her mind off Giles, I asked quickly, 'Does Vincent spend much time with Piers?'

'Not really.' She pursed her lips. 'I can't make that boy out. When he's in, he says very little. When he and his father go riding together, Vincent always returns exhausted. He says the boy wears him out, and I can quite believe it. Vincent prefers a quiet life, you see. He rides a little, writes letters, reads, walks, but most of all, he enjoys conversation.' She paused for a moment. 'In fact, the only person who seems to get on with Piers is Mr Reevers.'

'Mr Reevers?' I echoed in disbelief.

'Well, I think it must be so. Before Mr Reevers went to London, he and Piers were always out together.'

I could not believe Piers and Mr Reevers spent time together; they had nothing in common, and the very idea made me shiver, but Marguerite didn't notice, all her thoughts being centred on her new gown. As she hated crossing the Solent, her clothes were made at a highly fashionable, luxurious establishment in London, and delivered by a senior seamstress, who made any tiny adjustments necessary. These were few in number, as the head of this enterprise sensibly had Marguerite's measurements checked every year.

We went up to her dressing room where she held this stunning silk creation against her body, and I saw the material was the exact same shade of violet blue as her eyes. 'It's absolutely heavenly,' I said. 'You will set every male heart pounding.'

She gave a little giggle of pleasure. 'Do you really think so?'

I looked at her and laughed. 'You know perfectly well you will.' When she put on the matching hat, I said, quite truthfully, that I had never seen her in anything quite so fetching. It also gave me the perfect chance to tell her of my visit to Portsmouth. 'I must purchase a decent hat for the wedding or I shall look a positive frump beside you,' I declared cheerfully.

She never liked me to be away and when, on returning downstairs, we saw Vincent coming out of the library, she told him my plans in a most dejected manner.

'I shall be back in a week,' I said. 'You'll barely notice my absence.'

'On the contrary, you will be greatly missed,' Vincent insisted, and turning to Marguerite he put his hand lightly on her arm. 'Won't she, my dear.'

'I always miss Drusilla when she's not here,' she answered simply. 'I don't know why it is, but everyone seems to be leaving the Island at present. First Giles, then Mr Reevers, and now you and your uncle.' But a moment later her eyes lit up. 'Still, Giles will be back soon.'

I walked down to the stables rather than wait for Orlando to be brought up to the house, and saw Leatherbarrow sitting in the sun. He stood up as I approached, and I waved him back onto his seat. 'You should be taking it easy.'

'I'm almost as good as new now, my lady.'

I smiled. 'I see you've rid yourself of your bandages.'

'My memory came back too, like the doctor said it would.' And he told me how he came to be attacked. 'I was passing the track leading to Dell Farm when I heard someone yelling for assistance. I turned down the track, but couldn't see anyone, so I dismounted, and I was just looping the reins round a branch, when I was struck down. It's not much help I'm afraid, my lady.'

'No,' I agreed. After a moment, I asked, 'Can you remember which gentlemen were out when you set off for the yacht?'

His brow furrowed in thought and it was a minute or two before he answered. 'The horses belonging to Mr Vincent and Mr Piers were in the stables, my lady. And Mr Reevers set off for Norton House ten minutes before I left.'

'Really?' Norton House was a mile or so past Dell Farm. Thinking aloud, I said, 'In that case, he should have passed Dell Farm before you.'

'I expect he had some business elsewhere first. It was lucky he found me my lady, or I don't think I'd be here now.'

After dinner, leaving my aunt, uncle and cousin to spend a quiet family evening together, I went up to my bedchamber. My clothes were packed ready for the trip, but I opened one of the bags and stuffed in some things I'd kept locked in a drawer. Then, going down to the workroom, I went over my plans for meeting the Gosport man, thinking of the busy days ahead of us.

On the first of those days, my uncle and I, accompanied by Mudd, enjoyed a leisurely journey to Cowes. We had, with some difficulty, persuaded my aunt there was no point taking my maid, or my uncle's valet, just for a couple of days, when neither of them liked crossing the water, and would only be a nuisance if they were ill.

In Cowes we put up at the best inn, arranging for the stabling of the horses until our return. After an excellent dinner, we took a stroll around the narrow streets of the town before retiring. But I had forgotten how noisy an inn could be, what with horses and people passing by, and the shouts of late arrivals in the stable yard.

Sleep came eventually, and we were up very early in the morning, making our way down to the harbour soon after daybreak. The sea was a little choppy, but a fair wind made for an easy passage, and a pleasant one too with the waves sparkling in the sunshine. Standing on deck, I watched the Island's church spires and green hills slowly receding into the distance. Leaving always filled me with sadness, and I knew I could never live anywhere else.

I had written to bespeak rooms at the 'George' in the High Street, and on our arrival we were shown to spotless bedchambers. Our appetites sharpened by the sea crossing, we ordered a meal, and while that was being prepared, I unpacked my bags myself, declining the services of a maid servant. A substantial cold collation was set out in our private parlour, and after hunger had been appeased, my uncle leant back in his chair, sighing with satisfaction. 'Well, I must say, I was ready for that.'

Laughing, I said, 'I wonder why sea air makes one so ravenous?'

'I don't know, but if all the meals here are up to this standard, I shall find some excuse to come again.' The waiter came in to remove the dishes, returning immediately with coffee, and once he'd gone, my uncle asked, 'What do you mean to do now, Drusilla? Shouldn't we find this inn first?'

'Mudd can do that, Uncle. I don't want to draw attention to myself.' Acknowledging ruefully, 'Being so tall, people do tend to notice me. In any case, having visited Gosport with father on several occasions I know the town well, although I don't recall this particular inn. It's important that we walk straight to it tomorrow, rather than stumble around in the dark looking for it.'

He didn't miss my use of the word 'we,' and eyed me thoughtfully before speaking. 'Drusilla, I understood Mudd was to meet this man, and arrange a suitable place for us to speak to him.'

Finishing my coffee, I put my napkin on the table. 'I've been thinking about that, Uncle. The problem,' I murmured, unconsciously pushing some crumbs together on the table-cloth, 'is that there is nowhere he and I *could* meet. Every establishment is either unsuitable for me as a woman, or for him as a smuggler.' I spoke in apologetic tones, having real-ised this from the outset, but had not said so in case he refused to escort me. 'I do have a solution. Only I'm afraid you won't approve.'

27

A long silence ensued as he took in all I had said. 'You mean to go into this inn, don't you.'

I smiled, grateful for his quick comprehension. 'I must speak to this man myself, Uncle.'

He looked at me, greatly troubled. 'Drusilla, you are a sensible woman. If you went into an inn full of drunken sailors, workmen and probably thieves, everyone would gape at you, and our informant would disappear in a trice.'

'Yes, I realise that. But a man in old clothes would be acceptable, surely? If you put on those clothes I asked you to bring, and Mudd wore-----'

'No, Mudd and I wouldn't cause a stir.' His whole face relaxed, and he gave a hearty chuckle. 'Do you know Drusilla, for one awful moment, I thought you meant--------' He stopped, for my face told him his first reaction had been the right one.

'I'll be wearing my father's shabbiest clothes.' He stared at me, dumbfounded. 'It'll be all right, Uncle. My height will help, and luckily I have a slender figure. I'll tie my hair back and wear a large hat, although I don't suppose there will be much light in such a place.'

He leant forward, his elbows on the table, his brows drawn together in obvious anxiety. 'I understand why you want to do this, but you cannot have thought what it will be like. The oaths, the coarse jests, the drunken behaviour, the - er - loose women. You would be greatly shocked.'

'Yes, I've thought of all that. I shall pay no attention to it. I----'

'Pay no attention,' he spluttered. 'My dear child, you can have no notion of-----'

'I will ignore it Uncle, I promise you. I must hear for myself what this man has to tell us. How else can I judge what manner of man he is, or if he is speaking the truth?'

He shook his head from side to side in despair. 'I beg of you to reconsider, Drusilla.'

'I'm sorry, Uncle,' I said kindly, 'but my mind is made up.'

He tried another tack. 'I dread to think what your aunt would say-----'

I smiled. 'I have no intention of telling her. And I strongly recommend you don't either.'

That brought forth a short laugh, followed by a resigned sigh. 'Your father always said you were headstrong, now I see what he meant.' Reaching across the table, he put his hand over mine. 'But will you not be afraid, my dear? This could be very dangerous---'

'I don't think it will be. He's only interested in the money.'

'Have you considered the possibility that he knows nothing? That we might be set upon and robbed of the five hundred pounds?'

'I have thought of that. But I have father's pistols with me. He taught me to shoot and I'm not afraid to use them.'

'I've brought pistols too,' he admitted. 'And a knife, which I gave to Mudd. I trust we won't need any of it, but I must warn you Drusilla, that shooting a man is not the same as firing at a target in the orchard.'

I nodded, being aware of that myself. 'I will do it if I have to.' Sighing, he asked where I had hidden the money and I told him, 'In a bag round my waist.'

My uncle chuckled. 'You are a most resourceful woman.'

'I'm glad you think so,' I murmured with a smile. I had been very worried that I would not be able to persuade my uncle to let me go with him and Mudd, but with that fear overcome, my hopes rose considerably. Now I might, at long last, find out who was responsible for the murders.

Having despatched Mudd to look for the Gosport ale-house, my uncle and I set off for the bootmaker my father had patronised. In this fashionable shop, a style was chosen, measurements carefully taken, and the riding boots promised for Thursday morning.

'It wouldn't do to go home without them,' my uncle said, his eyes twinkling. 'Your aunt is no fool, you know.'

That was very true, and he reminded me I needed to buy a hat, my excuse for coming to Portsmouth. I promised to do so the following day, as I could see he was tired, and he did no more than purchase some perfume for my aunt and cousin, while I bought my aunt a pair of gloves, and a novel for Lucie.

Back at the inn, he went to rest in his bedchamber, while I sat by the window of our private parlour watching the comings and goings in the busy street. Ordinary citizens out taking the air, sailors going to and from ships and taverns, tradesmen selling their wares, besides horsemen, carriages and carts clattering by. Urchins dodged in and out of the throng, Naval officers walked purposefully in the direction of the harbour, and I was laughing at a young man's attempt to shake off a stray terrier yapping at his heels, when I saw Mudd returning.

When he tapped on the door, I bade him enter, instantly demanding, 'Did you find the place, John?'

'Yes, my lady. The New Inn is down a narrow alley off Middle Street, close to the harbour, and it's full of sailors, like my father said. I did look around the town for a more suitable meeting place, but----'

'There isn't anywhere this man and I could both go,' I finished for him. When I told him how I meant to solve that difficulty, his eyes almost came out of their sockets.

'But, my lady, you can't----'

'I wish it wasn't necessary,' I admitted with a rueful grimace. 'But I must speak to this man myself.' I pointed out I wouldn't be there long, that it would be dark, and my uncle knew about it.

'But - but, this is a common alehouse, my lady,' he objected, convinced I had not understood.

'I shall keep my head down and my ears shut.' And I closed the subject with a smile. 'Now that you're back, I should like to look at the harbour. Wait here while I collect my pelisse.'

Still shocked, he bowed. 'Very good, my lady.'

I liked Portsmouth despite the dirty streets and raucous, drunken sailors rolling out of the taverns at all hours of the day. The town bustled with life, and father and I had loved to watch the ships sail in and out of the beautiful harbour, which was large enough, he had said, to shelter the whole of our Navy. The last time we had come here, the sea and sky had been so grey we could hardly tell where one ended and the other began. Father would have loved it today, I thought, with the sea glistening in the sunlight, giving the whole harbour a most attractive appearance.

I spent an hour watching an array of vessels making their way in and out and around the harbour. Small boats taking sailors and officers to Navy ships at anchor, watermen ferrying passengers across the harbour to Gosport, wherries, fishing boats, a customs cutter, and a frigate sailing out to sea, its sails filling with the breeze.

As I watched, I told Mudd the arrangements for the following day, and I was about to return to the inn when he said, 'There's something I ought to tell you, my lady. In Gosport I bumped into a groom in the employ of a Naval gentleman in Yarmouth, and when they were setting out to cross the Solent this morning he saw Mr Reevers mooring Mr Giles's yacht in the Yar.'

My heart began to pound and I took a deep breath. 'Was Mr Giles with him?'

'No, my lady. He was alone.'

So many awful possibilities came into my head that I reached the inn without any clear recollection of the streets we had walked through. Why had Mr Reevers come back without Giles? What did it mean? Was he still in France? I didn't want to think about that, but I couldn't help it. Yet, I couldn't allow myself to dwell on such things, at least not until I returned from Gosport, for I would need all my wits about me when I met this man.

Finding my uncle much refreshed by his rest, I did not mention Mr Reevers, for there was nothing to be gained by doing so. We enjoyed an excellent dinner, eating rather later than was our custom, our conversation inevitably revolving around tomorrow's meeting.

'Drusilla, how are we to leave the 'George' in those old clothes?'

'We'll sneak out the back way, by the servants' door. Mudd says it's dark there, and he'll tell us when it's safe.'

He admitted in a constrained manner, 'You seem to have thought of everything, my dear.'

'I wish that was true. When I was out earlier, I was idly observing the very proper attentions Portsmouth gentlemen exhibited towards the ladies, when it suddenly struck me how very odd it would look tomorrow, when I'm wearing father's old clothes, if you handed me into, or helped me out of the boat, when we cross the harbour. Or for that matter, if you opened a door, allowing me to pass through first, or put a chair for me at the alehouse, assuming they have chairs in such a place.'

'I hadn't thought of that.' He looked at me in horror. 'Nor can I address you as Drusilla.'

I laughed. 'Indeed not. I thought Andrew would be suitable - with Drew being the first syllable of Drusilla.'

'That's an excellent idea.'

Another thought occurred to me. 'Heavens, I'd better instruct Mudd not to call me, "my lady."'

My uncle started to laugh. 'Promise me one thing, Drusilla.'

'What's that?'

'That I can be there when you tell him. I want to see his face.' But Mudd, having already foreseen the problem, mentioned it himself, much to my uncle's disappointment.

My uncle retired early, although I wondered how he would sleep through the noise from the street. I sat by the window going over my preparations for the following evening to ensure I'd missed nothing of importance, but my fears for Giles kept intruding into my thoughts.

That night I did not sleep well, even when the noise abated, and I woke early, disturbed by someone shouting in the street. Looking out the window, I saw a water cart stationed outside, and a large woman haranguing the man selling the water for, in her view, charging too much.

Yawning, I turned away, decided any attempt to sleep now would be pointless, and rang for some hot water. Having washed and dressed, I went down to breakfast, to find my uncle awaiting me. Thankfully he'd slept like a baby, and after breakfast we strolled out to the shops, attended by Mudd, to search for my new hat. I wanted something cream or white, to go with my pale green gown, and found the very thing at the third establishment I tried. A large and very expensive creation, with a long white feather, which suited me rather well. Very different, I thought, as I tried it on, from the battered old hat I was to wear that evening, and a considerable improvement on the one I had originally bought for the wedding. This one would please both my aunt and Julia.

I sent Mudd back to the inn with the hatbox, telling him he could do as he pleased until five, when we were to prepare for the evening ahead. Meanwhile, my uncle and I strolled round the ramparts, and had the good fortune to witness a ship of the line leaving port.

'Look at the speed our sailors scramble up the rigging,' I declared in some awe.

'Yes,' he said thoughtfully. 'Let's hope they're faster than the French.' Despite his French birth, he was an Englishman at heart; even more so since his recent experiences.

Luckily the sun was out, for there was a cool north westerly wind blowing. We ambled along the spacious Grand Parade where, observing the grime and dust gathering along the hem of my walking dress, I remarked that, while I liked Portsmouth, the state of the streets left much to be desired. Concerned that my uncle should not tire himself out, we returned to the inn in good time for nuncheon, after which I persuaded him to rest for an hour or two.

To allow plenty of time to dress for the evening ahead, I had arranged for us to dine early, although we did not say much during the meal, our minds being on what lay ahead.

After dinner, up in my bedchamber, I dressed with care. I had taken in the breeches round the waist, despite my lack of skill as a needlewoman, and removed the lace from the shirt. I tied back my hair, fixed a large battered old hat firmly on my head with two strong hatpins, and pulled on an ancient coat which had a high collar that hid the length of my hair. Only the shoes were my own, an old, plain and sturdy pair.

A few minutes later, hearing my uncle's light tap on the door, I bade him to come in. When he shut the door behind him, I asked breathlessly, 'Will I do?'

He didn't answer at once, but walked slowly round inspecting my appearance, and I soon saw he was grinning. 'You look every inch a young man.' And I breathed a sigh of relief. 'Someone who has fallen on hard times, I would say. Your face is smooth, of course, but that's often the case with very young men.'

I asked if he had the money, which I had given him, at his suggestion, as it was best carried close to the skin, and therefore wiser that he remove it when needed.

He patted his waistline. 'Yes. All safe and sound.' His own clothes were the ones he'd worn in prison, kept as a salutary reminder of what he'd suffered, in case he'd said, he ever had a fit of the dismals in the future.

Mudd was punctual as usual, and following him down the back stairs to the servants' entrance, we waited here briefly, pretending to adjust our hats, as two grooms walked in chatting. They took no notice of us, and we were soon outside walking in the direction of Broad Street and Portsmouth Point, to take a boat across the harbour.

To gain confidence in my appearance, I took it upon myself to deal with the watermen. The normal fare across to Gosport was one penny, but it was high tide, and I was informed that the strong north westerly wind meant rowing three quarters of a mile in difficult conditions, and they wouldn't do it for less than threepence per passenger. Eyeing our clothes, they also insisted on being paid beforehand. Unused as I was to this kind of treatment, I handed over the correct amount without a quibble, grateful to be accepted for what I appeared to be.

A choppy sea and spray from the waves did not make for a comfortable crossing. The watermen got the worst of it, of course, yet despite that and a biting wind, perspiration began to run down their faces, and every pull on the oars made them grunt with effort. When we finally reached Gosport, I got out of the boat first, gauging my leap at exactly the right moment. My uncle and Mudd quickly followed, and we headed for Middle Street, in the manner of people who knew where they were going. Gosport was a growing town; many officers in the Navy resided here, and there were numerous thriving businesses and shops.

Walking into Middle Street, Mudd soon led us down a dim and dirty alley. A pale shaft of light allowed us to see the inn at the far end, the sign outside creaking as it swung in the breeze. A woman lounging in a doorway, a clay pipe in her mouth, stared at us as we walked past. Two dogs snarled at each other in a corner, then we heard people running up the alley behind us, and my heart began to pound. Just before they reached us, three men appeared out of the darkness, and our pursuers stopped and ran back the other way. By now, I was more than a little frightened, and thankful to reach the alehouse, I quickly removed my hatpins, slipping them into a pocket as we hurried inside.

The air had been foul enough out in the alley but inside, the powerful smell of stale ale and gin, mixed with the stench of unwashed bodies and clothes, almost me knocked backwards. The floor looked as if it hadn't been swept in weeks, smoke from clay pipes thickened the air, and the place seemed to be frequented by sailors, watermen, working men in rough clothes, and for all I knew by pickpockets and thieves too.

Serving girls laughed and joked with these vulgar men in the most brazen way, but having promised my uncle I would ignore it, I forced myself to do so, difficult though it was not to stare. Mudd led the way, and we squeezed through the crowd to the table where we had been instructed to wait. Sitting down, I soon saw why that particular table had been chosen; for it was in the lightest part of this gloomy establishment, and enabled him to take a good look at us first. The other customers clearly knew not to sit there, for while most tables were crowded, this one remained empty. A fact that made me finger the pistol concealed in the belt under my coat.

The noise was considerable, even this early in the evening, with people singing raucous songs, the words of which I was glad I could not quite make out. People glanced at us, as they do at strangers, and my uncle said, 'We had better buy some ale, or it will look odd.'

He attracted the attention of a serving girl, who soon returned with three tankards of ale. The girl threw me a saucy look and winked. Thankful at being accepted as the man I appeared to be, I winked back and took a large swig of ale. With a merry laugh, she went off to serve her other customers, and I turned to look at my uncle, the ale still in my mouth, for it was so ghastly I could not bring myself to swallow it. My uncle, summing up the situation in a trice, murmured with dancing eyes, 'Vile stuff, isn't it. But you must swallow it.'

Somehow I forced it down without showing distaste, but it was a minute or two before I could bring myself to speak.

'I've never yet tasted ditch water, but I cannot image it to be any worse.'

A few minutes later someone told us to join a man seated alone in a dark corner. Then those who had looked at us, turned away, as if understanding why we were there. And I guessed this was where the Gosport man conducted his smuggling business.

Picking up our tankards we threaded our way across the room, coming face to face with a large, strongly built individual wearing seafaring clothes. An ancient black hat was perched on his dark sleazy hair, he was unshaven, pock marked and had filthy fingernails. Yet, in the dim light, I caught a faint glimmer of intelligence in those dark eyes.

I'd already told Mudd not to behave as a servant, but to sit with us, and act as if we were friends, which he managed very well. The table was a small one, and placing my tankard on it, I sat to the left of the man, with my back to the wall, so that he had to look sideways at me. My uncle settled opposite him, with Mudd facing me. The man looked round at us all, his eyes resting on me longer than the others. I did not lower my gaze, and he grunted as if satisfied.

'Have you got the money?' His voice was deep and harsh, his accent local. My uncle said that we had. 'Five hundred?'

'If you tell us what we want to know,' I promised, speaking in the low voice I had practised. He turned to look at me again, and I asked what he knew about the deaths of Thomas and his son.

'I didn't do no killing,' he declared at once, shaking his head at us in a convincing manner. 'I was only brought in to sink the yacht. Boats I sink are never seen again, and they knew that.' So that was why no wreckage had been washed ashore. 'It was the others. They took the man and the boy out to sea—'

'The French smugglers?' I asked.

He nodded. 'I don't know what they did, only that their orders were it had to look like an accident, or they wouldn't get paid.'

I looked down at the table, desperately trying not to think of what the kind Thomas and young Tom must have suffered. 'How did you know where to find the yacht?'

'He told us.'

'He?' I reiterated.

'The man who paid us.'

My heart began to pound. 'And who was that?'

'I don't know his name.'

I groaned inwardly, for I had pinned all my hopes on being given a name. 'Did you see him?'

'No, I was told to keep out the way. He didn't want any English involved.'

'Were the others all French?' I said, thinking of the man found with the Saxborough ring round his neck.

A wary look crept into his eyes. 'Yes, but I only met them once and I don't know their names.'

'The Englishman - did------'

'I didn't see him. I just heard him talking to the Frenchies. Gabbling away like a Frenchman he was. Mind, he was English all right, the others said, and a gentleman by his clothes.'

I asked where and when this meeting had taken place. 'In France,' he said. 'On the fifteenth of September.'

'You're very precise.'

'That was the day he fixed. And I never forget when I'm being paid. All I know is he was ranting on about some ring he said we'd stolen, and how he should have known better than to trust a bunch of Frenchies. I didn't know anything about this ring, and I'd done my job properly, but I still only got half of what I'd been promised.' And he spat on the floor.

So that was why this man was willing to speak to us. But far from certain he was speaking the truth, I tried to catch him out. 'What was the name of the yacht?'

'The "Augusta."'

'How do you know that? Can you read?'

'No, but I heard the others talking about it. It was a lovely boat. If I'd known I wasn't going to get what I was promised, I'd have kept it and sold it.' He looked round at us all. 'I've told you everything I know. Now I want my money.'

'Willingly,' I said. 'If you give us the name of the Englishman.'

He gave a shrug. 'He was a gentleman, that's all I know.'

My uncle said, 'We were told you had proof of what you knew.'

Without a word he took something from his pocket and put it on the table. 'This was in the cabin.'

It was a penknife. My uncle looked at me in puzzled fashion, for it meant nothing to him, never having seen it before, but I would have recognised those distinctive markings anywhere. My hand shook as I picked it up, for it was the penknife I had given Tom on his fourteenth birthday.

28

I stared at the penknife, unable to speak, and glancing across at Mudd, saw the colour drain from his face, for he remembered it from my father's study. My uncle said later that one look at me had told him who it had belonged to.

The man went on, 'In the cabin there was a tiny painting of a lady, but one of the others took that.' Having been on Thomas's yacht a few times I'd seen the pretty miniature of his wife.

In the end, we gave him the money. Preferring to hand it over rather than risk being attacked in the alley, as I was certain we would be, otherwise. We left the inn then, glad to be out, even into the stale air of the alley. None of us spoke until we reached the relative safety of Middle Street, when I told my uncle not to worry about the money. The most important thing was we had met someone willing to talk about the murders, and I believed we had learnt at least some of the truth.

With the wind behind us the return crossing to Portsmouth was swift, and we made our way back to the inn in silence, lost in our own thoughts. My uncle, having seen me safely to my bedchamber, said that if I didn't mind, he would go straight to bed, as he was feeling very tired. 'We can talk about it all in the morning, my dear.'

Once he had gone I changed into my own clothes, packed father's old things in one of the bags, hiding them under my dirtied walking dress. Then I rang for some hot water, and also ordered supper. I wasn't surprised at my uncle's tiredness, as I felt decidedly weary myself. The strain had been much greater than I'd expected, and far more frightening too. Only now did I allow myself to think of the risk we had taken by going to such a foul and unsavoury place, for I had never so much as walked past such a low inn before. I shuddered at the thought of what could have happened if that man had seen through my disguise, or if we had been attacked and robbed. I had been very foolish, I saw that. Yet, I'd had to go; it was the only thing to be done.

When the water came, I had a thorough wash, including my hair, desperate to be rid of the disgusting stink from that tavern. I changed into my night attire, put on my dressing gown, and had just finished dragging a comb through my long hair, wishing my maid was here to make it more presentable, when a maidservant arrived with some cold meat, bread and butter, and hot chocolate. I felt better when I'd eaten, and after the dishes had been removed, a servant came in with a warming pan to take the chill off the sheets.

Climbing into bed, I was glad of that warmth, as I went over everything the Gosport man had told us. I believed what he'd said about Thomas and young Tom being taken out to sea by the French smugglers. And that he had sunk the yacht. For it explained the lack of wreckage, and how the bodies came to be found at Hokewell.

Once again, I was struck by the care with which the whole thing had been planned. I thought about that for a long time. I thought about why the Gosport man had been willing to speak; his insistence that he didn't know the Englishman's name, only the date he'd been paid, and that he'd produced Tom's penknife. He had told his story convincingly, without faltering and I had not been able to catch him out. Had he really done it for revenge? Was it true that he'd received only half the money promised, despite doing what was asked of him? Had he truly had no hand in stealing the Saxborough ring? Was it just the French smugglers? I didn't know, and I was still turning it all over in my mind long after the sounds in the street had finally died away.

I reflected too on how extraordinarily smoothly everything had gone. The Gosport man had not asked who we were, the men running up the alley had been stopped from attacking us, and no-one had bothered us in the inn. Things that made me very uneasy. As with so much else in this business, I had the distinct feeling everything had not been quite what it seemed.

My uncle, however, had no such doubts. 'In my opinion Drusilla, the man's a scoundrel,' he said over breakfast. 'Smugglers can be very devious when there's easy money to be had.' I bit into my toast and nodded in acceptance. 'At least you know what happened to the yacht now.'

'True.' And I reminded him, 'He did say French smugglers committed the murders.'

'Yes, but we already knew that.' He shook his head sadly. 'The truth is Drusilla, we learnt very little, and you are the poorer by five hundred pounds.'

I sighed, agreeing it certainly looked that way, but it had been a chance and as such, had to be investigated. Pouring us both another cup of coffee, I went over the evening again at great length, for he would have thought it odd if I hadn't. Eventually he said he could see how very cast down I was, but it would be best to put the whole episode behind us. I did not argue, nor did I speak of my own doubts, not wanting to worry him unnecessarily. Instead I reminded him we must collect his riding boots before we left for home.

When we set off for the shop shortly afterwards I took the opportunity to tell him what Mudd had said about Mr Reevers returning to the Island. 'Giles wasn't with him, Uncle,' I said, unable to keep the anxiety out of my voice.

He looked at me. 'You're afraid he's still in France?' I nodded dumbly, and he said, 'Try not to worry, Drusilla. In my opinion, Giles is very well able to look after himself.'

Crossing the Solent that afternoon, the gulls shrieking around the boat, I thought how very little of our trip we could repeat to my aunt and cousin; but thankfully they would only expect to hear of the shops, our walks, and the prettiness of the harbour.

It was well after dark when we reached Cowes, the late dinner provided at the inn being a welcome sight. My uncle retired soon afterwards, and I was so tried, I did not stay up for long. Even so, I still couldn't sleep; but it was anxiety over Giles, rather than the noises in the street, that kept me awake.

Things always seemed worse at night, yet I felt no better in the morning and rode home fearful of what I would learn when I arrived. My uncle insisted I was worrying unnecessarily, and so it proved. Walking into the drawing room I saw Lucie's eyes shining with happiness, and knew Giles was back, which filled me with the most enormous sense of relief.

'Giles arrived home late yesterday,' Lucie said on greeting me, eager to relive that moment of joy. 'And came over to see me this morning.'

I said everything that was appropriate, and my uncle gave Lucie a hug. 'Just two more weeks, and I will have lost my daughter.'

She laughed gaily. 'Don't be silly, Papa. You will never lose me, and Giles will be like a son to you.'

To which he exclaimed in teasing fashion, 'Now, why didn't I think of that?'

My aunt, who had been upstairs, came bustling into the room, and having greeted her, I left them to a family reunion. Badly needing a moment or two to myself, I crossed the hall to the workroom. Sinking into the one comfortable chair I kept in that room, I sat back, closed my eyes and allowed that blessed feeling of relief to seep right through my body. Giles was alive and back on the Island. Tears threatened, and I told myself not to be so silly, but the truth was I had been terrified he might never come home.

It was some ten minutes before I felt fully in control of myself again. On going into the hall, I saw Jeffel and asked if all was well at Westfleet.

'Yes, my lady, everything is much as usual. Cook's rheumatism is starting to play up a bit with the colder weather. Oh, there was one thing – Jess caught a pigeon-----'

'A pigeon?' I exclaimed, astonished.

He nodded. 'She sneaked it into the kitchen just as cook was preparing dinner. The bird was still alive, and when Jess let go of it, the poor thing panicked, flying into everything in sight. You should have seen it, my lady. There were feathers everywhere. Some even went into the soup - I'm afraid cook was in quite a state.'

'I'm not surprised,' I said, laughing. 'Dinner was late, I imagine?'

He gave a chuckle. 'By more than half an hour, my lady. Cook had to make fresh soup.'

'Oh dear,' I sighed. 'Mrs Frere will be demanding Jess's head on a plate soon if she keeps on like this.'

'I'm afraid she wasn't best pleased, my lady, but Miss Lucie told cook not to worry.'

I nodded, grateful I could rely on Lucie to show some common sense. 'I'll have a word with cook. Anything else I should know, Jeffel?'

'I don't think so, my lady.' He asked if I'd had a pleasant trip, and I told him what we had seen in Portsmouth, as he liked to hear about the places I visited

Having mollified cook, I went to find Lucie. She was sitting by the drawing room fire reading the newspaper, but put it down on seeing me, and told me happily, 'Giles says all the legal matters are settled now.' When she insisted on being shown my new hat, we went up to my bedchamber, where I took it from the box, put it on and turned to face her. Instantly she broke into a wide smile. 'It's beautiful. I like the feather, and it will go perfectly with your gown.'

'Yes, that's what I thought.' Removing the hat, I sank wearily into a chair. The trip to Portsmouth, all that had happened there, worrying whether Giles was dead or alive, and the sheer lack of sleep, had finally taken it out of me.

'Is something wrong, Drusilla?' Lucie asked in concern. 'You don't look at all well.'

Blinking in surprise, I assured her, 'No, I'm fine. I'm just a little tired, that's all.'

'Tired? You?' She exclaimed in astonishment. 'I've never heard you say that before. I do hope you're not sickening for something.' Lucie naturally wanted everything to be perfect for her wedding, and I reassured her, saying that having been woken early every morning by the noises in the street, I just needed a good night's sleep. And I asked how my godmother was.

'Tolerably well, I think. I called on her every day, and Vincent drove her over to dine with us on Wednesday. On Thursday, Mama and I joined them for a drive in the sunshine. You know, Drusilla,' she mused thoughtfully, 'I believe Vincent enjoys the company of women.'

'Without a doubt,' I agreed with a chuckle. 'It seems to me you've had a riotous time while we've been away.'

'Well, I wouldn't call it riotous exactly, but it has been pleasant.'

She told me her wedding dress would be delivered in a few days. 'It's absolutely perfect,' she sighed happily, her face flushed with excitement now that the day was drawing near. When she finally left me to dress for dinner I found her happy chatter had relaxed me a good deal.

Dinner was a cheerful affair; my aunt expressing satisfaction with my uncle's new boots, and that I'd bought a suitable hat. She wanted to see it for herself, of course, and later, when I put it on, she instantly declared, 'Now that's what I call a hat, Drusilla. You should give the other one away.'

When we all retired to the drawing room, my uncle and I presented Aunt Thirza and Lucie with the small gifts bought in Portsmouth. I stayed talking for an hour, then left them to themselves, saying I had some things to see to, and went into the workroom to write down everything the Gosport man had told us. I had just put the sheet back on the wall, when Jeffel came in to say Mr Arnold wished to see me. I told Jeffel to show him into the library, and pulled the shutters over the charts, not wanting anyone to see what I had just written.

On entering the library I found Jeffel lighting some extra candles, and talking to Mr Arnold about the warmth of the evening. Mr Arnold declined my offer of refreshment, and when Jeffel had left the room, explained, 'I have just come from dining with Captain Wilson, and if I drink one more glass of wine, my wife will have just cause to accuse me of becoming a tippler.'

'That I do not believe,' I said, laughing. 'I trust Mrs Arnold is well?'

'Very well, thank you, ma'am.' There was no mistaking the pride in his voice, and that he considered himself fortunate in his choice of wife. 'But I mustn't trespass on your time. Indeed you must be wondering why I have called at such a hour.' I assured him, quite truthfully, that I was pleased to see him at any time. 'It concerns the murders of Thomas Saxborough and his son, and------'

'You have some new evidence?' I asked eagerly.

'Would that I had, ma'am. But the subject came up over dinner and Mr Orde told us the official position.' Thomas Orde, Governor of the Isle of Wight, was a particular friend of the Arnolds. 'It will soon be common knowledge, so I am not breaking a confidence, but I'm afraid it is not what you will wish to hear. Officially it is thought the smugglers who carried out the murders did so in order to steal not only the Saxborough ring, but the yacht as well. Either to sell, or to use for smuggling purposes. As you know, it had quite a turn of speed. Personally I find it hard to believe smugglers would go to such lengths, but I may well be wrong. It would certainly explain why no wreckage has been found.'

'Indeed,' I agreed in a neutral tone, not wanting to mention what I had learned in Gosport until I'd had more time to consider it all.

'I'm afraid the general opinion is that Thomas and his son were simply thrown overboard,' he continued unhappily. 'It is not a pleasant thought.'

From what the Gosport man had said, I was quite certain they were drowned first, and left where they would easily be found. Imagining how this might have been achieved was one of the things that had kept me awake for the last two nights.

'I was told,' Mr Arnold went on, 'that with these smugglers being French, nothing more can be done.'

I sighed. 'I had hoped the search for evidence would not be given up so soon.' A sudden gust of wind rattled the windows and the candles flickered in the ensuing draught. 'Do you know if Giles Saxborough has been informed?'

'I understand the situation was explained to him this morning.' After a slight hesitation he said, 'There is one other thing, ma'am. It concerns Smith - his tongue ran away with him over the business of hiding contraband on his farm. He gave us the names of everyone involved. But he is still protesting he had nothing to do with that piece of cliff falling on you at Hokewell Bay. Vehement, he is.'

I shrugged. 'The man was always a liar.'

'Very true. But in this instance he may be speaking the truth. He said he was at Dittistone market that morning with his son, Daniel. They bought some hens and came back about noon with the carrier who transported them. The carrier confirmed it, and the farmer who sold him the livestock remembered it because it happened to be his birthday.'

29

'I see,' I said, frowning. 'Did you speak to Daniel?'

'Yes. In view of my involvement in the smuggling charge, I went along with the constable. Daniel said his father was with him all morning, and they didn't hear of your accident until they got back.'

'I see,' I said thoughtfully, certain Daniel would not cover up for his father. 'Then it cannot have been Smith.'

'No, ma'am. That is our opinion too.'

When Mr Arnold took his leave, I went over what had happened on that terrifying day. I had tethered Orlando to Smith's gate and been attacked within half an hour. Much too quickly for it to be his Guernsey friends. A week earlier I'd lost my temper with Smith, warning him no smuggler was going to tell me what I could, or couldn't do, on my own land. Sensible reasons for believing it was Smith.

I went back into the workroom to look at my charts, for if Smith hadn't attacked me, then it must be the man behind the Saxborough murders. The night before that attack, someone had broken into my workroom and read my charts. But as they showed only the bare facts, which were known to everyone closely involved, plus some background details, I hadn't connected the break-in with the attack. In fact, I was convinced the intruder, having seen how very little I knew, would realise I was not a danger to him. Therefore, I'd seen no reason for him to attack me.

Besides which, his 'accidents' had been planned with meticulous care, and the attack had not, for I'd gone down to Hokewell Bay on impulse. Perhaps he'd been watching the house, seen me leave alone, followed me, and grasped the opportunity. But why had he taken such a chance? Why was he so desperate to be rid of me?

Was there something on my wall charts that gave away his identity? Eagerly I went through those facts again, searching for what he might have seen. And found nothing. Eventually I concluded he was simply worried that I was trying to solve the murders. Yet, every instinct within me said it wasn't so. Unfortunately, this useful insight failed to indicate what I should look for on my charts.

In the morning, still none the wiser, I rode over to Ledstone, where Parker informed me that only Giles and Marguerite were in the house. 'Mr Reevers has gone to Norton House, and Mr Vincent and Mr Piers left half an hour ago to visit friends near Brading.'

Brading being over on the east of the Island, I asked, 'How long will they be away?'

'Only until tomorrow, my lady.' I nodded and asked to see Giles, if it was convenient.

A few minutes later Parker ushered me into Giles's study, having first explained, in a confidential manner, that Mr Saxborough was busy catching up on estate matters this morning, but that in his opinion, too much pouring over figures never did anyone any good. Giles, greeting me with affection and pleasure, seemed to be bursting with good health. Just as if he really had spent all his time away in London.

I settled myself in the chair on the other side of his desk, saying how pleased I was to see him back at Ledstone. He scrutinised what I knew to be my somewhat haggard appearance and asked anxiously, 'Drusilla, are you quite well?'

'Of course. When am I ever anything else? I haven't been sleeping well, that's all.' He didn't comment, and I stripped off my riding gloves, putting them on the arm of the chair. 'I hope you're not too busy. I have a great deal to say to you.'

He laughed out loud, as if he hadn't a care in the world. 'Straight to the point as usual, Drusilla.' He glanced at the clock. 'I've promised to drive Mama to Yarmouth in an hour. Will that be long enough do you think?' he inquired tongue-in-cheek. Not being in a mood for joking I said it should suffice, and he leaned back in his chair waiting for me to speak.

First I thanked him for getting my uncle out of prison, explaining I'd prised the information out of Leatherbarrow.

'Yes, I know about that.'

'I trust you're not angry with him, Giles. I----'

'Of course I'm not. He wasn't in a position to do anything else.'

'How is he, by the way?'

'Almost recovered, and itching to get back to his duties, he tells me.' Affection for his groom clear in his voice.

'I'm glad to hear it.' I took a deep breath and begged him to tell me how he got my uncle out of prison.

He looked at me from under his brows. 'It wasn't difficult.'

'If it was that easy,' I retorted caustically, 'prisoners would be escaping all the time.'

Grinning, he shook his head at me. 'I suppose you won't be happy until I have told you the whole.' He brushed a wayward hair from his forehead. 'I meant to hold up the coach on the road to Paris, but changed my mind. In fact, we stopped it in a wood on its way to the prison, tied the guards to trees, having first borrowed their uniforms.'

I thought of what that would have involved. Pistols and probably masks. Just like a common highwayman, only rather more dangerous. 'Who was with you?'

'My French friend, the one who discovered where your uncle was.' He grimaced. 'But I didn't mention the change of plan until the last minute. He's a rogue, Drusilla. I'd paid him well, but I made one mistake. I told him this was the last time I would need his services.'

My heart pounded in alarm. 'You speak as if you've employed him many times before.'

'Oh, he's had his uses,' he replied offhandedly. 'But after that his manner changed. He made such strenuous efforts to prevent me changing my plan, I guessed that now I was no longer a source of income to him, he meant to add to his fortunes by informing the French authorities of my intentions. So I warned him, that should I be arrested, I would still manage to shoot him first.'

Horrified, I whispered, 'How could you take such a risk?'

Giles laughed in his carefree way. 'There was no risk after that. He understood, believe me. When I doubled the sum I'd promised him, he was only too happy to do as I wished. He did the talking at the prison, although as he was well aware, my French is excellent, but no-one suspected we weren't the real guards. Your uncle was handed over without a quibble, and we headed for the coast, where French smugglers brought him to the Island. It was as simple as that.'

I raised an eyebrow at him. 'So you never did have any friends in Normandy. It was this----'

'The Frenchman, yes. Smugglers usually know what's going on. I'd hoped your uncle was in hiding and thus easily got out of France. When I learned he was in prison, and was soon to be taken to Paris, I thought only of what Lucie would suffer if I did nothing. Her father's life would end in a swift trial, a ride through the streets of Paris in a tumbril being jeered at by howling mobs, before climbing the steps to the guillotine. When I saw a way to save him, how could I not do so? I want no sadness on my wedding day, Drusilla.'

If he'd failed, both he and my uncle would have been guillotined, causing Lucie even greater suffering. But he had not failed, so I said nothing.

He thanked me for what I had done for his groom, and I remarked casually, 'Leatherbarrow said he was to meet you somewhere on the Normandy coast. After he was attacked, Mr Reevers went off in your yacht and--------'

'Yes, Radleigh told me all about that in London.'

'He must have got there before you did.'

'Indeed.'

'Didn't he think that odd?'

A smile flickered on his lips. 'He did seem a trifle put out. But Radleigh rarely stays angry for-----'

I cut in, 'Giles, the attack on your groom was meant to----'

'Stop him picking me up. Yes, I realise that. But—'

'Who else knew where your groom was going?'

He gazed at me for a moment, then stared down at his hands. 'It so happens I couldn't wait for Leatherbarrow anyway.'

I gave a little gasp. 'What do you mean? Why couldn't you wait?'

'Well, as you know, before the war, I used my own yacht to go to France, and paid my French friend to meet me in

Normandy with a good horse.' So that's why he'd employed
the Frenchman before. I was inordinately relieved.

'When I was ready to come home, I arranged to meet
the Frenchman at daybreak on the beach where I was being
picked up. He was to collect my horse, and I'd pay what I
owed him. But I'd still underestimated the man's greed,' he
confessed, with a grimace. 'Quite by chance, I was about
an hour early. Eager to get back to Lucie you see,' he owned.
'There was very little wind that morning, and I could hear
every sound. The noises I heard came from horses. A snort
or two, the jingle of harnesses as they shook their heads.
Too much for the single horse I'd expected, so I waited and
watched for a while. When I saw soldiers moving across
the beach, I knew the Frenchman had betrayed me.'

I stared at him in horror. 'How did you get away?'

He gave a rather wry smile. 'I was lucky. It was still dark,
so I rode back along the coast to a fishing village and borrowed
a boat.'

'You stole a boat?'

'It was either that or the guillotine. Don't look at me like
that, Drusilla. The boat has been returned. And I am safely
home.'

'Yes, thank heavens.' I sat looking down at my fingernails, thinking of the terrible danger he had been in, yet no
remembered strain showed in his face. It was almost as if he
had enjoyed it. And I asked, 'Why did you stay in France after
you knew my uncle was safe?'

He began tidying the papers on his desk. 'Oh, you know
me, Drusilla. Being so close to Paris, I wanted to see what was
happening there. Not everyone has the opportunity to witness a revolution, and I saw no reason -----.'

'No reason?' I spluttered. 'When you had just removed my uncle from prison?'

He grinned. 'You forget, I was disguised as a French soldier.' And he told me something of what he'd seen. 'Those who criticize the revolution are considered enemies of liberty and must be eliminated,' he said, irony in his voice. 'I could virtually smell the fear on the streets.' His lip curled in distaste. 'And there were these dreadful old hags, who sat knitting at the foot of the guillotine.'

I felt my jaw drop. 'Good God, did you actually watch one of these executions?'

He hesitated. 'I didn't mean to, believe me. But I got caught up in the crowd and it wasn't wise to be seen leaving.' He closed his eyes momentarily. 'Frankly Drusilla, I was glad to get out of Paris. There is no respect for life in France any more. I think that's why those French smugglers murdered Thomas and Tom----' A butterfly fluttered in through the open window; Giles carefully caught it and put it outside again. 'Before this revolution, they would never have snuffed out two lives as if they were of no more importance than that butterfly.'

'I don't believe the revolution had anything to do with it.'

A startled expression sprang into his eyes. 'Whatever makes you say that?'

I told him about my trip to Gosport and he stared at me in growing alarm. 'You should never have done such a thing. Anything could have happened to you?'

'I had my uncle and Mudd with me.'

'A frail old man and a groom----'

'Giles, stop preaching and listen to me. This man said his job was to sink the yacht so that it would never be found.'

'How much did he want for this information?' When I told him, he shook his head from side to side in despair. 'And you believed him?'

Taking Tom's penknife from my pocket, I handed it to him. 'He gave me this.'

Giles turned it over and gasped. 'But this is the penknife you gave Tom.' He looked across at me. 'Where did he get it from?'

'He said it was in the cabin.'

Giles put the penknife on his desk and sat gazing at it, a stricken look on his face. 'Did he tell you who paid these French smugglers?'

'An Englishman, he said.'

'Did he give you a name?'

When I shook my head, Giles gave a grim smile. 'I thought not. Could he describe this man?'

'No. He heard him talking to the French smugglers, but couldn't see him in the dark.'

Giles's lips twisted in a manner that suggested it was exactly the answer he'd expected. 'Is that all?' When I nodded, he picked up the penknife and held it in the palm of his hand, pain in his eyes. 'Perhaps he did sink the yacht and steal the penknife, but the rest is probably a fairy tale. These rogues will say anything for that kind of money.'

This was what my uncle had said, and I was well aware of it myself. But I didn't think that was the real reason the Gosport man had told me those things. Giles seemed less concerned than I'd expected by what I'd said, and a new suspicion rose in my mind.

'Giles, do you know what is going on in your family?'

Looking up, he answered quietly. 'Yes, I believe so.'

I was very thankful to hear it, and before I could stop myself, I blurted out, 'Does Mr Reevers have any part in it?'

He stared at me in utter astonishment. 'Radleigh?' Suddenly he began to laugh. Going on so long he had to mop his eyes with his handkerchief.

'I'm so glad to have amused you,' I muttered acidly. But he didn't react, and I urged, 'At least have the decency to tell me why it's so funny.'

He gazed at me for a moment. 'I thought you two got on rather well. I didn't expect you to accuse him of----'

'He's very short of money,' I pointed out abruptly, my temper still a little frayed.

Giles shook his head at me. 'He is also one of my greatest friends. I thought you knew that.'

I grunted. 'Well, who do you suspect then?'

Rising from his chair, he came round the other side of his desk, perched himself on the edge of it and took my hands lightly in his. 'Drusilla, I beg of you not to involve yourself in this any more. You've taken too many risks already.' When I began to protest, he squeezed my hands. 'You always were far cleverer than anyone else of my acquaintance, but whatever possessed you to go into a low inn carrying five hundred pounds? Half the men there would have killed you for such a sum. Didn't you think of the dangers?'

I lifted my shoulders a little. 'I hoped there was a chance of finding out the truth.'

'Brave, but foolhardy,' he said affectionately. 'From now on you must leave it all to me.'

I said nothing and he, knowing me of old, insisted with an urgency I was unused to from him, 'Promise me you'll stay out of it, Drusilla. I do not want to spend the rest of my days with your death on my conscience.'

30

Before I could answer Giles, his mother burst into the study, ready for her outing, a smart black hat perched on her curls. 'Drusilla,' she exclaimed with delight. 'I didn't know you were here.'

I stood up and greeted her with affection. 'I hear you're going to Yarmouth this morning.'

'I'm spending the day with Maria Ross,' she told me, her eyes alight with anticipation. 'She's been in London for the past month, and I can't wait to hear all the latest gossip.'

With my godmother eager to be on her way, I soon took my leave, wishing I'd had more time to discuss the murders with Giles. Still, he'd made it clear he didn't want me involved; his sense of chivalry would not allow it. I did not, however, have any intention of keeping out of it.

Back at Westfleet, I strolled into the drawing room where I found my aunt, uncle and cousin engrossed in wedding arrangements. The ceremony was to be held in Westfleet's ancient Norman church, with the wedding breakfast at the Manor. My uncle had insisted I should bear none of the expense and I had, therefore, left my aunt to organise the day as she wished.

Everything seemed to be in hand, but when my aunt maintained she didn't know how she was to get everything done in time, I asked, 'Is there anything I can do to help?'

She threw me a grateful look. 'That's kind of you Drusilla, but it's mostly sewing -- some things for Lucie's wedding trip. I thought I had plenty of time, but somehow-----'

I agreed I certainly could not assist with that. She had already refused my offer to purchase some new gowns for Lucie; naturally I respected her wish to be independent; and in any case once Lucie was married Giles would provide for her.

Leaving them to get on with things, I went into the work-room, where I spent a good deal of time studying the evidence on my charts, and thinking about the man who had planned the murders. An Englishman, the man in Gosport had said; which he had to be, I reasoned, no matter how much I wished otherwise. Someone highly intelligent, yet devious, and while there must be evil in him, no murderer could be sinister all the time. He must have other sides to his nature; perhaps someone who could make me laugh, who shook his head over the French, and complained of the government, as we all did on occasion. He might, I thought with a shudder, be a man I liked.

Strolling through the gardens in some welcome October sunshine that afternoon, I had just stopped to enjoy the fragrance of a late flowering rose, when I saw Mr Reevers striding down the path in my direction. My heart lifted with a joy that overwhelmed me in its intensity, for I had not seen him in three weeks.

On reaching me, he bowed. 'Your butler said I would find you here.'

'Did he indeed?' I remarked a little wryly, trying not to show how happy I was to see him. 'It is a source of wonder to me that my movements can be so accurately forecast by my servants, when I don't know which direction I will take from one minute to the next.'

He chuckled. 'Yes, it is annoying, isn't it. But let us not concern ourselves with minor irritations on such a day as this. I rather hoped you might invite me to stroll in the gardens with you, as I have no desire to play gooseberry to Giles and Lucie, or---'

'Giles is here?'

He nodded. 'We rode over together. Jeffel said your aunt and uncle were discussing wedding arrangements. So you see---' And he jiggled his bushy eyebrows at me.

'Oh, I see perfectly,' I replied, choking back a laugh. 'I am the best of a poor set of choices. Frankly, I'm surprised you bothered to accompany Giles here at all.'

'Yes, I quite surprised myself. But the truth is I had nothing better to do,' he drawled lazily, his eyes dancing. 'Mrs Saxborough is in Yarmouth, and Vincent and Piers have gone to Brading.'

Strolling round the walled garden, I remarked casually that I gathered he and Piers had become quite friendly. He turned and stared. 'Who told you that?'

'Mrs Saxborough. She informed me you and Piers were often out together.'

He drew his bushy eyebrows together and said in a cold voice, 'Mrs Saxborough is mistaken, Lady Drusilla. We may be out at the same time. I assure you we are never together. I do not care for people of a dour disposition.'

Leaving the walled garden and heading for the orchard, he began to talk of the weather, and amused at the abrupt change of subject, I remarked, 'If you do not wish to talk about Piers, surely you could think of a topic more original than the weather.'

His bottom lip quivered. 'Ah, but I assumed you would take the hint, like any other well-bred female.'

'Did you?' I murmured dryly. 'I had no idea you could be so foolish.' He immediately assumed such a chastened expression that I choked.

'I humbly beg your pardon, ma'am. As you clearly wish it, we shall speak of Piers. Though I can find little to say, except that he rides like a slug, cannot draw, has no conversation, is devoid of charm, lacks a sense of humour, and his eyes are too close together. But, of course, if you admire the fellow—'

Torn between exasperation and laughter I spluttered, 'W-will you p-please be quiet!'

'Certainly.' Smiling down at me, he murmured in a low, caressing voice, 'I should be happy to sit quietly in your company all day, if you wished it.'

I gasped, and though I did not look at him, his very nearness made me breath faster. Quickly turning away, I drew his attention to the beauty of a bank of Michaelmas daisies, inwardly cursing the tremble in my voice.

At which he whispered softly, 'Who is changing the subject now?'

I shook my head at him. 'You are too audacious, sir. It will not do.'

He bowed, and after a moment inquired, 'Tell me, why are you still unwed?'

I turned and stared at him, my eyes widening. 'Frankly sir, I do not think that is any of your concern.'

'Perhaps not, but I should like to know all the same,' he reiterated, undaunted.

Taken aback, I didn't answer at once. Glancing at him, I saw he was watching me, a half smile hovering on his lips. 'Are you always so direct?'

'Only with people I like.'

He looked at me expectantly, and with a shrug, I answered his question. 'It's quite simple really, Mr Reevers. No-one has ever made me an offer.'

'So if a respectable man made you an offer, you would accept?' And he raised an eyebrow as if in polite interest.

It was impossible to guess what was in his mind, but he needed money badly, having sold his family home to pay his father's debts, and I was a very wealthy woman. I liked him far more than any man I had ever met, but he clearly knew how to make himself agreeable to any gentlewoman, and afraid my growing feelings for him were overcoming my judgement, I fought to regain control of the situation. Primly I informed him, 'There are two reasons why I have not married. I have never met anyone I wished to marry--'

He nodded in acceptance. 'And the second reason?'

'I am used to being my own mistress, and no man, however amiable, would allow me the independence I am accustomed to. And that is something I am not prepared to give up.'

Having reached the end of the orchard we climbed the short, steep hill to the Downs, where I told him how much I enjoyed this quiet spot.

'I can see why,' he said. 'No-one will disturb you here, and you have the perfect view of everything going on.' And he asked if the wood beyond the shrubbery to our left, was part of my land.

'No, that belongs to Vale House, but now old Mr Jenkins has died, the estate is to be sold.'

I thought it wisest not to linger here, and he followed me back down the hill, stopping to admire the old oak tree that had stood close to the end of the path, probably for centuries.

'You have a beautiful home,' he observed without a trace of envy in his voice.

'I think so, of course.'

A leaf fell from the tree onto his shoulder and he brushed it off. 'Tell me, are you ever lonely?'

Again his boldness made me gasp. 'That is not a question one asks in genteel conversation.'

'No, it isn't, is it. But are you?'

I shook my head at him, half laughing. 'If you must know, I never used to be when my father was alive. Now, I have my family at Westfleet, yet there are times when-----'

Realising my tongue was running away with me, I stopped, for I was admitting things I rarely spoke of to anyone, except perhaps Julia and Giles. When I didn't continue, he murmured softly, 'I too have discovered it is possible to be lonely in any number of unlikely situations.'

I looked up, and he held my gaze in a manner that gave me a severe jolt, for his eyes bore an expression I could not mistake. My heart began to thud alarmingly, for he did not seem to want to look away, and I could not. We were virtually at the furthest point of Westfleet's extensive gardens and no-one, not even a gardener's boy, was in sight. We were still under the oak tree, and so close that one short step would take me into his arms.

I had never had the slightest desire to be in any man's arms before, and to find that, at this precise moment, it was something I wanted very much, came as a considerable shock. For a minute neither of us spoke, then he reached for my hand, murmuring my name in a soft caressing voice. But determined not to throw caution to the winds, and take what would be an almost irrevocable step towards marriage, somehow I pulled myself away, swung round on my heel, and without a word, left him standing there. For, there were too many unanswered questions, too many things I was unsure of.

Most of the extremely honourable gentlemen I had met over the years had been more interested in my fortune than myself, and there wasn't one I hadn't very soon found boring. I certainly did not find Mr Reevers boring; far from it. He, being an astute and observant man, was no doubt aware I was becoming increasingly attracted to him. If I was ever to think of marriage, it wasn't his financial difficulties that would make him ineligible to me, but the fear that he saw me only as a means of resolving those problems.

He had never made any reference to my fortune, nor did he attempt to flatter me as other men did. His manner, whatever the provocation, was invariably calm and pleasant. He was, by far, the most interesting man I had ever met, and one who listened to my views without the superiority some men adopted.

His looks were not exceptional, his thick, wavy black hair had being allowed to curl carelessly round his ears. But, to me, a man's personality was of far greater importance than a handsome face. Those dark eyes of his were his best feature; full of intelligence and laughter, they seemed all too often to know what I was thinking.

What it was that attracted me I didn't know, except that there seemed to be an affinity between us, and what amused him made me laugh too.

I half expected him to follow me, but when I reached the other end of the orchard and looked back, he was leaning against the tree watching me, a curious smile on his lips.

Returning via the stables, I found Giles on the point of leaving, having promised to collect his mother from Yarmouth in good time for dinner. 'Have you seen Radleigh?' Before I could answer, however, he saw that gentleman walking towards us. Farewells were made in the usual fashion, and I went back indoors not knowing what to think.

That evening, sitting in the library reading, I found it impossible to concentrate on my book. I kept thinking of what Giles had said earlier; that he knew something I didn't, and I should leave everything to him now. But what was it that I knew nothing about?

In the end I made my mind to ask him. It was ridiculous to go on like this. If he wanted me to stay out of things, he would have to tell me why. But when I arrived at Ledstone the following morning Parker informed me Giles had gone to visit one of his tenants. Removing my riding gloves, I inquired if my godmother was in, and on being ushered into her drawing room, I found Vincent and Piers with her. Marguerite greeted me with joy, and as the gentleman rose from their chairs and bowed, I asked if they'd had an agreeable visit with their friends near Brading.

Vincent answered, 'It was delightful, thank you, ma'am. Piers was eager to explore that area before leaving the Island.'

'When do you mean to leave?' I asked.

'The day after the wedding, provided the sea promises a smooth crossing.' And he chuckled, 'I don't want Piers turning green again.'

'You shouldn't tease Piers in that way,' Marguerite chided. 'He can't help being sea-sick.'

Piers punctiliously thanked her for her concern, and said, 'Papa, it is time we left for Newport.'

They were both dressed for riding, and Vincent glanced at the clock on the mantle shelf.

'What will Lady Drusilla think of us, dashing off the moment she arrives.'

'Please don't delay on my account,' I smiled.

'Ten minutes won't matter one way or the other. We have some shopping to do, that's all.'

Marguerite asked him, 'What's this I hear about your valet? Parker said he's in quite a state. Is it true his father is very ill?'

'I'm afraid he's dying. Wistow showed me the letter he'd received. He was so upset, I sent him off to London straightaway. Although I have to say it couldn't have come at a more inconvenient time, with the wedding so near.'

Piers said, 'I told you Papa, my man will look after you.'

'Yes, and I am grateful Piers, believe me. But even you will admit your man is not a patch on Wistow.'

I asked Vincent, 'Is he likely to re-join you soon?'

'When we reach London I expect. We're spending a few days there before going home, and the doctor was of the opinion Wistow's father would not linger more than a week.'

'How will you make your way back to Italy?' I inquired, conscious of the difficulties of travelling during a war.

'By sea, I think.'

Marguerite looked at Piers, thinking of his problems with seasickness, and said impulsively, 'Oh, isn't there some other way? Your poor son-----'

Piers said, 'I'm not returning to Italy yet, ma'am. I mean to go to Paris first.'

'Paris?' Marguerite burst out. 'But is that wise? The French are our enemies and-----'

'I lived in France for many years ma'am, and I have only friends there, not enemies.'

Vincent shuddered. 'Personally, I intend to steer well clear of the place. Too much blood being spilt for my liking.'

'I couldn't agree more,' I said, and asked Piers, 'Is it true every patriot in France wears a red hat?'

'It's called a 'bonnet rouge,' ma'am.'

Marguerite announced, 'Well, I'm glad I'm not in Paris. Red really isn't my colour.' Vincent and I laughed. Piers did not seem to find it amusing. She said to Vincent. 'When you get back to Italy, you mustn't forget us. Promise me you'll visit us again soon.'

'Of course,' he said easily. 'Next summer.'

'Then I must be content,' she sighed. The gentlemen took their leave then, promising to be back in good time for dinner.

After they had gone, our conversation inevitably turned to the wedding, and it was about half an hour later that Parker entered to say the housekeeper wished to see Mrs Saxborough urgently. 'What is it, Parker? Can't it wait?'

'She's very agitated, ma'am. A housemaid was dusting Mr Vincent's bedchamber when she accidentally smashed the glass on the miniature painting he keeps beside his bed.' Marguerite gave a cry of alarm, and he explained, 'She knocked it onto the floor, ma'am. Very upset the girl is. What with Mr Vincent always being so kind to her.'

Marguerite dealt with the matter, accepting it had been an accident, but the instant we were alone again, she became visibly flustered. 'What am I to do?' she said, looking at the painting her housekeeper had handed to her. 'This is the only portrait he has of his wife. He'll be terribly upset.'

'Glass can be replaced,' I said. 'Is the painting damaged at all?'

She held it up close to her eyes. 'Oh dear, where are my spectacles?' Passing the miniature to me, she urged, 'You look

Drusilla, your eyes are so much better than mine. I don't know how I shall face him if that silly girl has ruined it.'

I studied the portrait carefully. 'There's a tiny scratch in one corner, probably caused by the broken glass, but the lady herself is unharmed.' Only then did I take a proper look at the woman for whom Vincent had given up everything. 'She's incredibly lovely, isn't she,' I said, gazing in admiration at a pair of huge honey coloured eyes set in an oval face, and long golden tresses reposing against a neck that was as graceful as a swan's. Returning it to Marguerite, I said, 'I can see why Vincent fell in love with her.'

'Yes. It is *such* a pity she was only an actress.' And added, 'Giles must arrange for the glass to be replaced.' She looked at me, still worried. 'What on earth am I to say to Vincent?'

'I'm sure he'll understand. After all, the portrait itself is unharmed.' She put it on the table beside her, and I glanced at the lady again, saying a trifle enviously, 'What wouldn't I give for hair like that.'

Marguerite shook her head. 'Blonde hair wouldn't suit you at all.' Her thoughts still on Vincent she spoke of what was uppermost in her mind, that he would soon be leaving Ledstone. 'I shall miss him so very much, Drusilla. But I am determined to make the best of the time left to us. In fact I've decided to hold a Farewell Party for him and Piers.'

'That's a splendid idea,' I declared, eager to encourage this optimistic outlook. She wanted everyone at Westfleet to come and we settled on Tuesday as being the most suitable day.

'I'd like to give him a memento, to remind him of us. What would please him, do you think?' I deliberated for a moment or two, shook my head, promising to give it some thought, and she went on despondently, 'I believe he'd stay longer if it wasn't for Piers. Do you know, I actually overheard

Piers talking of these dreadful executions in Paris, and saying how much he wished he could be there.'

She gave a shudder, and we agreed that no sane person would choose to be in Paris during this awful revolution. Yet Giles had gone, and I'd always thought him sensible. Guillotines were set up all over France, but it was in Paris that the King and many members of the nobility had lost their lives.

Later, as Parker was seeing me out, Mr Reevers came down the stairs. He wore a dark green coat, fawn breeches, and carried a riding crop. At the sight of me, his eyes lit up. 'I heard you were here,' he smiled, eagerly crossing the hall. 'I hoped I might see you before I left.'

'You're leaving Ledstone?'

'Only for a few days. The sale of my home has to be completed, and the clothes I mean to wear at the wedding are still in Lymington. Will you walk with me in the garden for a few minutes, there's something I particularly wish to say.'

31

My heart began to thud, and once we were away from the house, he said, 'Giles asked me to speak to you. He's afraid you are putting yourself in great danger. He told me about your trip to Portsmouth. And he's right to be worried. Murderers are utterly ruthless, your research into history told you that. The difference is, this one has not been dead for centuries. You are a highly intelligent woman, but you have almost no experience of what a villain will sink to in order to stay alive. If he even suspects you have evidence that will send him to the gallows, he will kill you without a second thought. But I believe you know that.' When I didn't answer he asked, 'Do you have that kind of evidence?'

I met his look. 'No, I do not.'

He seemed to relax a little. 'Can you obtain it, do you think?'

I gave shrug. 'Giles insists I leave it in his hands now. And I believe that would be best.'

He groaned. 'You should never tell lies. Your voice gives you away. Besides, you're not the type to give up that easily. I wish you'd tell me what you mean to do.'

'I'm sure you do.'

'We are on the same side,' he said, frowning.

'How can I be certain of that?'

He shook his head at me sadly. 'I thought you were a good judge of character, Drusilla.'

'I did not give you permission to use my name, sir.'

'No. I beg your pardon.' Taking out his pocket watch he said, 'I wish I could stay, but I shall miss the tide if I don't go now.'

Forcing a smile, I said lightly, 'Will you be back in time for the party?'

'I'm afraid not.' News which left me feeling unaccountably dejected. He lifted my left hand to his lips. 'Be careful, my dear.'

Riding home, I refused to think about Mr Reevers, concentrating instead on the memento Marguerite wanted to give Vincent. Remembering Vincent's promise to visit the Island again next summer, I was delighted for Marguerite's sake, and for my own too, as I enjoyed his company. Although I hoped he would not bring his son with him next time. And thinking of Piers, I suddenly had the perfect idea for a memento.

An hour later, I was in the library when Giles called in on his way home from visiting his tenant. 'Lucie's gone for a walk with her mother,' I told him and took the opportunity to ask what he was giving Lucie as a wedding present.

He looked across at me, his eyes glowing. 'It's a surprise, Drusilla.'

'So I imagined,' I said, smiling. 'You're not the only person who can keep a secret, you know.'

He grinned at me. 'Yes, I do know. To be truthful I'm dying to tell someone. I've bought her the most delightful, spirited bay mare you ever saw. Radleigh is bringing her to the Island when he returns.'

'You bought her on the mainland?'

He nodded. 'The last time I stayed with Radleigh.'

Without thinking I blurted out, 'Oh, but that was the night--------'

'When Thomas and Tom died?' He sighed and went on, 'It was also when I bought the mare and barely got home in time for the outing to Carisbrooke. Once the horse is in my stables I shall have to swear all the grooms to secrecy. I expect that will cost me a pretty penny.'

I laughed. 'Well, you can afford it. In any case by this time next week you'll be married.'

He nodded eagerly and said, a quiver of excitement in his voice, 'I didn't know it was possible to feel this happy.'

I hesitated, not wishing to spoil the moment, then said, 'Anything can happen in a week. You will take care, won't you, Giles.'

He smiled at me. 'Of course I will, but I've told you before, nothing is going to happen to me.'

I took a deep breath. 'Giles, there's something I must ask you.' I was determined to find out what he knew about the murders that I didn't. 'The thing is—' I stopped, for he was no longer listening, having seen Lucie walking back to the house with my aunt.

'You will excuse me, won't you, Drusilla,' he grinned, hurrying towards the door. 'Perhaps we can talk later.'

Giles spent the afternoon with Lucie and was easily persuaded to stay to dinner. I sent a message to Marguerite so that she wouldn't worry; a sensible precaution, for it was well after ten when Giles finally left. The others went straight up to bed, but having failed to speak to Giles alone again, I was in no mood to settle. Collecting a cloak, I left the house though a back door. Physical exercise always had a calming effect on me, and crossing the lawns to the right of the house, I climbed the steep rise beyond. There was very little moon, but looking down towards the village I could just make out the church and the cottages around the green. A faint light bobbed about in the churchyard, suggesting local smugglers were busy.

I caught the faint sound of voices on the breeze, but it wasn't smugglers I could hear, the churchyard was too far away. Quietly making my way down the hill, I realised the voices were coming from the other side of the wall bordering my land. There was a hillock close to the wall, and climbing it, I could just make out a man on a horse speaking to someone standing beside him.

'Someone's been talking to Lady Drusilla, Jacob.' The softly spoken voice was so well known to me I had to bite my lip to stop myself gasping out loud.

'So I heard.' Jacob was the smuggler Giles had employed to collect my uncle's letters from France, and to bring his own message to me. 'What did he have to go and do that for?'

'Money, of course.'

Jacob grunted. 'Been dealt with has he?'

'Naturally.' Giles sounded remarkably untroubled. 'His usefulness came to an end the moment he opened his mouth.'

The wind kept taking their voices away, but I heard Jacob ask Giles what would happen now. 'Well, unless I'm much mistaken, Mr Piers means to have me arrested.'

Jacob muttered an oath. 'He knows you did it then?'

'Oh yes. He's known for some time.'

'You'd be topped for sure if you were arrested, and then he'd get his hands on Ledstone.'

'Quite so.' His horse moved restively, and Giles calmed him with a word. 'Only Ledstone is mine now Jacob, and I have no intention of letting anyone take it away from me. So Mr Piers must be stopped.'

Jacob laughed unpleasantly. 'Just say the word and I'll-------' A sudden gust of wind caused the leaves to rustle and I missed the rest. A moment later Giles rode off, while Jacob headed for the churchyard.

I couldn't seem to move, and I thought, vaguely, that if I tried my legs would give way. I don't know how long I stood there staring into the darkness, but eventually I stumbled blindly back to the house. Shutting the door, I leant back against it, shaking with shock.

The house being in darkness, I felt my way into the drawing room, where the fire was still glowing. Stirring the embers with a poker, I threw on a log, and sinking into a fireside chair, sat staring at the sparks, the conversation I'd heard repeating itself over and over again in my head.

It wasn't possible, I told myself. *It just wasn't possible.* Giles could not have done those terrible things. Yet, he'd admitted it. I'd heard him say so. Heard him say that Piers knew he was guilty. And that the Gosport man, having opened his mouth to me, had been dealt with. I put my head into my hands and groaned, for I had told Giles what the man had said.

Ever since Cuthbert Saxborough's death I had tried to keep an open mind as to who had killed him. Sticking to the facts, just as I had when assisting with father's work. Facts did not lie. Only people did that. The Gosport man told me an English gentleman had paid French smugglers to murder Thomas and Tom. He'd even given me the date they received their money - the fifteenth of September. When all the gentlemen, except Giles, had been at Ledstone. Giles, as I well knew, had been in France on that date. But I'd decided that was a subtle attempt by the man behind the murders to make me think Giles was guilty. Now, it seemed, I was wrong.

Numb and trembling, I sat by the fire for a very long time, until things finally became clearer in my mind. And I saw that, whatever my own feelings were, I had to decide what I should do. Which was so awful a thing to contemplate that, in the end, I resolved to write everything down on my wall charts first. Perhaps then I would be able to think more clearly.

Taking a spill from the mantle shelf, I thrust it into the embers of the fire, lit a branch of candles, threw the spill into the fire, and carried the candelabra into the workroom, placing it on the table. Removing a sheet from the wall, I first added the small background details learned earlier in the day, before forcing myself to record the conversation I'd overheard between Giles and Jacob. This being so fixed in my memory, I wrote it word for word. When it was done, and the ink had dried, I returned the sheet to the wall, and went through every fact I had concerning the deaths of the three Saxboroughs, including the whereabouts of every member of the family at those times, where it was known. Then there was the background information; the part played by smugglers in the murders, and in my uncle's rescue, Vincent's letters, Piers's obsession with sketching, Mr Reevers' lack of money, and a great deal more. No circumstance was too small to my mind.

As I slowly studied it all again, I gave a sudden gasp. For, one of the minor facts I'd just added contradicted a trivial background detail I had noted down soon after Cuthbert's death. I checked it again, but there was no doubt.

And in that instant so much became clear. This small insignificant fact was the reason I had been attacked at Hokewell Bay. He feared it would eventually lead me to the truth. As, indeed, it had now. To me, it was absolute proof of guilt; as he had known it would be.

Slowly, bit by bit, I came to see how the murders had been planned and carried out. I recalled too the reminder father had written to himself, that solving a mystery was often a matter of asking the right question. Now, at long last, I saw what that question was. And if I had asked it when I'd had the opportunity, before I left for Portsmouth, everything I'd overheard Giles say tonight would have been obvious to me long ago. But that question had simply not occurred to me then. And it was too late to ask it now.

Eventually, sheer exhaustion got the better of me, and going up to my bedchamber, I undressed, climbed into bed, and fell into a troubled sleep. When I woke some hours later, the curtains had been drawn back, and I heard Gray, my maid, busying herself in my dressing room. The sky was a clear blue, and as the first shaft of golden sunlight fell across my bed, a blackbird on the tree below my window burst into song. The kind of morning that would normally have had me leaping eagerly out of bed. Instead, the events of last night came rushing back into my mind, and I lay there some time with my eyes closed.

When I opened them again, I sat up and gazed round my bedchamber at all the things I loved. The old wood panelling, the small bookcase holding some of my favourite books for when I couldn't sleep, the brightly patterned curtains that matched those around my four poster bed. On the mantle shelf above the fireplace was the first fossil I ever found, when I was four. I'd asked father how the tiny shell had got into that stone, and his answer had fired my interest in his hobby.

The old screen standing in front of the fireplace had belonged to my mother, and I loved too the ormolu clock bought in Paris when travelling with father. Portraits of my parents hung on the wall opposite, painted soon after their marriage. The delicate looking mother I couldn't remember, and beside her the father I had adored, his laughing gray eyes smiling down at me, as they had all my life. With the passing of the years, the slender figure portrayed here had filled out, he'd acquired laughter lines on his face and his thick brown hair had become tinged with grey. And I sighed deeply, thinking he couldn't help me now.

It was then an odd thing struck me. It was true that, in the early days of the Saxborough troubles, I had longed for his help, for we had worked so well together; but at some point, that feeling had passed without my being aware of it. What I really yearned for was his physical presence, as I still missed his companionship deeply. As for the business of the murders, I already knew what I had to do. A man responsible for the deaths of three members of his family could not be allowed to profit from his crime. No matter who he was.

Now I knew who, how and why, I had decisions to make. After breakfast I went straight to the workroom, informing Jeffel that on no account was I to be disturbed. For, I had to be quite certain I hadn't missed anything last night. Going through the facts again, I recognised the meticulous skill with which everything had been planned. In the calm of daylight I also realised the tiny detail that had explained it all to me last night, would not, by itself, be sufficient to prove guilt in a court of law.

I spent an hour or two making plans, and as these involved Mr Arnold, I resolved to call on him first thing Monday. Today, being Sunday, he would not be at work. Meanwhile, it was vital that I should be seen to be carrying on my life as normal. Thus, resolutely putting all other thoughts out of my mind, I went to see my godmother about the memento for Vincent.

Marguerite often enjoyed an afternoon nap in her drawing room, and when Parker announced me, she sat up with a start, the book on her lap slipping onto the floor. 'Did I wake you?' I murmured apologetically.

She straightened her cap, insisting she had not been asleep. 'I was reading.' Reaching down for the book, I was astonished to find it was a volume of sermons. Until I lifted it up and another much slimmer book, one the romances Lucie loved, fell out. Marguerite immediately feigned surprise. 'How on earth did that get there? One of the servants must have----' But I was laughing so much she soon gave up the pretence.

I sat down, declaring affectionately, 'I can't stay long. It's just that I had an idea for a keepsake you could give Vincent.'

'Oh, do tell me. I can't think of a thing.'

'Well, you remember that lock of his son's hair we found in one of those old letters?' she nodded, puzzled. 'He might like that - perhaps set into the handle of a quizzing glass.'

Instantly she clapped her hands together. 'Drusilla, how clever you are. That's the very thing.'

She talked excitedly about how and where to get it done in time, but when I pointed out Vincent would wonder how she came by it, she bit her lip in vexation.

'Well, I shan't tell him I've kept his old letters. It would be too unkind to remind him of what he wrote then. I shall say I found the lock of hair among my keepsakes, and thought he might like it.' She looked at me appealingly. 'The letters are in my dressing room. I could ring for my maid I suppose, but she's bound to bring the wrong box or—'

'Shall I fetch them for you?' I asked, laughing.

'Would you?' She bestowed her best smile on me, and I went off to do her bidding, as I had so often before, happy that she liked my solution to her problem. For, in a day or two, I would have no time for trivialities, and I wanted to keep her mind occupied. As for the murders, I would withhold the truth from her as long as I could. And I wished with every fibre of my being that I could do so for ever.

On opening the door of her dressing room, I was greeted by the familiar smell of roses, from her favourite perfume. Her maid wasn't in the room, but I found the bandboxes in a corner of a clothes closet, and removed the bundle of letters tied up with blue ribbon, written in Vincent's unmistakable handwriting. Returning to the sitting room, I watched her go through them, until she eventually found the right one.

'I have a lock of Giles's hair that is very similar,' she said, smoothing Piers's hair with her finger. 'I cut it during one of his dreadful illnesses. I was so afraid he would die, and I wanted something I could touch and-----' She broke off, looking up as Parker entered the room.

When he informed her the parson had called, begging the favour of a few moments of her time, she groaned, 'On a Sunday?' She turned to me. 'You'd think he'd be too busy to bother me, wouldn't you.' With a sigh, she told her butler, 'I had better see him, I suppose. It's bound to be about the wedding. Where have you put him, Parker?'

'In the green room,' he told her. Which amused us both, for it was the coldest room in the house, and not one where visitors cared to linger. 'The fire has not been lit,' Parker added.

'Good,' Marguerite said, rising from her chair and pulling her shawl tightly round her shoulders. 'I won't be long, Drusilla.'

'Shall I return the letters to your dressing room while you're gone?'

'Would you? I'd be so grateful.'

In her search for the lock of hair, she had let many of the letters fall onto the floor, and I picked them up in order to fold them. The one that had contained the hair was still spread open on the couch, and I glanced at it again. Reading the loving descriptions of Vincent's wife and son, and his financial difficulties of that time, I saw how right Marguerite was not to remind him of what he had written long ago.

Packing up the letters, I retied the blue ribbon and took them back to her dressing room. When Marguerite returned, she was in high dudgeon. 'That dreadful man only wanted to know why I wasn't in church to hear the banns read.'

I felt my lip quiver. 'What did you tell him?'

'Oh, I soon put him in his place. I told him I hadn't thought it wise to go when I could feel a sore throat coming on. I said I hoped he wouldn't catch it.' I laughed, asking how long he stayed after that. 'Not more than a minute. He couldn't wait to get out the door.'

I left soon after, for pretending everything was perfectly normal when it was far from it, was an increasing strain. I kept thinking of all Marguerite had gone through this year, and what I now knew lay ahead of her. I longed with all my heart to spare her the pain of it, but there was no way out. No way at all.

32

O n Monday, I woke to some pleasant hazy sunshine, but that had disappeared by the time Mudd and I left for East Cowes, and I arrived at the Customs House in a torrential downpour.   This building stood close to the water's edge, as it had done for more than 200 years. There was very little else here, apart from wharves and warehouses, and I remembered Mr Arnold saying how inconvenient a situation it was, when he, and most of his men, lived at West Cowes. But that was how it had always been, and such things were not easy to change.

The Customs House had been extensively altered in recent times, Mr Arnold having gained the Commissioners' approval to have the work done, provided so he'd told me, he shared in the expense. He seemed a little disconcerted at my visiting him alone, but quickly placed a chair for me, expressing his concern that I had ridden there in such bad weather.

'I do trust you won't catch cold—'

'Luckily, I am rarely ill,' I smiled 'And I came because I need your help.'

He inclined his head. 'I am always at your service, ma'am.'

'Thank you.' I explained first about the Gosport man, and my fear that he might now be dead. After a slight hesitation

Mr Arnold admitted, 'A smuggler was found stabbed to death in an alley in Ride a few days ago.'

'An Island man?'

'No, ma'am. Jake Blandford came from Gosport. He was about thirty, muscular, dark haired with a badly pock-marked face.'

'That sounds like the smuggler we met.' As Giles had told Jacob, the man had indeed been dealt with. 'Do you know who killed him?'

Mr Arnold shook his head. 'The local constables are doing their best, but it's thought to be a case of thieves falling out.'

I told him then what I'd overheard Giles say to Jacob, what I meant to do about it, why I needed his help, and why I did not want to involve any other authorities. It took a long time, and he agreed the courts wouldn't convict anyone on the evidence I had. It was too circumstantial, and he sat staring at me, a shocked expression on his face. After a few minutes, he asked one or two sensible questions, shaking his head in sorrow at my answers. 'It pains me greatly to learn that a man I like and respect is nothing but a common murderer. But, as I have observed all too often in my profession ma'am, greed can make decent men do things they would never consider normally. Nonetheless, no man is above the law, not even the King himself.'

Getting up, he walked to the window, where he stood looking out for a while without speaking. When he turned back, he said, 'I believe you are right, ma'am. The plan you described to me may indeed be the only way to get evidence that would satisfy a court of law.' He heaved a heartfelt sigh. 'Well, you can rely on me to do everything possible. But I must beg you not to put yourself in danger.'

I promised I would try not to. 'I shall have Mudd with me.'

He bowed. 'Then I must be content.'

Thankfully it did not rain on the day of the Farewell Party, although there was a stiff south westerly breeze blowing when we rode to Ledstone.

Marguerite had surpassed herself with a delectable meal, the two courses embracing a vast number of dishes, including such delights as soup Lorraine removed with salmon, beef olives, lobster pie, stewed soles, a variety of roast meats, fricassee of chicken, stuffed calves ears, oyster loaves, her own favourite blackberry pie, a lemon tart, orange creme and even mince pies. Sitting down to the first course of this huge repast, much praise was heaped on my godmother, who confessed that Vincent had helped her choose the dishes.

I turned to him with a smile. 'Should I ever decide to hold a Venetian breakfast, then I shall know where to come for advice.'

He looked at me, an amused glint in his eyes. 'I am, of course, always at your service ma'am, though I must say I cannot imagine you indulging in any such fanciful entertainment.'

A favourable comment by my aunt on the merits of French cuisine led to a discussion on foods from other countries. The conversation moved on to travel in general, during which Marguerite stated that, in her opinion, there was nowhere like the Isle of Wight, and she didn't mean to leave it, ever.

Once the laughter this remark produced had died down, Lucie said she had never gone beyond Normandy and announced, her eyes shining, 'I should so like to travel.' She turned to Vincent, saying she envied him his year in America. 'Tell me, what kind of weather did you encounter there?'

'All kinds,' he replied in his pleasant fashion. 'Stifling heat in the south, cooler in the north, of course. When we first arrived in New York the summer heat was truly oppressive, but returning at Christmas, it was bitterly cold. Great extremes of weather, of a kind we do not see here.'

'No, thank heaven,' Marguerite agreed. 'The climate on the Island is usually very agreeable. We see very little in the way of snow----'

'And not much sun either,' Giles cut in with a laugh, as the servants finished removing the remains of the second course.

When Giles then began to talk of the war, his mother protested, 'Oh must we discuss the war today? I'm sick and tired of hearing about it. And that wretched revolution, with all those dreadful French peasants. Sans— oh whatever they call themselves----'

'Sans-culottes,' Giles said, and looking across at Parker, quietly gave permission for the servants to leave the room.

'Yes. Them. They are ruining their beautiful country and----'

Piers interrupted curtly. 'You are mistaken, madam.'

'My son always sides with the underdog,' Vincent sighed, reaching for his glass of wine.

Piers retorted, 'French peasants have been starved and oppressed for too long, and now they are fighting in the name of liberty---'

'Liberty?' Marguerite echoed in disgust. 'For whom, pray?'

Giles said, 'No, Piers is right---'

'Right?' came a chorus of disapproval.

'Yes,' Giles insisted. 'The French aristocracy only have themselves to blame. Neither they, nor the middle classes, ever paid their fair share of taxes, which placed the burden, most unfairly, on the peasants. And some noblemen treated their workers like cattle. I've seen the hovels they were obliged to live in, and believe me, my pigs enjoy better conditions. Many peasants were forced to bake their bread in the landowner's ovens, grind their corn at his mill, use his wine press for their grapes, and pay handsomely for the privilege. Such families were literally starving.'

Appalled, we sat dumbfounded, and Marguerite dabbed her eyes. I commented, 'No-one can justify that Giles, but you don't approve of what is going on now, surely?'

'No. Of course, those are not the only reasons behind this revolution, but if the aristocracy had paid fair taxes and not made life insupportable for their dependents, perhaps it might not have happened, and we wouldn't be at war now. The sad thing about the revolution is that the good are condemned with the bad, the innocent with the guilty.'

Lucie burst out indignantly, 'Like Papa, who is not capable of treating his dependents badly. He harmed no-one, and yet he only just escaped with his life.'

Aunt Thirza nodded in agreement. 'If Giles hadn't got him out of that dreadful prison, he'd----' She broke off, realising too late what she had said.

A stunned silence followed, broken by Marguerite demanding in bewilderment, 'Whatever do you mean?' Aunt Thirza chewed her lip, but did not answer. Vincent looked baffled, while Piers sat twisting the stem of his wine glass.

My uncle broke the silence, speaking in contrite tones. 'I'm sorry, Giles. Since you arrived home safe and sound, I haven't watched my tongue as I should have.' I wasn't really surprised, for my aunt would have latched onto any careless remark, and in a marriage it must be difficult to keep such a secret.

'No matter,' Giles murmured quietly.

Marguerite turned a worried face to Giles. 'Why won't anyone answer me?'

'It's not important, Mama.'

'What do you mean, not important. I want to know what----'

My uncle broke in, 'I think it best Giles, if I explain.'

Giles gave a slight shrug. 'Very well.'

Looking round the table, my uncle said, 'Well, we are all friends here, and just between ourselves, the truth is I owe my freedom to Giles.'

Marguerite spluttered, 'But I don't understand.'

'Nor I,' agreed Vincent, brows raised in curiosity. 'What *have* you been up to, my dear boy?' Piers sat staring at Giles too, but Lucie's lack of concern suggested she also had been enlightened.

Giles said modestly, 'I did very little. Indeed, anyone could have done it. There was no danger.'

Marguerite whispered in a frail voice. 'You mean, it's true? You helped Charles to escape?' The colour drained from her face and Aunt Thirza quickly took some smelling salts from her reticule, left her place and wafted them under Marguerite's nose, begging her not to distress herself. 'None of us knew what he meant to do and, thankfully, he's quite safe now. Believe me, I cannot express to you how grateful I am.'

'Yes, but----' She turned to her son, her eyes wide with fear. 'You could have been killed.'

Giles lied calmly, 'There was never a chance of that, Mama. Or I wouldn't have done it. Now let us talk of something more interesting.'

Unsurprisingly, no-one was prepared to talk of anything else, until Giles explained how the escape had been accomplished. He did so reluctantly, skilfully skimming over the risk to himself, making it appear that his role was a minor one, and that his French accomplice was the real hero. Which slowly brought the colour back into Marguerite's cheeks, and apart from admonishing him for taking such risks, she said very little more. I guessed that now he was safe and about to be married, she saw no further cause for worry. And I suspected that once over the initial shock, Marguerite would be really rather proud of her son.

'Well, my boy,' commented Vincent jovially, 'you won't return to France in a hurry, eh?'

Which, not unnaturally, reactivated Marguerite's fears, until Giles answered in a decisive manner, 'No, you can be very sure of that. I mean to settle down to a happy married life, looking after my estates and tenants, as a man in my position should. In fact, I doubt I shall leave the Island, except to take my beautiful wife to London. Or wherever else she desires to travel.'

'I'm very thankful to hear it,' Vincent remarked. 'Not every young man is as wise. Or I might add, as fortunate to win the hand of such a lovely girl as Lucie.' He winked at her, making her blush furiously. 'Talking of the wedding,' he went on. 'Is Mr Arnold invited?'

'Of course,' I said. 'He has been a good friend to the Davanishes of Westfleet. Why do you ask?'

Vincent chuckled. 'Well, I bumped into a very worried sexton this morning. The brandy that should have been removed from its hiding place in the crypt, is still there, and can't now be shifted until after the wedding.'

Laughing, I said, 'I hardly think Mr Arnold will be looking for contraband during a wedding ceremony.'

'That's what I told him, but the fellow is already a bag of nerves. As he said, he has his position to consider.'

From smuggling, the conversation turned to wines chosen for the wedding breakfast, which led to other subjects concerning the happy occasion. Marguerite seemed in no hurry to leave the gentlemen to their port, and even when she did signal to the ladies, the gentlemen rejoined us within half an hour. It was altogether a memorable occasion, and even Piers was seen to smile from time to time.

Mr Reevers returned to the Island the following morning, and came over to Westfleet that very afternoon. Determined to keep him at arms length, I nevertheless couldn't resist his offer of a ride across the Downs. I sent a message to Mudd to have Orlando saddled, instructing him he was to accompany us.

Amused, Mr Reevers mocked, 'Observing the proprieties, ma'am? Your aunt will be pleased.'

'True,' I said, pulling on my gloves. 'I must make a point of telling her.'

Some minutes later, crossing the courtyard to the stables, he said, 'Are you afraid to be alone with me? Is that it? You need not be you know.'

He spoke in such soft caressing tones, my heart began to thump alarmingly. I made the mistake of looking up at him, and the expression in his eyes made me catch my breath. I looked away, answering in as dignified a voice as I could manage, 'If you remember, after that business with the cliff fall I promised my aunt I would not ride anywhere without Mudd.'

'So you did.' He carefully removed a horse hair from his sleeve. 'But surely Smith was behind that? And he's in prison.'

'I did think it was him, only I was wrong. Smith has a cast-iron alibi.' I did not tell him how willingly I was sticking to my promise to my aunt, or how hard it was to appear outwardly calm, for I knew there would be another attempt on my life, that being the only way to stop me investigating these murders. And the next one might not fail. I literally shook every time I thought of it. Reinforcing the sad fact that, far from being the brave person I'd hoped I was, when it came down to it, I was really rather a coward.

Yet I had to go on, no matter what the cost. If I sat back and did nothing, I would have to live with the consequences for the rest of my life. But, for the moment, I forgot all that, revelling in the delight of a gallop across the Downs with a man who enjoyed riding as much as I did.

We made our way back along the cliff top, and on reaching the highest point above Hokewell bay, Mr Reevers asked if I would care to walk a little. 'Mudd can stay here and look after the horses.'

'Provided,' I insisted in my primmest voice, 'we don't go out of his sight.'

He looked all around, and raised an amused eyebrow at me; from here we could see a considerable distance in every direction. 'That would be difficult.' Handing the horses over to Mudd, we set off toward Hokewell village, and he began telling me about the beautiful mare Giles had bought for Lucie as a wedding present. He spoke of the animal's good points and perfect behaviour when he brought her over the Solent, but I was only half listening, my mind on what I knew must happen before the wedding.

Suddenly he stopped talking and asked, 'Am I boring you?'

I gave a slight start. 'I do beg your pardon.' Pointing to the beach immediately below us, I reminded him that was where I had been knocked out by a piece of cliff. 'I was thinking it was fortunate you came along when you did.'

'Mudd wasn't far behind. He would have saved you.'

'I could have drowned by then.'

He hesitated, then asked, 'Did you know who tried to kill you?'

Unable to trust myself to speak, I simply shook my head.

He didn't comment, merely saying, 'I came over today as I doubt I'll have the pleasure of seeing you again before the wedding. Giles has a list of things for me to do, and I have to work on my speech.'

'Have you been a groomsman before?'

'No. And it terrifies me.'

I turned to him. 'You don't look terrified.'

'I expect that's your calming influence.'

I couldn't help laughing. 'Are you able to turn everything I say to your advantage?'

'Oh, it's not just you, ma'am. I'm the same in the company of any beautiful woman.'

Foolishly I fell straight into the trap. 'I'm not beautiful.'

His eyes gleamed. 'Fishing for compliments, ma'am?'

I choked. 'Don't be so absurd. Lucie is beautiful. I am merely passable.'

'Hmm. Let's see, shall we.' He stopped and studied my face carefully. 'Expressive eyes, straight nose, good complexion, a very kissable mouth and------'

'*That* will do,' I said firmly.

He turned his palms upwards in a helpless gesture. 'I was only trying to be truthful.' But his eyes were dancing. 'I think I would describe you as attractive, possibly even adorable-----'

'Mr Reevers, this has gone far enough.'

He ran a hand round his chin. 'Yes, you're right. Adorable isn't the right word. Now let me think-----'

'Will you please be sensible.'

'If you insist.' And before I knew what he was about, he lifted my left hand to his lips and kissed the tips of my fingers one by one.

Pulling my hand away, I demanded, 'H-how – how is that being sensible?'

He looked at me with those bright intelligent eyes and murmured, 'You are forgetting I said you had a very kissable mouth.'

By now I was feeling decidedly breathless. 'You will stop this nonsense now, sir.'

He grinned at me. 'If that is your wish. Personally I found it most agreeable. You see, you were looking so despondent, I thought you needed cheering up.' I opened my mouth twice without saying a word, and he laughed. 'You're not usually stuck for words.'

'Do you ever mean anything you say?'

'I always mean exactly what I say.' He moved so close I could feel the warmth of his body, and he said in a caressing voice, 'What's troubling you, my dear? I wish you would tell me.'

33

He was watching me intently, but the lump in my throat made speaking impossible. I dared not trust him, no matter how much I wanted to. As if he'd read my thoughts, he said, 'I am very trustworthy, I promise you. Ask Giles.'

I thought of the facts on my charts in the workroom. His lack of money, how he saved me after the cliff fall, and the incident when Leatherbarrow was attacked. 'You're quite mistaken,' I said, 'there's nothing bothering me. Apart from the fact the wedding is this Saturday and there's still a great deal to be done.'

Last time we met he had been very concerned for my safety, but he hadn't even mentioned it this time, and I wished I knew why.

That night the strong south westerly winds that had blown across the Island for several days now, freshened into a ferocious gale, and by morning we were in the thick of it. An outside door slammed shut, trees creaked and groaned, and cold draughts seemed to find their way into every corner of the house. Logs crackled and blazed in the fireplaces, fallen leaves swirled around the garden, and it felt as if winter had come.

The wedding was two days away, and when I came down to breakfast, Jeffel commented, 'It seems a pity the bad weather couldn't have waited until next week, doesn't it, my lady.'

'It does indeed,' I agreed with a rueful smile. 'Still it will probably blow itself out before Saturday.'

I had slept badly, my senses still in turmoil from the events two days earlier. There could be no doubt of the truth now, and at last I saw how it all fitted together. I even understood the purpose of the Gosport man. But as Giles had warned me not to interfere, I tried to behave as if I had finally taken his advice to heart, at least when in his company.

Over a family nuncheon, discussing wedding arrangements, we tried to settle the allocation of rooms for the three couples who were to stay at Westfleet. Two bedchambers were of a good size, the difficult was deciding who should have the third much smaller, north facing room, when all three couples were of similar social standing and age. As it was impossible to please everyone, I suggested the matter should be settled by the turn of a card.

Aunt Thirza was outraged, but my uncle quickly cut short her protests. 'Drusilla is right, my dear. That will resolve the difficulty without upsetting anyone.'

Still bristling, my aunt declared that if his mind was made up, there was nothing more to be said, but if their friends were shocked at such cavalier treatment, it would be no fault of hers.

My uncle's eyes twinkled merrily. 'I will tell them you refused to be associated with so ridiculous a scheme.'

They were travelling down from London together and crossing to Cowes today. My uncle had procured rooms in the best inn and having arranged to escort them to Westfleet tomorrow, he soon set off for Cowes on horseback, accompa-

nied by his valet. The chaise, which was to convey the ladies
and their maids to Westfleet, had left earlier in the charge of
two reliable grooms. The men and their valets would travel on
horseback, extra horses having been hired in Cowes.

Now my uncle had gone, I'd hoped to avoid further dis-
cussions about the arrangements, as I had my own plans to
make. Plans I had not mentioned to my uncle, for if I had, he
would have refused to leave the house.

But my aunt, naturally unaware of what was going on
in my mind, insisted I inspect every guest bedchamber for
myself. In the course of which she managed to find either a
window with a smear on it, a speck of dust under a bed, or
draughts she was certain would send smoke down the chimney
to choke her friends. She demanded to know what I meant
to do about the gardens, the gale having undone much of the
gardeners' previous efforts. And had I realised the carriage
that was to convey Lucie and my uncle to the church, needed
a coat of paint?

It was well into the afternoon before I finally escaped, and
only then on the pretext of speaking to Mudd about the carriage. Putting on a warm pelisse, I went to look at the carriage
for myself, and as I'd expected, found nothing wrong with the
paintwork. Knowing perfectly well that Mudd would ensure
there wasn't a speck of dirt to be seen on the day of the wedding, I left it in his hands, casually mentioning to him that
I meant to walk up the hill at the back of the orchard. By
now the gale had moderated somewhat, but in any case, I had
always loved the feel of the wind on my face.

I strolled down to the walled garden first, past lawns and
flower beds strewn with leaves, which the gardener's boys were
collecting, restoring some semblance of order. The walled
garden, stripped of its summer colours, looked rather bleak,

and leaving by the north gate, I walked up through the long border, past the greenhouse and through the orchard. The gale had brought down most of the remaining apples, and these still lay on the ground, for so many other things needed attention they hadn't been collected yet. I strode on, climbing up the hillside to the point where I could see the whole of Westfleet and the gardens laid out below me.

There was no better place to see how beautifully positioned the Manor was, nestling at the foot of the Downs, sheltered from northerly winds. A thick shrubbery bordered my land to the left of the orchard, on the far side of which was a wood; to the right, lay Westfleet village, with its cluster of cottages around the green, and the church nearby. Beyond that was the sea.

Many people had lived at Westfleet before me, and I wondered if they had come up here too when they needed to think. Had they loved this view? Had they adored my beautiful manor house as much as I did? Giles, of course, loved Ledstone Place in the same way. It had always been his home, but now, with Cuthbert, Thomas and Tom all dead, he had the riches and consequence that went with it. And after his wedding on Saturday he would have everything he had ever wanted. But I knew Giles could not be allowed to marry.

For an arrest to be made, there had to be proof of guilt. What I'd overheard Giles say to Jacob would not, on its own, convince a court of law. And although that small detail on my charts might be proof to me, I saw how easily it could be made to look trivial and unimportant.

Like Mr Arnold I believed no man was above the law; thus my personal feelings, the sadness, the sheer disbelief, had to be ignored. I could see only one opportunity to obtain evidence that no-one could dispute, a plan that required Mr

Arnold's co-operation, and one that made me acutely uneasy, for so much could go wrong. And if I failed, I would not get another chance.

The afternoon light was fading fast now, and heaving a long sigh, I stood up and brushed a leaf off the skirt of my pelisse before heading back towards the house. I had just reached the orchard when a pistol shot rang out, and a bullet smacked into a tree no more than twelve inches from my head. Instinctively I threw myself on the ground, but I wasn't quite quick enough, and a second shot just grazed my forehead. I felt a searing pain, and as I hit the ground, blood trickled down my face onto the grass beside me. Guessing the shots had come from the shrubbery running along the edge of my land at the far side of the orchard, I did what seemed most sensible. I scrambled behind the nearest tree on my hands and knees.

I was too far from the house to make a run for it. If I tried, I would be hampered by my skirts, and my assailant would by now have reloaded his pistols. This time I was quite sure I would not be so lucky. For I knew him to be an excellent shot. If I had been a fraction slower in throwing myself on the ground, I would already be dead.

After the cliff fall incident, I had promised my aunt I would not ride anywhere alone, and apart from the occasional mile long daylight outing to see Julia, I had kept my word. Since then too, Mudd and I had both carried a pistol. My mistake had been to assume I was safe in the grounds of my own home. For I had stupidly left my pistol in my bedchamber.

The only protection I had now was the none too thick trunk of this apple tree, and slowly rising to my feet behind it, I leant against it, shaking uncontrollably, convinced my last moments had come.

In the fast gathering gloom, I heard the swish of his boots as he ran through the damp grass. When he stopped, he was so close I could actually hear him breathing, and I froze with fright. Then came the unmistakable sound of a pistol being cocked.

All at once, anger swept away fear. I wasn't just going to let this thing happen, like some rabbit caught in a trap. I looked around for something, anything to defend myself with, but there was nothing except the apples brought down by the gale.

In one swift movement, I bent down, grabbed an apple and threw it across the orchard as far as I could to distract his attention. When he swung round to see what had caused the disturbance, I quickly scooped up several apples, and stepping out from behind my tree, hurled one at him with all my might, striking him on the head. In the twilight I could not make out his features, and that made it easier. He let out a cry of anguish, put a hand over his face and reeled backwards, whereupon I quickly threw another apple, and another. He ducked the last one and steadied himself, but before he could fire at me again, I leapt back behind the tree.

I knew I wouldn't catch him by surprise again, which left me no choice but to run. Better that than waiting for him to come up and put a pistol to my head. He started to close in on me and I lifted my skirts a trifle, ready to run, when I heard a horse galloping towards the orchard. My assailant heard it too, and as he wheeled round, I ran towards the house as fast as I could, trying to keep trees between us. Hearing a pistol shot, I flinched instinctively, and hurled myself to the ground again. A few moments later I heard Mudd's anxious voice calling out to me, and I gave way to a sob of relief.

As I told him, I had never been so glad to see anyone in my whole life. Mudd escorted me safely back to the courtyard, where he explained that, having heard that first shot, and knowing I'd gone up to the hill, he'd thrown himself onto the nearest horse. Riding bareback, he'd galloped past the side of the house, across the south lawn, jumped a wall into the bottom end of the orchard, and seeing a figure cutting stealthily through the trees, had fired at him.

'He turned and ran through the shrubbery before I could reach him. I lost sight of him then and -----'

'Did you recognise him?'

He shook his head. 'It was too dark. All I saw was a shadowy figure.' And added apologetically, aware of how everything was meant to be just so for the wedding, 'I'm afraid I've cut up the south lawn, my lady. But I didn't think of that at the time.'

I laughed shakily. 'I'm very thankful you didn't, John. Frankly, I thought my last hour had come. At least you had the sense to keep your pistol on you. I was foolish enough to think I was safe at Westfleet.'

Everyone from my aunt down to Jeffel made a great fuss when they saw my face and learnt what had happened, but I refused to call the doctor for a mere graze, and my aunt cleaned it up for me.

'Who was it, Drusilla?' she demanded, a tremble in her voice. 'You must have seen him.'

I shook my head. 'He was in the shrubbery, Aunt.'

'No, but when he came out into the open----'

'It was too dark then.'

She looked at me, pale and drawn with worry. 'I think you know more than you are saying. You have a good deal of courage, but —'

'On the contrary, I was terrified.'

'Yes, well, it's not to be wondered at.' Still greatly troubled, she went on, 'What is it that you're not telling us, Drusilla? First, two men tried to rob you when you were caught out in the mist, then there was that cliff fall business at Hokewell Bay, which I always thought odd. And now this.'

I shook my head at her, and Lucie who had been sitting by the fire listening, cut in gently, 'Mama, I think Drusilla needs to rest for a while. We can talk about it later.' And she asked if I would prefer a tray to be brought to my bedchamber rather than join them for dinner.

But having been alone out in the orchard for what had seemed a lifetime, it was the last thing I wanted now, and I declined. 'Frankly, I'm so thankful to be alive, I cannot bear to let either of you out of my sight. As for dinner, well to tell the truth, I am quite extraordinarily hungry.' And I knew that doing something as ordinary as changing for dinner would help to restore me to some semblance of normality.

I had never given much thought as to how I would react if my life was seriously threatened. I suppose, like most people, I hoped I'd acquit myself creditably. In fact, I had been reduced to a quivering wreck when those two smugglers dragged me to the edge of the cliff, unaware their object had been merely to frighten me.

But the two attacks since then were meant to kill me. At Hokewell Bay I had been lucky to escape; I had also been more scared than I imagined it was possible to be. I thought afterwards, that if I ever had to face another attempt on my life, my earlier experience would serve to lessen the terror. Regrettably that had not been the case. Instead, I'd scuttled behind the nearest tree, quaking in every limb. In the end, two things had saved me. My own anger; and Mudd's bravery. Anger had given me strength and resolve. Pelting him with apples had stopped him shooting at me for a few precious moments. But the truth was, he would have prevailed if it hadn't been for Mudd. It was Mudd who had shown great courage, risking his own life to save mine. It was a sobering thought.

By the time we all retired for the night, the calmer weather of the afternoon had gone. The wind had got up again, and that night, as I lay awake listening to the rattling of the leaded windows, I doubted that even the local smugglers would try to bring a boat ashore in such conditions. And that meant Mr Arnold could safely relax.

But when that gentleman called the following morning, far from being relaxed, he seemed decidedly agitated. I received him in the library, where he bowed and said, 'Lady Drusilla, I trust I'm not disturbing you—'

As Jeffel closed the door, I assured him, 'Not in the least.'

Taking a seat opposite me, he spoke in anxious concern, 'I was never more shocked than when I heard what had happened to you yesterday. And in your own grounds too. I had to see for myself that you were not injured.'

I smiled. 'I am quite recovered, and have only a graze to show for my adventure.'

'Adventure?' he echoed, shocked. 'My dear ma'am------'

'Yes. Well, I don't admitting to you, that it was a most alarming experience.'

'I should just think it was. Did you see your assailant, ma'am?'

'No. It was too dark, I'm afraid.'

He leaned back in his chair, running a hand across his forehead in a weary fashion. 'What is to be done, ma'am? The wedding is tomorrow---------'

'I am certain Giles will leave the house tonight on some pretext, and -----------'

'What if he doesn't, ma'am?'

'He will leave, Mr Arnold, believe me. Nothing in this awful business has been left to chance. And when he does, Mudd and I will follow him. What happens after that will, I believe, provide evidence the courts will accept without question.'

Still highly distressed, he shook his head. 'It will shock a great many people when it becomes known. But my duty is clear, ma'am. My men already have their orders, and I have impressed on them the seriousness of the situation, although naturally I haven't told them what's at stake. Everything that can be done, will be done.'

We spoke further on the subject, the many uncertainties of the situation being the greatest worry. In fact, I was confident of only two things. That Giles would leave Ledstone sometime after dark. And I would follow him. But, as I was soon to learn, it is never wise to be too sure of anything.

34

M r Arnold stood up to take his leave. 'I imagine you will have little time for going out today, ma'am.'

'I think it most unlikely. We have several wedding guests arriving later.'

He smiled. 'I must say, I am glad to hear it, ma'am. You will be much safer in your own home.'

I did indeed mean to stay in, knowing I must conserve my strength for what lay ahead that evening. Although I hated to admit it, I was still rather shaken by the second attempt on my life. I tried not to think of how close those bullets had come to ending my existence. For I had been lucky twice now, and could not expect to be so again. I shivered at the thought of what might happen tonight. Yet I had to go. There was, quite simply, no other choice.

For some time after Mr Arnold had departed, I sat by the fire in the library, going over the plans for that evening. Seeing nothing I could improve on, I went to look out the window at the weather. The gale had blown itself out by daybreak, and there was hardly a breath of wind now. Thick cloud covered the Island, and I prayed it would clear, as I needed moonlight later. The opening of the door disturbed my thoughts, and I turned to see Jeffel coming in with a note. As I took it somewhat absently from the salver, he informed me, 'It's from Ledstone Place, my lady.'

In spite of everything, I couldn't help smiling. The previous evening I had sent a groom to Ledstone with a letter for Marguerite, telling her about the shooting incident, knowing that word of it would reach her, as such things did in small communities. Not wanting her to hear some garbled, exaggerated version of the truth, I explained I had disturbed a man in the orchard, who had foolishly fired two shots, but I was quite all right. She had written back immediately, distressed and worried, as I had known she would be.

This morning, however, her mind was clearly back on the wedding, and also on Vincent's imminent departure, for I had already received two notes from her. The first concerned the lock of Piers's hair which she'd had incorporated into a quizzing glass, as I'd suggested. She'd presented it to Vincent after breakfast, and believed I would wish to know that he had been moved to tears. The second note begged me to seat the parson and his wife as far away from her as possible at the wedding breakfast.

'Is the groom waiting for a reply?' I asked Jeffel.

'Yes, my lady.' He went on to say that my uncle had sent a messenger on ahead to warn us that he and our wedding guests expected to arrive within half an hour.

I nodded. 'Good. Inform my aunt and cousin please, Jeffel.' I sat down at my writing desk again, and began to unfold the note. 'I'll ring when I've answered Mrs Saxborough's letter.'

He bowed. 'Very good, my lady.'

As he shut the door, I spread open the single sheet, smiling to myself, wondering what she'd thought of this time. What I saw, however, was not my godmother's large, open scrawl, but Giles's clear, neat hand.

'*My dear Drusilla,*

We were all greatly shocked to hear what happened last night, but thankful that you escaped unscathed. Mama sends her love, and Radleigh meant to call, but has had to go over to Norton House on a pressing matter. Vincent and Piers too begged me to express their deep concern. They are busy with preparations for their departure on the day following the wedding. Drusilla, I am writing as I must speak to you on a matter of the utmost urgency. Come to Ledstone as soon as you possibly can after three. Do not fail me, and do not, under any circumstances, come without Mudd.'

I shivered, wondering what it meant. Glancing at the library clock, I saw it wanted some twenty minutes to three, and I simply couldn't leave now when my aunt's closest London friends, three couples as yet unknown to me, were about to arrive. Good manners alone demanded I should be here to greet them. Thus, I took a sheet of writing paper from the drawer, wrote a brief note explaining the situation, and that I would be over as soon as I could. I read it through, rang for Jeffel, and gave him the note to hand to the groom.

Then I checked my hair, ensuring it covered the graze on my head, before joining my aunt and cousin in time to greet our guests. My uncle had already explained my proposal for choosing their bedchambers by the turn of a card, and highly amused, they all entered into the spirit of the thing, the losing couple accepting their lot with good humour. Aunt Thirza and Lucie, at my suggestion, showed them to their bedchambers, enabling me to speak to my uncle.

'I have to go to Ledstone,' I said, explaining Giles wanted to see me on an urgent matter.

His brows drew together in a frown. 'Did he say what it was about?' When I shook my head, his frown deepened. 'Is this wise, Drusilla?'

'I think it will be all right. Mudd will be with me, and we have our pistols. I'll be safe enough at Ledstone with so many people about.'

We were standing in the hall, and the sound of conversation and laughter drifting down the staircase seemed inappropriate somehow. My uncle said, 'Does your aunt know about this?'

'No, the note came just before you got home.'

He chewed his lip. 'I think I'd better come with you.'

I shook my head. 'You're needed here, Uncle. I'll leave around four, when everyone is changing for dinner. My godmother has already sent two notes about the wedding today, and my aunt will instantly assume this one is from her too. If you let her think that, she'll go on about my godmother fussing over nothing as usual, but she'll understand I still had to go, and will explain that to everyone else.'

He gazed at me for a long moment, a wry smile on his lips. 'You know Drusilla, I had no idea you could be so underhanded.' I laughed, but in truth I had been even more devious than he thought, for he did not yet know of the second attempt on my life, and this certainly wasn't the time to tell him.

When Mudd and I rode into the stable yard at Ledstone, an hour or so later, Leatherbarrow was waiting for us. 'Mr Giles has had to go over to Norton House, my lady. He asked me to say he is very sorry, but could you meet him there.'

I wheeled Orlando round slowly. 'Well, it's not very convenient, but I suppose I'd better go, Leatherbarrow. Is something wrong at Norton House?'

'I couldn't say, my lady. All I know is, Mr Reevers returned a while ago, and Mr Giles went back with him.'

It was some five miles to Norton House, and by the time we got there the light was beginning to fade. Having stabled the horses next to those belonging to Giles and Mr Reevers, Mudd accompanied me to the front door. After he'd knocked twice without anyone answering, I suggested, 'Perhaps they're in the garden.'

We walked past the side of the house to the extensive rear gardens that ran right down to the beach. A hedge bordered the whole area, except at the bottom right hand corner where the boathouse stood. Thomas had kept his yacht here in the winter, and as we approached it, I saw the doors were open.

'They must be inside,' I said. The boathouse was of a strong construction, and as with anything that concerned sailing, Thomas had kept it in pristine condition.

The big double doors faced the sea, and walking round to them, I noticed how calm the sea was now the wind had dropped. I went inside, followed by Mudd, and called out. 'Giles, are you in here?'

It was, necessarily, a large boathouse, and there were no windows. A lamp glowed in the far corner, but I couldn't see anyone. As I peered into the gloom, the door was suddenly slammed shut, and the key turned in the lock.

'Giles?' I shouted. 'Is that you? '

Two planks of wood, stretched across the outside of the doors, reinforced the lock in severe weather, one about a third of the way down, and another two thirds down. Hearing these being slotted into place, I banged my fist furiously on the door.

'Let me out, Giles. At once - do you hear?'

'I'm sorry Drusilla, but you leave me no choice. I did warn you not to interfere. I'll send a message to Westfleet that you are staying to dinner, so they won't miss you.'

Desperately I yelled out again, begging him to listen to me first, but there was no answer. I heard the sound of his riding boots scrunching on the stones as he crossed the small patch of beach between the boathouse and the garden. And then, silence. He had gone.

'How the devil are we to get out, John?' I fumed. 'And it's so dark with the door shut.' I wasn't frightened, only annoyed that I couldn't see.

'I'll fetch the lamp, my lady.' Having done so, he held it up, carefully studied the doors and gave a grimace. 'It's good, strong oak.'

I looked at him in dismay. 'Well, we have to find a way out.' Taking the lamp from Mudd, I carefully examined every inch of the boathouse. In one corner there were some old sails and ropes, which Mudd lifted up, but there was nothing that could help us to get free. Marks in the ground suggested there had been other things in here recently which Giles, in his usual meticulous manner, must have taken out.

'Well,' I said, removing my hat for comfort, 'I have pistols, but nothing else of use, unless you count these hatpins.' I laid these on a small shelf nearby and Mudd, having put his own pistol beside mine, turned out his pockets, finding a hoof-pick, a few coins and a clasp knife. I looked at him helplessly, for I couldn't see how such things would be of use, and I burst out more in desperation than belief, 'There *must* be a way, John.' Everything depended on it. I didn't want to think of what would happen if we failed.

'I could try shooting the lock out, if you stand well back, my lady.'

I nodded, for Giles would be half way to Ledstone now and well out of earshot. The report was deafening, but thankfully he was successful first time. Then, using the barrel of the pistol, he knocked the lock right out, leaving a hole in the door. Looking through it I saw it was completely dark now. The door barely moved when Mudd pushed it, the two planks of wood remained firmly in place across the doorway, stopping us from getting out.

There was little chance anyone had heard the pistol shot as Norton House was fairly isolated, indeed there was no sound now apart from the gentle lapping of waves on the stony beach. There were a few bits of metal around the hole where the lock had been, which Mudd prised out with the hoof-pick and clasp knife. It was just possible to make out, through the tiny space where the doors met, the position of the two outside pieces of wood, and I saw a slight chance.

'John, if you could enlarge that hole with your clasp knife, enough to get an arm through it, we might be able to lift the wood out of its slots.'

He studied the hole, and the thickness of the wood again. 'I could try, my lady, but it will take some time. Those doors must be two inches thick.'

'Can you think of any other way?'

'No, my lady, I'm afraid I can't.'

I told him to take his jacket off to make it easier to work, and as he started whittling away at the wood with the knife, I held the lamp to enable him to see what he was doing. The wood was so solid he could only shave it off in tiny slivers, and the effort needed caused perspiration to form on his forehead, which soon began to run down his face. Every few minutes he stopped to wipe his brow, and after what seemed an absolute age, he'd cut enough wood away to get his fingers into the hole.

On and on Mudd worked, the perspiration running down his face, for hour after hour, or so it seemed to me. Then, quite suddenly, he slumped against the door, utterly exhausted.

'You hold the lamp John, and let me try.' I expected him to protest, but he didn't, and when he gave me the knife, I saw his right hand was red raw and bleeding where the skin had blistered. Appalled, I gasped, 'Why on earth didn't you tell me?'

'It's not as bad as it looks, my lady.' And he urged, 'I think you could get your hand through the hole now.' I tried, and found I could, just. Eagerly I tried to enlarge the hole but could make no impression at all. Mudd said, 'The blade is getting a bit blunt, my lady.'

I refused to think of that, only of what would happen if we didn't get out, and that made me attack the wood with renewed vigour. I managed to cut away a small sliver, and Mudd grinned, praising my efforts in much the same manner as he had when I'd achieved something as a child. I tried again and made a little progress, but I was much slower than Mudd. After some minutes he said he was ready to take over again.

I protested, 'But your hand—'

'Begging your pardon, my lady, but this needs a man's strength.'

He was right, of course, and picking up my hat, I ripped out the soft inner lining and insisted on wrapping it round his hand. Thanking me, he began to slog on again. If only I knew what the time was, I thought, and prayed we would not be too late, that Giles would not have left Ledstone yet. And I had to stop myself urging Mudd on, for no-one could have worked harder.

As he worked, I talked to him about the murders; what I thought about the Gosport man, what I'd heard Giles say to

Jacob, and how I believed Cuthbert Saxborough had died.   I told him everything I knew; who, how, and why.   And that unless we got out of here soon, it would be too late to stop Giles adding to the family deaths.

35

The next time Mudd tried putting his arm through the hole, he got past his elbow. 'I think I can reach the lower piece of wood,' he said. Somehow, he managed to get the wood out of its slot, tipping it over onto the ground. With a broad grin, he stood up and mopped his face. After a moment or two, he tried to remove the higher piece of wood, and although he could reach it and push the plank upwards a trifle, he couldn't get his muscular upper arm through the hole far enough to lever the plank over the top of the slots holding it in place.

'My arms are thinner and longer than yours,' I said. 'Let me try.' Being tall, I had to stoop a little to push my arm through, and ignoring the jagged edges catching on my sleeve, I found I could do so right up to my shoulder. I easily reached the plank of wood, and pushed it up with all my might, only for it to fall back into the slots again.

'You have to push it up and then out over the top of the slot, my lady,' Mudd advised. I nodded and tried again. On my third attempt the wood toppled over and hit the ground. The planks of wood had landed close to the doors, but Mudd managed to open the doors far enough to push them out of the way, and at last we were free.

Thankfully our horses were still in the stables, and we set off for Ledstone. Mudd's hack couldn't keep up with Orlando, and I arrived first, riding straight into the stable yard where Leatherbarrow was saddling a horse.

He looked up as I reined in, waiting only until I had dismounted and looped Orlando's reins round a rail, before blurting out, 'Thank goodness you've come, my lady. I don't know where Mr Giles has gone and----'

'Start at the beginning, Leatherbarrow,' I ordered quietly, sounding much calmer than I felt.

'I beg your pardon, my lady.' He took a deep breath and explained, 'Mr Piers went out at about half past seven, and I thought nothing of it, what with him being on his own. Then, an hour or so later, a message came down that Mr Giles and the other two gentlemen were going out too, and their horses were to be saddled at once. When Mr Vincent got here, he was in quite a state-----'

'How do you mean?'

He hesitated. 'I hardly like to say----'

'Just tell me, Leatherbarrow.'

'Well, my lady, he was almost in tears.'

Startled, I asked if he knew why, but was not surprised that he didn't. 'What happened then?'

'Mr Giles said I was to stay here. But they've been gone well over an hour, my lady-----'

'An hour?' I echoed in dismay. 'What time is it, Leatherbarrow?'

'Why, it must be nearly ten,' he said, giving me a look of surprise. 'I didn't want to worry Mrs Saxborough—'

I cut in quickly. 'On no account.'

'And I didn't expect to see you, my lady.'

'I don't suppose you did. So you decided to look for Mr Giles.'

He nodded. 'I'm that worried, my lady. The only trouble is, I don't know where to start.'

'Well, I think ----------' and I stopped, for I could hear someone riding rather slowly towards the stables.

Leatherbarrow listened for a moment. 'That's Mr Vincent's horse,' he said, with the confidence of a man who knew the sound of every animal in the stables.

Vincent rode into the yard, slipped off his horse and handed the reins to Leatherbarrow without a word. I don't think he saw me in the darkness until I spoke his name. He turned and stared at me, before saying in a colourless voice, 'Lady Drusilla. You here? I should have known.' He turned to go indoors, his usual good manners deserting him, for he showed no interest in why I'd come to Ledstone at this late hour.

Abruptly I demanded, 'Mr Saxborough, where is Giles?'

He stopped, looking round at me wearily. 'He and Mr Reevers are out looking for my son. Piers wasn't at Dittistone, so I tried Yarmouth, while they went along the coast to Hokewell. They'll be back soon, I have no doubt. But I am disgraced, ma'am. Utterly disgraced.' And with shoulders sagging, he walked on into the house.

By this time Mudd had arrived, and I told him and Leatherbarrow I was going inside to find out what had happened. 'I want you both to look for Mr Giles. Try Hokewell Bay first.' I didn't tell them I intended to follow as soon as I could, or Mudd would have refused to go.

Hurrying indoors, I found Vincent in the drawing room pouring himself a large glass of brandy. His hands were shaking so much he spilt a good deal of it on the sideboard. Refusing his offer of refreshment, I insisted on being told what had happened. Vincent looked at me, and I saw his eyes were filled with a kind of shocked horror.

'Why not?' he shrugged. 'I may as well tell you, the whole Island will know soon enough.' Swallowing a large measure of the brandy, he slumped into a chair, and sat gazing into the glass, trembling so much he had difficulty in holding it steady. His speech was reasonably coherent, however. 'Earlier this evening, realising Piers had forgotten to inscribe his name on the card accompanying our wedding gift, I went to his bed-chamber, only to find the room empty. Guessing he had gone to Yarmouth and might be back late, I decided to leave a note. I was searching for some paper in a drawer when I found it.' His voice broke up then, and he put his head in his hands.

'Found what?' I asked quietly, when he failed to go on.

He looked up at me, almost as if he'd forgotten my presence, and taking something from his pocket, threw it on the table. 'That,' he denounced in a mixture of loathing and despair.

I picked up the folded paper, and opened it to find a large detailed map of the Isle of Wight with a good deal of writing on it. All in French. Certain coastal areas were marked out, including I was horrified to see, Dittistone, Hokewell Bay and Luckton.

'This is an invasion plan,' I gasped, for it didn't take much intelligence to see these were landing areas.

Far from denying it Vincent took another large gulp of brandy. It was obvious Piers approved of the aims of the French Revolutionaries, but I had not thought him actively involved. To find he meant to assist the French to march across our Island, killing, burning, plundering - well, it turned my stomach. I studied the map again, learning little more, my French being too poor. But much else became clear to me.

'Piers explored the Island to discover what defences we had,' I said, 'and the best beaches to land an invasion force.' That was why he'd tested the sand at Hokewell bay with that long stick. 'And he'd questioned the local fishermen about their welfare hoping they'd assist an invasion.' · Furious, I burst out, 'Piers only came here to spy for the French.'

Bowing his head in shame, Vincent said, 'When I saw that map I called Giles at once. Mr Reevers, hearing my distress, came too. They were as shocked as I.' He drained his glass. 'My son is a traitor, ma'am. You cannot imagine how I feel.'

'Do you think the French mean to invade tonight?'

He looked at me, almost as if it didn't matter. 'Giles found a screwed up note on the floor, written in French, telling Piers to be at Dittistone Bay at eight tonight. We rode like the wind, but it was almost nine when we arrived, and the place was deserted.' I glanced at the clock; it was well past ten now. If there had been an invasion we would know about it by now. Vincent's thoughts, however, were elsewhere. 'I pray Piers will be found before he does anything further to shame me. To think that my own son could betray our country------'

Frankly I didn't think the message had any connection with a possible invasion. That an invasion was being considered, I did not doubt, but it wouldn't come tonight. The message was related to something else that was meant to happen tonight; something I could have prevented if Giles hadn't locked me in the boathouse.

Vincent rose unsteadily to his feet, crossing to the sideboard to refill his glass. While his back was turned, I quietly left the room, and a few minutes later I rode out of the stable yard, heading for the coast.

It was a particularly dark night, no moon or stars, and there being little wind, the sea was calm. Riding between Dittistone and Hokewell, I saw no signs of smugglers, no lights flashing on shore signalling it was safe to land, and if there were boats waiting off shore, it was too dark to see them. Nor did I find Giles, but I had not expected to now. I already knew I was too late.

I had planned to follow Giles when he left Ledstone, obtain the evidence needed to satisfy a jury, and thus stop him adding to the family deaths.

But Giles had made his own plans, and he never left anything to chance. Fearing I was still involving myself in his affairs, despite warning me to keep out of it, he'd made sure I couldn't interfere. He guessed I would be prepared for a third attempt on my life, but perhaps not for a simple trick designed merely to remove me from the scene. And how right he had been. That possibility had not crossed my mind.

On reaching Hokewell I found Mudd and Leatherbarrow talking to Thorpe, the Riding officer. Thorpe informed me four of his men patrolling the coast from Dittistone to Hokewell had gone missing a couple of hours ago.

'I've just found them ma'am, in a ditch, trussed up like chickens.'

I groaned inwardly. 'What, all of them?'

'They were patrolling in pairs, some distance apart, and were pulled off their horses by a gang of French smugglers who attacked them with clubs.'

I swallowed hard. 'When was this?'

'Some time between eight and nine.' When Mudd and I were still incarcerated in that wretched boathouse.

Leaving Thorpe to continue his duties, the two grooms and I carried on searching for Giles, but it was too dark to see anything, and eventually we went back to Ledstone, where I hoped Giles, Mr Reevers, or Piers might have returned. I was not surprised to find none of them had.

At my behest, Leatherbarrow gathered all the Ledstone grooms together outside the stables, where I explained the situation to them in simple terms, and immediately despatched them with messages asking the local gentry to assist with a thorough search at first light. After which I went back into the house, and found Vincent sitting where I had left him hours before.

The brandy decanter was now almost empty. The branch of candles on the table flickered in the draught of the open door, and the fire had all but gone out. Vincent had removed his coat despite the chilliness of the room. He looked up at me in a decidedly befuddled fashion, and remembering his manners, tried to rise. Swaying, he put his hands on the table to steady himself, attempted a bow, hiccupped, and slumped back into the chair. Lifting a hand, he slurred a greeting, added something to the effect that I ought not to be there, raised his glass to me, and in doing so, spilt brandy down his shirt front. I wrinkled my nose in disgust. Vincent swallowed what liquid remained in the glass in one gulp, and his eyes began to glaze over.

Aware I would not get any sense out of him tonight, I was about to leave when I saw the invasion plan and the note to Piers, still on the table. I don't think he noticed when I picked them up and slipped them in my pocket. Even if he had, I thought, he wouldn't remember it in the morning. Then, without a word, I turned and left the room.

Out in the hall I found the butler hovering. 'Parker, has Mr Vincent been in the drawing room since I left?'

'Yes, my lady. I didn't hear you come back, or I would have warned you he wasn't in a fit state to----'

'That's all right, Parker. As long as he hasn't informed Mrs Saxborough that Mr Giles is missing.' I didn't need to explain why it was better to keep her in ignorance of that fact. Parker, who had been at Ledstone Place some thirty years, understood all too well. She would have to be told sometime, but I could at least spare her one night of anguish.

Parker said, 'Mrs Saxborough retired early tonight to recruit her strength for the wedding tomorrow.' His face was lined with anxiety, but he didn't ask if the wedding would still go ahead. His fears were far more fundamental. 'I keep thinking of Mr Thomas and Master Tom my lady, and well - what I mean is - do you think Mr Giles is – is he still alive?'

I answered him truthfully. 'I'm quite sure he is, Parker.'

Thankfully, Marguerite's ability to sleep through any disturbance meant I did not have to face her tonight. But Lucie would have to be told. When I returned to Westfleet, however, I found everyone, except my uncle, had retired for the night. Glancing at the clock, I saw why. It was already past two. My uncle had waited up for me and fallen asleep in a chair in the drawing room. Quietly, I put more logs on the fire to keep the room warm, tiptoed out and crossed the hall to the library.

Having lit some candles, I rekindled the fire here too, for it was a cold night, and I had things to do. Watching a flicker of flame taking hold, I thought of what would happen at daybreak. Of the Island gentry, snug in their beds at this hour, who would arrive at Ledstone Place at first light to begin the search. I could picture them now, gathering in the stable yard, sombre-faced, stamping their feet in the chill early morning air, their breath mingling with that of their horses, speaking in hushed tones of old Cuthbert Saxborough, who had taken a tumble from his horse, and how they had always suspected there was something fishy about it.

Then Thomas and young Tom had been murdered, but had the Frenchies really been responsible, like everyone said?

Now Giles had disappeared on the eve of his wedding. There would be much sighing and muttering of what was the world coming to, as they speculated on who was behind it. But I was ready to swear that not one of them would come close to guessing the truth.

Once the fire was ablaze, I took the invasion plan and the note to Piers from my pocket. Locking the note in my writing desk, I spread out the map on the library table, holding the corners down with heavy books. Placing the branch of candles beside it, I tried to translate the written detail. Although I could read French better than I could speak it, many of the words were beyond me.

When the library clock chimed three, the wind began to pick up a little, stirring the leaves that always collected in one particular corner outside the window. I looked out to see if the weather had changed, but an overcast sky still obscured the moon.

Returning to the plan, I saw, thanks to the French words for infantry and artillery being similar to our own, that the proposed invasion force included twentyfour battalions of the former, and eight companies of the latter. I didn't know how many men that signified, but I took it to be a considerable number. I soon gave up struggling with the language though, and went to wake my uncle. He was the person I needed here.

When he opened his eyes and saw me smiling down at him, he murmured, 'Thank heavens you're safe, Drusilla. You must have been very late home.'

'I was.' I told him what had happened at Ledstone, but did not mention the boathouse episode at that time.

His eyes were full of anxiety. 'Is anyone out looking for Giles?' I shook my head, explaining a search was planned at first light, and asked him to look at the invasion plan. Following me into the library, he studied the plan carefully, and whispered aghast, 'Vincent found this in his son's room?'

I nodded. 'If you remember, the sketches Piers made of the beaches included every rock he could see.'

'To aid the French with their landings,' he muttered in disbelief. 'How must Vincent feel, knowing his only son is a French spy?'

'He seemed to feel it deeply. In fact he was drowning his sorrows when I left him.'

He looked down at the plan again, his face grave. 'Have you worked out what it says, Drusilla?'

I shook my head. 'That's why I woke you.' I told him the few fragments I had made out. 'But what does this mean?' I said, pointing to the first words I'd puzzled over. 'Whatever they are, there's two hundred of them.'

'Oyster ketches,' he said. 'They have very shallow draughts. Perfect for landing on a beach.' He studied the written details, translating as he went along. 'French warships will protect the fleet, with smugglers who know the Island directing the force to their landing places.' And he exclaimed, 'Well of all the nerve - once they've captured the Island, they will send the most influential inhabitants to France as hostages. Anyone not needed to work the land or build their fortifications will be transported to the mainland. Their dragoons, it seems, will bring their own saddles, bridles and pistols, but use Island horses.'

'I'd shoot mine first.'

He gave another gasp. 'Drusilla, this monstrous thing is planned for next month.'

We looked at each other in horror, and I asked, 'Does it explain how they intend to capture the Island?'

'Oh yes, it's all here. Good God, they mean to land at Dittistone, Hokewell and Luckton.' He read on again and muttered, 'Damned cheek. Oh, I beg your pardon Drusilla, but it seems they expect little or no resistance, and to capture the Island in a single day. After which they'll load fifty ships with huge boulders and sink them in a manner that will force all our ships to use the narrow Needles channel—'

'Where there are shoals and sandbanks, and dangerous tides and currents,' I put in. 'They know what they're doing, Uncle.'

'I'm afraid so. Once Gosport is captured, they'll bombard Portsmouth dockyard until it's totally destroyed.' He straightened up saying, 'There's a good deal more, but that's the main gist of it.' And he looked at me. 'Mr Pitt must be informed at once. If we take this to the Governor of the Island—'

'That's what I had in mind. I'll see Mr Orde has it later this morning. For the time being it should be safe enough in my desk.' And I locked it in the secret drawer. 'First, I must look for Giles,' I ended in a choking voice.

Putting his hand on mine, he murmured compassionately, 'My dear, that's no task for a woman.'

'He must be found Uncle, and I cannot sit here doing nothing. I should go mad.'

He walked across to the fire and stood, one foot on the fender, gazing into the smouldering embers. After a moment, he said, 'You'll take Mudd with you?'

'Of course.'

Which left my uncle with the appalling task of breaking the bad news to my aunt and cousin when they woke up, for there was nothing to be gained by rousing them any earlier. My heart went out to Lucie, who instead of waking to the happiest day of her life, would have to be told Giles had disappeared. As for how my godmother would react, I could not bear to think of it. And if it came to a public trial------------ Resolutely I pushed such awful thoughts from my mind. It was imperative that I kept a clear head.

36

This being the day of the wedding, much of the household was up earlier than usual. Wanting to be away at first light, I rang for hot water to be brought to my bedchamber. I washed, changed my clothes, and felt a little better. Looking out the window, I saw the faintest suggestion of light on the horizon. Going back downstairs, I found Jeffel in the hall, and asked him to come into the library, where I explained briefly what had happened overnight, and that I was joining the search for Giles. I told him my uncle and cousin would go to Ledstone to be with Mrs Saxborough, but I didn't know what my aunt would do, in view of our guests.

'If she does go Jeffel, you will be in charge of the house.'

He bowed. 'Very good, my lady.'

'Look to the needs of our guests, and do whatever you think necessary.'

He nodded. 'Don't you worry about the house, my lady. I can see to it all.'

'I know that Jeffel,' I said, forcing a smile. 'In fact I don't know what I would do without you.'

His cheeks grew a little pink, but all he said was, 'Do take care, my lady.' And noticing I'd left my pistol on the table, he pointed it out to me.

Picking it up, I put it in my pocket. 'If there's any news, I'll send word at once.'

'Thank you, my lady.'

I realised, as I walked down to the stables, that Jeffel had not asked for specific instructions on the wedding arrangements, or the food for the wedding breakfast. If by some extraordinary chance the wedding went ahead, I realised I would find the arrangements in order. If it did not, he knew it would not matter. Such welcome common sense left me free to concentrate on what was important.

Mudd had the horses saddled ready, and as the first grey light appeared we rode out towards Westfleet village. The morning air was cold, the overnight clouds having finally given way to clear skies. As we trotted past the church where the wedding was due to take place later that morning, I found myself thinking, incongruously, of the brandy hidden in the tomb, and of the nervous sexton. And his concern that Mr Arnold might find it. He couldn't know that Mr Arnold had something far more important to do.

To Mudd, I said, 'We'll start at Hokewell and work along the bay.' If there was anything to be found, I was sure it would be along this coast. Men were already making their way out into the fields as we cantered down the road, and those we passed touched their forelocks. On reaching the bay, we rode slowly along the cliff top in the direction of Dittistone, where in the growing light, I could just make out the magnificent chalk cliffs.

Shrieking gulls wheeled and dived overhead, the morning dew clung precariously to the short, springy downland grass, and unconsciously I filled my lungs with the sea air, the familiar taste of salt on my lips. A light breeze had sprung up, billowing out the sails of the vessels at sea as they went about their business. I saw a number of fishing boats, a man o' war, and one of Mr Arnold's smaller revenue boats, though there was no sign of the cutter, 'Swan III.'

The tide was coming in, and would soon cover the sand. Up on Hokewell Down, flocks of sheep grazed, and looking behind me I saw the sun just beginning to edge over the eastern horizon. Lucie, like all brides, had so hoped the sun would shine on her wedding day. At first, where the cliffs were quite low, it was easy enough to look down onto the beach, but as the land rose higher in the great sweep of the bay, it became difficult, at least on horseback, to see into some of the deeper crevices. Mudd dismounted in order to search them, while I took the reins of his horse, and in this manner we progressed slowly along the cliff top, until the long stretch of beach that led to the Hokewell chine came fully into view. When, suddenly, Mudd stopped dead in his tracks.

'What is it?' I hissed, my heart pounding. He neither answered, nor moved, but just stood staring straight ahead. I urged Orlando nearer the cliff edge, bringing the whole beach into view. And saw for myself.

There was a body on the beach. A man in riding breeches and a green coat, who lay face down in the wet sand. Even from the cliff top, I could not mistake the Saxborough blond hair. Orlando, sensing my tension, shook his head restlessly. While I, like Mudd, just stared. I tried to speak, but found I could not.

I start to shake, and aware of a roaring in my ears, imagined it to be the sound of the sea, for I had no idea I was actually holding my breath, and close to fainting. I wondered, vaguely, why the waves still moved, when I could not. I sat in the saddle, motionless, gazing fixedly at the body, my mind refusing to comprehend.

I saw, but did not believe, could not believe, that Giles, one of my dearest friends, who had survived childhood against all the odds, who had risked his life to rescue my uncle from a French prison, was now dead. Yet, in the same instant, I knew I had to believe it. And that, somehow, I must also endure it. For there was no other choice.

Becoming aware that Mudd was speaking to me, I took a deep gulp of fresh air, and automatically handed over the reins of his horse, as he requested. There were beads of sweat on his forehead, and remounting, he blurted out, 'He may still be alive--' I gazed at him helplessly, for we both knew there was no life left in the body on the beach.

A sudden gust of wind agitated Orlando and quite unconsciously calming him, I followed Mudd to the chine. On the cliff top above, he handed over his hack's reins again. 'I'd best go alone, my lady.' He pointed towards Hokewell Down, where a small group of horsemen, other searchers, were riding in my direction. 'Someone must tell them.'

'Yes,' I whispered, running a tongue round my dry lips. 'You go on.'

Mudd looked up at me, hesitating. 'Will you be all right, my lady?'

It was very many years since he had asked such a question, and I blinked. 'Yes,' I said, not knowing if it was true.

The approaching riders were still some distance away, and I watched Mudd scramble down the chine, loose clay and shale bouncing and scuttling ahead of him. When he reached the beach he looked up at me anxiously, before running towards the body, his boots leaving a trail of deep footprints in the wet sand.

Watching him bend over the body, I felt the sting of unaccustomed tears in my eyes and mechanically brushed them away. Waves still rolled in on the sand, the sun continued to rise in a clear blue sky, and a bee buzzed dozily around Orlando, causing him to shake his head. Everything around me going on as normal. As if nothing had happened.

Late yesterday evening I'd told Parker I was sure Giles was still alive, but it seemed I had been wrong, his body must have been here even then. I shuddered at the thought of Giles all alone, hidden by darkness, last night's gentle waves sweeping up the sand and over his body, the foaming surf draining through his tangled blond hair and across his sightless blue eyes.

The riders were almost upon me, and mechanically, I turned Orlando to face them. Vincent led the group, but close behind him was a man I had not expected to see. Vincent brought his horse to a halt, his face etched with anxiety over the whereabouts of Piers, and explained that Mr Reevers had returned an hour ago. 'He and Giles were set upon by a band of Frenchies soon after I left them at Dittistone.'

Mr Reevers, grey-faced and haggard, told me, 'It was Giles they wanted, I'm afraid. They left me tied up on Hokewell Down. Regrettably it took some considerable time to get out of my bonds.'

'So you escaped,' I whispered. 'While Giles lies dead on the beach.'

'Dead?' he echoed, as if he'd misheard. With a gulp, I pointed to the body. Vincent looked down and covered his face with his hands, while Mr Reevers sat stonily in his saddle, watching Mudd climb back up the chine to the cliff top.

Mudd ran towards us, the breeze tousling his hair. Wet sand clung to the knees of his riding breeches, where he had knelt by the body. He looked straight at me, and I saw his eyes were alight with hope. Nevertheless he spoke in grave tones. 'It's not Mr Giles, my lady. It's Mr Piers. Shot through the heart.'

'Piers?' I repeated in a whisper, my senses reeling. Giles often wore a green coat, that being his favourite colour, whereas Piers preferred maroon. In fact, I couldn't recall ever seeing him in green. Both had blond hair, and it was Giles, not Piers, whose life had been at risk. Or so I had thought.

'Are you sure?' It was a fatuous question, yet I could not help myself. Mudd simply nodded, and I asked, 'Is there any sign of---'

'There's nothing else, my lady,' he answered firmly. 'Not even a pistol.'

I could not believe Piers was dead. It was the last thing I'd expected. On hearing Mudd's words, Vincent had uttered a cry of anguish. Dismounting, he stood reins in hand, his eyes on my groom. 'There must be some mistake.'

Mudd said, 'I'm very sorry, sir. It's Mr Piers right enough.'

Vincent stared at him blindly for some seconds before saying in dignified tones, 'Then I must go to him.'

Out of respect we waited on the cliff top, watching as he hurried down to the beach and ignoring the fast encroaching waves, knelt beside the body, as Mudd had done. His shoulders began to shake with grief, and I turned away. His loss meant Giles might still be alive, and I asked Mr Reevers if he knew where the Frenchmen had taken him.

He started to shake his head but quickly stopped, wincing. 'I have a lump on the back of my head the size of an egg,' he grimaced. 'All I can tell you is we were set upon by about ten Frenchmen. One of them knocked me out with a club, and when I came to, I was alone.'

Gazing down at Vincent I saw he hadn't moved. 'I won't wait,' I said. 'I'll carry on looking for Giles.' Frankly I did not expect to find him, but I had already been wrong once this morning.

Mudd and I searched the west coast without finding Giles or anything connected with his disappearance. There was nothing to do then except return to Ledstone and join the family gathered in the drawing room. Mr Reevers, who had taken over the organisation of the search, had drawn up a map of the areas covered, and those not yet searched.

It wasn't until the searchers had been dispatched again that Vincent, who had been sitting with his head in his hands, looked up and said, 'It's my belief Giles isn't on the Island.'

Marguerite, who had refused to go and lie down, cried out, 'Whatever do you mean? Giles must be on the Island.'

Crossing to her side, Vincent took her fluttering hands in his. 'You must be brave, my dear. As we both must. I believe I know where Giles is.'

A chorus of voices demanded, 'Where?'

'I fear he has been kidnapped.'

Marguerite gave a little sigh and fainted clean away. Aunt Thirza, who thought it her duty to be here, dismissed Vincent's suggestion as nonsense, but my uncle drew his brows together in a worried frown, and said nothing. Lucie, wafting some smelling salts under Marguerite's nose, demanded to know why he should think that.

As my godmother began to come round, he said, 'Well, my poor boy is dead, so it cannot hurt him,' he said, his voice filled with sadness. I stood by the window opposite, and Vincent looked across at me. 'Piers told me Giles was wanted in France for a crime against the revolution.'

'Removing my uncle from prison?'

He inclined his head. 'Piers made some wild remarks about wanting to see justice done. If only I had known then that he was spying for the French. I didn't take his ramblings seriously you see, for after all, Giles was here, not in France.'

'What are you saying?' Marguerite whispered fearfully.

'My dear, I wish I could spare you this, but I'm afraid there's no help for it. I believe Giles has been abducted by a bunch of French revolutionaries and is, at this moment, on his way to France to face trial.'

Marguerite gasped, her left hand clutching at her throat. 'No - you cannot mean that. No-one would do such a wicked thing.' She looked up at me pleadingly. 'Drusilla, it isn't true, is it?' I could not bring myself to answer her, for I knew it to be true.

'If only I had realised sooner what Piers meant to do,' Vincent said, 'I might have saved them both. Your son, my dear Marguerite. And mine.'

Marguerite was very pale. 'I do not believe Giles is dead.'

'Nor is he, as yet, my dear. Perhaps you may be luckier than I. He may even now be rescued before they-----' He stopped, but we all knew what he meant.

In France today, justice was dispensed by the guillotine. Giles had known of the risk, for I'd overheard him telling Jacob that Piers knew what he'd done and meant to have him arrested. For one terrible hour I'd thought Giles had been speaking of the Saxborough killings, until that piece of contradictory evidence on my wall charts had shown me who was really behind the murders.

Which told me Piers had to get Giles to France before the wedding, before there was a chance of an heir. Or the murders would have been for nothing. Therefore some pretext was needed to persuade Giles to leave Ledstone last night. I had to admit that an invasion plan and a note suggesting Piers was assisting a French force to land was masterly, for Giles would never consider his own safety if he believed the Island, and England itself, was in danger. Severe gales had prevented anyone sailing to France over the last few nights. But, yesterday, the winds had dropped away almost to nothing. If that had not happened, if the weather hadn't changed, there would have been another plan. I was quite sure of that.

Giles had sensibly taken Vincent and Mr Reevers with him last night, but after Vincent went off to Yarmouth, French smugglers had attacked them. The worst part of it all was that I could have prevented it. And gained the evidence needed for an arrest. If Giles hadn't shut me in the boat-house. I mentioned this quietly to my uncle, while Vincent, Lucie and my aunt were comforting a now highly distressed Marguerite.

He said, 'Giles did it for the best, Drusilla. He was convinced someone would be watching Westfleet after dark yesterday. If you and Mudd had not left until then, he believed you would both be killed. And I think he was right.'

I stared at him. After two attempts on my life I'd expected a third. Yet, stupidly, I'd thought myself safe, provided I wasn't alone. 'When did Giles tell you this, Uncle?'

'He rode over just after sunset yesterday to tell us you were not in any danger. He meant to release you later, when he was sure it was safe.' So that was why my family hadn't worried where I was.

Giles, of course, aware of what Piers meant to do, believed he could outwit him. I was, however, virtually certain Giles was unaware of one vital fact. It wasn't Piers he had to outwit.

Marguerite being a little calmer now, I smiled at her encouragingly, but stayed where I was, in order to ask the one question no-one had mentioned. 'Who do you think killed Piers, Mr Saxborough?'

'Why those revolutionary scoundrels he was meeting, of course. Once they had Giles in their clutches, Piers was of no further use to them. So they shot him.' He began to sob quietly, 'My poor boy - all that revolutionary nonsense led him astray.'

'But,' I murmured softly, 'he wasn't your son, was he?'

37

A stunned silence filled the room, but I didn't miss the fleeting flicker of shock in Vincent's eyes. Marguerite looked up at me as if I'd gone mad. 'What are you saying, Drusilla? Of course Piers was Vincent's son.'

Vincent had come to mean so much to her in the past few weeks, I wished I didn't have to show her the kind of a man he really was when she was already worried sick about Giles. But I could see no other way. 'I'm afraid Mr Saxborough has not been telling us the truth,' I told her gently. 'Do you recall showing me his letters?'

Marguerite's hands flew up to cover her flushing cheeks. 'Drusilla, those letters were private. Whatever must Vincent think of us.'

To which that gentleman said, 'Do not distress yourself, my dear Marguerite. I don't pretend to understand what Lady Drusilla means, but------'

'I am referring to the letters you wrote to your brother in the years following your estrangement from the family.'

He stared at me for several seconds before turning to Marguerite in understandable astonishment. 'You mean, you kept them?'

'Of course. I am persuaded Cuthbert would not have liked me to throw them away.'

He looked from Marguerite to me, his brow furrowing, and I said, 'When you wrote to my godmother back in the summer, she remembered those old letters of yours, and allowed me to read some of them.'

'*Drusilla*,' Marguerite gasped. Opening her pretty fan, she employed it with unaccustomed vigour. 'Whatever will you say next?'

Vincent shrugged. 'Really Lady Drusilla, I cannot see that letters I wrote a quarter of a century ago can be of any significance.'

I raised my brows slightly. 'You think not, Mr Saxborough?' And I took a folded sheet from my pocket.

Marguerite's eyes widened in alarm. 'If that is one of Vincent's letters you must give it to him at once.' I glanced at Vincent, and although he said nothing, a slight wariness had crept into his eyes. When I carefully unfolded the sheet, Marguerite became even more agitated. 'It is true I allowed you to read those letters Drusilla, and that was very wrong of me, but I *know* I did not give you permission to keep any of them.'

I inclined my head in apology. 'No, indeed you did not, and I must beg your forgiveness.' For, what I had to say would cause her great pain, and I longed with all my heart for a kinder way. 'If you remember, I was at Ledstone when one of the housemaids accidentally broke the glass on the miniature Mr Saxborough kept in his bedchamber. The only keepsake he has of his wife. The portrait showed a beautiful woman with honey coloured hair and eyes, and you asked me to see if it was damaged.'

'Of course I remember, Drusilla. But I don't see what that has to do with anything.'

'No, neither did I at the time.'

I paused, deliberating on the best way to continue, but no-one spoke, or even moved. Everyone waited, as if mesmerised, for me to go on. I explained how I'd used the wall charts in my workroom to record the facts about the Saxborough deaths, including some background information copied from one of Mr Saxborough's old letters. 'But the miniature showed me one of those small details didn't mean what I'd thought.'

This glaring discrepancy told me who was behind the murders, and why I had been attacked at Hokewell Bay, and in my own orchard.

'I didn't think I'd made a mistake when copying the letter, but I needed to be certain. There was a lock of Piers's hair with that particular letter. So,' I said, addressing my godmother, 'when you decided to return the lock to him-----'

'But that was your idea,' Marguerite burst out. 'I didn't know what to give Vincent as a memento, and you suggested-------- She stopped and after a moment, accused, 'I suppose that's when you stole the letter.'

'I slipped into my pocket, yes.' One glance had confirmed I'd correctly copied what Vincent had written, which meant that the Piers we knew, could not be his son.

When I carefully flattened out the letter Marguerite begged in distress, 'You are surely not going to read it out loud.'

'Just one small paragraph, that's all.'

Lucie took her hand, and my uncle said, 'I believe we should trust Drusilla's judgement, ma'am.'

Throwing him a grateful look, I went on, 'I should explain that Mr Saxborough wrote the letter when his wife and son were dangerously ill with a fever. He asks his brother to help him provide the good food and decent lodgings the doctor recommended.'

Vincent sat, apparently indifferent to the proceedings, one leg crossed over the other. Calmly he tapped the top of his snuff box, flicked it open and took a pinch of the contents. Brushing a speck of snuff off his riding breeches, he commented in sardonic fashion, 'Do not, on any account, spare my feelings, ma'am.'

Mr Reevers, who had not spoken throughout, quietly crossed the room to stand guard by the door as I read the paragraph.

'*I beg of you to help me Cuthbert, for my son is as much a Saxborough as your own beloved Giles. At four years of age, Piers bears a remarkable resemblance to the portrait of your good self that hangs in the gallery at Ledstone. The one Mama had done when you were five. Piers, like so many of his Saxborough ancestors, has blond hair, as you can see from the lock I have enclosed. He is fortunate too in that he has inherited his mother's beautiful eyes, and like her, has the most charming nature.*'

Folding the sheet, I put it back in my pocket.

Marguerite was the first to speak. 'I don't understand, Drusilla. There can be nothing to object to in that. Indeed it shows a sensitivity that can only please.'

Glancing at Vincent, I saw that he understood all too well, and turning back to my godmother, I reminded her in a placid tone, 'The Piers we met had gray eyes.'

She looked up at me, puzzled. 'Why, yes, so he did.' She still didn't grasp the significance, and I asked quietly, 'What colour were the eyes in the miniature?'

'Oh, Vincent's wife had the most gorgeous honey-coloured eyes. As soon as I saw the painting I remembered. Everyone

commented on them at the time. Even Cuthbert said.......'
Her voice trailed away as she finally saw what it meant, and
she turned to Vincent, murmuring his name in a stunned,
questioning way.

The letter stated Piers had inherited his mother's beautiful
eyes, and as his were gray, I'd assumed hers had been too. It
had been on my charts so long, I barely noticed it any more.
Even when I saw the miniature of Vincent's wife, it had not
come to mind. It wasn't until I looked through my charts that
night that I realised how we had been deceived.

Vincent had introduced the man with him as his son Piers,
and we had accepted it without question, as he had known we
would. Even though Piers's features and build were quite different to Vincent's, and as I later saw, to his wife's too. If I
had taken the lack of resemblance into account much sooner,
I might have questioned some of the other things Vincent had
told us.

For in working out who was responsible for the murders,
I knew it wasn't Giles. He simply wasn't capable of such a
thing, which left Mr Reevers, Vincent and Piers. Piers didn't
have the intelligence to devise so clever a scheme. The other
two gentlemen had exactly that kind of mind.

I didn't know what to think where Mr Reevers was concerned, for he desperately needed money, and at the time of
the murders had thought himself next in line after Giles. But
when we learnt Vincent was alive, that changed the family
tree, making him the heir to Ledstone Place until Giles and
Lucie married and had children.

Vincent's answer was dismissive. 'Gray eyes, brown eyes.
Men don't notice such things. I was distraught when I penned
that letter. I hardly knew what I was writing. My wife and
son were very ill, the walls of our lodgings ran with damp, and

I hadn't enough money to buy the food they needed. Cuthbert chose not to answer my letter, and my dear wife died. I feared my son would be taken from me too, but---- '

'And you did lose your son, didn't you?' I murmured softly. 'He died. The man we knew as Piers had the blond hair of a Saxborough, and gray eyes not too far removed from the blue of so many of your ancestors. A man educated in England, who would be accepted as your son.'

Vincent shook his head in disbelief. 'I fear the events of today have unhinged your mind, ma'am.'

He spoke in his usual charming manner, more in sadness than anger. All along I had accepted it was impossible for him or Piers to be involved with the murders, when voyages between England and America might take six or seven weeks, and often more in bad weather. And I had grown to like Vincent. He was excellent company, an intelligent conversationalist, a man of good sense who showed considerable kindness to my godmother. Even when I realised the truth, he had remained all of those things. At no time displaying the loathsome, callous or unfeeling traits of a man who had cold bloodedly planned the murders of three members of his own family, and devised two attempts on my own life. A fact I found totally unnerving.

But, charming or not, he was guilty, and had to answer for his actions. I thought of the lives he'd cut short, of young Tom in particular, and responded to his derision with an abrupt, 'There is nothing wrong with my mind, Mr Saxborough. As I shall prove to-------- '

'Lady Drusilla, I beg of you,' he drawled, still well in command of himself. 'Do please allow me to stop you making a fool of yourself. Piers and I were in America until the first of July. Correct me if I am wrong, but Cuthbert died in April and the yachting tragedy occurred at the end of July. We didn't reach------'

He stopped, for I had lifted my brows at him, because at no time had I accused him of killing his brother. He had associated the two incidents himself, and any lingering doubts I had as to how Cuthbert had died, disappeared. I remained silent, however, and after a moment's hesitation, he carried on, his most pressing need being to establish his innocence. 'We didn't reach London until the fifteenth of August,' he pointed out. 'Captain Kettlewell can vouch for that. Indeed, you were present when I met the captain again, quite by chance, I might add, at Westfleet. And we talked of the crossing then, if you remember.'

At the time I had indeed accepted that as absolute proof that Vincent and Piers were not involved with the murders. 'Yes, I admit that baffled me for a while. Until I recalled that Captain Kettlewell said Piers kept to his cabin---'

'He was seasick----'

'So you maintained. But it's my belief it was Wistow, your valet, who occupied that cabin, not Piers. The perfect servant who had to be paid an exorbitant salary.'

This, I suspected, was the man Vincent had ensured I'd seen in the library, dressed in one of Piers's maroon coats, the day Piers attacked Leatherbarrow. And when Wistow went to visit his sick father in London, Vincent and Piers had ridden off within half an hour of his departure, supposedly to Newport. I doubted the valet ever left the Island, or that his father was really ill. Wistow had simply known far too much.

Father had believed that solving a mystery was often a matter of asking the right question. I saw now that I should have asked Captain Kettlewell to describe the man who sailed home with Vincent on his ship. For the tall, slim, fair-haired

Wistow, bore little resemblance to the short, stocky Piers. But it hadn't occurred to me then, for I'd seen no reason to doubt that Vincent and Piers had travelled back to England together. When I did think of it, the captain was well on his way to New York.

Vincent dismissed my suggestion with an airy wave of his hand. 'Oh, really, Lady Drusilla, I think you have been reading too many novels.'

Marguerite, pale and bewildered, turned to Vincent uncertainly, and when he smiled at her, her features relaxed. For, despite everything I had said, she found it impossible to accept that this charming man, who had been such a comfort to her, was capable of harming anyone. And, in that moment, she persuaded herself that, somehow, I must have got it all wrong.

'Drusilla is very fond of reading,' she agreed uncertainly. 'Oh dear, I do hope I am not to blame. I did lend her a novel recently in which some very odd things happened.' And she found another excuse for my behaviour. 'She hasn't really recovered from the death of her dear father either. Do promise me you won't hold this against her.'

'Of course not,' Vincent promised with all his customary gallantry. 'I understand only too well how bereavement can affect the mind.' He looked across at me, smiling confidently. 'Now ma'am, let's stop this nonsense, shall we.'

'Yes, you would like that, wouldn't you,' I countered, icily calm. 'You once told me you couldn't stand the sight of blood, which meant you needed someone to carry out the murders for you. A man who could also masquerade as Piers.' Vincent gave a loud despairing groan, which I ignored.

'When you heard of Giles's betrothal, you had to stop him getting married and producing an heir, or you would never become Mr Saxborough of Ledstone Place. Piers agreed to do his part so that he could assist those cut-throats governing France, and then you had the good fortune to meet William Arnold's brother-in-law, John Delafield in America. Finding he corresponded with the Arnolds, you introduced Piers to him in February, stating you would both be touring the southern states before returning to England in the summer. To ensure he would mention you in his letters, you bumped into him several times, both then and in late June. Indisputable proof that you could not have been in England when the murders took place. And, by inference, that gave Piers an alibi too.'

I took a deep breath, as what I had to say next would distress my godmother. 'You and Piers probably did leave New York together, but he sailed home in February, no doubt under another name, while you toured the south. And following your orders, he murdered your brother.'

A strangled cry escaped Marguerite's lips, and she fell back in a swoon. Lucie and my aunt rushed to her aid, but Vincent barely glanced at her. It was so unlike him to ignore her distress, I knew he must be badly rattled. He hid it well, however, answering me with a languid, 'What a vivid imagination you have to be sure, ma'am.'

With my godmother still in a faint, I hurried on, hoping to spare her the ordeal of hearing how her husband had died. 'Everyone thought it was an accident, for that was how it looked, even to me. But your brother was an expert horseman. He didn't rush the schooling of new horses, and would never have jumped the east gate on a nervous young animal, bought three days before. That's what first made me suspicious.'

'Really, Lady Drusilla, this is quite absurd. How else could----'

'I believe the gate was open and Piers stretched something across it - probably a rope.' Again his eyes flickered. 'And he closed the gate afterwards to make it look like an accident.' If the fall hadn't broken Cuthbert's neck, I was certain Piers would have instantly rectified the matter, but as Marguerite was coming round, I kept that thought to myself.

A hint of sarcasm entered his voice. 'I suppose Piers single-handedly murdered Thomas and his son too, and stole the Saxborough ring.' At the mention of young Tom I looked at him with such loathing he lowered his eyes.

'French smugglers were paid to do it,' I said, almost choking over the words. 'It's my belief you meant to use the ring and Tom's penknife to make it appear Giles had murdered them. Then Piers learnt from his revolutionary friends that Giles had rescued my uncle from prison, and you had a much better idea. If Piers could get Giles to France, he'd face the guillotine for such a crime. No-one could blame you for his death, and you would inherit the estates, which has been your aim all along.'

A faint smile twisted Vincent's lips, and he inquired in amused fashion, 'Is there anything else? Could you not find a way to blame me for the bad harvest, or the weather?'

Marguerite, listening dumbfounded and white-faced, finally found her voice. 'Drusilla, I do not believe Vincent would harm Giles. Or anyone else.'

'No?' I smiled grimly. 'Who do you think killed Piers?'

Aghast, Marguerite burst out, 'No, Drusilla. Not his own son---'

Gently I reminded her that the man we knew as Piers wasn't his son. 'Once Giles was on the boat bound for France, Vincent had no further need of Piers.'

A muffled sob escaped Lucie, but she leapt up and faced Vincent, her eyes blazing. 'Drusilla is right, and all the time you pretended to be my friend.'

He held out his hand to her. 'My dear child-----'

Lucie hissed, 'You won't inherit Ledstone. If Giles dies, I'll shoot you myself.'

'My dear girl, it was Piers who-----'

'Piers put Giles on the boat,' I cut in, 'but you planned it all. Piers wasn't capable of inventing the devious schemes you contrived.'

He still did not appear discomforted. And I knew why. A court might agree that Vincent's letter proved Piers was an imposter; and Captain Kettlewell's evidence would show Piers had not returned to England with Vincent. Which suggested a conspiracy of some sort, but there wasn't one shred of actual proof connecting either of them with the murders.

Last night, I'd hoped, with the help of Mr Arnold's men, to catch Piers in the act of forcing Giles onto a boat bound for France. Evidence no court could dismiss. Piers, once arrested, would unquestionably have implicated Vincent. And I would have succeeded too, if Giles hadn't locked me in the boathouse.

Now, if Giles died on the guillotine, Vincent would inherit Ledstone Place and its estates. For, how could I prove he was guilty? The men who could provide the evidence were all dead. Piers. Almost certainly Wistow, the valet. And the Gosport man.

The purpose of the Gosport man had puzzled me at first. He hadn't told me the name of the Englishman who'd hired him, only the date he'd been paid. The fifteenth of September. A day when Vincent, Piers and Mr Reevers were at Ledstone. Giles, as I well knew, had been in France then. The subtlety of giving me a date, rather than Giles's name, showed a far greater intelligence than the Gosport man possessed. When I thought about it all later on, I recognised the hand behind it.

Once the Gosport man had done his part, Piers killed him, probably when he and Vincent were supposedly visiting friends near Brading. When Piers had fulfilled his purpose, Vincent couldn't let him live, for he knew everything.

I looked up to see Vincent watching me, the faintest suggestion of smugness in his smile. He knew I couldn't prove it, and that I didn't know what to do next. If Giles was in France now, as seemed all too likely, he could expect a swift trial and execution. All Vincent had to do was wait.

38

My aunt and cousin were too devastated to speak, and even my godmother was quiet. My uncle stood by the window, staring out, while Mr Reevers kept his eyes on Vincent, his face grave and alert. I still didn't know if Mr Reevers was involved in the murders in any way.

No-one spoke; in fact, it was so quiet that when the door suddenly burst open, it startled us all. Mr Reevers swung round, the others raised despairing eyes, and I turned to see a highly dishevelled looking gentleman striding in. One of medium height and angelic features.

'Giles!' chorused Marguerite and Lucie together. As they both rushed to hug him, Vincent's blue eyes flash murderously.

Mr Reevers moved swiftly towards him, saying to me, 'Don't worry, I'll see he does not leave this room.' I nodded and turned away, utterly unable to speak, for I had seen the thankfulness and joy on his face when Giles walked in, and the relief of knowing which side he was on, along with the fact that Giles really was safe at last, completely overwhelmed me.

Silent tears streamed down my cheeks, and taking out my handkerchief, I dried them with trembling fingers. It was some moments before I felt able to face them all again, and when I did so, I saw Mr Arnold standing in the doorway.

Realising he had brought Giles home, I pulled myself together and went to greet him.

He bowed. 'I don't wish to intrude, ma'am. I just wanted to ensure you were all safe.'

'As you see.' I smiled a little shakily. 'Now you have returned Giles to us, I do not think we have anything further to fear. But will you not come in? I have so much I wish to ask you.'

Thus, while Marguerite and Lucie, aided by my aunt and uncle, fussed over Giles, I sat in a quiet corner of the room with Mr Arnold, listening to him relate, in his modest way, how his men had prevented Giles from being taken to France. 'The day you told me Vincent Saxborough was behind the murders, I was greatly shocked. He always seemed such a charming gentleman.' Glancing at Vincent, he shook his head in disbelief. 'To think of the terrible fate he planned for his own nephew ----'

'He deceived us all, Mr Arnold. But tell me, are all your men safe?

He nodded. 'Yes, I'm thankful to say. I gave Sarson, the captain of the cutter, strict orders to patrol the coast from Dittistone to Hokewell, as you suggested, but what with last night being as black as pitch, and the Frenchies hoisting dark sails, they almost slipped through our fingers. Their boat was making its way out to sea before my men spotted them. It was quite a chase, Sarson said, and our cutter didn't catch them until sometime after midnight, but they gave up without a struggle.'

'Without a fight?' I repeated in surprise.

'The French were heavily outnumbered,' he explained with a smile. 'Sarson and his crew reached Cowes around dawn, and very thankful I was to see Giles Saxborough safely back on our Island, I can tell you.'

'As we all are, believe me,' I said, glancing at the happy faces around Giles. 'I am most grateful to you, Mr Arnold. We shall always be in your debt.'

'My goodness, ma'am,' he protested, embarrassed. 'I did nothing, except give the orders. And my men did their duty, as I expected.'

Giles, emerging from being hugged by those who loved him, demanded, 'Where's Piers? I saw him on the beach before I was thrown into the hold. But he wasn't on the boat when the revenue cutter stopped us.'

'Dead,' Mr Reevers declared. 'Vincent shot him. He hatched the whole plan too. The murders, everything.' And explained briefly why Piers could not be Vincent's real son.

Giles stared at him, utterly stunned. 'That I had not suspected. Frankly I thought Piers arrived here from America, heard I'd rescued Lucie's father, and saw a golden opportunity to snatch Ledstone for Vincent and himself. These revolutionaries preach equality, but given the chance they are as greedy as anyone else.'

Mr Reevers said, 'It was Lady Drusilla who fathomed it all out.'

'So I understand from Mr Arnold.' Giles turned to me, smiling. 'I owe you a great deal, Drusilla. I should have listened to you.'

Such an admission silenced me for a moment and Vincent muttered, all pretence gone now, 'I congratulate you, ma'am. You appear to have thought of everything.'

I asked curiously, 'Why did you do it, Mr Saxborough?'

'Why? Oh that's quite simple.' His eyes glittered with bitterness. 'Cuthbert refused to acknowledge my wife and son. Even when they became desperately ill, he ignored all my pleas for help. Money could have saved them.' Vincent removed a speck of snuff from his sleeve. 'As it was, they died of the fever, and I swore that, one day, I would take my revenge. That I would own Ledstone Place and its estates.'

'So,' I said, 'I take it your brother didn't set you up in business.'

Vincent's lip curled. 'Not he.'

'You told Mrs Saxborough----'

He shrugged. 'I wanted her to think I was grateful to Cuthbert, and therefore not after Ledstone. There never was a gaming club. The truth is, six months after my wife died I met a rich widow and married her. She died some years ago and------' Seeing our expressions, he held up his hands in protest. 'Of natural causes, I swear. Piers was her son. I never did take to the boy, but believe me, killing is not in my line. I had to consume a considerable quantity of brandy before I could shoot him.' He shuddered. 'Never again.'

Mr Reevers ground his teeth. 'You won't get the chance. It's the gallows for you.' He turned to Giles. 'Where shall I put him? In the cellar?'

'No, really, Giles,' Vincent protested. 'I'm too old to be stuck in some damp, cold cellar for hours on end.'

I urged strongly, 'I think the cellar would be the ideal quarters for a man whose sole aim was to take your place, Giles.'

'But what could I do now, Lady Drusilla?' Vincent protested. 'If I shot Giles, which I promise you I could not, for I really rather like him, everyone would know it was me. What would I gain?'

I looked at Giles. 'Vincent also tried to kill me on two occasions.'

Vincent shuddered. 'Not I, Lady Drusilla. That was Piers, I assure you.'

'He may have carried out the attacks,' I retorted softly, 'but you told him how to go about it.'

'I agree with Lady Drusilla,' Mr Reevers said. 'The cellar it must be.'

Giles nodded decisively. 'Very well. We'll deal with him later.'

Throwing up his hands in capitulation, Vincent begged, 'I trust I won't be left there to starve. I have not yet had breakfast and-----'

Giles stared at him. 'My father, brother and nephew are dead, and you tried to have me killed, and I'm supposed to care whether you starve or not?' He shook his head in disbelief. Then, observing Vincent's dejected face, gave a harsh laugh and shrugged. 'I'll see Parker brings you something.'

When he tugged the bell-pull, Parker appeared so quickly, I suspected him of hovering outside. Giles said, 'Parker, it seems Mr Vincent organised my trip to France last night.'

'So I understand, sir,' he said gravely.

'You know about it already do you, you old reprobate. Tell me, how is it that the servants always know everything that goes on in this house?'

Parker replied loftily, 'I really couldn't say, sir.'

'Won't, more like,' Giles laughed. 'Well, as you know so much, you won't be surprised to hear Mr Vincent is to be incarcerated in the cellar until after the wedding.'

'Very wise, if I may say so, sir.'

'I'm glad you approve. Take a tray of food and drink to the cellar, if you please, and then we'll lock him in.'

Casting Vincent a look of disfavour, Parker answered with a dignified, 'If that is your wish sir, I will see to it immediately.'

As Parker shut the door behind him, Mr Reevers glanced at the clock. 'I don't want to rush you Giles, but if you mean to get married today shouldn't you take a bath? You're quite disgustingly grubby you know.' A statement that started a buzz of comment, with Mr Arnold saying he must be going if he was to get to Cowes and back in time for the ceremony.

After he'd left, Lucie came up to Giles, 'Are you sure you're all right?'

Taking her hands in his, he smiled down into her eyes. 'Of course. Thanks to Drusilla. But for her, I would be in a French prison by now.'

Lucie turned to me, but before she could speak, I reminded her affectionately, 'It's time you went back to Westfleet, if you're to be ready for the wedding.'

'Aren't you coming with us?'

'I'll come when I've seen Vincent safely locked up.'

When Parker returned to report, with more than a hint of disapproval, that he'd taken food and drink to the cellar, Giles locked Vincent in.

Riding home across the Downs, accompanied by Mudd, I told him everything that had happened.

Greatly relieved, he declared, 'I can't believe it's all over, my lady.'

'Nor I.' And I said, with a smile, 'I owe you a great deal, John.'

His weather-beaten cheeks flushed a little. 'My lady—'

'But for you, I would not be here.'

He said gruffly, 'It was nothing, my lady. Besides I promised his lordship to make sure you didn't come to any harm.'

I arrived home to find everything being set out for the wedding breakfast, and much furious activity going on in the kitchen. Despite the appearance of chaos, Jeffel assured me he had it all under control. And, somehow, despite much shouting for servants, doors being banged and a great deal of rushing about, everyone managed to be ready in time.

The sun shone, the bride was radiant, and my uncle proud. The carriage taking them to the church was as spotless as my aunt could possibly have wished. Even the parson was in good humour, and Giles greeted his bride with such joy Marguerite had to dab her eyes with her handkerchief. The wedding breakfast went off without a hitch, speeches were given, people laughed in all the right places, and a huge quantity of food and wine was consumed.

Lucie had just gone to change her dress when I saw a groom riding up to the house. A moment later Jeffel brought in a note on a salver, presenting it to Giles. He read it, frowned, slipped the note into his pocket, and quietly made his way to my side. 'Could we go into your library?'

'Of course.'

Giles brought Mr Reevers with him and having shut the door, took the note from his pocket and said, 'I'm afraid Vincent has escaped.'

'Escaped?' I gasped in disbelief. 'But how? The cellar door was locked.'

'I know,' Giles agreed ruefully. 'Only as you discovered Drusilla, under that veil of charm lies an exceptionally cunning and resourceful man.'

Mr Reevers asked curiously, 'Who is the note from?'

'From Vincent himself. He has been kind enough to explain how he means to escape justice.' Unfolding the note, he read it to us.

'*My dear Giles,*

May I first congratulate you on your wedded state. I wish I could have been there, my dear boy, but by the time you receive this I shall be crossing the water to Lymington. When Lady Drusilla was so insistent that I should be locked in this ghastly cellar, she quite forgot I have a way with locks—'

Giles looked up at me. 'What does he mean?'

I gave a heartfelt groan. 'I'd quite forgotten, but the night before I was attacked at Hokewell Bay, someone picked the lock on my workroom door, broke in and looked at my wall charts. At the time, I didn't know who it was. Later I decided it must have been Piers. I'm sorry, Giles.'

Giles gave a wry grimace. 'Well, it can't be helped.' And he read on:-

The lock on this door is simplicity itself. I have already picked it, and mean to leave the instant I have finished this note. When I reach Yarmouth, I will arrange for your horse to be returned to Ledstone, and this letter to be delivered to you.

You need not worry about me any more, for I shall never return to the Island. I have been a gambler all my life, and I gambled everything on becoming Mr Saxborough of Ledstone Place. I shall not try again, nor ever return to England. I freely admit I persuaded Piers to murder Cuthbert and Thomas and Tom, and that Piers then died by my own hand. But I do not intend to end on the gallows.

I shall return to my villa in Italy, which is quite out of the way. Frankly, I do not believe you would ever find it. In any case, I am sure you have no wish to drag the Saxborough name through the courts. Really, my boy, it will not do. For what would you gain? You already have everything you could ever want. So allow me to bid you a fond farewell.

Yours etc.

Vincent.'

None of us spoke for a moment, then Giles muttered savagely, 'So I have everything I could ever want, have I? Does he really believe I wanted to inherit Ledstone in such a way? I'd give it all up this instant if my father, brother and nephew could be restored to me.' He looked at me with so much pain in his eyes I lowered my gaze. 'It was my father he hated. Yet he had Thomas and Tom murdered too. Tom was just an innocent b-boy-------' he stopped, his voice breaking, and he turned to look out the window, his hands on the sill, his knuckles white.

After a minute or two, I said quietly, 'I'm not making excuses for what he did, but his own son was just a boy when he died too. As Vincent saw it, his brother could have saved his wife and child, but chose not to. That doesn't justify murder, but it may explain it.'

Giles stood staring down at the note, then carefully folding it, he looked up at me, in control of himself again. 'I'll pass this on to the proper authorities. They can deal with it as they will.'

Mr Reevers urged, 'I should keep a copy, Giles. It's the only admission of guilt you have.'

'Yes, I'll do that. Frankly though, I don't think they'll catch him.'

I said with some regret, 'I suppose the whole story will be in the newspapers.'

'Perhaps,' Giles said. 'And - er - perhaps not. I - er - do have some influence in high places.'

I stared at him. 'Whatever do you mean?'

'Well, there is something Radleigh and I haven't told you.'

I eyed him with suspicion. 'Why do I have the feeling I am not going to like this?'

Which only made Giles laugh. 'Do you remember asking me why I went to Paris after your uncle was safely on his way to the Island?'

'Of course. You said you were curious.'

'I'm afraid I lied, Drusilla. The thing is --- Radleigh and I, we - er - work for the government.'

I looked at him, puzzled. 'How do you mean? How can you possibly work for the government?'

He fidgeted with the folded note, turning it in his fingers, before putting it into his pocket.

'Well, Mr Pitt wanted a first hand account of the situation in Paris, and I could hardly ignore a request from the first minister in the land, now could I.'

'Mr Pitt?' I repeated in disbelief.

'Yes, but I must ask you not to speak of this to anyone.'

'Indeed not,' murmured Mr Reevers feelingly. 'Think of my skin, my dear fellow.'

Giles chuckled. 'Quite so. Now that I'm getting married, I have resigned. But Radleigh hasn't retired. So you will be careful, won't you.'

Incredulous, I spluttered, 'Are you telling me that you are a spy?'

He lifted his shoulders. 'Government agent, Drusilla.' And he grinned at me sheepishly.

'Don't split hairs, Giles. How long has this been going on?'

'Since I came down from Oxford.'

I thought of the years he had spent supposedly travelling for pleasure. 'And you never even gave me a hint.'

'I couldn't, could I. Be reasonable, Drusilla.'

But I was in no mood to be rational. 'Don't you realise, I thought Mr Reevers might be involved with the murders at one time?'

'Yes, I know.' Giles began to look a little uncomfortable. 'I told you he was innocent, but you obviously didn't listen----'

'Oh,' exclaimed Mr Reevers acidly, 'so you're to blame for the frosty reception I have received from this lady on more than one occasion. Well, let me tell you Giles, next time you get stuck in France with a horde of sans-culottes yelling for your blood, I shall leave you to your fate.'

I turned to Mr Reevers hardly able to believe my ears. 'You went to France in Leatherbarrow's place?' I had been so sure no-one but Giles's groom knew where to pick him up.

It was Giles who answered. 'Radleigh and I often work together. But as I explained to you Drusilla, I wasn't able to wait for anyone.'

'Being unaware of that,' Mr Reevers told me sardonically. 'I spent a whole day dodging the Frenchies, risking life and limb, waiting for him to turn up. Something,' he reiterated, 'I shan't do again.'

'You forget,' Giles pointed out shamelessly, 'there won't be a next time.'

'When you two have quite finished,' I intervened, choking on a laugh. 'There's one thing you have both forgotten.' Going to my writing desk, I unlocked the secret drawer, took out the French invasion plan and handed it to Giles. 'You must get this to Mr Pitt.' Giles looked at the document for a moment, then having glanced at me, lifted a questioning eyebrow at Mr Reevers. This gentleman's lips twitched, and he gave a slight nod. Watching this meaningful exchange,

I eyed the pair of them warily. 'What are you two scheming now?'

Giles said, 'We think you should take it to Mr Pitt, Drusilla.'

'Me?' I gasped.

He nodded. 'You'll find he'll want to hear how it came into your hands. Tell him the whole story. How you unmasked Vincent and-----'

Mr Reevers broke in, 'And how you prevented one of his best agents from ending up on the guillotine.'

'Yes,' Giles agreed feelingly. 'Make sure you tell him everything.'

I stared at them, speechless, and Mr Reevers said, 'I should be honoured ma'am, if you will allow me to escort you to Downing Street. Properly chaperoned, of course. Your aunt and uncle perhaps?'

I did not answer at once, for until today I had feared Mr Reevers might be involved with the murders in some way, and that my feelings for him were affecting my judgement. To have those fears banished filled me with joy, and the thought of being in his company in London, without such worries, was infinitely appealing.

Looking across at him, he smiled in a way that caused my heart to lurch alarmingly. Giles glanced from Mr Reevers to me, and having missed nothing, asked in his most matter-of-fact voice, 'Well, what do you think, Drusilla? Would you like to meet Mr Pitt?'

I didn't stop to consider where such a decision might lead. I simply turned to Giles and said happily, 'Yes, I do believe I would.'

THE END

25462204R00246

Printed in Great Britain
by Amazon